6—

DEVIL ON THE CROSS

DEVIL ON THE CROSS

Ngũgĩ wa Thiong'o

Translated from the Gĩkũyũ
by the author

LONDON

HEINEMANN

IBADAN · NAIROBI

Heinemann Educational Books Ltd
22 Bedford Square, London WC1B 3HH
PMB 5205, Ibadan · PO Box 45314 Nairobi

EDINBURGH MELBOURNE AUCKLAND
HONG KONG SINGAPORE KUALA LUMPUR
NEW DELHI KINGSTON

Heinemann Educational Books Inc.
70 Court Street, Portsmouth, New Hampshire 03801, USA

ISBN 0 435 90200 8 (paper)
ISBN 0 435 90651 8 (cased)

© Ngũgĩ wa Thiong'o 1982
First published in Gĩkũyũ by
Heinemann Educational Books (East Africa) Ltd 1980
First published in
African Writers Series 1982
Reprinted 1983, 1985

Set in 10 point Times
by Coats Dataprint, Inverness
Printed in Great Britain by
Richard Clay (The Chaucer Press) Ltd,
Bungay, Suffolk

*To all Kenyans
struggling against the
neo-colonial stage of imperialism*

Chapter One

1

Certain people in Ilmorog, our Ilmorog, told me that this story was too disgraceful, too shameful, that it should be concealed in the depths of everlasting darkness.

There were others who claimed that it was a matter for tears and sorrow, that it should be suppressed so that we should not shed tears a second time.

I asked them: How can we cover up pits in our courtyard with leaves or grass, saying to ourselves that because our eyes cannot now see the holes, our children can prance about the yard as they like?

Happy is the man who is able to discern the pitfalls in his path, for he can avoid them.

Happy is the traveller who is able to see the tree stumps in his way, for he can pull them up or walk around them so that they do not make him stumble.

The Devil, who would lead us into the blindness of the heart and into the deafness of the mind, should be crucified, and care should be taken that his acolytes do not lift him down from the Cross to pursue the task of building Hell for the people on Earth . . . .

2

I, even I, Prophet of Justice, felt this burden weigh heavily upon me at first, and I said: The forest of the heart is never cleared of all its trees. The secrets of the homestead are not for the ears of strangers. Ilmorog is our homestead.

And then Waríínga's mother came to me when dawn was breaking, and in tears she beseeched me: Gícaandí Player, tell the story of the child I loved so dearly. Cast light upon all that happened, so that each may pass judgement only when he knows the whole truth. Gícaandí Player, reveal all that is hidden.

At first I hesitated, asking myself this question: Who am I – the mouth that ate itself? Is it not said that an antelope hates less the one who sees it than the one who shouts to alert others to its presence?

It was then that I heard the pleading cries of many voices:

Gīcaandī Player, Prophet of Justice, reveal what now lies concealed by darkness.

Then for seven days I fasted, neither eating nor drinking, for my heart was sorely troubled by those pleading voices. Still I asked myself this: Could it be that I am seeing phantoms without substance, or that I am hearing the echoes of silence? Who am I – the mouth that ate itself? Is it not said that the antelope conceives more hatred for him who betrays its presence with a shout?

And after seven days had passed, the Earth trembled, and lightning scored the sky with its brightness, and I was lifted up, and I was borne up to the rooftop of the house, and I was shown many things, and I heard a voice, like a great clap of thunder, admonishing me: Who has told you that prophecy is yours alone, to keep to yourself? Why are you furnishing yourself with empty excuses? If you do that, you will never be free of tears and pleading cries.

The moment the voice fell silent, I was seized, raised up and then cast down into the ashes of the fireplace. And I took the ashes, and I smeared my face and legs with them, and I cried out:

I accept!
I accept!
Silence the cries of the heart.
Wipe away the tears of the heart . . . .

This story is an account of what I, Prophet of Justice, saw with these eyes and heard with these ears when I was borne to the rooftop of the house . . . .

I have accepted.
I have accepted.

The voice of the people is the voice of God.

That is why I have accepted.
That is why I have accepted.

But why am I lingering on the bank of the river?

To bathe is to strip off all clothes.
To swim is to plunge into the river.
It is good so . . . .
Come,
Come, my friend,

8

Come and let us reason together.
Come and let us reason together now.
Come and let us reason together about
Jacinta Waríínga before you pass judgement on our
   children . . . .

Chapter Two

1

The Devil appeared to Jacinta Waríínga one Sunday on a golf course in the town of Ilmorog in Iciciri District, and he told her — Wait! I am leaping ahead of the story. Waríínga's troubles did not begin at Ilmorog. Let us retrace our steps . . . .

Misfortune and trouble had trailed Waríínga long before she left Nairobi, where she worked as a secretary (typing and shorthand) at the offices of the *Champion Construction Company*** in Tom Mboya Street near the *National Archives* building.

Misfortune is swifter than the swiftest spirit, and one trouble spawns another. On Friday morning Waríínga was dismissed from her job for rejecting the advances of *Boss* Kíhara, her employer, who was the managing director of the firm. That evening Waríínga was abandoned by her sweetheart, John Kimwana, after he had accused her of being *Boss* Kíhara's mistress.

On Saturday morning Waríínga was visited by her landlord, the owner of the house in Ofafa Jericho, Nairobi, in which she rented a room. (A house or a bird's nest? The floor was pitted with holes, the walls gaped with cracks, the ceiling leaked.) The landlord told Waríínga that he was increasing her rent. She refused to pay more. He ordered her to quit the premises that instant. She objected, declaring that the matter should be referred to the *Rent Tribunal* for settlement. Her landlord climbed into his Mercedes Benz and drove off. Before Waríínga could blink, he had returned with three thugs wearing dark sunglasses. The landlord stood at some distance from Waríínga, arms akimbo, taunting her: 'There, I have brought you your *Rent Tribunal*.' Waríínga's things were thrown out of the room, and the door was locked with a new padlock. One of the henchmen tossed a piece of paper at the girl, on which was written:

We are the Devil's Angels: Private Businessmen.

Make the slightest move to take this matter to the authorities, and we shall issue you with a single ticket to God's kingdom or Satan's – a one-way ticket to Heaven or Hell.

---

*In the original work, written in Gíkũyũ, certain words and phrases appear in English, French, Latin and Swahili. In this translation all such words and phrases are printed in *italic* type.

They all climbed into the Mercedes Benz and disappeared.

Waríínga gazed at the scrap of paper for a little while, then tucked it into her handbag. She sat down on a box and held her head in her hands, wondering: Why should it always be me? What god have I abused? She took a small mirror out of her handbag and examined her face distractedly, turning over her many problems in her mind. She found fault with herself; she cursed the day she was born; she asked herself: Poor Waríínga, where can you turn now?

It was then that she decided to go back to her parents. She stood up, collected her things together, stacked them in the next-door room belonging to a Mkamba woman and started to make preparations for the journey, a cauldron of worries seething in her mind.

Waríínga was convinced that her appearance was the root cause of all her problems. Whenever she looked at herself in the mirror she thought herself very ugly. What she hated most was her blackness, so she would disfigure her body with skin-lightening creams like *Ambi* and *Snowfire*, forgetting the saying: That which is born black will never be white. Now her body was covered with light and dark spots like the guineafowl. Her hair was splitting, and it had browned to the colour of moleskin because it had been straightened with red-hot iron combs. Waríínga also hated her teeth. They were a little stained; they were not as white as she would have liked them to be. She often tried to hide them, and she seldom laughed openly. If by mistake she laughed and then remembered her teeth, she would suddenly fall silent or else she would cover her lips with her hand. Men would sometimes tease her, calling her Waríínga, the angry one, because of her lips, which were nearly always firmly pressed together.

But when Waríínga was happy and forgot to worry about the fading whiteness of her teeth and about the blackness of her skin and laughed with all her heart, her laughter completely disarmed people. Her voice was as smooth as perfume oil. Her eyes shone like stars in the night. Her body was a feast for the eyes. Often, when she walked along the road without self-consciousness, her breasts swaying jauntily like two ripe fruits in a breeze, Waríínga stopped men in their tracks.

But she could never appreciate the sheer splendour of her body. She yearned to change herself, in covetous pursuit of the beauty of other selves. Often she failed to dress in harmony with her body. She rushed to copy the ways in which other women dressed. Fashion, whether or not it flattered the shade of her skin or the shape of her figure, was what governed her choice of clothes. Sometimes

Waríínga distorted the way in which she held herself by trying to imitate another girl's stride. She forgot the saying: Aping others cost the frog its buttocks.

Insistent self-doubt and crushing self-pity formed the burden that Waríínga was carrying that Saturday as she walked through the Nairobi streets towards a bus stop to catch a *matatū* to take her to her parents' home in Ilmorog.

Even after many days had passed, and her life had changed in ways that she had never dreamed of, Waríínga was not able to explain clearly how she had managed to walk right along River Road and to cross Ronald Ngala Street, to find herself standing at the edge of *Racecourse* Road, between *St Peter's Clavers Church* and the sewing-machine shop, at the Kaka Hotel bus stop.

A city bus came speeding towards her. Waríínga shut her eyes. Her body shuddered. She swallowed a lump, and her heart began to beat as if to the rhythm of prayer: In times of trouble, do not, O Father, look the other way. Do not hide your face from me at this time of tears .... Now ... receive me ....

Suddenly Waríínga heard a voice within her head: Why are you trying to kill yourself again? Who has instructed you that your work on Earth is finished? Who has told you that your time is up?

Waríínga quickly opened her eyes. She stared from side to side. She could not see the owner of the voice. And now she felt shivers running from her toes to her hairline as she recalled what she had been about to do.

Instantly she felt dizzy. Nairobi – people, buildings, trees, motor cars, streets – began to swirl before her eyes. Her ears were blocked. All noise ceased as the country retreated into a vast silence. Her legs weakened at the knees; strength ebbed from her joints; Waríínga sensed that she was losing consciousness and balance. But as she was about to fall, she felt someone grab her by her right arm to support her.

'You nearly fell,' said the man who was holding her. 'Come and sit in the shade of the building. Come out of the sun.'

Waríínga was in no state to refuse or even to discover who was talking to her. She let herself be led to the steps of the Kaka *Heavenly Massage and Hairdressing Salon*. The door to the salon was shut. Waríínga sat down on the second step. She held her head in cupped hands, her fingers touching her earlobes. She leaned back against the wall. All at once the last bit of strength left her, and she slid into depths of darkness. Silence. Then she heard whistling noises, then sounds that were not whistles: they seemed more like voices singing far away, sound carried on the waves of the wind:

12

I mourn over my own body,
The one I was given by God, the All-Powerful.
I ask myself:
When they bury me,
With whom shall I share my grave . . .?

Then the sound was not a song, and the voices were no longer identifiable. They had disintegrated into cacophony, a well-spring of the foam and froth of meaningless noise.

And now Wariinga was revisited by a nightmare that she used to have when, as a student at *Nakuru Day Secondary*, she attended the *Church of the Holy Rosary*.

She saw first the darkness, carved open at one side to reveal a Cross, which hung in the air. Then she saw a crowd of people dressed in rags walking in the light, propelling the Devil towards the Cross. The Devil was clad in a silk suit, and he carried a walking stick shaped like a folded umbrella. On his head there were seven horns, seven trumpets for sounding infernal hymns of praise and glory. The Devil had two mouths, one on his forehead and the other at the back of his head. His belly sagged, as if it were about to give birth to all the evils of the world. His skin was red, like that of a pig. Near the Cross he began to tremble and turned his eyes towards the darkness, as if his eyes were being seared by the light. He moaned, beseeching the people not to crucify him, swearing that he and all his followers would never again build Hell for the people on Earth.

But the people cried in unison: 'Now we know the secrets of all the robes that disguise your cunning. You commit murder, then you don your robes of pity and you go to wipe the tears from the faces of orphans and widows. You steal food from people's stores at midnight, then at dawn you visit the victims wearing your robes of charity and you offer them a calabash filled with the grain that you have stolen. You encourage lasciviousness solely to gratify your own appetites, then you put on robes of righteousness and urge men to repent, to follow you so that you may show them paths of purity. You seize men's wealth, then you dress in robes of friendship and instruct them to join in the pursuit of the villain who has robbed them.'

And there and then the people crucified the Devil on the Cross, and they went away singing songs of victory.

After three days, there came others dressed in suits and ties, who, keeping close to the wall of darkness, lifted the Devil down from the Cross. And they knelt before him, and they prayed to him in loud voices, beseeching him to give them a portion of his robes of

13

cunning. And their bellies began to swell, and they stood up, and they walked towards Warĩĩnga, laughing at her, stroking their large bellies, which had now inherited all the evils of this world . . . .

Warĩĩnga started. She gazed about her. As if it had been on a journey far away, her mind slowly returned to her. She saw that she was still on *Racecourse Road*, still at the Kaka Hotel bus stop near *St Peter's Clavers Church*, and that the sounds she had heard were nothing but the hooting and revving of cars. She asked herself: How did I get here? Which wind has carried me here? I remember boarding the 78 bus from Ofafa Jericho. It passed through Jerusalem, Bahati, and it joined Jogoo Road, past Macaakũ *Country Bus Station* . . . and . . . *oh, yes* . . . I was on my way to the university to see John Kĩmwana, my love, for one last glance . . . . I got out at the bus stop outside the *National Archives* building, near the *White Rose* drycleaners. I walked down *Tom Mboya Street* and past the Koonja mosque. I crossed the *Jeevanjee Gardens*, past the *Garden Hotel*, and I stopped at the corner of Harry Thuku and University streets, facing the *Central Police Station*. Was that where I turned back? For when I looked at the university buildings, and especially at those of the Engineering Department, I remembered the dreams of my youth, when I was at school at Baharini *Primary* and *Nakuru Day Secondary*, and I recalled how later my dreams were trampled into the dust by the Rich Old Man from Ngorika. When those memories fused with thoughts of John Kĩmwana, who abandoned me last night, knee-deep in the mire of my troubles, I suddenly felt my brain and heart burn with pain, and my anger seemed to suffocate me . . . . Now, what did I do next? Where did I go? Ah! My God, where is my handbag? Where did I leave it? Where will I find the fare to Ilmorog?

Once again, Warĩĩnga stared about her. It was then that her eyes met those of the man who had taken her by the right hand and had made her sit on the steps of the massage parlour.

'Here. Here is your bag,' the man said, stretching out his hand to give her a black bag decorated on one side with a piece of zebra hide.

Still seated, Warĩĩnga took her handbag from him. She glanced at him inquiringly. He had a youthful build, though his face displayed maturity. He had a mass of jet-black hair and a beard like that of a small he-goat. His dark eyes shone with the light of a wisdom that sees many things hidden in the distance . . . . He had on khaki *jeans* and a brown leather jacket. Under his left arm he carried a black leather bag. He explained how it was that he had Warĩĩnga's bag.

14

'You dropped it in River Road, near *Tearoom*, the Nyeri and Murang'a *matatū* stop, and I picked it up for you and followed you. You have been very lucky today – you could easily have been run over. You were crossing the streets and dodging the traffic like a blind man who has been smoking dope and is filled with reckless courage. I caught up with you as you were swaying on the kerb. I took you by the hand and led you into the shade. Since then I've been standing by idly, waiting for you to return from whichever land you'd been transported to by the trials of the heart.'

'How did you know that I was far away?' Waríínga asked.

'From your face, your eyes, your lips,' the young man replied.

'I'm very relieved to get my handbag back,' Waríínga said. 'I didn't even realize that I'd dropped it. And I haven't got as much as half a cent in my pocket.'

'Open it and check that all your things are there, especially the money,' the young man told her.

'There wasn't much money in it,' she said ruefully.

'Even so, you'd better check. Don't you know that it is the thief who steals twenty-five cents who is usually hanged?'

Waríínga opened the handbag, looked inside without much interest and then said: 'Everything's there.' A question was troubling her. Was this the man whose voice had intervened when she was about to throw herself into the road? How had he fathomed her thoughts? How had he known that this was not the first time she had attempted to kill herself? She asked: 'Are you the person who spoke to me just before I fainted?'

He shook his head. 'I arrived as you were about to fall. Are you ill?'

'No,' Waríínga answered quickly. 'Just weary, body and soul, of Nairobi.'

'You are right to be weary,' the young man said. 'Nairobi is large, soulless and corrupt.' He moved nearer to Waríínga, leaned against the wall and went on: 'But it is not Nairobi alone that is afflicted in this way. The same is true of all the cities in every country that has recently slipped the noose of colonialism. These countries are finding it difficult to stave off poverty for the simple reason that they have taken it upon themselves to learn how to run their economies from American experts. So they have been taught the principle and system of self-interest and have been told to forget the ancient songs that glorify the notion of collective good. They have been taught new songs, new hymns that celebrate the acquisition of money. That's why today Nairobi teaches:

> Crookedness to the upright,
> Meanness to the kind,
> Hatred to the loving,
> Evil to the good.

Today's dance-song proclaims:

> That which pecks never pecks for another.
> That which pinches never pinches for another.
> That which journeys never journeys for another.
> Where is the seeker who searches for another?

Turn these matters over in your mind, and ask yourself: That kind of song – where is it leading us? What kind of heart is it nurturing in us? The kind that prompts us to double up with laughter when we watch our children fighting it out with cats and dogs for leftovers in rubbish bins?

> The wise can also be taught wisdom,
> So let me tell you:
> Gīkūyū said that talking is the way to loving.
> Today is tomorrow's treasury.
> Tomorrow is the harvest of what we plant today.
> So let us ask ourselves:
> Moaning and groaning – who has ever gained from it?
> Change seeds, for the gourd contains seeds of more than one
>   kind!
> Change steps, for the song has more than one rhythm!
> Today's *Muomboko* dance is two steps and a turn!'

The young man suddenly fell silent, but his voice and his words rang in Warīīnga's ears.

She did not understand all the things that were hinted at in the arcane language of the young man. But here and there she could sense that his words approached thoughts that she herself had had at one time. She sighed and said: 'Your words have hidden meanings. But what you say is true. These troubles have now passed beyond the limit of endurance. Who would not welcome change in order to escape from them?'

As she spoke, Warīīnga felt her tongue loosen. She began to talk as if she were lifting a heavy burden from her heart. She spoke in a level voice, neither strident nor muted, neither breathless nor halting. It was a voice, however, laden with pain, sorrow and tears.

16

'Take a girl like me,' Warĩĩnga said, gazing down at one spot as if she were talking to herself. 'Or take any other girl in Nairobi. Let's call her Mahũa Kareendi. Let's assume that she was born in a village or in the heart of the countryside. Her education is limited. Or let's say, perhaps, that she has passed CPE and has gone to a high school. Let's even assume that it is a good school and not like those Haraambe schools where the poor pay good money even when the classrooms boast no teachers.

'Before she reaches *Form Two*, Kareendi has had it. She is pregnant.'

'Who is responsible?'

'A student, say. The student doesn't have a cent to his name. Their friendship has been a matter of lending each other novels by James Hadley Chase, Charles Mangua or David Maillu. It has been a question of singing songs from the records of Jim Reeves or of D. K. or of Lawrence Nduru. Kareendi, where can you turn now?

'On the other hand, we could imagine that the man responsible for the pregnancy is a loafer from the village. The loafer is jobless. He hasn't even a place to lay his head. Their love affair has been sustained by guitar playing and evening dances in the village. It has been conducted in borrowed huts or in the open fields after dark. Little Kareendi, where will you turn? The baby will need food and clothes.

'Perhaps the loafer has a job in the city, but his salary is five shillings a month. Their love has been nourished by Bruce Lee and James Bond films – by five minutes in a cheap hotel on their way home by *matatũ*. Who will wipe away Kareendi's tears now?

'Or let's say that a rich man is the father of the child. Isn't that kind of affair the fashion these days? The rich man has a wife. The affair has been a question of a rendez-vous in a Mercedes Benz on a Sunday. It has been fuelled by small amounts of cash that Kareendi has received as *pocket money* before returning to school. It has been lubricated by hard liquor drunk in hotels far away from the village.

'Student, loafer, rich man – their response is the same when Kareendi tells them about her condition: "What! Kareendi, who are you claiming is responsible for the pregnancy? Me? How have you worked that out? Go on and pester someone else with your delusions, Kareendi of the easy thighs, ten-cent Kareendi. You can cry until your tears have filled oil drums – it will make no difference.... Kareendi, you can't collect pregnancies wherever you may and then lay them at my door just because one day I happened to tease you!"

'Say Kareendi needs no borrowed tongue. She stands there, arms akimbo, and lashes out at yesterday's sweetheart. "You think you are sugar itself? I'd rather drink tea without sugar. You imagine that you're a bus? I'd rather walk. You think you are a house? I'd prefer to sleep in the open air. Or the bed itself, perhaps? I choose the floor. I've lost my faith in silken-tongued gigolos." But Kareendi is only trying to put a brave face on things. Inside, her heart is dancing with rage.

'Let's say Kareendi refuses to take drugs. It is appalling that babies should emerge from their mothers' wombs as corpses. Kareendi has the baby. And she doesn't throw it into a latrine pit, nor does she abandon it at the roadside or in a bus. Nor does she leave it in the forest or on a rubbish tip. Kareendi places on the shoulders of her mother or her grandmother the burden of bringing up this baby, who has come into this world in spite of the fact that her parents have neither welcomed nor prepared for her arrival. But Kareendi's mother and grandmother warn the girl not to make a habit of this: "Be on your guard from now on, Kareendi. Do not forget that men have stings, vicious and corrosive, the poison of which never leaves the flesh of their victims."

'And Kareendi now knows only too well that no one repents on account of another's sins. There is no one who regrets the going as much as the returning. To be smiled at is not to be loved. So Kareendi bites her lips decisively and goes back to school. She makes steady progress and reaches *Form Four*. She sits the Cambridge or *School Certificate* and she gets her EACE, a certificate to indicate that she has passed in English, Swahili and Religion.

'So far so good.

'But problems don't have wings to bear them away. Once again Kareendi's parents have to dig into their pockets. They pull out the cents that they have been saving, the stick put by in reserve in case they should meet a rat unexpectedly – and now just such a rat has appeared. They speedily enrol Kareendi at the *Nairobi Secretarial College* so that she can learn typing and shorthand. At the end of nine months Kareendi can pound a typewriter, thirty-five words a minute, and she is now an expert at shorthand – she has reached the speed of eighty words a minute. The language of the eye is not the language of the ear. Typing and shorthand: Pitman's certificates for the two skills are in Kareendi's pocket.

'Kareendi now tramps all over Nairobi looking for a job. Armed with her Pitman's skills, she enters one office after another. In one she finds *Mr Boss*, who leans back in his chair for greater comfort. He eyes Kareendi from top to toe. "What do you want? A job? *I see.* I'm very *busy* right now. Let's meet at five." Kareendi waits impatiently for the hour to come. She rushes back to the office, panting. Now *Mr Boss* smiles at her, and he offers her a chair, and he asks her what her names are, the one she was given at birth and her acquired English one, and he inquires into the things that are troubling her, and he listens with attentive patience. Then *Mr Boss* taps the desk top with his finger or with a pen, saying, "Ah, Kareendi, jobs are very hard to come by these days. But a girl like you ... it shouldn't be too difficult to find something for you to do. But, Kareendi, a matter like this can't be finalized in the office. Let's go across to the Modern Love *Bar and Lodging* to discuss the question more fully." But Kareendi recalls the venomous stings of her early years: he who has seen once knows thereafter, and he who has drunk from a calabash can gauge its size. So Kareendi declines all invitations to meetings at hotels designed for love, old-fashioned or modern. The next day she is still combing the city for a job.

'She enters another office. She finds there another *Mr Boss*. The smiles are the same, the questions are the same, the rendez-vous is the same – and the target is still Kareendi's thighs. The Modern Love *Bar and Lodging* has become the main employment bureau for girls, and women's thighs are the tables on which contracts are signed. A maiden once drowned in a sea of sweetness. Our new Kenya, however, sings only one song to Kareendi: Sister Kareendi, the case of a fool takes a long time to settle. Sister Kareendi, every court session opens with feasting. Sister Kareendi, no man licks an empty hand. Take care of me, and I will take care of you. Modern problems are resolved with the aid of thighs. He who wishes to sleep is the one who is anxious to make the bed.

'Kareendi is determined to make no beds: she would rather leave her case unsettled. And because God is truly no *ugali* eater, one morning Kareendi lands a job without having to visit any hotel for modern love. *Mr Boss* Kīhara is the managing director of the firm. He is middle-aged. He has a wife and several children. On top of that, he is a member of the committee that runs the Church of Heaven. Kareendi carries out her office duties meticulously.

'Before a month is up, Kareendi finds herself a Kamoongonye.* The young man is a university student. He holds modern, progressive views. When Kareendi confesses to him that she has a child at home, Kamoongonye silences her with kisses of love. He tells Kareendi: "A child is not a leopard, capable of wounding people. Besides, giving birth is proof that you're not a mule!" Hearing this, Kareendi weeps tears of happiness. Then and there, she swears loyalty, with all her heart: "Because I am very lucky, and I have looked for and found a Kamoongonye, a young man with modern views, I, Kareendi, will never anger him or argue with him over any issue. If he shouts at me, I will remain silent. I will simply look down like the shy leopard or like a lamb cropping grass. I will help him with his keep so that he can finish his education without trouble or delay and so that together we can make a home that has solid roots. I will never look at another."

'The other girls, Kareendi's friends, envy her, and they offer her bits and pieces of advice: "Kareendi, you'd better change your ways: the seeds in the gourd are not all of the same type," they tell her. Kareendi replies: "A restless child leaves home in search of meat just as a goat is about to be slaughtered." But the girls tell her: "Friend, this is a new Kenya. Everyone should set something aside to meet tomorrow's needs. He who saves a little food will never suffer from hunger." She replies: "Too much eating ruins the stomach." They taunt her: "A restricted diet is monotonous." Kareendi rejects this and tells them: "A borrowed necklace may lead to the loss of one's own."

'Now, just as Kareendi is thinking that her life is running very smoothly, *Mr Boss* Kĩhara begins to sound her out with carefully chosen words. One day he comes into her office. He stands by her typewriter, and he pretends to examine the sheets of paper that Kareendi has typed. He says: "*By the way, Miss* Kareendi, what are your plans for *this weekend*? I would like you to accompany me on a small safari – *what do you say to that*?" Kareendi declines politely. Rejection wrapped in civility arouses no ill feelings. *Boss* Kĩhara waits, hoping that Kareendi will eventually yield. Too much haste splits the yam. One month later, he again accosts Kareendi in the office. "*Miss* Kareendi, this evening there's a *cocktail party at the Paradise Club*." Once again Kareendi disguises her refusal with polite phrases.

*Kamoongonye is a character in a Gĩkũyũ ballad about a young girl whose father wants her to marry Waigoko, a rich old man with a hairy chest, while she prefers her own choice, a poor young man, Kamoongonye.

'The day comes when *Boss* Kīhara reasons with himself in this way: The hunter who stalks his prey too stealthily may frighten it off in the end. Begging calls for constantly changing tactics. Bathing involves removing all one's clothes. So he confronts Kareendi boldly. "*By the way, Miss* Kareendi, I've got a lot of work to do today. There is a pile of letters to be answered, all very important and very urgent. I would like you to stay behind in the office after five o'clock. The firm will pay you *overtime*."

Kareendi waits. Five o'clock. *Boss* Kīhara is in his office, drafting the letters, perhaps. Six o'clock. Everyone else has gone home. *Boss* Kīhara calls for Kareendi. He asks her to take a seat so that they can talk. After a minute or two, *Boss* Kīhara stands up and sits on the edge of his desk. He smiles slyly. Kareendi now finds her tongue. '*Please, Mr Boss*, do dictate the letters to me now. I was planning to go out this evening, and it's getting dark.'

"'Don't worry, Kareendi. If it gets late, I will give you a lift home in my car."

"'*Thank you*, but I really don't want to inconvenience you," Kareendi answers levelly, to hide her irritation.

"'Oh, it will be no trouble at all. I could even ring home to instruct *my personal chauffeur* to collect you and drive you to your place."

"'I enjoy travelling by bus. *Please* – where are the letters?

'*Boss* Kīhara leans slightly towards Kareendi. A certain light is shining in his eyes. He drops his voice.

"'Kareendi, darling, mine are letters dictated by the heart."

"'By the heart, did you say?" Kareendi asks quickly, pretending not to understand the implication of his words. "Is it wise for you to dictate such letters to an employee? Wouldn't it be better for you to type them yourself, so that the secrets of your heart will not be read by someone for whom they are not intended?"

"'Beautiful Kareendi, flower of my heart. No one but you can type them. For I want to send them care of the address of your heart, by the post of your heart, to be read by the eyes of your heart, thereafter to be kept within your heart, sealed there forever and ever. And you when you receive the letters, I beg you, don't write *Return to sender*. Darling, flower of my heart, see how my love for you has weakened me?"

"'*Mr Boss, sir, please* . . .!" Kareendi tries to slip in a word. One part of her is scared as she sees how *Boss* Kīhara is panting. But another part of her feels like laughing when she contrasts the words that are tumbling from the *Boss*'s mouth with the bright, shining bald patch on his head. Kareendi is searching for words that will put this old man to shame: "Suppose your wife heard you saying such things! What would you do?"

"'She doesn't count. One doesn't use scentless perfume when going to a dance. *Please*, Kareendi, little fruit of my heart, listen to me carefully so that I may tell you beautiful things. I will rent a house for you on *Furaha Leo Estate*, or in the city centre, *Kenyatta Avenue*, or any other part of the city. Choose any flat or house you like. I will have the place decorated with furniture, carpets, mattresses, curtains from Paris, London, Berlin, Rome, New York, Tokyo, Stockholm or Hong Kong. *Imported furniture and household goods*. I will buy you clothes, for I want you in the latest fashions from *Oxford Street*, London, or from the *haute couture* houses of Paris. High heels and platform shoes will come from Rome, Italy. When you step out in those shoes which you people have nicknamed 'no-destination-why-should-I-hurry?' I want everyone in Nairobi to turn round and whistle with envy, saying: That is *Boss* Kĩhara's *sugar girl*. If these pleasures last, if you keep me happy with all earthly delights, I will buy you a small basket for the market, for shopping, or for jaunts on a Sunday – I think an Alfa Romeo is the kind of car that would be fitting for a bride. Kareendi, my little fruit, my little orange, flower of my heart, come to me and say *bye-bye* to poverty . . . ."

'Kareendi is now holding back her laughter with great difficulty. She says to him: "'*Mr Boss, please* may I ask you one question?"

"'Ask a thousand and one!"

"'Are you saying that you want to marry me?"

"'Ah! Why are you pretending not to understand the way things are? Can't you see that . . . . My little fruit, be mine now, be my girl."

"'No. I have never wanted affairs with my *bosses*!"

"'My little fruit, what are you afraid of?"

"'Besides, I wouldn't want to break up your home. A borrowed necklace may make a person lose his own."

"'Didn't I tell you that one doesn't go to a dance wearing old, scentless perfume? Kareendi, my new necklace, my tomato plant growing on the rich soil of an abandoned homestead! What are you afraid of? What is the problem?"

"'I have a Kamoongonye, a young lover."

"'Ha! Kareendi, don't make me laugh. Are you really so *old-fashioned*? Are you talking about one of those boys who pretend to be men? Those boys, are they even circumcised?"

"'The yam that one has dug up for oneself has no mouldy patches. The sugar cane that one has picked out has no unripe edges. Those whom one loves do not squint. The young man who you claim is uncircumcised is my chosen one."

"'Kareendi, listen. I'll tell you something,' *Boss* Kīhara says to her, panting. He gets off the table. He comes closer to Kareendi. "These days the question of a choice between Waigoko, the man with the hairy chest, and Kamoongonye, the young lover, is no longer valid. Waigoko's hairy chest has been shaved by money . . . . But because it is true that the heart is hungry only for what it has chosen, I won't press the matter of your becoming my mistress. You have refused a nice house. You have refused expensive clothes. And you have refused a shopping basket. All right. *As you like*. But allow me this one request. Don't refuse me."

"'Aren't you a member of the Church of Heaven? Do you ever read the Bible? When you go home, read *Romans*, Chapter XIII, line fourteen: 'Make not provision for the flesh, to fulfil the lusts thereof . . . .'"

"'But in the same book it is also written: 'Ask, and it shall be given you; seek and ye shall find; knock, and it shall be opened unto you: For every one that asketh receiveth, and he that seeketh, findeth; and to him that knocketh it shall be opened . . . .' My little fruit, my love, we need not even bother with accommodation. This office floor is adequate. If these offices could talk, they would tell many tales. A smooth cement floor makes a fantastic bed. It straightens the back and all the bones of the spinal cord right up to the neck."

"'I don't want my back straightened!' Kareendi snaps back, concealing her anger no longer.

'*Boss* Kīhara now tries to embrace Kareendi. The two nearly trip over the chair. Kareendi gets up, hangs her handbag over one shoulder and begins to walk backwards. *Boss* Kīhara reaches for her. They circle one another in the office as if they were dancing the dance of the hunter and the hunted. *Boss* Kīhara has abandoned all pretence at dignity.

'And suddenly *Boss* Kīhara pounces on Kareendi. One hand holds Kareendi by the waist. The other tries to feel for her body. Kareendi attempts to free herself from the man's grip, at the same time beating her fists on his chest and also trying vainly to open her handbag to take out the folding knife she normally carries. The sound of their heavy breathing fills the office. Kareendi senses that she is about to be overcome. Suddenly she forgets that this is her *Boss* and cries out: "If you don't let me go, I will shout for help!"

'*Boss* Kīhara pauses. He remembers his wife and children. He recalls that often on Sundays he is the one who reads the Bible at the altar in the Church of Heaven, and that from time to time he gives

23

talks at weddings, advising newlyweds about the need for parents and children to live together in love and harmony. He recalls all these things simultaneously. He imagines the scorn of the whole country if he were charged with raping his secretary. The fire suddenly dies. Ardour retreats. He releases Kareendi. He takes a handkerchief from his pocket and wipes away the sweat. He looks at Kareendi. He tries to say something, then he stops. He is trying to find words to save his face. He tries to laugh, but the laughter fades. For the sake of saying something he asks: "Does this mean, Kareendi, that at home nobody teases you? *Anyway*, don't jump to hasty conclusions. This was only a joke between father and daughter. Go home now. You'd better do the letters early tomorrow morning."

'Kareendi goes home, still thinking about the joke between father and daughter. How well she knows that joke. It's a joke between a leopard and a goat . . . .

'In the morning Kareendi comes to work as usual. She is five minutes late. She finds that *Boss* Kīhara has already arrived. *Boss* Kīhara summons her to his office. Kareendi goes in. She feels a little awkward as she recalls their struggle last night. But *Boss* Kīhara does not even raise his eyes from his newspaper.

'"*Miss* Kareendi, it looks as though you're your own boss these days."

'"I am sorry, *sir*. The bus was late."

'Now *Boss* Kīhara looks up from the newspaper. He leans back in his chair. He fixes Kareendi with a look full of bitterness.

'"Why can't you admit that the trouble is the rides you are offered by young men? *Miss* Kareendi, it seems as though you don't much care for work. I feel I should let you follow the promptings of your heart. It would be better for you to go home for a while. If ever you feel that you need work, as other girls do, I haven't closed the door. Take this month's salary and next month's too *in lieu of notice*."

'Our Kareendi now has no job. Once again she roams the streets in search of work. She goes home to sorrow in silence. She sits in her room until evening, waiting for her young man. Her heart pulses to the rhythm of happiness as she recalls the sound of her young lover's voice. Everyone cares about those whom he loves. Her Kamoongonye will give her strength to endure this sorrow through words of love. At long last Kamoongonye comes home. Kareendi pours out the whole story of Waigoko, whose bearded chest has been shaved by money. There is no greater love than this, that a modern girl should reject Waigoko's money because of Kamoongonye! Kareendi finishes her story. She waits for a sympathetic sigh. She anticipates kisses that will brush away her tears.

24

'But no.

'Kamoongonye is the one who lowers his eyes like the shy leopard or like a lamb cropping grass. But he is motivated by hypocrisy. He lectures Kareendi. He declares that he knows very well that Kareendi has rumpled Waigoko Kīhara's bed, that Kīhara is not even the first to eat from Kareendi's thighs, that a girl who has sipped at the delights of money can never stop drinking. He who tastes develops a penchant for tasting. A chameleon will always be a chameleon. A girl who starts going with men old enough to be her father while she is at school, to the extent of giving birth to babies when still a student, how can she stop herself? "Tell me this, Kareendi of the easy thighs, if you had allowed Waigoko to rub off his soot on your thighs, would you have come to tell me? No. You are spinning me this yarn only because Waigoko has refused to let you continue making his bed in hotels for modern love."

'Kareendi is speechless.

'Tears flow down her cheeks, and she does not wipe them away. Bitterness rages in her heart.

'Kareendi asks herself many questions without answers. The grade cow has stopped yielding milk. So is it now fit only for slaughter?

'For Kareendi, the sword is burned at both ends. She is back where she started.

'So tell me, you who held my hand so that I shouldn't fall again: does this mean that the Kareendis of modern Kenya have only one organ? What will prevent Kareendi from roaming the streets as if she were sister to the legendary Cain?

'For today Kareendi has decided that she does not know the difference between

> To straighten and to bend,
> To swallow and to spit out,
> To ascend and to descend,
> To go and to return.

Yes, for from today she'll never be able to distinguish between

> The crooked and the upright,
> The foolish and the wise,
> Darkness and light,
> Laughter and tears,
> Hell and Heaven,
> Satan's kingdom and God's.

25

Who said that in a man's life on Earth there are only two days? Days

> Of honey and acid,
> Of laughter and tears,
> Of birth and death?

To the Kareendis of modern Kenya, isn't each day exactly the same as all the others? For the day on which they are born is the very day on which every part of their body is buried except one – they are left with a single organ. So when will the Kareendis of modern Kenya wipe the tears from their faces? When will they ever discover laughter?'

3

When Warĩĩnga had finished her story, she looked up to study the young man's face. Then she gazed down the length of *Racecourse Road*, and she observed that people were still busily going about their business and that cars were still hooting to get past each other and that Nairobi had not changed a bit since she had been thrown out of her house in Ofafa Jericho.

Just then the bells of *St Peter's Clavers Church* began to toll, reminding believers of the angelus before sunset. Warĩĩnga and the young man turned towards the peal of bells. As if the bells themselves were chanting, Warĩĩnga heard these words:

> Come, come,
> Hold fast to your plough
> And don't look back.
> Come, come . . . .

She asked herself: These voices I keep hearing – where do they come from? Where will they lead me? Although she had not entered a church for a long time, she found herself muttering a prayer:

> O Holy Virgin Mary, Mother of God and our Mother,
> And you, Holy Joseph,
> And you, my guardian angel,
> And all you Holy Ones,
> Pray for me

That I may give up
The sin of wanting to end my life
Before I have completed my span on Earth.
Watch over me today
And all the days of my life
To the day of my death.
Amen.

When the bells of *St Peter's* fell silent, Warĩĩnga turned to the young man and said: 'Thank you for listening to me so patiently. My heart feels lighter, just as it used to feel after I had confessed to the Catholic priest.'

'Maybe I'm a priest who has not yet been ordained.... But I belong to an order that has been called to serve by the poverty of the people of Kenya. That story of yours – I mean, about Kareendi, Waigoko and Kamoongonye – pierced my heart like a spear. There are countless Kareendis in Kenya, as you say. But I don't agree with you that our children will never know laughter. We must never despair. Despair is the one sin that cannot be forgiven. It is the sin for which we would never be forgiven by the nation and generations to come. Where are you going now? Where are you heading?'

'Ilmorog.'

'Ilmorog? Is that where you come from?'

'Yes, Ilmorog is home. Why?'

'Because ... er ... no particular reason. I was just asking. But buses for Ilmorog don't stop here. This stop, Kaka, is for buses to Kĩambu, Nduumbeeri, Ting'aang'a, Ngeemwa, Ikinũ, Karia-inĩ and Gĩthũngũri. *Matatũs* for Ilmorog halt at the same stop as those bound for Nakuru, over there at Nyamakĩma.'

'I know. In fact, that was where I was going. I don't know which ill wind blew me to this side of the road.'

Warĩĩnga stood up, like a person emerging from a deathly day dream, and she slung her handbag over one shoulder. '*Well*, take care,' she said to the young man. She was happy, but also a little ashamed.

'Look after yourself. I hope the dizziness doesn't strike again.'

As Warĩĩnga turned to make her way towards Nyamakĩma, the man called out to her: 'Wait a moment....'

Warĩĩnga stopped and looked back, asking herself: Could he be another Kamoongonye who thinks he has found a Kareendi of the easy thighs?

The man opened the bag he was carrying. He searched inside it, took out a card and gave it to Warĩĩnga, explaining: 'I told you that

27

your story, or the parable about Kareendi and Waigoko and Kamoongonye, pierced my heart. If you would like to know more about the conditions that breed modern Kareendis and Waigokos, go to the feast advertised on the card when you get to Ilmorog.

The man strolled away. Wariinga walked down *Racecourse Road*, through the grounds of the *Esso* petrol station, across River Road and on to Nyamakima. She only looked back once, just to see if the man was following her. She did not see him. And I never asked for his name, Wariinga thought. It might be on the card he gave me. But all men, whoever they are, are soothing blood-suckers. He tells me to go to a party. I don't want to go to any parties. I don't want any more affairs, be they with Waigokos, old and hairy-chested men, or with Kamoongonyes, young lovers.

At Nyamakima there were no *matatūs* bound for Ilmorog or Nakuru. Waringa leaned against the wall of a shop selling onions and potatoes, near the Nyamakima Bar . . . .

After a while Waringa caught herself fingering the card she had been given. She remembered that she had not even read it. She paused, then she took it out of her pocket and examined it closely. This is what she read:

The Devil's Feast!

Come and See for Yourself –
A Devil-Sponsored Competition
To Choose Seven Experts in Theft and Robbery.
Plenty of Prizes!
Try Your Luck.
Competition to Choose the Seven Cleverest
Thieves and Robbers in Ilmorog.
Prizes Galore!
Hell's Angels Band in Attendance!

Signed: Satan
The King of Hell
c/o Thieves' and Robbers' Den
Ilmorog Golden Heights

Wariinga felt as if she had been stabbed in the stomach with a razor blade. She gazed about her, from side to side, in front of her and behind her, to establish whether her body really was at Nyamakima or if she was dreaming again. Questions assaulted her mind's ear like a swarm of bees on the move. And just as a single bee is sometimes left behind by the others, one question in particular remained lodged in Wariinga's mind: Who was that young man who had taken her by the hand? And did this mean that her handbag had been retrieved for her by a thief? She trembled. She felt for the card again. She leaned against the wall of the onion and potato shop to prevent herself from falling.

But her heart was beating fast. A devils' feast at Ilmorog! A competition for thieves and robbers at Ilmorog! Tomorrow, Sunday? Who would believe that such miracles could happen?

Chapter Three

1

Nyamakīma, like so many *matatū* stops and bus stops in Nairobi, is very congested with people and cars – people coming from or going to Grogan Valley, where it is said one never fails to find spare parts for any and every type of vehicle; people coming from and going to River Road, said to be the street where workers and peasants, especially those from the rural areas, go shopping on Saturdays and Sundays. Some are just buyers of potatoes and onions and *sukuma wiki* vegetables; others want to visit the bars and restaurants to have a beer and fill their bellies before going home to the locations: Kariokor, Eastleigh, Pumwani, Shauri Moyo, Bahati, Makaandara, Ofafa Jericho, Kariobang'i and Dandora. But the majority are travellers waiting for *matatūs* bound for Naivasha, Gilgil, Olkalou, Nyahururu, Nakuru, Rūūwa-inī and Ilmorog. Nyamakīma, when the place is full of people and cars, resounds with the din of seven markets.

That Saturday there weren't many vehicles bound for Rūūwa-inī and Ilmorog. Whenever she heard the rumble-tumble of a *matatū*, Warīīnga would look up in expectation. But on hearing that only passengers for Nakuru or Nyahururu were being called, her heart would sink. When six o'clock came, she began to pity herself, and she silently prayed: 'O, Virgin Mary, Mother of God, have pity on me. I don't want to spend another night in Nairobi. Help me to find a bus, even a donkey cart, anything that will take me away from Nairobi and home to Ilmorog. Praise be to the Father, and the Son, and the Holy Spirit, as it was in the beginning, is now and will be for ever and ever. Amen.'

She had barely finished her prayer when an Ilmorog-bound *matatū* arrived. But on looking at it, Warīīnga was appalled: had this thing just been collected from a rubbish heap in Grogan Valley? Certainly, it was old: but the owner had tried hard to disguise its age by painting on its sides many eye- and mind-catching ads: IF YOU WANT GOSSIP OR RUMOURS, RIDE IN MWAŪRA'S MATATŪ MATATA MATAMU. YOUR WAYS ARE MY WAYS. TOO MUCH HASTE SPLITS THE YAM. CRAWL BUT ARRIVE SAFELY. HOME SWEET HOME.

Just before she had finished reading all the ads, Warīīnga saw the driver jump out and start praising his *matatū*, calling attention to it with words and songs that were intended to distract people's eyes from its decrepit condition.

'Get in, get into Matatū Matata Matamu Model T Ford, and you'll find yourself in Limuru, Satellite, Naivasha, Rūūwa-inī, Ilmorog, before you've have blinked twice. I once heard young men sing

> If God's kingdom were near,
> I would take you whores to court.
> Something given you free by the Lord
> You now sell for twenty shillings.

Young men, let me tell you a secret: God's kingdom has been brought closer by Mwaūra's Matatū Matata Matamu Model T Ford. Even the journey to the Devil's place is nothing to Mwaūra's Matata Matamu Model T Ford. Get in! Get in! Ilmorog is here, no further than the eye is from the nose.'

On hearing the mention of the word 'devil', Warīīnga once again experienced an eerie sensation. She remembered her invitation to the Devil's feast and the competition in theft and robbery, and she again asked herself: What kind of a feast is this? What does the competition consist of? Someone who was so good to me – how can he possibly have joined a band of thieves and robbers? Why didn't he steal my handbag? But as she listened to the words that were gushing from Mwaūra's mouth, for a while she forgot the load she carried in her heart.

By now dozens of people had come out of bars and shops and were standing on the kerb to see the owner of the matatū for themselves, egging him on: '*Yes! Yes! Tell us everything!*'

2

It looked as if Mwaūra's Matatū Matata Matamu Model T Ford, registration number MMM 333, was the very first motor vehicle to have been made on Earth. The engine moaned and screamed like several hundred dented axes being ground simultaneously. The car's body shook like a reed in the wind. The whole vehicle waddled along the road like a duck up a mountain.

In the morning, before starting, the matatū gave spectators a wonderful treat. The engine would growl, then cough as if a piece of metal were stuck in its throat, then it rasped as if it had asthma. At such times Mwaūra would open the bonnet dramatically, poke here and there, touch this wire and that one, then shut the bonnet equally dramatically before returning to the steering wheel. He would gently press the accelerator with his right foot, and the engine would start groaning as if its belly were being massaged.

But the *matatū* had a public relations officer in Mwaŭra. People would ask him: Mwaŭra, does this vehicle belong to the days of Noah? Mwaŭra would laugh, shake his head, lean back against the car, then try to intoxicate his audience with proof of the car's excellent qualities.

'I tell you honestly, there is no modern car that can match the Model T Ford construction-wise. Don't simply contrast the gleam of the bodywork. Beauty is not food. The metal from which modern cars are made – models like Peugeots, Toyotas, Canters, even Volvos and Mercedes Benzes – fall to pieces as easily as paper soaked in rain. But not the Model T Ford, oh no! Its metal is the kind that is said to be able to drill holes in other cars. I'd rather keep this old model. A stone hardened by age is never washed away by the rains. A borrowed necklace may cause one to lose one's own. The new models come from Japan, Germany, France, America. They trot with vigour for two months, then they disintegrate and leave the Model T Ford right in the middle of the road.'

Yet Mwaŭra's aim was to make money as quickly as possible in order to buy a bigger vehicle which would carry more passengers, so that more cash would flow more quickly into his pockets.

Mwaŭra was one of those who worshipped at the shrine of the god of money. He used to say that there was no universe he would not visit, no river that he would not cross, no mountain that he would not climb, no crime that he would not commit in loyal obedience to the molten god of money.

But it looked as if his prayers were not heeded or even kindly received, because Mwaŭra had never owned any vehicle but that *matatū*, which had been left to him by a European they used to call Nyaangwĩcũ. Once in a while Mwaŭra would bury himself in grief, asking himself: 'Have I been on the road all this time, the fruits of success hanging here above my very eyes, only to find that when I stretch out my arms to pick them, I see them recede to a point so far distant that I can't reach them even if I stand on my toes?'

Mwaŭra would tell people: 'This money that has been brought here by Europeans is wholly evil. When you think that it was money that caused the Son of Mary to be crucified on the Cross, even though he was the first-born of the God of the Jews, what else can you say? As for me, I would sell my own mother if I thought she would fetch a good price!' People used to think that this was the idle boast of a light-hearted businessman. Only one man knew that Mwaūra never joked where money was concerned, but he never came back to tell the tale. He and Mwaūra had quarrelled over five shillings. The man had refused to pay, and he had even taunted Mwaūra: 'You will always make shift like a beetle in rain-soaked dung, and you'll never acquire riches!' Mwaūra told him: 'You have refused to pay me my five shillings, although you know very well that we agreed that you would hire the car for seventy-five shillings, just because you say I took on two other passengers. Were you hiring a seat or the whole car? I challenge you to make off with my money. The Mwaūra you see has not been sharpened on one side only, like a matchet.'

One morning the man was found hanged in his own house. Near the body had been left a piece of paper on which these words were scribbled: NEVER PLAY WITH OTHER PEOPLE'S PROPERTY. We are the *Devil's Angels – Private Businessmen.*

But driving Matatū Matata Matamu Model T Ford, registration number MMM 333, was the job for which Mwaūra was best-known.

3

There is a saying that when a bird in flight gets tired, it will land on any tree. When Warīīnga saw that there was no other vehicle bound for Ilmorog, she entered Mwaūra's. And, seeing Warīīnga enter, Mwaūra added more embellishments to his songs and words:

> Young maiden, if I should beg,
> Don't say you'll get pregnant,
> For as I know how to brake a motorcycle,
> Do you imagine that I could not apply the brakes to you?

He paused. He heaved a sigh. He surveyed the people who had now surrounded him. He smiled, standing with his hands on his hips. Then he shook his head and said: 'A loafer's brakes are false brakes. There are no brakes to match the strength of those that belong to Matatū Matata Matamu Model T Ford. . . .'

People were beside themselves with laughter and whistled loudly. Mwaūra went on touting for passengers. '. . . Limuru, Naivasha, Rūūwa-inī, Ilmorog! Let's go now. Remember: your ways are my ways. . . .'

That Saturday Mwaūra had been up and down the Limuru – Nairobi route without picking up enough passengers to cover even

33

the cost of the petrol. It was late in the afternoon when he decided to go to Nyamakīma to see if he could pick up a few passengers to pay for the petrol for Ilmorog. That's why he was now shouting so vigorously. ' ... Remember: This is your country! This is your *matatū*! Forget all about those Peugeots that bounce along the road, causing our women to have miscarriages. Crawl but arrive ....'

Another passenger got into the car. He had on blue overalls, which were worn out at the knees and elbows. His shoes were covered with ashy dust. He sat down facing Warīīnga. Mwaūra also climbed in, sat down in the driver's seat and revved the engine a little. Then, leaving it running, he went outside again. He felt as if everything would come to nothing. Just the two passengers ....

Irritably, he wondered: Am I really going to end up dying, bleating like a sheep? Will there never come a time when I'll be able to afford a new car like other men? Today people with pushcarts and donkey carts, the shoeshine boys, those who roast maize and those who sell rabbits and fruit and sheepskins to tourists by the roadside will take home more money than I will. What will eventually become of me, Robin Mwaūra? I'd better give up these night journeys. I'll rent a room in Nairobi and go to Ilmorog tomorrow morning.'

But remembering the loss he had already incurred over the petrol, Mwaūra felt as if a sharp knife were being driven into him. Mwaūra was one of those men who can never leave a shining coin lying in their path – even a five-cent piece. He would rather fall into a pit in an attempt to reach it. He said to himself: Me, sacrifice the fares of these two? No! Before I get to Limuru I may find passengers stranded on the road at night, or some who normally wait for the OTC buses at the Mūtarakwa stage, and I can win them over with sweet words. Besides, I'd really like to spend tonight in Ilmorog so that tomorrow I will be among the first there. He who searches carefully never fails to find.

His hope of riches instantly revived, his heart began to beat hard, and he shouted with great gusto: 'You're about to be left behind! You're about to be abandoned by Matatū Matata Matamu! I am your servant. Give me the order to speed you to God's or to Satan's place! Let there be peace! We'd better be off. You should get yourselves to Ilmorog so that afterwards you won't have to depend on hearsay. You ought to be in Ilmorog to see for yourselves and to hear for yourselves .... Fortune may be hiding just on the other side of the bush! Let this *matatū* take you around the bush that now stands between you and good fortune! Now is the hour – we must be off to Ilmorog, for good fortune can change to ill fortune, and good luck never makes an early visit twice ....

'Is he going to start, or is he going to keep us here all night with his stories?' the man in the blue overalls asked.

'A *matatū* is the home of gossip, rumour and idle talk!' Warīīnga replied.

Mwaūra climbed into the vehicle, revved the engine, hooted and then began to pull out.

Suddenly on every side the crowd broke into a chorus of high and low-pitched whistles, warning the driver to stop. Mwaūra braked.

A young man with a suitcase ran up to the vehicle, panting, and climbed in to join Warīīnga and the man with the blue overalls. 'Is it going to Ilmorog?' he asked still breathless.

'Yes, yes, home to Ilmorog!' Mwaūra said, in a jovial mood.

'Ah, I almost missed it!' the man with the suitcase said, but nobody responded. There was a pause.

'Were you with another passenger?' Mwaūra asked.

'No!' the man with the suitcase replied.

The man laid the suitcase across his knees. Warīīnga glanced at it briefly and saw that the lid of the suitcase bore both his name and his address: Mr Gatuīria, *African Studies, University of Nairobi.*

The university! Warīīnga sensed an unpleasant sinking feeling in her belly.

Mwaūra drove off with his three passengers, Warīīnga, Gatuīria and the man with the blue overalls. He passed the Macaakū and railway bus stops without picking up any other passengers. He drove along *Haille Sellasie* Road, then joined Ngong Road. He had given up all hope of finding any more passengers.

The man called Gatuīria opened his suitcase and took out three books, *The Lives of the Great Composers,* by Harold C. Schomberg, *Introduction to Kamba Music,* by P. Kavyu, and *Musical Instruments of East Africa,* by Graham Hyslop, looked at each, then began to read *The Lives of the Great Composers.*

What is fated to be yours will always belong to you. When Mwaūra reached Dagoretti Corner, near Wanyee's Clan's place, he was stopped by a woman wearing a kitenge upper garment that covered a sisal basket she was carrying. She wore no shoes.

'Ilmorog?' she asked.

'Step right inside!' Mwaūra said, happily. 'Mother, come in. We're off. Is there anyone else?'

'No,' the woman said, getting into the car. Once seated, she cupped her chin in her left hand. Mwaūra drove on, whistling.

At Sigona bus stop, near the Golf Club, Mwaūra picked up another passenger, bringing the total to five. He was a man in a grey suit and a tie with a pattern of red flowers. In his right hand he held a small, black, leather suitcase with a shiny aluminium lining. His eyes were shielded by dark glasses.

Mwaũra felt his heart swell. After we have travelled a little further, I may get another five to make ten and that will give us enough for petrol, he counselled himself.

But when he go to Mũtarakwa, at Limuru, despair seized him. There was not a soul going westwards. Doubts and indecision repossessed him. Should I go on to Ilmorog in the dark just because of five passengers? he mused. Shouldn't I lie to them, tell them that the vehicle has broken down and that we will have to sleep at Kamĩrĩĩthũ and resume the journey tomorrow? But another voice told him: 'Mwaũra, don't snub good fortune. While you sleep, fortune can change her mind. Don't look down on a fragment of a coin. The volume of a fart is increased by the seat. In the belly one small portion joins another to form a whole meal. Single cents gather together to make whole shillings in the pockets of a property hunter.'

Mwaũra stepped on the accelerator and headed towards Ilmorog with his five passengers: Warĩĩnga, Gatuĩria, the man in the blue overalls, the woman with the kitenge garment and the basket and the man with dark glasses.

Travelling is what makes a journey.

4

The woman with the garment and the basket was the first to speak. The *matatũ* had passed Nguirũbi and was just coming to Kĩneenĩĩ when the woman cleared her throat. 'Driver!' she called out.

'Call me Robin Mwaũra,' Mwaũra told her jovially.

'Friend, let me pour out my problem to you before we have gone too far.'

'Knock and it shall be opened,' Mwaũra replied, thinking that the woman wanted to start the kind of conversation that is usual in a *matatũ*. 'Wisdom hidden in the heart can never win a law suit,' he added.

'That is the spirit, friend. In this world there is nothing as important as helping one another. I am riding in your vehicle, but I haven't so much as a cent that I can offer you as the fare,' the woman said sadly.

'What?' Mwaũra shouted.

'I can't pay the fare!'

Mwaũra braked abruptly. On the side where the man with the dark glasses was sitting the doors opened. It was only the quick reflex of the man in the blue overalls that saved the man with the dark glasses from being thrown out on to the Kĩneeniĩ slopes, for it was he who saw the danger and sprang forward to grab the other man.

Mwaũra stopped by the roadside.

'Why are you taking this one to Ngong?'* the man in the blue overalls asked Mwaũra. 'Have you been bribed by his enemies?' he added. The man with the dark glasses did not have a chance to say anything – to rebuke Mwaũra or to thank the man in the blue overalls.

'It is all this woman's fault!' Mwaũra replied quickly, and he turned to her. 'I do not want any wrangling between us. This vehicle does not run on urine.'

'When we get to Ilmorog, I won't fail to find someone to lend me the fare.'

'Nothing is free in Kenya. Kenya is not Tanzania or China.'

'Elderly one, I have never lived by the sweat of another.... But if you only knew what I have seen and been through in this Nairobi of yours....'

Mwaũra cut her short. 'I don't want any tales about one-eyed ogres. Cough up the money or get out.'

'You really mean to leave me here in the wilderness?'

'Woman, you must get out and continue to Ilmorog on foot. I repeat, this car does not run on urine.'

'I am telling the truth when I say that I fought for this country's independence with these hands. Am I now supposed to spend the night here, sharing the dark forest with wild beasts?' the woman asked with a heavy heart, as if posing a problem with which she was familiar, but to which she had so far failed to find an answer.

'These days the land rewards not those who clear it but those who come after it has been cleared,' Mwaũra told her. 'Independence is not tales about the past but the sound of money in one's pocket. Don't joke with me. Get out or let us hear the sweet sound of coins so that we can continue.'

It was the man in the blue overalls who settled the dispute. 'Let us go on, driver. No animal cries out in pain unless it has been hurt. I'll pay for her.'

The man called Gatuĩria spoke up: 'Yes, start the engine and let's move. I will also contribute a few cents to her fare.'

---

*Meaning 'Why are you trying to kill this man?' The phrase came into use after the J.M. assassination on Ngong Hills in 1975.

'I would like to contribute as well,' Waríínga said quickly, remembering that she too would have been without money for the fare if her handbag had been lost in River Road.

'We can divide the amount by three to make the load lighter. A large task becomes a burden only when people refuse to do their share,' the man in the blue overalls said.

Mwaúra started the car and drove away from Kíneeníí.

They travelled a short distance in silence. It was the woman who broke the silence with words of gratitude.

'I'm very happy. But there is nothing I can do to let you know how I feel about your help. My name is Wangarí. I come from Ilmorog – Njeruca village. When we get to Ilmorog, I'll try somehow to get the money to pay you back. But I have showered a little saliva on my breast. May you always cultivate fertile fields.'

'Don't worry about my share,' the man in the blue overalls told her. 'If we don't help each other, we'll become like the beasts. That's why in the days of Mau Mau we took the oath, swearing: 'I'll never eat alone . . . .

'*Even mine . . . I mean*, mine also, *forget it – sorry, I mean*, forget about my share,' Gatuíria said. Gatuíria was always ashamed of mixing English and Gíkúyú words, and he tried hard not to do it. 'As for me, I agree with what this man says,' Gatuíria added. 'But what is your name, so that I can stop calling you "this man"? *My name . . . I mean* mine is Gatuíria.'

'And I am called Mútri,' the man in the blue overalls replied. 'I'm a worker. I specialize in carpentry, stone-working and plumbing – I'm a *plumber, carpenter and mason* – but I can do anything that involves using my hands. Work is life.'

'What about you, young lady?' Wangarí asked Waríínga.

'I am called Waríínga, Jacinta Waríínga, and I come from Ilmorog.'

'Which part?' Wangarí asked.

'From the village called Ngaindeithia near *New Jerusalem* Njeruca', Waríínga replied.

'You know, what you were saying . . .,' Gatuíria began, directing his words at Mútri. He paused, cleared his throat, then asked Mútri: '*Can you please tell me, I mean*, can you tell me . . .' He paused once more, as if he did not quite know what he wanted to ask. He tried again. 'Can we say that the idea of Haraambe has its roots in the goals and aims of the Mau Mau?'

'Haraambe?' Mútri said, laughing a little. 'Haraambe? Haven't you heard what the Nyakínyua dancers sing?

38

The Haraambe you now see,
The Haraambe you now see
Is not for gossipers and rumour-mongers.

So it isn't proper for me to gossip and spread rumours about anything to do with modern Haraambe. Modern Haraambe? H'm! I'll shut up, for it is said the people from the land of silence were once saved by silence. But if I were to be asked my advice, I'd tell the Nyakīnyua dancers to sing this:

The Haraambe of money,
The Haraambe of money
Is for the rich and their friends.

When we were fighting for independence, Haraambe — or let's call it organized unity – took two forms. There was the organization of home guards and imperialists, and there was the organization of patriots under Mau Mau. The organization of patriots used to sing these words:

Great love I found there
Among women and children.
A bean fell to the ground –
We split it among ourselves.

The organization of home guards and imperialists used to sing the song like this:

Self-love and the love of selling out
Among the traitors of the land.
The bean we steal from the people –
We struggle to see who can grab it all.

You people, the Haraambe of home guards and imperialists was an organization designed to encourage bestiality: a man would throw children and the disabled into the fire as he rushed for the debris and leftovers of the imperialists. The Mau Mau's Haraambe was an organization designed to spread humanitarianism, for its members used to offer their own lives in defence of children and the disabled. The home guards' organization aimed to sell our country to foreigners: the Mau Mau's aim was to protect our country. You, young man! I told you, I'll not talk about modern Haraambe. The modern Haraambe has its owners.'

Mũturi stopped abruptly. He swatted a fly that was crawling across his overalls. In the car complete silence reigned again. Mwaũra negotiated the bends and the corners of the slopes of Kĩneeniĩ as he drove towards the bed of the *Rift Valley*. The darkness had now started to deepen, and Mwaũra switched on the headlights.

Wangarĩ clicked her tongue, cleared her throat and started talking in a voice full of bitterness. 'You say that if a bean falls to the ground, we split it among ourselves? That we shed blood because of the great movement that belonged to us, the people of Kenya, Mau Mau, the people's movement, so that our children might eat until they were full, might wear clothes that kept out the cold, might sleep in beds free from bedbugs? That our children should learn the art of producing wealth for our people? Tell me this: who but a fool or a traitor would not have sacrificed his own blood for those glorious aims? I, the Wangarĩ you see before you, was a small girl then. But these legs have carried many bullets and many guns to our fighters in the forest . . . and I was never afraid, even when I slipped through the lines of the enemy and their home guard allies. Our people, today when I recall those things, my heart weakens and I want to cry! Mũturi, what did you say? That the modern Haraambe is for the rich and their friends?

You have said well.
You have said well.
If I had milk,
I would wash you in it.

'It doesn't matter. . . . It doesn't matter. . . . But, our people, I keep asking myself: this money, thousands and thousands of shillings donated day after day – from what depths of the sea does it come? The man who is able to give away hundreds of thousands day after day – how much is he leaving behind in the store for himself and his children? This garden of endless harvests – what kind of garden is it? This spring whose water never dries up – what kind of spring is it? And the friends of this man; the friends who never come out in the open to be seen – who are they? These friends whose names are never disclosed in public – who are they? These people who like to give only under cover of darkness – who are they? But every secret act will one day be exposed on a mountaintop, in full view of the people. I say this: when we fought for independence, it was not money that did the fighting: it was love. Love for Kenya, our country, was what gave our young men courage to face the prospect

40

of being mowed down by enemy bullets – and they would not let go of the soil. When we fought for independence, we did not look at the way a person dressed and say: 'This one is dressed in rags. Let him be thrown into jail.' In fact, the man in rags was the one in the front line, and he did not know the word retreat. But the man in the tie would run to pick up the hat of the imperialist felled by the bullets from our front line and reserve forces! And when you hear me talk like this, our people, don't think that I've been drinking alcohol or smoking bhang. No. I'm speaking in this way because of what I have gone through in the Nairobi we have left behind. Modern Haraambe ... I don't know where it is leading us, the Kenyan people....'

Wangarĩ paused. Mũturi, Warĩĩnga and Gatuĩria felt compassion because of the sorrow and the bitterness in Wangarĩ's voice. The man in dark glasses shrank further into his corner. Mwaũra stepped on the accelerator, hoping that the car would whisk them all away from Wangarĩ's story.

'Tell us, what has Nairobi done to you to make your heart so heavy?' Mũturi asked her.

'I wonder if I should describe it as astonishing, or horrifying enough to make the heart and body tremble,' Wangarĩ replied quickly.

Wangarĩ told them then of the unspeakable horrors she had experienced in Nairobi, the capital city of Kenya.

'That Nairobi – even now I don't know what spirit transported me from Ilmorog to Nairobi. For today is there a single corner, even in the most far-flung reaches of Kenya, where a poor man can run to escape poverty? Ilmorog, Mombasa, Nairobi, Nakuru, Kisumu – the water in all these places has become bitter for us peasants and workers....

'My small piece of land, two acres, had just been auctioned by the *Kenya Economic Progress Bank*, as I had failed to pay back a loan I had burdened myself with so that I could keep grade cows. It was a loan of 5000 shillings. I bought posts and fence wire. I bought a cow that was six months pregnant. Then I used some of the money to pay my son's school fees. The cow gave birth to a bull. The milk brought in only enough money to cover the monthly interest payments to the bank. My cow caught gall fever. The vet did not arrive until after the cow had died and had been buried. I had not even paid a quarter of the debt.

'So when the piece of land was sold, and I saw that I had no land to cultivate and that I would not get a job in Ilmorog, I thought I should go to the capital city of Kenya to look for work. Why? Because when money is borrowed from foreign lands, it goes to build

41

Nairobi and the other big towns. When peasants grow food, it goes to Nairobi and to the other big towns. As far as we peasants are concerned, all our labour goes to fatten Nairobi and the big towns. So, alone in my hut, I told myself this: I can't fail to find a job in Nairobi. At least I could sweep out offices or wipe children's bottoms. I don't mind what job I do, for he who is given a piece of meat does not expect fat as well. And perhaps in Nairobi there won't be any thieves and robbers like the ones who have been disturbing and harassing Ilmorog workers and peasants night and day.

'So I tied a few cents in my cloth and set out.

'Really! I've never seen so many cars flowing on the tarmac road like floods in the plains – and buildings taller than the legendary Cain, who could touch the clouds, it is said. Nairobi is like a big garden of stones, tar and cars. When I saw the shops, hotels and cars, I said to myself: Our Kenya has certainly made progress. Surely I will find a job here. So I went into the first shop I came across. The clothes in the shop shone with all the colours of the rainbow. I found an Indian in charge. I asked him if I could work for him, sweeping out the shop. He told me that he didn't need anyone to do that in his shop. I begged him to let me clean up after his children. He said that he couldn't offer me that job either. I went out into the streets again, looking only for tall, tall buildings. It was then that I entered a hotel. It was a big hotel, the size of Mount Kenya. There, at the tables, sat no one but Europeans. I went into an office. I found a European there. He told me that there were no jobs. I told him that I didn't mind dusting the shoes of these whites, numerous as locusts though they were. He laughed and told me that it was impossible. What about cleaning out toilets for the whites? No. There I was, still jobless.

'Then I wandered into shop after shop, looking for one that employed black men. One's own family and age-group are never disowned: and we black people, aren't we all of one kin, one clan? I entered a shop which looked like a store for household goods and garden tools. Hoes, matchets, garden forks, kettles and saucepans were crammed on to the shelves. A black man. There was a black man in the shop. My heart lifted with hope. I told him all my troubles. Can you believe it? He collapsed with laughter! He told me that the only job he could offer me was that of spreading my legs, that women with mature bodies were experts at that job. I felt a tear drop to the ground.

'I roamed the streets, not knowing what to do or where to turn. Then I saw another hotel. I went straight in. I asked for the office. I found a black man. I asked him for work. He said to me: "You,

42

woman, weren't you here a little while ago? And weren't you told by the European owner that there were no jobs here for the likes of you?' I was very shocked and frightened. I had walked in a circle, back to the very hotel that I had tried before. I was about to leave when the man called me back. He asked me to sit down on a chair while he rang up a place that he knew was never short of jobs for people like us. My heart beat with joy. *Independence* had truly come to our land. I waited for my good fortune with the patience of a fisherman.

'Oh, our people, what can I tell you? Before I could sneeze twice, I saw policemen enter the office. The black man gave me up to the police, who were black like me, and told them that I had been keeping a watch on the hotel. And when the European owner was called, he said the same thing: that I had spent the whole day going round and round the hotel in a way that clearly indicated my intention to steal. He patted the black man on the shoulder and said to him, in a voice that seemed to come through his nose: "Good work, Mr Mũgwate, good work," or something similar. And the police inspector kept saying: "*Yes, yes,* it is women like this one who are now employed by thieves and robbers to spy on shops, hotels and banks."

'I was then pushed into a police vehicle and taken to a cell. But was it a cell, or rather a lair for mosquitoes, lice, fleas and bedbugs? I slept in that cell for three nights. I, Wangarĩ, who have never stolen so much as a single potato from anybody! I, Wangarĩ, who offered my life for my country! I, the Wangarĩ you now see before you dressed in a kitenge garment and carrying a basket, spent three nights suffocated by the stench of shit and urine!

'I was taken to court this very morning, charged with intending to steal and with roaming about Nairobi without being a resident of the city, without a job, without a house and without a permit. Vagrancy or something like that, that is what they called it. But, our people, think: I, Wangarĩ, a Kenyan by birth – how can I be a vagrant in my own country? How can I be charged with vagrancy in my own country as if I were a foreigner? I denied both charges: to look for work is not a crime.

'The judge was a European, with a skin that was red like a pig's. His nose was peeling, like a lizard's body. He wore glasses with big arms.

'The European owner of the hotel acted as a witness. Mr Mũgwate, that slave of foreigners, was also a witness.

'The judge asked me: "Have you anything you want to tell this court before I sentence you?"

'Even now, I can't say where I found the courage that suddenly gripped me. (Was it courage or pain?) I told the judge: "Look at me properly. I am not a foreigner here like you. And I am not a vagrant here in Kenya, and I will never be a foreigner or a vagrant here in Kenya. Kenya is our country. We were born here. We were given this land by God, and we redeemed it from the hands of our enemies with our own blood. Today you see us clothed in rags, but we, the peasants and the workers, are the same people who were around at the time of Kĩmaathi. Now, look at me closely again. I am not a thief. I am not a robber. If you want to know who the real thieves and robbers are, follow me and I will show you their lairs and caves in Ilmorog. Give me a few policemen, and we'll go right now to arrest the thieves and robbers who have always troubled us. I don't know about Nairobi or other places, but in Ilmorog, our Ilmorog, thieves and robbers don't even bother to hide."

'I sat down.

'The judge took off his glasses. He wiped them with a red handkerchief. Then he put them back on his peeling nose. He eyed me again. And I kept saying in my heart: *Yes*, look at me properly if you have never heard the tongue of a Wangarĩ, the tiller. If we were still living at that other time, you would be looking down the barrel of a gun, you devil. He asked me to repeat what I had said about Ilmorog thieves and robbers. I told him: "Really! Why should I lie to you? Who would be happier, you or I, to hear that those thieves and robbers were gnashing their teeth in jail? Give me some policemen, and I will show them where the thieves hang out."

'The judge said that because I had offered to co-operate with the police in rooting out theft and robbery in the country, the court would not jail me. I would only have to pay a fine because I had been wandering about Nairobi without a permit and hence breaking the vagrancy laws.

'Can you believe it? I ask you to turn over the matter in your minds. Is it right that I should need a permit to enter Nairobi, just like in the days of the Emergency, when our European tormentors used to make us carry pass books?

'The judge told the police chief to make arrangements to catch all the thieves and robbers in Ilmorog. My ready co-operation was what had saved me from six months in jail.

'From the courtroom I was taken first to the police station. Mark you, now I was being soothed with tongues of honey. I was flattered. I was told that if *all the citizens* were like me and joined hands with the police like the yam and its supporting tree, the whole country would be cleansed of theft, robbery and similar crimes and those

44

who had would be able to enjoy their wealth in peace and sleep soundly without any worries.

'We agreed that I should return to Ilmorog first, on my own, to find out exactly when and where the thieves and robbers normally gather. When I'd gleaned that information, I would go and report to Ilmorog police station. The Nairobi police, for their part, would inform the chief of Ilmorog police station, a Superintendent Gakono, about what was going on and would give him my name, so that my report would be acted on promptly.

'That's how we parted. But they never even gave me half a cent for the fare!

'I tell you, all my money – 200 shillings in all – was left at the court. And I was turned out to foot it to Ilmorog. Now, but for the fact that you were blown by God's wind in my direction, where would I have slept tonight? What would I have eaten?

'Today, this very day, as you and I are sitting here together, if someone were to drop from the skies and ask me to sing the praises of the Haraambe of money, I would offer him two or three words he would never forget. . . .'

Wangarĩ stopped abruptly, as if her thoughts were still lingering on police cells and courtrooms, judges and policemen.

Warĩĩnga made as if to open her handbag to take out the card she had been given at the Kaka bus stop. Did Wangarĩ know about the Devil's feast in honour of theft and robbery in Ilmorog? The question made Warĩĩnga pause. She looked at Wangarĩ and asked her in a slightly tremulous voice: 'Tell me . . . would you honestly say that there are lairs and caves for thieves and robbers in Ilmorog?'

'What? And you claim that you come from Njeruca in Ilmorog! Which part?' Wangarĩ replied with a question.

'It is . . . I honestly did not know. . . .' Warĩĩnga replied, hesitantly.

'Now you know the truth,' Wangarĩ told Warĩĩnga and fell silent.

5

The other passengers also remained silent, as if they had nothing to add to Wangarĩ's story or to Warĩĩnga's question. But after they had travelled in silence for a short distance, Mũturi started up a conversation.

'This country, our country, is pregnant. What it will give birth to,

45

God only knows .... Imagine! The children of us workers are fated to stay out in the sun, thirsty, hungry, naked, gazing at fruit ripening on trees which they can't pick even to quieten a demanding belly! Fated to see food steaming in the pantry, but unable to dip a calabash into the pot to scoop out even a tiny portion! Fated to lie awake all night telling each another stories about tears and sorrow, asking one another to guess the same riddle day after day: "Oh, for a piece of one of those!"'

'Ripe bananas!' Wangarĩ replied, as if Mũturi had asked her a real riddle.

'Oh, for some of that!' Mũturi said.

'Fresh, cool water in a cave that belongs to another,' Wangarĩ replied again.

'Wangarĩ, your story shows that this country, our country, should have given birth to its offspring long ago.' Mũturi was repeating what he had said earlier. 'What it lacks now is a midwife,' he added. 'The question is this: who is responsible for the pregnancy?'

'It's the Devil doing his work.' Robin Mwaũra suddenly plunged into the discussion.

Mwaũra had been a little embarrassed by the ill-will he had shown at Kĩneeniĩ. Since the moment Mũturi, Warĩĩnga and Gatuĩria had agreed to pay Wangarĩ's fare, Mwaũra had been trying to find an opening to change the subject, to steer it away from Wangarĩ and her problems. Now he started singing:

I shall knock-a-knock the Devil.
I shall knock-a-knock the Devil.
I shall tell him: Leave me alone
I do not belong to demons!

Warĩĩnga felt her whole body heat up as she recalled all the things that had occurred that day. She asked herself: Why is it that today events seem to be repeating themselves? Or is all this mere talk?

Gatuĩria glanced at the driver as if he would have liked Mwaũra to continue with the song. Gatuĩria was very disturbed by Wangarĩ's story, and it had made him ask himself over and over again: Is it really possible that such things happen in Kenya today? Then, remembering that there were indeed vagrancy laws in Kenya, he believed Wangarĩ's story. But what made him hope Mwaũra would continue with the song had something to do with the load he himself was carrying inside him and another he was carrying in his suitcase.

The man with the dark glasses withdrew still further into his corner, as if he feared that he would be set on by the others, for he thought they were together.

Mwaũra suddenly stopped singing, leaving the song hanging in the air.

Mũturi asked him: 'What! Have you cut the thread?'

'No, I'm throwing the thread to you,' Mwaũra replied.

Mũturi said: 'We ourselves used to sing the song this way, or perhaps I should say, we used to sing the same tune with these words:

> I shall knock-a-knock the whites.
> I shall knock-a-knock the whites.
> I shall tell them: Go home now!
> Kenya does not belong to imperialists!'

As Mũturi was about to sing the next verse, Wangarĩ joined in. Now the two sang with voices that blended together beautifully, like a mixture of perfume oils of the same kind.

> Kenya does not belong to you, imperialists!
> Kenya does not belong to you, imperialists!
> Pack up your bags and go!
> The owner of the homestead is on his way!

Mũturi and Wangarĩ finished their duet together, like experts.

Mwaũra said: 'As for me, there was no song I wouldn't have sung then. Even today there's no song that I wouldn't sing. I say this world is round. If it leans that way, I lean that way with it. If it stumbles, I stumble with it. If it bends, I bend with it. If it stays upright, I stay upright with it. If it growls, I growl with it. If it is silent, I am silent too. The first law of the hyena states: Don't be choosy; eat what is available. If I find myself among members of the Akũrinũ sect, I become one of them; when I'm with those who have been saved, I too am saved; when I'm with Muslims, I embrace Islam; when I'm among pagans, I too become pagan.'

'Gĩkũyũ said that no one can cook two pots of food simultaneously without burning the contents of one of them,' Mũturi said. 'But you, Mwaũra, seem to be able to cook a couple of thousand pots at the same time! Are you really able to watch over the food in all of them, or do you end up with charred remains?'

'The mouth that ate itself!' Mwaũra said and laughed. His heart had felt light and gay from the moment he heard the talk move away from Wangarĩ and her problems. 'It seems as if it was because of us matatũ drivers that the saying was coined. We are known for our loud mouths and our wagging tongues. Why? Because the fisherman does not know exactly where in the stream he will make his catch, so he casts his line here and there. For us *matatũ* drivers, our tongues are our hooks — '

'For catching money?' Mũturi cut him short.

'Yes, for catching money,' Mwaũra agreed at once. 'And people. Or let's say our tongues are bait for human beings along with their money. For money comes from human beings. So if you pay too much attention to what we say, you could get lost in broad daylight. Take a woman like this one here. She might have thought I really meant it when I said earlier that I would abandon her to the beasts in the forest. No, I just wanted to frighten her a little. We often have to work ourselves up into a state because there are passengers who like to cheat us. I normally carry two bags: one of honey and one of bitters.'

'Of life and death?' Mũturi pressed, with a trace of sarcasm in his voice.

'You've put your finger on it,' Mwaũra replied simply, as if he had not noticed the sarcasm. 'What do you think allows us to survive on these roads?'

'I grant that what you've said could be true,' Mũturi said, and then he added pointedly: 'because when we were at Nyamakĩma, you were singing out that there was nowhere you would refuse to take a passenger in pursuit of money: to God's Heaven or to the Devil's Hell. But tell me, whose side are you on?'

'God's or the Devil's?'

'That's the question,' Mũturi replied.

'I'm equally at home on either side. Didn't you say just now that I was someone who cooks two pots simultaneously? You were quite right. Only I don't like burning the food in either pot. Let's go back to the question of God and Satan. I have never set eyes on either of them. But let's agree they both exist. Each has his own powers. And it is true that both have always sought votes on this Earth, the votes that are cast in the hearts of men. Can't you see, then, that each is capable of improving or ruining your fortunes on this Earth? Just as you find candidates vying with each other as they tout for votes during elections, so we businessmen play off God and the Devil against each another. We don't like to anger either of them. We pray to both.'

'You are speaking like a traveller who has lost his way. Haven't you heard it said that no man can serve two masters? Even the voter eventually casts his vote for one politician.'

'A businessman has many masters. And he must obey them all. If this one calls me, I run to him. If that one calls me, I run to him.'

They both fell silent. Mwaũra was driving carefully because he was nervous of the bends and corners on that road. The road was heavily used by oil tankers and by trailers and lorries loaded with charcoal, potatoes and vegetables.

They had passed the road leading to Kijabe Mission and the church built by the Italian prisoners during the Second World War, and they were now descending to the bottom of the *Rift Valley*.

Mũturi pressed Mwaũra with another question: 'Don't you believe in anything? Isn't there anything that your heart considers bad or good?'

Mwaũra was quiet at first, as if he had not heard the question clearly. Am I carrying a religious fanatic, a Jesus-is-My-Saviour type? he asked himself.

The other passengers waited in silence for Mwaũra's reply because they too were turning over Mũturi's question in their hearts.

Mwaũra was conscious of the eagerness with which his reply was awaited. He cleared his throat. 'You ask me about my beliefs, is that right? The affairs of the heart are difficult to fathom.* The hearts of men do not open up to each other like mole holes. The affairs of the heart are a dense forest, which no one can penetrate. First, ask yourself this: what's a heart? Where does it reside? Is the heart an organ made of flesh, or is it mere breath? Once when I was a child my grandmother told me a story about a sick lion which, after eating a donkey's heart, was cured of its illness. I was very sad. I asked my grandmother: "What will that donkey do when Jesus comes back and wakes the dead?" My grandmother told me: "Don't bother me with chatter; your animals won't be resurrected."

'A man may return to a homestead he once abandoned. The other day I came back to the very question I asked as a child when I read in a newspaper, *Taifaleo*, that these days a heart can be removed from one person and planted inside someone else. The question is this: that person, is he the same man as the one who was there before, or is he now a new person as he has a new heart? When the Day of Resurrection comes, what will the two people do when both bodies claim the same heart? Think about the heart that has been

*It must be remembered that in Gĩkũyũ the word 'heart' means many things: soul, spirit, conscience, mind, inner man, essence and so on.

shared by two bodies. Suppose the heart is upright, obedient, clean. What will prevent both bodies from scrambling for it?

'I am full of doubt. When a heart is transferred from one body to another, does it emigrate with all the integrity or wickedness of the first body, or does it assume the corruption of the new body?

'Now, let us consider a land peopled with rich and poor citizens. A rich man may indulge in all sorts of wickedness, but when he is about to die, he goes to a hospital and he buys the heart of a poor but upright person. So the rich man goes to Heaven because of the righteousness of the poor, and the poor man goes to Hell because of the wickedness of the rich or because he is now without a soul! Ha! ha! ha!'

Mwaũra cut short his own monologue with laughter. He laughed and laughed like someone who is about to say something funny but, as he is trying to say it, is struck by the humour of it. Still laughing, Mwaũra resumed. 'I would like to start a heart business, a market for human hearts, a shop for human hearts, a *supermarket* for human hearts, *Permanent Sale....* I wonder how much money a heart like mine would fetch?'

With that, Mwaũra collapsed with laughter.

But not a single passenger joined in.

By now they had gone past the road to Nare Ngare and Narok. The satellite station was to their left, Kijabe hills to their right. Mount Longonot lay ahead. Darkness had embraced the whole land. But the lights from Mwaũra's Model T Ford and from the other vehicles going in the same or in the opposite direction cleared a passage, splitting the darkness into two halves. Some drivers did not dim their lights. When Mwaũra's eyes were blinded by these lights, he would swear by his mother, would use long, unmentionable words to curse the drivers. Once he said: 'Those driving licences that are for sale are breeding danger on the roads! Can you believe that today a mere babe in arms is able to tuck a driving licence into its pocket on paying 500 shillings? Even though it may never have set eyes on a steering wheel!'

'The water has become sour!' Mũturi told him.

'And the hearts of men have become empty!' Wangarĩ added. Mũturi and Wangarĩ began to sing together:

> Famine has increased in our land,
> But it has been given other names,
> So that the people should not discover
> Where all the food has been hidden.

Two bourgeois women
Ate the flesh of the children of the poor.
They could not see the humanity of the children
Because their hearts were empty.

Many houses, and acres of land,
And mounds of stolen money –
These cannot bring peace to a person,
Because they have been taken from the poor.

Now look away from the rich
At the poor, and at the children.
They are all stagger-a-staggering on the highway
Because their hearts are empty.

Mũturi said: 'The rich stagger because they over-eat.'
Wangarĩ added: 'And the poor because they are starving.'
They sang in unison: ' . . . Because their hearts are empty. . . .'
Again Mwaũra asked himself: What kind of religious fanatics have
I burdened myself with? Could they all be members of the sect of
Deep Waters?
'Have you returned to the problem of the human heart?' Mwaũra
asked, in a tone that betrayed his impatience with Mũturi and
Wangarĩ. 'Hearts, hearts, hearts! What is a heart? A breeze, a breath
of wind, a voice? No! The heart is a passing cloud that is transformed
by the dreams of a man crushed by poverty into a golden ladder that
reaches to God's Heaven or a ladder of redhot coals constructed to
guide His enemies' descent into Hell. Where is the market in which
I can sell my heart to a fool for any sum he cares to name?'
Mũturi quickly replied: 'The human heart? A breeze, a breath of
wind, a passing cloud? A dream ladder in the mind of person made
sleepless by poverty? No! The human heart is flesh and it is not flesh.
The heart makes a man and it is made by man. The heart is borne
by the body and in turn becomes the body. There is in man an organ
called the heart. That organ is a kind of engine that pumps blood into
the arteries and veins that carry food to all the cells of the body and
remove the waste from all parts of the body. The organ co-operates
with all the other organs of the body. These organs have to work
together to make a human being see, touch, hear, smell, taste, talk,
swing his arms, walk, start building his life.
'What he himself builds is the other heart. That other heart is the
humanity we fashion with our hands, aided by our eyes, our ears,
our noses, our mouths. That other heart is the product of our work

51

and our actions, which are guided by our mind – the work and actions involved in modifying nature to make things to meet our needs, like shelter to keep out rain, clothes to keep out cold and sun, food to make the body grow and many other needs.

'That humanity is in turn born of many hands working together, for, as Gĩkũyũ once said, a single finger cannot kill a louse; a single log cannot make a fire last through the night; a single man, however strong, cannot build a bridge across a river; and many hands can lift a weight, however heavy. The unity of our sweat is what makes us able to change the laws of nature, able to harness them to the needs of our lives, instead of our lives remaining slaves of the laws of nature. That's why Gĩkũyũ also said: Change, for the seeds in the gourd are not all of one kind.

'That humanity, fruit of the work of our hands and minds striving together to subdue nature, is what distinguishes a human being from a beast, a tree and all the other creatures in nature's kingdom.

'Tell me this: is any other creature able to trap and yoke the wind, water, lightning, steam? Able to tie their legs and arms with chains and lock them up, making them prisoners, submissive and obedient to its needs? No. Human nature and animal nature are quite different. Animals stoop low before nature, allowing themselves to be turned this way and that by her, just as sausages are turned casually in the fire by little boys. But the human being wrestles with nature and strives to command her.

'Look at the fruits of the combined labour of many hands: roads, and rails, and cars, and trains, and many other types of wheel that permit man to run faster than the hare or the swiftest animal in the forest; aeroplanes that give man wings more powerful and faster than those of any bird in the sky; missiles faster than sound and lightning; heavy ships that float, miraculously, on deep seas without sinking the way Peter did in the Sea of Galilee; telephones, radios, televisions, devices that are able to capture the voice and substance of a human being, so that his face and his voice remain alive even after his body is dead and buried and has decayed. What marvel could be greater than that? Look at the towns we have built with our hands: Mombasa, Nairobi, Nakuru, Eldoret, Kitale, Kisumu, Rũũwa-inĩ and Ilmorog. Look at the coffee, and the tea, and the sugar cane, and the cotton, and the rice, and the beans, and the maize we have grown out of a handful of seeds. Look at the fire trapped inside copper wires that stretch from the Rũirũ, Athi and Sagan Rivers, so that we can have suns and moons and stars in our towns and in our houses after nature's sun, moon and stars have gone to bed! If the fruits of that co-operation had not been grabbed by the clan of parasites, where do you think that we, the clan of producers, would be today? Would we still know the meaning of cold, hunger, thirst and nakedness?

'That humanity is the heart of man because the heart of man is linked irrevocably with the growth of his nature as a man. Can you tell us the price of a heart now, you cheap and foolish merchant?'

Mũturi was panting a little because of the fervour of his argument and the thoughts in his head. He had often turned over such thoughts in his mind, but never before had he managed to clothe them in words. He was surprised at himself, for he could not identify the source of those philosophical thoughts.

Mwaũra appealed to his passenger. He said to Mũturi: 'According to your outlook, there are no good or evil hearts. They are all part of our humanity. For remember, we were talking about good and evil. Now, your outlook and mine are identical. In this world there is no good or evil. In this world there are no good or evil hearts. A heart is a heart. Talk of Heaven and Hell is nothing more than a collection of stories that are intended to frighten children. What are we arguing about? Let there be peace! Let there be money!'

'Heaven and Hell?' Mũturi jumped back into the debate. 'Both exist, and there is a difference between them, just as there is a difference between good and evil, a good heart and an evil heart. Listen. Our lives are a battlefield on which is fought a continuous war between the forces that are pledged to confirm our humanity and those determined to dismantle it; those who strive to build a protective wall around it, and those who wish to pull it down; those who seek to mould it, and those committed to breaking it up; those whose aim is to open our eyes, to make us see the light and look to tomorrow, asking ourselves about the future of our children, and those who wish to lull us into closing our eyes, encouraging us to care only for our stomachs today, without thinking about the tomorrow of our country.

'It is a war without spectators. For each man is part of the forces that have been recruited for creating, building, making our humanity grow and blossom in order to nurture our human nature and create our own Heaven, thus taking on the nature of God – these are the forces of the clan of producers; or he is part of the forces of destruction, of dismantling, of harassing and oppressing the builders and the creators, the forces that seek to suppress our humanity, turning us into beasts in order that we should create our own Hell, thus taking on the nature of Satan – these are the forces of the clan of parasites. Each of the two forces builds a heart that reflects the nature of its clan. Therefore there are two hearts: the heart built by

53

the clan of parasites, the evil heart; and the heart built by the clan of producers, the good heart.

'It is our actions that show which side we are on and therefore what kind of heart we are building. For our hands, our organs, our bodies, our energy are like a sharp sword. This sword, in the hands of a producer, can cultivate, make food grow, and can defend the cultivators so that the blessings and the fruits of their sweat is not wrested from them; and the same sword, in the hands of a parasite, can be used to destroy the crops or to deny producers the fruits of their industry.

'In the hands of the producer the sword of fire has the capacity to do good. And in the hands of the parasite the sword of fire has the capacity to do evil. Its actions illustrate both the evil and the good nature of the sword of fire. The same is true of the labour of our bodies.

'Gĩkũyũ once said: The leopard did not know how to scratch; it was taught. True, but it always had the claws and the power to scratch. Does it scratch to kill its children? Or does it scratch to kill its enemies?

'One thing is certain. What is done cannot be undone. Our actions are the bricks that we use to construct either a good or an evil heart.

'The heart in turn becomes the mirror through which we can look at ourselves and our work on this Earth. If you do not want a mirror that will reflect both good and evil, you have no place here on Earth. Be quick about it: rush your heart to the market, and you will remain a shell of a man. In those days that you are all aware of, we used to sing a certain song. It went like this:

> Even if you sob and weep
> Because of your sins,
> Until you enter into patriotic service to help the nation
> You will never find peace.
> When you were lost and couldn't see the way
> To life,
> The guide used to point out the only way:
> Organized unity of the people.

'Driver! There are two ways: the one that leads people to death, and the one that leads people to life. Show me the way to death, and I will show you the way to life. Show me the way to life, and I will show you the way to death. For the two meet in the actions of every man, as he builds the heart he wants. . . . Mwaũra, you have just told

54

us about the first law of the hyena, is that right? I ask you: the hyena that tried to walk along two paths simultaneously – where did it end up? Mwaũra: choose one path and stick to it.' Mũturi finished talking.

'I chose my path a long time ago,' Mwaũra replied.

'Which one is it?' Mũturi asked.

'The road to death!' Mwaũra replied, laughing a little, as if he were joking. 'Where do you think you are heading now?' Mwaũra asked mockingly. Total silence gripped the *matatũ*.

6

Waríĩnga heard a buzzing sound in her head, as if a mosquito were trapped inside. And her heart was beating like the heart of someone who has spent the whole day going round and round the Mtego-wa-Panya enclosure in the *City Park* in Nairobi, looking for an escape route. She had not followed the argument between Mwaũra and Mũturi clearly, where it had come from and where it had led, because in the midst of listening she would suddenly find herself back with her own troubles: John Kĩmwana, *Boss* Kĩhara, the job she no longer had, her eviction from her house, her attempted suicide, the young man who had held her hand, the invitation to the Devil's feast, the competition in theft and robbery – and now all this talk about death, life and the soul. She wondered: When will I reach home so that I can rest my mind and body? Will my problems ever end? When did they all start? Where? And with whom?

Waríĩnga remembered the Rich Old Man from Ngorika, Nakuru, a long time ago, and she felt her whole body fill with bitterness....

Gatuĩria now cut off the flow of Waríĩnga's thoughts. 'Please, wait a moment!' he said, loudly.

Mũturi, Wangarĩ, Waríĩnga and the man in the dark glasses looked at him. Mwaũra turned his head slightly, then he looked back at the steering wheel and the road.

Gatuĩria lowered his voice: '*Please*, permit me to ask a question!'

Gatuĩria hesitated, like a man burning to get to the kernel of an important matter but uncertain about where to begin.

'Go ahead, ask!' Mwaũra encouraged him. 'No one's jailed for asking questions!'

'Ah, but in the Kenya of today?' Mũturi muttered.

'Don't worry,' Mwaũra encouraged Gatuĩria. 'When you are inside Mwaũra's Matatũ Matata Matamu Model T Ford, you are in the heartland of democracy!'

'Oh, yes, there you are right,' Wangarĩ supported him. '*Matatũs* are the only places left where people can discuss things freely. In a *matatũ* you can speak your thoughts without first looking over your shoulder to see who is listening.'

'When you are in my *matatũ*, you could be inside a prison or a grave. There's nothing you can't say.'

'Your argument, *sorry*, your discussion.... *Excuse me*....' Gatuĩria paused again.

Gatuĩria spoke Gĩkũyũ like many educated people in Kenya – people who stutter like babies when speaking their national languages but conduct fluent conversations in foreign languages. The only difference was that Gatuĩria was at least aware that the slavery of language is the slavery of the mind and nothing to be proud of. But in the heat of discussion Gatuĩria was able to speak his language without pausing, hesitating or reverting to English.

'It is said that differences of opinion breed hatred. But often where there is conflict, shoots of truth spring up,' Wangarĩ told Gatuĩria, by way of encouragement.

Gatuĩria cleared his throat, then he tried again. 'I can't quite see the *difference* ... *sorry*, I mean, the difference between your two positions.... *Let me ask* ... *sorry*, *I mean*, let me ask you this question. Do you believe that God and Satan exist, *I mean*, that they are alive, like you and me?'

'If God exists,' Mwaũra rushed in, 'then Satan exists. But personally I don't know.'

'But what about believing? What do you believe?' Gatuĩria persisted.

'Me? Young man, I don't belong to those churches of yours. Business is my temple, and money is my God. But if some other God exists, that's all right. Sometimes I pour out a little liquor for him, so that he won't be tempted to do to me what he once did to Job. I don't examine the world too minutely. What did I say before? If it leans this way, I lean with it. The Earth is round, and it changes. That is why Gĩkũyũ said that the sun does not rise the way it sets. Caution is not a sign of cowardice. I don't have that many questions to ask. Show me where the money is and I'll take you there!'

'What about you?' Gatuĩria asked Mũturi, after Mwaũra had had his say.

'Me? I believe.'

'What?'

'That God exists.'

'And that he's alive?'

'Yes.'

'And Satan?'

'Yes, he exists too.'

'And he's also alive?'

'Yes, he's alive.'

'Do you really believe these things?'

'Yes, I really do.'

'But you have never seen either of them with your own eyes?' Mwaũra asked Mũturi.

'This young man was asking about belief,' Mũturi replied. 'I believe that God and Satan are images of our actions in our brains as we struggle with nature in general, and with human nature in particular, in our search for something to eat, to wear and to shelter behind to keep out the sun, the cold and the wind. The nature of God is the image of the good we do here on Earth. The nature of Satan is the image of the evil we do here on Earth. The question is this: what are evil actions, and what are good actions? Young man, you are making me repeat the words I have already said and put behind me. There are two kinds of man: he who lives by his own sweat and he who lives by the sweat of others. The riddle lies there, so take a forfeit* and solve the riddle for us, because you seem familiar with books.'

'"In the sweat of thy face," Wangarĩ spoke as if she was reading from a Bible open in front of her, "in the sweat of thy face shalt thou eat bread, till thou return unto the ground."' Wangarĩ closed the Bible that was in her mind and turned to Gatuĩria: 'That is another riddle, and you must solve that one too, so that we can all hear the answer. Take a forfeit from me too.'

'I won't take too many forfeits because you are a clanswoman,' Gatuĩria replied, laughing a little.

'Oh, so you do speak good Gĩkũyũ, and I thought that you only knew this language of "Good morning",'* Wangarĩ told him, lightheartedly.

Gatuĩria felt himself relax somewhat.

'I used to listen to riddle competitions long ago,' Gatuĩria replied, 'but now I wouldn't be able to solve even the simplest one. If you

*A forfeit (kĩgacawa) is an imaginary piece of property that is surrendered by someone who has failed to solve a riddle to the person who posed the riddle.
*She means English.

57

and I were to compete, you would win all the forfeits until you had won all my property. But let's go back to the root of the matter. I must say, I felt that your talk raised doubts and conflicts that I've had in my heart for a long time. *I mean*, I have a knot in my heart, and I would be very glad if you would help me to untie or loosen it a little.'

Gatuīria paused again.

Warīīnga sensed that Gatuīria's voice had changed. She felt suddenly apprehensive, as if she had heard that voice somewhere else, a long time ago, but she could not place it. She decided that the apprehension was prompted by a burning desire to know what knot was troubling Gatuīria.

All the other passengers were sitting attentively, anxious to hear the story. It was as if they feared that Gatuīria's knot might be similar to the one they each carried.

Gatuīria cleared his throat again. He looked at Mūturi. 'You talk as if you knew I came from the university, and it is true. I am from there. I'm a kind of research student in culture. I'm *a junior research fellow in African culture. Our culture . . . sorry, I mean*, our culture has been dominated by the Western imperialist cultures. That is what we call in English *cultural imperialism*. Cultural imperialism is mother to the slavery of the mind and the body. It is cultural imperialism that gives birth to the mental blindness and deafness that persuades people to allow foreigners to tell them what to do in their own country, to make foreigners the ears and mouths of their national affairs, forgetting the saying: Only he who lives in the wilderness knows what it is like. Hence a foreigner can never become the true guide of another people. It is about our generation that the singer sang:

> The deaf man, the deaf man,
> The deaf man is he who can't hear for the nation!
> The blind man, the blind man,
> The blind man is he who can't see for the nation!

'Let us now look about us. Where are our national languages now? Where are the books written in the alphabets of our national languages? Where is our own literature now? Where is the wisdom and knowledge of our fathers now? Where is the philosophy of our fathers now? The centres of wisdom that used to guard the entrance to our national homestead have been demolished; the fire of wisdom has been allowed to die; the seats around the fireside have been thrown on to a rubbish heap; the guard posts have been destroyed;

58

and the youth of the nation has hung up its shields and spears. It is a tragedy that there is nowhere we can go to learn the history of our country. A child without parents to counsel him – what is to prevent him from mistaking foreign shit for a delicious national dish?

'Our stories, our riddles, our songs, our customs, our traditions, everything about our national heritage has been lost to us.

'Who can play the gĩcaandĩ for us today and read and interpret the verses written on the gourd? Today who can play the wandĩndĩ, the one-stringed violin, making it sound like the voice of a young man wooing his love as she comes back from picking peas in the field, or fetching water from a cave in the valley, or digging up arrowroot, or cutting sugar cane in the slopes of the valley? Today who can play the bamboo flute, whose sound makes the hearts of a young man and a maiden beat in unison as they go to the fields to scare birds from the millet fingers while the moon casts its light over the land?

'That's why some people at the university, students and teachers, are now attempting to unearth the roots of our culture. The roots of Kenyan national culture can be sought only in the traditions of all the nationalities of Kenya.

'I, for instance, work in the Department of Music, which concerns itself with music and musical instruments and their uses. I study traditional instruments mostly – drums, flutes, jingles, rattles, oryx horns – and all kinds of string instruments, like the lyre and the one-stringed violin.

'I am also a composer. My ambition and dream is to compose a piece of music for many human voices accompanied by an orchestra made up of all kinds of national instruments: skin, wind, string and brass. I have composed a number of songs. But I have not yet found the tune or the theme of the music of my dreams. Day and night I have searched for the tune and the theme, but in vain.

'You can't know the pain I carry about in my heart.

'Often, when I'm alone in a hut thatched with grass and bracken and it is raining or the wind is blowing, or when I'm on my own at night and the moon is shining down on the land, I can hear the many voices gone, the many voices now living, the many voices to come, all singing to me in whispers. At times like those I feel I am just about to catch the tune, the rhythm and the theme of the music I have always longed to write. But it drifts away, carried on the waves of the wind.

'At other times, lying under the shade of a spreading tree or walking all alone in the plains or by the seaside, I often hear with the ears of my heart flutes and trumpets blown by a choir of herdsmen in the plains, the drums of the whole land calling on the youth of our country to go to war, then a thousand jingles, and rattles swung by our national heroes as they sing victory songs, and then the voices of women ululating in praise of their victorious sons. And suddenly I hear the sound of the national horn blown in victory, and oryx horns and others responding in joy. And then I hear the voices and the sounds of all the men and all the instruments come together, finishing with one voice in many voices, with many voices in one voice, like a choir of earthly angels proudly celebrating the heroic deeds of the nation.

'I seize pen and paper to write down the message of the voices before they are carried away by the wind.

'People, what can I tell you now?

'Have you ever dreamed of fruit hanging just above your head when you are very thirsty, under a scorching sun during a dry month, and when you raise your hands to pick one to cool your parched tongue, the fruit slowly rises out of reach and disappears into the sky? "Here I am! Here I am! But as you have refused to pick me, I am going away. . . ." Or that's what they seem to be saying, teasing you merely to whet your appetite and desire. That is how the voices and the instruments whet my appetite. But when I start to write the music down, alas, the music and the flutes are no longer there.

'I console myself by claiming that it does not matter: who has ever gained by moaning?

'I begin the search all over again. I myself ask a question that I have posed many times: what can I do to compose truly national music for our Kenya, music played by an orchestra made up of the instruments of all the nationalities that make up the Kenyan nation, music that we, the children of Kenya, can sing in one voice rooted in many voices – *harmony in polyphony?*

'I have spent many sleepless nights. A composer who is unable to snare the tune, the theme and the rhythm of his music is a shell of a human being.

'For a year or so after coming back from abroad, I was like a farmer trying to uproot a blue gum tree with a blunt digging stick. I could not get to the bottom of the root I was after. . . .'

Gatuīria cut short the story of his endless search. Nobody spoke.

Warīīnga felt restless, but she did not know why – was it Gatuīria's words, or the way he told his story, or simply his voice? His voice was like that of a man who has been carrying a load of deep troubles for several days and who has spent sleepless nights wrestling with questions for which he cannot find answers. Why had he ended the story at that point? Waríínga kept asking herself. What was the knot he had wanted help in untying?

Gatuíria turned to Waríínga as if he could read her thoughts. But before he could take up the story again, the man in dark glasses spoke in English: '*So you are on the staff of the university?*'

The other passengers were startled by the voice. These were the man's very first words since he entered the *matatū* at Sigona bus stop. Throughout the journey he had remained in his corner as if he were afraid that he would be murdered in Mwaūra's *matatū*.

'*Yes, yes, I'm on the research staff*,' Gatuíria replied in English.

'So you know *Professor* Ngarikũũma and *Professor* Gatwe Gaitumbí?'

'Yes, *Professor* Ngarikũũma is in the Political Science Department, and *Professor* Gatwe Gaitumbí is in the Department of Commerce and Economics.'

'What about *Professor* Kĩmenyiũgeni?'

'He is in the Department of History. But he only knows European history.'

'And *Professor* Bari-Kwĩrĩ?'

'He's in the Department of English – English literature. But he sometimes gives lectures in the Department of Philosophy and Religion.'

'I see, I see,' the man in dark glasses said, in a voice that indicated a heart more at peace with itself.

They waited for him to ask another question or to add something else, but he didn't speak again. It appeared that he was now much less afraid, however, and he even sat back, more relaxed. Gatuíria resumed his story.

'The day came when I thought I could at last see the light. A certain old man from Bahati village in Nakuru — '

'Bahati, did you say?' Mwaūra shouted. 'Bahati, Bahati in Nakuru?'

'Yes,' Gatuíria replied. 'What's the matter?'

'Nothing . . . nothing much. Go on with your story,' Mwaūra said in a worried voice.

'*Anyway*, the old man from Nakuru, from Bahati, was the one who showed me the way. I had gone to him and I had begged him: "Father, tell me old stories – tales of ogres or animals." He was silent. He looked at me. Then he laughed a little. He told me: "There is no difference between old and modern stories. Stories are stories. All stories are old. All stories are new. All stories belong to tomorrow. And stories are not about ogres or about animals or about men. All stories are about human beings. Young man, I can't understand the kind of education you all receive these days, or the kind of learning you want to acquire overseas during the course of so many years. How many? Fifteen years? Did they ever teach you that literature is a nation's treasure? Literature is the honey of a nation's soul, preserved for her children to taste forever, a little at a time! Gĩkũyũ said that he who has put something aside never goes hungry. Do you think Gĩkũyũ was a fool when he said that? A nation that has cast away its literature is a nation that has sold its soul and has been left a mere shell. But it is good that you have come. Say yes, and I'll tell you the stories I can remember.'

'It was evening, soon after darkness had fallen. The tongue of the glassless tin lamp was waving like a red flag in the wind, making our two shadows play on the walls of the man's square room.

'The old man told me first of a peasant farmer who used to carry an ogre on his back. The ogre had sunk his long nails into the neck and shoulders of the peasant. The peasant was the one who went to the fields to get food, the one who went into the valleys to fetch water, the one who went to the forest to get firewood and the one who did the cooking. The ogre's job was to eat and thereafter to sleep soundly on the back of the peasant. As the peasant became progressively thinner and more depressed at heart, the ogre prospered and flourished, to the extent of being inspired to sing hymns that exhorted the peasant to endure his lot on Earth with fortitude, for he would later find his rest in Heaven. One day, the peasant went to a diviner. The diviner told him that the only solution was for the peasant to boil some oil and to pour it on to the nails of the ogre when he was fast asleep. The peasant said: "What if I should burn my neck and shoulders?" The diviner said: "Nothing good was ever born of perfect conditions. Go home." The peasant was saved from certain death only when he did what he had been advised to do by the diviner.

'The second story was about a girl, an ebony beauty with an appealing gap between her teeth. She was named Nyanjirũ Kanyarari for three reasons: she was black; she was truly beautiful; and she had rejected the hand of all the young men in her country. But when Nyanjirũ saw a young man from a foreign country one day, she immediately claimed that he was the one for whom she had been waiting. She followed him. And do you know what? The young foreigner was a man-eating ogre. He tore off Nyanjirũ's limbs one by one and ate them.

'The third story was the one that left a indelible mark in my heart. How am I going to tell it to you? I wish I could even approach his manner of telling it, the way he raised and lowered his voice, for instance. But no, I can't even try. The kind of education bequeathed to us by the whites has clipped the wings of our abilities, leaving us limping like wounded birds. Let me tell you briefly the story that the old man from Bahati told me, so that you can see where the knot I talked about comes in.

'He started off with several proverbs. I can't remember them all. But they were all about avarice and conceit. He told me that though it is said that the fart of a rich man has no smell, and that a rich man will cultivate even a forbidden, sacred shrine, still every man ought to know that he who used to dance can now only watch while others do it, and he who used to jump over the stream can now only wade through it. To possess much encourages conceit; to possess little, thought. Too much greed may well prompt one to sell oneself cheaply. "Young man," he said, "go after property. But never show God your nakedness, and never despise the people. The voice of the people is the voice of God." Why do I say these things?

'A long, long time ago there lived an old man called Nding'ūri. Nding'ūri did not own much property. But he had a soul that was richly endowed. He was much respected because of his courage whenever enemies attacked his village, and because of the wisdom of his heart and tongue. He preserved the culture of his nation and observed all the proper rituals. Many a time he would sacrifice a goat and pour a little beer on to the ground for the good spirits, asking them to deliver him from evils that might have been caused by his own failings or brought into the homestead through the ill–will of wicked spirits. He was not a lazy man, and he was able to provide enough food to eat and clothes to wear for himself and for his family. What he did not suffer from was greedy desire for other people's herds or land belonging to his clan or to other clans. His lack of greed, added to his famed generosity, prevented him from amassing the kind of wealth that made some elders wear rings on their fingers and leave the tilling of the fields and the grazing of herds to slaves, servants, labourers, peasants and their wives and children, while they themselves feasted daily off honey beer. Hands make a man: this was what Nding'ūri believed.

'But one day, a strange pestilence attacked the village. The pestilence destroyed all Nding'ūri's possessions and struck at his goat in its special pen. What could Nding'ūri do now? He asked himself: Why, when I have always sacrificed goats to the good spirits and brewed beer for them, have they now turned against me? Never again will I sacrifice to them.

'Early one morning, before dawn broke, Nding'ūri went to a

63

certain cave where the evil spirits dwelt. At the entrance to the cave he was met by a spirit in the shape of an ogre. He had long hair, the colour of mole skin, and the hair fell on to his shoulders like a girl's. He had two mouths, one on his forehead and the other at the back of his head. The one at the back of his head was covered by his long hair, and it was visible only when the wind blew the hair aside. The bad spirit asked him: "Why have you come to my cave with empty hands? Does a man take an empty basket to market if he is planning to barter his wares? Have you been abandoned by the spirits to whom you have always sacrificed? Do you think that we ourselves don't like sacrifices and some beer to wash down the meat?" Nding'ūri replied that it was poverty that had brought him there. The generosity of a poor man remains locked in the heart. The bad spirit laughed slyly and said: "But have I not heard that you possess a rich soul? Nothing good is ever born of perfect conditions. I will give you riches. But you must give me your soul, and you must never again sacrifice to the good spirits, for good and evil have never been friends." Nding'ūri asked himself: What is a soul? Just a whispering voice. He told the bad spirit: "Take my soul." The bad spirit said to him: "I have taken possession of it. Go away now. Go home and observe these conditions. First, never tell anybody that you are a man without a soul. Second, when you reach home, seize the child you love most, pierce one of the veins in his neck, drink up all his blood until his body is completely dry, cook the body, eat the flesh. Nding'ūri, I have turned you into an eater of human flesh and a drinker of human blood." Nding'ūri said: "What! How can that be? Am I to destroy the beauty of my own children?" The bad spirit told him: "Have you already forgotten that you no longer have a soul? That you have sold it for property? Listen: from today onwards you'll never be able to see the beauty of children, or of women, or of any other human being. You'll be able to see only the beauty of property. Go now, go home. Devour other people's shadows. That's the task I have given you until the day I come to fetch you!"

'From that day on, Nding'ūri began to fart property, to shit property, to sneeze property, to scratch property, to laugh property, to think property, to dream property, to talk property, to sweat property, to piss property. Property would fly from other people's hands to land in Nding'ūri's palms. People started wondering: How is it that our property slips through our fingers into the hands of Nding'ūri? Furthermore, he was now wearing iron rings on his fingers, which prevented him from working himself.

'Nding'ūri's character and behaviour altered. He became mean. He became cruel. He was always involved in lawsuits as he grabbed other people's land, extending the boundaries of his own property further and further. He had no friends. His meanness protruded like the shoots of a sweet potato. When people were dying from famine, that was when Nding'ūri was happiest because at such times people would dispose of their property as readily as they would give away broken pots.

'People in his village started asking themselves: Where has his kindly tongue gone? What is that thing he eats alone in the middle of the night, like a witch? When he sees another man's property, his mouth waters: when he acquires his own, his mouth quickly dries up. See now how his shadow grows bigger and bigger, while ours become smaller and smaller. Could it be that his shadow is swallowing our shadows, making us fall dead, one by one?

'A delegation of elders, Nding'ūri's age-mates, was sent to him to remind him that no one digs a deep hole in the yard of the village, for his own children might fall into it. They told him: "Nding'ūri, son of Kahahami, listen to the voice of the people. You have no wax in your ears – or if you have, take a splinter of wood and remove it.

'"The voice of the village is the voice of the Ridge, and it is the voice of the country, and it is the voice of the nation, and it is the voice of the people. Nding'ūri, the voice of the people is the voice of God. We come to bring you this message: avoid the ways of the witches and murderers. Allow yourself to be dazzled by the splendour of property, and you will be dazzled only by the splendour of the evil spirit. But in the glory of your nation you'll see the face of God. Happy is the man who willingly defends the shadow of his nation, for he will never die; his name shall live forever in the hearts of the people. But he who sells the shadow of his nation is damned, for his name shall forever be cursed by generations to come, and when he dies he will become an evil spirit."

'Nding'ūri just laughed, and he asked them: "What's a village? What's a nation? What's a people? Go away and tell all this to someone else. Why are you unable to take care of yourselves and your shadows? Why are you so lazy that you can't even bend down to remove a jigger from your legs? Go on talking until it rains or the heavens fall – your words will only be carried away by the wind. See, now, all my affairs are in perfect order. My fart never smells. Why? Let me tell you. Because property is the great creator and the great judge. Property turns disobedience into obedience, evil into good, ugliness into beauty, hate into love, cowardice into bravery, vice into virtue. Property changes bow legs into legs that are fought over by the beauties of the land. Property sweetens evil smells, banishes rot. The wound of a rich man never produces pus. The fart of a rich man never smells. Go back to your homes. Go back to your shacks, which you have the audacity to call houses; return to your strips of land, which you have the audacity to call farms. If you are unable to do that, come back here and work as wage labourers in my many fields. There is nothing you can do to me, Nding'ūri, son of Kahahami, because I have no soul!"

'When they heard that, the elders of the village were greatly alarmed, and they looked askance at one another: "So we have been harbouring a witch in our village? We have been sheltering a louse in our bodies? This one will drink up all the blood of all the people until there is no more blood left in the land." And then and there they seized him, and wrapped him up with dry banana leaves, and burned him and his house.

'From that day the village was rid of evil, and the shadows of the people grew healthy again. Many hands can lift the heaviest of loads!'

Gatuĩria paused again.

The Matatū Matata Matamu was still waddling along the road. By now it had left the road to Nakuru and had turned off on to the *TransAfrica Highway*, which passed through Rūūwa-inĩ and Il-morog. There was total silence in the car, each person wrapped in his own thoughts about the story, anxious to find out where Gatuĩria's knot fitted. Gatuĩria went on with his story.

'It was after I was told that story that I had a new thought and found a new theme around which I could now weave a new song. But was it really new, or was it the same one that I had always searched for? What I wanted to do now was to tell the same story in music. For what could beat the story I had been told by the old man from Bahati? What story could have a finer theme or teach a more important lesson than the tale of a man exchanging his soul for earthly riches? I wanted to compare Nding'ūri wa Kahahami with the Judas of Jewish literature, who sold the peace of his soul for thirty pieces of silver.

'I wanted the setting for the music to be a certain village before the advent of British imperialism in Kenya. I thought I would start by telling the origins of the village. I wanted one group of voices and instruments to represent the pastoral migrations of peoples before the feudal era. Another group of voices would represent the different ways in which the village produced and distributed its wealth. I wanted one set of voices to represent pastoralists, another the peasants, another the workers in metal and so on. Then I would introduce other movements of voices and instruments to symbolize famine, diseases, poverty and the beginnings of feudal rule. Then I would introduce the story of Nding'ūri, son of Kahahami.

'I started composing the music, a great fire burning inside me . . . . But after a few lines I felt the flames die, and the ashes of the work were left without even the tiniest spark.

'"Why? Why?" I cried, without knowing to whom I was appealing.

'In my heart I did not quite believe in the existence of ogres, spirits or creatures from any world but this. And then one night I heard a small voice whispering to me the real reasons for the death of the fire: "How can you compose music when you do not believe in the existence of the subject of your composition?"

'Belief . . . belief . . . where could I acquire belief? Belief is not for sale in a market. In my heart I reasoned this way: In the past, before imperialism, we had a system of age-groups, of extended families, of sub-clans and clans. In those days we had many types of people's organization. We had *Ujamaa wa Mwafrika*, for example – in English, *African socialism*. Where, then, did the eaters of men and the killers of men come from? My heart began to beat. Spirits, evil or good, do not exist. Creatures from other worlds do not exist. Kenya, our country, has no killers or eaters of men, people who drink blood and kidnap the shadows of other men. These days there is no drinking of human blood or eating of human flesh . . . . Spirits and ogres and creatures from other worlds, all those vanished a long time ago . . . . You who wish to compose music in praise of your country, look for roots and themes in true stories!

'And that's the state I've been in since then, restless, a thousand and one questions jostling inside me . . . .

'Our people, you can imagine how astonished I was yesterday when I went to my pigeonhole at the university where my letters are kept and found . . . oh, how can I tell you about it? Am I going to pretend that I didn't shake like a reed in the wind? Even now as I sit in this *matatū*, I can't quite believe the evidence of my eyes . . . .'

Wangarī interrupted, burning with a desire to know what it was that Gatuīria had seen. 'What extraordinary thing did you see that makes you forget what you are saying and keep pausing like the chameleon which once was sent by God to the people but never delivered the message it carried because it hesitated so long?'

'There in my pigeonhole,' Gatuīria hurried on with his story, 'I found a card inviting me to a Devil's feast in Ilmorog tomorrow. On the card were the following words.' Gatuĩria took out a card from his coat pocket and read out:

The Devil's Feast!

Come and See for Yourself –
A Devil-Sponsored Competition
To Choose Seven Experts in Theft and Robbery.
Plenty of Prizes!
Try Your Luck.
Competition to Choose the Seven Cleverest
Thieves and Robbers in Ilmorog.
Prizes Galore!
Hell's Angels Band in Attendance!

Signed: Satan
The King of Hell
c/o Thieves' and Robbers' Den
Ilmorog Golden Heights

Warĩĩnga shrieked and fell against Mũturi. Mwaũra turned his head quickly. The car started to lurch across the road.

'Stop the car! Who has got a light?' Mũturi shouted.

'What is it? What is it?' Wangarĩ asked, but nobody answered her.

'I haven't got a torch!' Mwaũra said, stopping the matatũ on the side of the *TransAfrica Highway*.

'I've got some matches,' Gatuĩria said.

'Give us a light! Strike a match!' Mũturi told him, and then they all fell silent, as if they were standing by the side of a grave.

Cars coming from and going to Ilmorog passed each other on the road, momentarily lighting up the plains of the *Rift Valley*. But the darkness that closed in behind the lights seemed denser than ever. The man with the dark glasses sat in his corner without stirring. Mwaŭra was still in his seat. The other three bent over Warĩĩnga.

The flame of a match would briefly light up Warĩĩnga's face, then it would flicker and die, and Gatuĩria would strike another. But when they saw Warĩĩnga open her eyes, and they found that she was still breathing and that her heart was still beating, they started talking, voicing their different opinions.

'I think this woman is ill,' Mũturi said. 'Probably malaria or pneumonia.'

'Her heart is beating very fast,' Gatuĩria said.

'It could be the woman's disease,' Mwaŭra said. 'Would you believe it? One woman recently gave birth in this very *matatŭ*.'

'Why don't you lift her out of the car for a breath of fresh air?' Wangarĩ suggested quickly, as if she wanted to put an end to Mwaŭra's story.

Then Warĩĩnga spoke in a faint voice, as if her tongue had been on a long journey.

'*Sorry*, but I suddenly felt very dizzy,' Warĩĩnga told them. 'Let's now go, *please*. Let's get out of this place.'

They resumed their seats. Mwaŭra tried to start the car. It would not start. Mũturi, Wangarĩ, Gatuĩria and the man in dark glasses got out and pushed. The engine roared into life. They climbed into the car, and they drove on a little way, the passengers silent.

Wangarĩ reverted to the subject of Warĩĩnga's dizziness. 'Was it the discussion we were having that brought on the illness?'

'It had something to do with it .... Yes, it was the talk ...,' Warĩĩnga replied.

'The subject scared you?' Mũturi asked.

'Yes ... and ... no,' Warĩĩnga said, doubtfully.

'Don't worry,' Wangarĩ said, 'those things no longer exist – ogres, killers and eaters of men, bad and good spirits, the Devil with seven horns. All those are mere inventions, which are meant to frighten disobedient children into mending their ways and encourage the obedient ones to follow the straight and narrow path.'

Mwaŭra started whistling a tune, like somebody who held

different opinions on the matter or knew a little more about it but did not want to reveal what lay hidden in his heart. Then he started singing:

> Maiden, should I ask you, grant me my wishes,
> And don't be stingy about it,
> So that when later you reveal that you are pregnant,
> I will not deny the responsibility.

He thought the passengers would laugh and move on to different topics, and abandon talk of killers, eaters of men, spirits and devils, feasts for competitors in theft and robbery. However, Warĩĩnga surprised them all by returning to the subject.

'But what if such things did exist? What if these were not mere stories told to children in the evenings? What would you do? Tell me, what would you do if bad and good spirits did actually exist, and if the Devil did exist, and if he visited Kenya, and if he hosted feasts on Earth and arranged competitions for his earthly disciples?'

'Me?' Mwaũra jumped as though the question had been directed at him. 'Me?' he asked again, as if he wanted to make sure. But before he had even received an answer, he went on: 'Let me tell you, I've seen some strange things. Well, once I was taken prisoner by some crooks in this very vehicle. But were they crooks or three young men dressed in fantastic suits? I found them at the *Farmer's Corner* in Limuru. It was in the evening, just before darkness fell. They told me they wanted to go to Kikuyu town. One glance at them and I thought I had stumbled across good fortune. I raised the hire fee. I tell you, by the time we reached Mũtarakwa I had begun to see through my mouth. They took out a pistol and jammed it against the back of my head, and they told me: "If you don't want fragments of metal to blast your head to smithereens, drive fast towards Kĩneenĩ forest, and don't you dare look back or sideways." No one can claim that all my money wasn't taken and all my clothes! I was left just as I was born – stark naked! But, fortunately, they did not steal my car keys.

'On another day an American tourist hired this car. This American was really old. His face was full of deep valleys. And on the other parts of his body, the folds of the skin lay in rolling layers. But he had with him an African girl, so tiny she could have been a schoolgirl. They sat in the back. I drove them all round Nairobi for an hour or so. They didn't talk much. And they didn't do a lot either. All he did was to keep pressing and pinching the little girl's thighs, and the girl massaged his face – sometimes her fingers got completely lost in the folds of his skin. When the girl pretended to feel pain and she cried out a little, the eyes of the American would light up with happiness. Foam dribbled out of the sides of his mouth, and he groaned as if the real deed were on. When I dropped them outside the *New Stanley* Hotel, the American took out a 100-shilling note and gave it to the girl, who walked away. The American tourist stayed behind, listing for me the virtues of the country as if I was the owner of Kenya: "*Kenya is a great country ... fantastic wild game ... and afterwards fantastic women, so beautiful .... Even I, an old man, I can get a chick .... I'll come back with even more tourists so that they can see Kenya's wild game and women for themselves .... Truly a beautiful country ... stability ... progress....*" And then he too walked away into the hotel. But he paid me well.

'So this world is full of many strange things. A man who doesn't travel thinks that it's only his mother who cooks wild vegetables .... Did you ask me what I would if I was invited to the Devil's feast? I would go, for I would never be satisfied with other people's accounts of it. To believe is to see and to touch. I am the modern Thomas. I, Mwaũra, have seen much and done much. Now leave me alone, woman! The sun never rises the way it set ....' Mwaũra finished in a tone that seemed to hint at many things and to hide much.

'What about you?' Warĩĩnga asked Mũturi. 'What would you do?'

'That's not easy to answer, I can tell you,' Mũturi replied. 'Gĩkũyũ once said: "Don't look down upon a drop of rain" and "There is nothing so startling that it cannot be faced by men." We workers have no home, or village, or even country. The whole Earth is our home, because for us it is a matter of where we can find someone to purchase our labour so we can earn a few cents to buy a bit of flour and cheap vegetables. But all the same, it is we who've built this Earth. How, then, could we possibly leave our Earth to the Devil and his evil spirits and their disciples, so that they can do whatever they liked with it? Let me ask you a modern riddle — '

'Do you think I can tell the difference between old and modern riddles?' Warĩĩnga replied.

'I walk this way and that way!' Mũturi said.

'The ways of hunters.' Wangarĩ answered for Warĩĩnga.

'No!'

'Take a forfeit!'

'The paths of builders! Answer another riddle!'

'I will!'

'I walk this way and that way!'

'The paths of builders.'

'No. Give me a forfeit.'

'It's yours.'

'The paths of workers. Answer another.'

'I will.'

'I walk this way and that way towards a revolution.'

'The paths of workers.'

'Yes and no. You owe me a forfeit, but I won't take everything, for you got half the answer.'

'I accept that.'

'The answer is the paths of resistance . . . and those are the paths made by workers. Why do I say that? Because this woman has asked me a difficult question. But it is also a simple question, because the things that are difficult are the ones that are simple . . . and the things that seem simple are the ones that are difficult. Now, I can tell you that I know of no devil worse than the employer for whom I have been working. As you know, I am a carpenter, a mason, a plumber, a painter, all that. I was really the foreman in charge of the site. My employer used to get building contracts worth tens of millions and more. He had a councillor who used to press his case in the committee that awarded the contracts. But the wages of those who made the tens of millions possible were *truly nothing* – just a few shillings, two hundred, three, five, not much more – and you know how prices have been rising. Our troubles began when we demanded an increase of fifty shillings and demanded too that thereafter wage increases were to be linked to the rising cost of living. Do you know, some people don't realize that when the price of things goes up and the wages remain the same, it is really the same thing as a drop in wages? But the profits of the employers increase at the same rate as the increase in prices – in fact, sometimes the rate of profit is higher than the price increases. So when the price of things goes up, the employers benefit, but the lot of the workers gets worse. When we decided to go on strike, our employer came to us, panting. He talked nicely to us, and he said that he would consider all our complaints and demands, and that we should all go back to work, and that he would submit a report to us a week later. On the day he was to let us have his report, he came back, accompanied by policemen armed with guns and batons and iron shields. The employer talked very bitterly, like a man who had quarrelled with his wife the night before. He said all strikes had been banned by presidential decree. He then said that anybody who was tired of working could go home because there were plenty of unemployed men looking for work. The ringleaders of the strike were dismissed. "Do you think that we in Kenya pick up money from the ground? As for you, Mũturi, don't think yourself so smart. Your record with the *Special Branch* is this long. We know that you are not alone." So we dispersed. One gun can only be confronted with another, and not with empty hands. That's why today you see me searching for work here and there. And that is only because I rejected slave wages. Just imagine living on a salary of 300 shillings a month in Nairobi!'

'Which company were you working for?' Warĩĩnga asked.

'The *Champion Construction Company*.'

'The *Champion Construction Company*?' Warĩĩnga repeated. 'The one managed by *Boss* Kĩhara?'

'Yes. Why do you ask? Why are you so surprised?' Mũturi asked Warĩĩnga.

'Because I worked for the same company.'

'In the city offices?'

'Yes. Kĩhara was *my boss*. *But what a boss*! Today I'm also on the road looking for another job.'

'Did you go on strike too?' Gatuĩria asked.

'No. I refused to be his *sugar girl*,' Warĩĩnga said.

'She went on strike all right – against the tyranny of the Boss's bedroom,' Wangarĩ said, as if the question had been directed at her.

'Do you see? Do you understand now?' Mũturi asked. 'Now you can see why I simply can't leave our Earth to the Devil for him to twirl this way and that as he fancies! The Devil's feast? I'd like to go to challenge the Devil!'

Warĩĩnga turned to Gatuĩria. 'What about you? Do you really believe in such a feast?'

'But I'm going to it,' Gatuĩria replied slowly. 'Tomorrow is the day of the Devil's feast.'

'Tomorrow? Sunday?' Wangarĩ asked.

'Yes, tomorrow, starting at ten.'

'And you aren't scared?' Warĩĩnga asked.

'Of what?'

'Of the Devil. Isn't he supposed to have seven horns?'

'That is precisely the centre of the knot I was talking about: does the Devil exist or not? I want to go there to put an end to all my doubts so that I can go on with my composition. Because I can't carry on with a mind troubled by endless doubts. Peace! A composer needs peace in his heart!'

73

'Oh, yes, let there be peace in all our hearts!' Wangarĩ responded.

'What about you?' Warĩĩnga turned to Wangarĩ.

'So you are still after an answer?' Wangarĩ asked. 'As for me, whether I am invited or not, if I were to come across this famous Devil, I would teach him never to oppress the true builders of this Earth! But tell me this: why are you asking these questions? What weight is burdening your heart?'

All the others had the same question in mind: what kind of woman was this? She had been quite silent after they had left Nairobi. Then she had suddenly shrieked. Then she had fainted. And now that she had recovered, she was asking endless questions.

'Yes, indeed, why are you putting the same question to all of us?' Gatuĩria asked.

Warĩĩnga said: 'Because I too have a knot in my heart.'

'A knot?' Wangarĩ and Gatuĩria asked together.

'I've also received an invitation similar to yours, and I don't know quite how it came into my hands.'

'What? Explain what you mean.'

'I too have an invitation to the Devil's feast at Ilmorog tomorrow. Today I've seen so many strange things that I now can't tell if I have been dreaming or if I've simply been ill and delirious. A man appeared to me in Nairobi at Kaka, near *St Peter's Clavers* church. I was about to . . . . Let me say simply that I wasn't feeling well in body or in spirit. The man gave me back this very handbag. I had dropped it in River Road without knowing it. But his face, his eyes, his voice made me open my heart to him at once, and I told him all my problems, and by the time I had finished my story, I felt that my heart was lighter. It was when we parted that he gave me the card. When I reached Nyamakĩma, I read what was written on it. Here it is!'

Warĩĩnga took the card out of her handbag. It was similar to Gatuĩria's invitation.

'What! This is beyond a joke!' Wangarĩ said. 'And we should not look down upon a droplet of rain. Didn't I speak to the police chiefs this very day? And according to these cards, the robbers and thieves are preparing to gather for a Devil's feast. Let them gather!'

Wangarĩ growled something that was partly a threat and partly a sigh. Then she began to sing.

> Come one and all,
> And behold the wonderful sight

74

Of us chasing away the Devil
And all his disciples!
Come one and all!

Mwaũra shouted: 'Hey! How I hope those rogues that stole my money and stripped me naked will all be there tomorrow!' But his voice carried a hint of sarcasm, as if he knew things that the others did not. Mũturi too did not display much surprise at the invitations to the Devil's feast.

Mwaũra was quiet. All of them fell silent now, conscious that Ilmorog town was not far away. And Mwaũra's Matatũ Matata Matamu Model T Ford, registration number MMM 333, bounced gently along the road, as though it was saying: Too much haste splits the yam. Patience brings wealth. It is better to arrive safely. It is safer to travel in Matatũ Matata Matamu. Ilmorog is to be preferred above all other towns.... We are going to attend the Devil's feast....

8

It was then that the man in dark glasses opened his mouth, like Balaam's ass in the Bible. 'Excuse me!' he said.

All of the travellers except Mwaũra turned towards him to catch what he was saying.

'Let me see those invitations,' he said to Gatuĩria and Warĩ-ĩnga.

Gatuĩria took out his card and passed it to him. The man asked Gatuĩria to light a match. He looked at the card, and then he turned to Warĩĩnga: 'Let me see yours too,' he told her.

Warĩĩnga opened her handbag and took out her card. She held it out, together with the piece of paper she had been given that morning by the *Devil's Angels*. She dropped the piece of paper at Mũturi's feet without being aware that she had done so. She handed the card to the man in dark glasses.

The man scrutinized the card, and he compared it with the one that Gatuĩria had given him. Then he opened his suitcase and took out another card, the same size as the ones belonging to Gatuĩria and Warĩĩnga. He handed it over to Gatuĩria and told him to look at it carefully, then to read it aloud to the others. Warĩĩnga took the box of matches and lit one for Gatuĩria. This is what Gatuĩria read:

A Big Feast!

Come and See for Yourself
a Competition to Select Seven Experts
in Modern Theft and Robbery.
Prizes Consist of Bank Loans
and Directorships
of Several Finance Houses.
Try Your Skills!
Try Your Luck!
You Might Take Home the Crown
of Modern Theft and Robbery!
Competition to Choose the Seven Cleverest
Modern Thieves and Robbers.
Prizes in Guaranteed Bank Loans
and Directorships
of One or Several Associations
of Finance Houses.
Hell's Angels Band in Attendance!

Signed: Master of Ceremonies
c/o Thieves' and Robbers' Den
Ilmorog Golden Heights.

'Do you see any difference between this card and yours?' the man asked Gatuĩria. 'The card I have just given you is the authentic one. I think you will have noticed that there isn't a single mention of the Devil or Satan. Let me tell you something else. The majority of those who will be attending the feast believe in God. I, for instance, go to the PCEA church at Thogoto, the *Church of the Torch*, every Sunday. Those who have printed the fake invitation cards are the enemies of modern progress. They just want to ruin the feast.'

'And who are these people who want to spoil the feast?' Gatuĩria asked.

'Who are they? I think they must be university students. It's just like students to think up this type of childish smear campaign against respectable people.'

'As for me, I don't see the difference between the two cards!' Wangarĩ said. 'How can students damage the reputations of thieves and robbers?'

'By claiming that this is the Devil's feast. And by claiming that it has been arranged by Satan, the king of Hell. And furthermore, on their cards they have not indicated that this is a competition in MODERN theft and robbery.'

'I can't see the difference either,' Mũturi said. 'Theft is theft, and robbery is robbery.'

The man in dark glasses seemed to be wounded by Mũturi's and Wangarĩ's attitude. He started to speak as if he were preaching to a people who had lost their faith.

'My name is Mwĩreri wa Mũkiraaĩ. I can't stand European names. I dropped my name, John, some time ago. As I said a little while ago. I am now heading towards Ilmorog. My car, a *Peugeot 504* (*with petrol injection*), stalled at Kikuyu. I left it outside the Undirĩ Hotel. I was given a lift to Sigona by a *friend*. I thought I would find other important guests travelling to the competition this evening. I met none. Many of the guests said they would be arriving tomorrow morning. But because one can never be quite sure with people who drink, I thought I should go ahead in a *matatũ*.

'I was educated in Siriana Secondary School and at Makerere when it really was Makerere, not the university it is today, ruined by Amin. At Makerere I read *economics* – that's the *science* or the study of how to create wealth in a country. In Uganda I graduated with a *B.Sc. (Econ)*. I didn't stop there. I enrolled at our university here. I was successful and emerged with a degree in commerce, that is, a *B. Comm.* Then, forward march. In America I went to the great university called Harvard. There I studied everything to do with business administration. I got another degree, a *M.Sc. (Bus. Admin.)* My full name is Mwĩreri wa Mũkiraaĩ, *B.Sc. (Econ.) (London); B. Comm. (Nairobi); M.Sc. (Bus. Admin.) (Harvard).* When I run through that list, I'm quite sure Gatuĩria understands fully the significance of what I'm saying. In those days my ambition was to teach at the university. Even today several *professors* are friends of mine. But then I looked around and saw *that there were far too few educated Kenyans in business*, so I opted for a career in commerce.

'Why have I introduced myself with such a fanfare?

'I've listened to all your talk, and I've heard all the arguments and all the doubts that some of you have been raising.

'I won't hide anything from you. It is your kind of talk that is ruining this country. That kind of talk has its roots in communism. It is calculated to sadden our hearts and make us restless. Such words can lead us black people astray, and you know how deeply we believe in God and in Christianity. Kenya is a Christian country, and that's why we are so blessed.

'First things first. This feast is not a Devil's feast, and it has not been organized by Satan. This feast has been arranged by the Organization for Modern Theft and Robbery in Ilmorog to commemorate a visit by foreign guests from an organization for the thieves and robbers of the Western world, particularly from America, England, Germany, France, Italy, Sweden and Japan, called the *International Organization of Thieves and Robbers*.

'Secondly, our university students have become very conceited. They have now devised ways of discrediting theft and robbery even before they know what modern theft and robbery really is. These students are spreading the kind of talk I have just heard from Wangarĩ and Mũturi, namely, that theft and robbery should end.

'So I would like to say this: I am very sure that people can never be equal like teeth. Human nature has rejected equality. Even universal nature herself has rejected any absurd nonsense about equality. Just look at God's Heaven. God sits on the throne. On his right side stands his only Son. On his left side stands the Holy Spirit. At his feet the angels sit. At the feet of the angels sit the saints. At the feet of the saints sit all the Disciples, and so on, one rank standing below another, until we come to the class of believers here on Earth. Hell is structured in the same way. The king of Hell is not the one who makes the fire, fetches the firewood and turns over the burning bodies. No. He leaves those chores to his angels, overseers, disciples and servants — '

'I say,' Mũturi interrupted him, 'have you ever been to Heaven?'

'No.'

'Or Hell?'

'No.'

'So this picture you have sketched for us – where did you get it from? Isn't a picture, like the shadow of a tree? Where is the tree itself?'

'If you look at this world, you'll see for yourself that what I am saying is quite true,' Mwĩreri wa Mũkiraaĩ replied quickly. 'Some people are tall; others are short. Some people are white; others are black. Some people lead a charmed life when it comes to matters of property; others have absolutely no luck, even with ten cents. Some are born lazy; others are born diligent. There are some who are VIPs by nature, natural managers of wealth, and others who are trash, natural destroyers of wealth. Some people know what civilization is; others have absolutely no idea. Some people know how to organize themselves; others can never take care of themselves. Some people, the majority, can only be dragged into modern society with a rope around their necks or a string through their noses, while others, the few, are born to do the pulling. There are two types of human being in every country: the manager and the managed, the one who grabs and the one who hopes for leftovers, the man who gives and the man who waits to receive.'

'Sir,' Wangarī interrupted him, 'don't you know that nothing lasts for ever? Haven't you heard what Gĩkũyũ said a long time ago, that he who used to dance can now only watch others doing it? And he who used to jump over the river can now only manage to wade through it? A pastoralist does not stay in one spot. Change, for the seeds in the gourd are not all of one kind!'

'I am talking about things that I have studied thoroughly,' Mwĩreri told Wangarī. 'Let's turn back to the question of business and economy and ask ourselves this: is theft and robbery a bad thing all the time, in all places, for all people?

'Believe me when I say that theft and robbery are the measure of a country's progress. Because in order for theft and robbery to flourish, there must be things to be stolen. And in order that the robbed may acquire possessions to be stolen and still be left with a few, they must work harder to produce wealth. *History* shows us that there has never been any civilization that was not built on the foundations of theft and robbery. Where would America be today without theft and robbery? What about England? France? Germany? Japan? It's theft and robbery that have made possible the development of the Western world. Let's not be fooled by socialist cant. To banish theft and robbery from a country is to stifle progress.

'So I'll finish by saying this: it's fitting that property should be in the hands of the nation's successful men, those born with the ability to manage wealth even in their sleep. Just imagine what would happen if a country fell into the hands of trash – the destroyers, the lazy, the idle, the wretched, those so feckless that they find it difficult to bend down to remove the jiggers on their toes, to kill the lice under their belts or even to frighten away fleas? Wouldn't this be the same thing as throwing precious pearls to pigs, which will only trample the stones into the mud? Long ago the Mũcũng'wa dancers used to sing:

79

The dancer's bell should be taken away from the weakling.
It should be given to the great hero.

'The question is: who are the modern heroes? We are – the people with money. It's we who have proved that we can beat foreign thieves and robbers when it comes to grabbing money and property. Our eyes are now wide open, and we are able to see clearly that theft and robbery are the true foundation of modern progress and development. That's why I myself attach great significance to the competition at Ilmorog, this competition that is being discredited by university kids. And that's why I would like to ask all of you here to attend the competition tomorrow to see for yourselves. And if any of us feels like entering the field to compete and to demonstrate his skills, he should feel free to do so. I personally believe in the democratic principle that states that he who is able to grab should be allowed to grab. You allow me to grab, and I allow you to grab. You grab, and I grab, and we'll see who beats whom at the game. Those who can bite should meet in the open to dispel all doubts about who has the sharpest teeth. But we should all stop this business of destroying other people's happiness by clandestine means. Throw away those fake cards printed by the university students, and I'll provide you with proper ones.'

Mwīreri wa Mūkiraaī paused. He took a handkerchief out of his pocket and wiped his face and then his nose. As for the other passengers, they were quite quiet, as if they could not believe the evidence of their ears.

Wangarī was the first to rouse herself out of the general stupefaction. 'It is quite true that the pain in the heart doesn't kill! You really dare to call us "trash"? You shamelessly call us peasants and workers "pigs"? You claim that we should be robbed of the pearls of our land? Who cultivates those pearls? He who sows and reaps, he who eats what others have grown – which of the two is the lazy one? Of the two, which produces the brightest pearls of the land?'

'You!' Mūturi added. 'You are very highly educated. But let me tell you this. When a monkey is robbed of its young, a mouthful of food is given it in return. But you people go too far. You rob us of the produce of our own hands, and you don't throw us even a small portion. You dam the river above us, so that not a drop of water gets through to us below. God never has a chance to see how strong your thighs are. I've heard it said that the Earth spins constantly and never rests at any one spot. Life is the circulation of the blood; death is the blood clogged in the veins. Life is the heart beating; death is the

80

heart stilled. We know that a baby in its mother's womb will not be still-born when it plays inside her and moves about. You! Something new may appear at dawn that was not there the night before. Don't despise the masses. The Iregi generation is still alive and rebellious. What did the Singer say the other day? That you people had better take care – it's we who were there with Kĩmaathi.'

Mwĩreri wa Mũkiraaĩ did not pay much heed to Wangarĩ's and Mũturi's outburst. He raised his voice a little, and he began to talk as if he were at the altar, preaching to a multitude with the Bible open before him.

'Why are you so amazed?' Mwĩreri wa Mũkiraaĩ began. 'Haven't you read the Book of God, the Book of Everlasting Life, brought to us by the missionaries? And haven't all these things been prophesied in that Bible? I say: he who has eyes, let him see, and he who has ears, let him hear . . . .'

Jacinta Warĩĩnga, Gatuĩria, Mwaũra, Mũturi and Wangarĩ leaned forward so they would not miss a single word. Matatũ Matata Matamu Model T Ford, registration number MMM 333, was like a church; the passengers were deaf to the noise of the vehicle as it waddled along the *TransAfrican Highway*, bearing them towards Ilmorog, the seat of the great competition in modern theft and robbery.

Mũturi heard the rustle of a piece of paper at his feet. He bent down, picked it up, put it in his pocket and went on listening.

Mwĩreri wa Mũkiraaĩ lowered his voice. He spoke gently, in a slow, soft voice, as if he were singing a lullaby to send their souls and minds to sleep . . . .

' . . . *For the Kingdom of Heaven is as a man travelling into a far country, who called his own servants, and delivered unto them his goods. And unto one he gave five talents, to another two, and to another one . . . .*'

Chapter Four

1

. . . For the Kingdom of Earthly Wiles can be likened unto a ruler who foresaw that the day would come when he would be thrown out of a certain country by the masses and their guerrilla freedom fighters. He was much troubled in his heart, trying to determine ways of protecting all the property he had accumulated in that country and also ways of maintaining his rule over the natives by other means. He asked himself: What shall I do, seeing that these people over whom I have always lorded are now about to expel me from these plantations and factories that I have taken from them? I can no longer cultivate the fields; I can no longer work with my hands. And if I wait until I am clubbed and gunned out of the country, I will live forever in shame because of all the hair-raising stories I have told them about the invincible might of my armoured cars and bombs, and because I have always tried to show them that the white race can never be dominated by the black race. And when the guerrillas win, and they seize the key to the country, I shall never be able to repossess these plantations and industries. This tea, this rice, this cotton, this coffee, these precious stones, these hotels, these shops, these factories, these fruits of their precious sweat – these and more shall be lost unto me. But now I know what I shall do, so that when eventually I go back to my own country through the front door, I shall be able to return here through the back door, and I shall be well received, and I shall be able to plant seeds that will take root more firmly than the ones I planted before.

He called his loyalist slaves and servants to him. He taught them all the earthly wiles he knew, and especially the trick of sprinkling theft and robbery with the sweetest-smelling perfumes, and the trick of wrapping poison in sugar-coated leaves, and many tricks for dividing the country's workers and peasants through bribery and appeals to tribe and religion. When he had finished, he informed them that he was about to leave for his home overseas.

When they heard that their lord and master was about to leave, the loyalist slaves and servants rent their clothes and smeared their bodies with ashes, and they knelt down and cried: 'How can you go away and leave us here, mere orphans, when you know full well how we have persecuted the masses and have perpetrated many other crimes in your name? Did you not vow that you would never leave this land? How can you now leave us to the mercy of the nationalist guerrillas?'

And the lord, their master, told them: 'Are you possessed of so little faith? Let not your hearts be troubled, for you must trust in the God I have taught you to know, and you should also trust in me, the interpreter of his Will. I have many ways of fulfilling my wishes in this land. If that were not so, I would have told you, so that you would have had time to flee or to find ropes to hang yourselves with before you are caught by the patriots. But what I wish to do now is to prepare positions of leadership for you, and to add a little more to the crumbs that you have been gathering from my table. And later I shall return with lots of money and many banks, and I shall also bring you more armoured cars and guns and bombs and aeroplanes, so that I shall be with you and you with me, so that we may love one another always and eat together, I sating myself on choice dishes, and you collecting up the precious remains.'

And it came to pass that as the ruler was about to return to his home abroad, he again called together all his servants and gave them the key to the land, telling them: 'The patriotic guerrillas and the masses of this country will now be deceived, because you are all black, as they are, and they will chant: "See, now our own black people have the key to our country; see, now our own black people hold the steering wheel. What were we fighting for if not this? Let us now put down our arms, and sing hymns of praise to our black lords."'

Then he gave them his property and goods to look after and even to increase and multiply. To one he gave capital amounting to 500,000 shillings, to another 200,000 shillings, and to another, 100,000 shillings, to every servant according to how loyally he had served his master, and followed his faith, and shared his outlook. And so the lord went away, leaving by the front door.

And the servant who had received 500,000 shillings immediately set out and bought things cheaply from the rural peasants, and sold them to the urban workers at a higher price, and in this way made a profit of 500,000 shillings. And the one who had received 200,000 shillings did the same: he bought cheaply from producers, and sold dearly to consumers, and so he made a profit of 200,000 shillings.

But he who had received only 100,000 shillings thought he was clever, and he reviewed his life and that of the masses of the land, and that of the master who had just left for a foreign country. And he began to talk to himself, saying: This lord and master has always bragged that he alone developed this country with the aid of the small amount of money that he came with, shouting, 'Capital! Capital!'

Now let me see whether capital will yield profit without being watered with the sweat of the worker, or buying cheap the labour of the peasant and worker. If it produces profit by itself, then I shall know beyond all doubt that it is money that develops a country. So he went, and he put the 100,000 shillings in a tin, and covered it well, and then dug a hole by a banana plant, and buried the tin there.

And it came to pass that before many days had elapsed, the lord came back to that country, through the back door, to check on the property he had left behind. He called his servants to account for the property and the money that he had given to each.

And the one who had been given 500,000 shillings came and said: 'My lord and master, you left me with capital of 500,000 shillings. I have doubled it.' And the lord was truly amazed, and he exclaimed, '100 per cent profit? *A fantastic rate of profit*. You have done well, you good and faithful servant. You have proved that you can be trusted with a little property. I shall now make you an overseer of many enterprises. Come and share in your lord's happiness and prosperity. I shall make you *managing director* of the local branches of my banks here and I shall appoint you a director of certain companies. You will also acquire a few *shares* in the same companies. From today I shall not let my face be too visible. You will represent me in this country.'

And the one who had been given 200,000 shillings came and told his master: 'My lord and master, you left me with 200,000 shillings. Behold, your capital has yielded another 200,000 shillings.' And the lord spoke and said: '*Wonderful, this is really wonderful: such a rising rate of profit! A stable country for investment*. You have done well, you good and faithful servant. You have proved that you can be trusted with a little property, so now I shall make you an overseer of many enterprises. Share in the happiness and prosperity of your master. I shall make you a *sales director* of the local branches of my insurance houses, and a director of the local branches of my industries, and a director of many other companies that I shall show you. You too will also acquire a few token *shares*. From today I shall hide my face. I shall stay behind the scenes, and you will stand at the door and at the windows, so that it is your face that will always be visible. You will the watchdog of my investments in your country.'

And the one who had been given 100,000 shillings stepped forward and told his master: 'You, lord and master, member of the white race, I have discovered your tricks! I have also discovered your real name. Imperialist, that's your real name, and you are a cruel master. Why? Because you reap where you have never sown. You grab things over which you have never shed any sweat. You have appointed yourself the distributor of things which you have never helped to produce. Why? Just because you are the owner of capital. And so I went and buried your money in the ground to see if your money would yield anything without being fertilized by my sweat or that of any other man. Behold, here is your 100,000 shillings, exactly as you left it. I now give you back your capital. Count it and check that not a single cent is missing. The most remarkable thing was this: my own sweat provided me with food to eat, water to drink and a shelter in which to sleep. Ha! I'll never kneel down before the lifeless god of capital again. I will be a slave no more. My eyes have now been opened. If today I joined hands with all the others who have opted to be masters over their own sweat, there would be no limit to the wealth we could produce for our people and country.'

The master looked at him with much bitterness in his eyes, with much pain in his heart. Then he spoke to him: 'You bad, unfaithful and lazy servant, member of a rebellious clan! Could you not have put the money into a bank or left it in the hands of those who trade in money, so that on coming back I would reap just a little interest? Do you know how it hurts me to find that you buried my capital in a grave, like a corpse? And who has revealed the secret of my name? Who has advised you to reject me, just because I reap where I have never sown and profit by things over which I have never shed any sweat? Who has told you that harvesting and husbandry is not hard work? No! You black people are incapable of such rebellious thoughts! No! You black people are incapable of planning and working out ways of cutting the ropes that tie you to your masters. You must therefore have been misled by communists. You must have got those dangerous thoughts from the party of the workers and peasants. Yes, your mind is poisoned with communist notions. Communism .... You have become a real threat to the peace and stability that used to exist in this country for me and my local representatives, the local guardians of my property. Now you are going to feel the heat of such a fire as will make you forget my real name forever. Arrest him, now, before he spreads these poisonous thoughts to other workers and peasants, and teaches them that the power of organized unity is stronger than all my bombs and armoured vehicles! Take away even the little that he has, and divide it among yourselves. For unto the man of property more will be given, but from the poor man will be taken even the little that he has kept in reserve. That is the most important of all my commandments. What are you people waiting for? Go and get the police and the military to arrest this fellow, who has had the audacity to reject slavery. Throw him into jail or into everlasting darkness, so that his family will harvest only tears and the gnashing of teeth!

'*Good! Good!* You people have done a fine job. Mete out the same treatment to all such rebels, so that the other workers will be too scared to strike for higher wages or to take up arms to smash the chains of slavery.

'As for you, from now on I shall no longer call you slaves or servants in public. Now you are truly my friends. Why? Because even after I had given you back the keys to your country, you continued to fulfil my commandments and to protect my property, making my capital yield a higher rate of profit than was the case when I myself used to carry the keys. Therefore I shall not call you servants again. For a servant does not know the aims and thoughts of his master. But I call you my friends because you know – and I shall continue to let you know – all my plans for this country, and I shall give you some of what I acquire, so that you will have the strength and the motivation to break the skulls of those who talk about the "masses" with any measure of seriousness.

'Long live peace, love and unity between me and my local representatives! What is so bad about that? You bite twice and I bite four times. We'll fool the gullible masses. *Long live stability for progress! Long live progress for profit! Long live foreigners and expatriate experts!*

2

When the master of ceremonies had finished talking in parables, all the thieves and robbers who had gathered in the cave for the competition stood up and gave him such an ovation that their clapping was like the sound of thunder. Some shouted, 'That shoe is a perfect fit for the foot . . . no need for any socks', while others tugged at one another's shirts and cuffs and whispered, 'Did you hear that? He who has will be given more . . . . The master of ceremonies has told the truth about the unity that exists between us and foreigners. They eat the flesh and we clean up the bones . . . . The dog that has a bone is better off than the empty-handed . . . but make no mistake, it is a bone with a bit of flesh on it . . . . *That's true African socialism . . . Ujamaa wa Asili Kiafrika* . . . not like that of Nyerere and his Chinese friends, the socialism of pure envy, the *Ujamaa* that seeks to prevent a man from holding a bone . . . . We don't want Chinese ways in our country. We want Christianity . . . .'

The master of ceremonies asked them all to sit down, and the noise and applause subsided. He had a well-fed body: his cheeks were round, like two melons; his eyes were big and red, like two plums; and his neck was huge, like the stem of a baobab tree. His stomach was only slightly larger than his neck. He had two gold teeth in his lower jaw, and, when talking, he opened his lips wide so that the gold teeth could be seen. He had on a silk suit which shone in the light, changing colour according to the intensity of the light and the angle of the beam. He offered his audience more details about the competition.

'Every competitor will mount the platform, and he will tell us how he first came to steal and rob and where he has stolen and robbed, and then he will tell us briefly his thoughts on how to perfect our skills in theft and robbery. But even more important, he must show us how we can develop the partnership between us and foreigners so that we can hasten our ascent into the heaven of foreign commodities and other delights. You, the listeners, will act as the judges, so you must clap each speaker to show how inspired you have been by his account of his earthly wiles.

'Now, speaking as chairman of the Ilmorog branch of the Organization for Modern Theft and Robbery, I would like you to note the following. Today's competition is the whetstone on which to sharpen our fangs and claws to enable us to gnaw at other people's wealth in unity and peace, for, as you know, a homestead with a whetstone at the gate never has a blunt knife. Therefore, those who lose should not despair. They too should continue to steal and rob, and should learn new tricks from the winners. The wise can also be taught wisdom. The leopard did not know how to kill with his claws until he was taught by the herdsman.

'And now, before I sit down, I shall call upon the leader of the foreign delegation from the International Organization of Thieves and Robbers (IOTR), whose headquarters are in New York, USA, to talk to you. I think you all know that we have already applied to become *full members* of IOTR. The visit of this delegation, plus the gifts and the crown they have brought us, marks the beginning of an even more fruitful period of co-operation. There are many tricks we can learn from them. We should never be afraid to acknowledge the fact that we don't know as much as foreigners do, and we should not feel ashamed to drink from foreign fountains of knowledge. Therefore, let's shower saliva on our breasts by way of asking God to pour blessings on our proceedings!'

The master of ceremonies now called the leader of the foreign delegation of thieves and robbers to the platform to address the crowd of competitors. The ovation accorded to the leader of the foreign delegation as he climbed the steps to the platform was louder than peals of thunder. The master of ceremonies left the platform to the foreign leader. The leader cleared his throat before starting his address.

'An Englishman was the first to say that *time is money*. We Americans believe the same: time is money. So I shall not waste your time with too much talk. The parable which the master of ceremonies told us contained all the most important points that need to be made.

'We have come from many countries, far and wide: from the USA, England, Germany, France, the Scandinavian countries – Sweden, Norway and Denmark – Italy and Japan. Now, let us pause and ponder about that. Different countries, different tongues, different skin colours, different religions – but one organization with one aim and one faith: theft.

'We have come to you as to our friends, who are also the local watchdogs who guard our investments. So when we are here, we feel very much at home. We have visited many caves and lairs owned by local thieves and robbers, and we are very pleased with the work that you people have done. Despite the fact that you were only very recently initiated into the ways of modern theft and robbery, you seem to have grasped and mastered the essentials very quickly. I think that if you continue along these lines, you will become real experts in modern theft and robbery, just like your counterparts in the Western world.

'What we want to do is to choose seven disciples. They will become the representatives of our representatives, thieves to teach other thieves, robbers to teach other robbers, experts to teach other experts, because, as the master of ceremonies was telling me, as we sat together at that table, you have a saying that there are iron tools that can bore through iron itself. The benefits that will accrue to the seven disciples are these: once they have been crowned, there will not be a single door to the local branches of any of our banks and insurance houses – let's say, the local branches of all our finance houses – that will ever be barred to them. Anyone who knows anything about modern theft knows very well that it is these financial institutions that govern everything today – industries and all other types of business. It's these finance houses that dictate the location of this or that industry, the expansion of this or that industry. They dictate ownership and growth – they determine whether an industry will be set up by Kamau or Onyango, whether it will expand or close down. The barons of finance houses are the governing voices in the world today. Money rules the world! These houses are also the only reliable safes in which to deposit the assets that one has grabbed from here and there. It will be the duty of the seven disciples to show other thieves and robbers, and particularly those without *experience*, the best ways of snatching and grabbing, the best ways of eating, drinking and snoring and the best ways of farting the rich man's fart, which is said by you people to be without smell.

'Now, before I sit down, I would like to leave you with a few words of wisdom.

'I think there is no one who does not know that theft and robbery are the cornerstones of America and Western civilization. Money is the heart that beats to keep the Western world on the move. If you people want to build a great civilization like ours, then kneel down before the god of money. Ignore the beautiful faces of your children, of your parents, of your brothers and sisters. Look only on the splendid face of money, and you'll never, never go wrong. It's far better to drink the blood of your people and to eat their flesh than to retreat a step.

'Why do I tell you all this? Because of our own experience. That is exactly what we have done in America and in Western Europe. When the Red Indians tried to protect their wealth and their property from us, we wiped them out with the sword of fire and with the gun, and we spared only a few, whom we later forced into reservations as a reminder of our history. Even before we had finished with them, we had turned to your own Africa, and we carried away a few million slaves. It is the blood of your people that raised Europe and America to where we now are. Why should I hide that fact from you, seeing that you are now our friends? Today we, the thieves and robbers from America, Western Europe and Japan, are able to roam the whole Earth, grabbing everything – though, of course, we do leave a few fragments for our friends. Why are we able to do this?

'Because our forefathers were not afraid to wallow in the river of the blood of their own workers and peasants and the blood of workers of other countries. Today we believe in the democracy of theft and robbery, the democracy of drinking the blood and eating the flesh of our workers. If you want to be like us, then hang your compassion from trees, and you'll never be scared of your workers and peasants. But as the master of ceremonies has rightly said, you should first try to hoodwink them with honeyed words and speeches. Now, what image was it that the master of ceremonies used? *Oh, yes*, you must learn to 'wrap poison in leaves of sugar'. But should they turn out to be obstinate, like the bad servant in the parable, who thought himself cleverer than his master, then you must grind them into the dust with hobnailed boots.

'Finally, you should develop the Uhuru of theft, and we shall help you to defend it with all the weapons we have at our disposal. That is my message. *Good luck in your proceedings.*'

As the leader of the foreign delegation sat down, the whole cave was thrown into confusion as it resounded with shouts and thunderous applause. 'The shoe doesn't need a sock! It doesn't need a sock! It fits the foot exactly! It is made for that foot! This foreigner really knows how to fit shoes!'

The *Hell's Angels* band struck up a tune, while the audience talked and drank. Some slapped one another excitedly on the shoulders, and others kissed their sweethearts on the lips, the nose, the eyes. The tune did not have a lilting rhythm. It was more like a psalm or a hymn. After a few minutes, everybody turned towards the band, and they all started to sing, as if they were in church:

> Good news has come
> To our country!
> Good news has come
> About our Saviour!

3

Wariinga turned to Gatuiria and asked him: 'Is it possible that people dressed in such expensive suits could be real thieves and robbers?'

'I don't really know what's going on,' Gatuiria replied.

'They are thieves! Of course they are thieves!' Wangari said.

'Modern thieves,' Muturi added.

'Those foreigners have very red skins,' Wariinga said, turning towards where the seven foreign thieves were sitting.

'Didn't you hear what their leader said?' Wangari asked, and then she whispered, 'It's because they drink the blood of their children and ours!'

'And because they bathe in it,' Muturi said. Wariinga, Gatuiria, Muturi, Wangari and Mwaura were sitting at a table at the very back of the cave, so whenever Wariinga wanted to get a better view of the foreigners, she had to crane her neck.

The table occupied by the foreigners was at the front of the cave, to one side of the platform. Right at the front of the platform was a small table with long legs. Each speaker stood behind it. In the right-hand corner of the platform, at the back, was the *Hell's Angels* band.

The seat taken by the leader of the foreign delegation was a little higher than the others. On his right sat three foreigners, and on his left the other three. As she stared at them, Waríínga noted that their skins were indeed red, like that of pigs or like the skin of a black person who has been scalded with boiling water or who has burned himself with acid creams. Even the hair on their arms and necks stood out stiff and straight like the bristles of an ageing hog. The hair on their heads was brownish, the colour of moleskin. It was long, and it fell to their shoulders as if it had never been shaved off or cut since birth. On their heads they wore hats like crowns. Each crown was decorated with seven metal objects shaped like horns, which gleamed so brightly that they almost blinded the eyes. All the crowns looked alike, but the leader's was a little larger than the others. The tips of the horns were twisted into the initial of the country that each delegate came from.

There were differences in the suits they wore. The one worn by the leader was made of dollars, the Englishman's of pounds, the German's of Deutschmarks, the Frenchman's of francs, the Italian's of lire, the Scandinavian's of kroner, and the Japanese delegate's of yen. Each suit was decorated with several badges, like those worn by scouts. The badges were made of metal and, like neon advertisements, they flashed on and off, illuminating the words that were inscribed on them. Each badge bore one or two slogans, like the following: *World Banks; World Commercial Banks; World's Exploitation Banks; Money-Swallowing Insurance Schemes; Industrial Gobblers of Raw Materials: Cheap Manufactures for Export Abroad; Traders in Human Skins; Loans for a Profit: Aid with Iron Strings; Arms for Murder; Motor-Vehicle Assembly Plants for Vanity Fair at Home & Bigger Profits Abroad; All Products Fair and Lovely to Keep Fools in the Dependent Chains of Slavery; Slave for Comfort, Deal with Me*; and many others in similar vein.

The table occupied by Gatuíria, Waríínga, Mũturi, Wangarí and Mwaũra was a little way away from where Mwíreri wa Mũkiraaí was sitting, so they could see only the top of his head. The night before, on their way to Ilmorog, they had all decided to meet at the feast to witness the competition for themselves. It was Mwíreri wa Mũkiraaí who gave them genuine invitation cards, for nobody was to be allowed into the cave without a card. And that was the way it turned out to be. When they had met that Sunday morning at ten, they had found guards at the door, who demanded to see their invitations before allowing them into the cave.

But was it really a cave or a house – the finest of houses?

The floor was smooth, as if it were polished constantly – so smooth, in fact, that if one looked down at the floor, one could see one's face reflected in it. The ceiling shone with painted cream. Chandeliers like bunches of glassy fruits hung from the ceiling. They were decorated with paper streamers all colours of the rainbow. From the ceiling hung more streamers, together with balloons. The balloons were also of different colours: green, blue, brown, red, white, black, deep brown.

Barmaids moved from table to table, taking orders for drinks. They were all dressed in catsuits of black wool. The suits were form-fitting: they clung to the contours of the girls' bodies so closely that a distant onlooker might have thought that the girls were naked. On the girls' bottoms were fixed small white patches shaped like rabbit's tails. On their breasts were pinned two plastic fruits. Each girl also wore a band around her head on which was written in English: *I Love You*. The girls looked like apparitions from another world.

Warĩĩnga was drinking whisky and soda. Gatuĩria, Mũturi and Mwaũra chose beer (Tusker), and Wangarĩ ordered a soft drink, Fanta. Gatuĩria and Mũturi paid the bills.

It was certainly a feast. The order of the day was drink your fill; indulge yourself by scattering bank notes about. It was an arrangement that pleased most of the competitors, for now everyone had a chance to display his wealth. When it was their turn, many of the guests would order rounds of drinks in measures that were generous – large bottles of whisky, vodka, brandy and gin, or whole cases of beer for each person. Such people would have bitten their lips in anger had they heard that at the table which they occupied there was someone who was ordering hard drink in tots or single bottles of beer. To order single bottles of beer or meagre tots of liquor, it was generally agreed, was the drinking style of the wretched.

Many of them had armed themselves with young women – *sugar girls* – who wore very expensive jewellery, like pearl and ruby necklaces around their necks or silver and gold rings on their fingers. It looked as if the women in the cave had dressed for a fashion parade, for a display of valuable stones. For their girlfriends the men ordered nothing but champagne, bragging: 'Let the champagne foam and flow like the Rũirũ River. If we can't drink it all, we'll bathe in it.'

'When are they going to start?' Waríínga asked Gatuíria.

'They are getting ready,' Gatuíria replied.

Wangarí was turning many things over in her mind: I'm very lucky. Only yesterday I was released after telling the police that I would search out the lairs of all the thieves and robbers so that I could play my part in serving the public at large. It was as if I knew all about this feast. What luck! Only twenty-four hours later I've found their lair. Aren't these people the villains, the ones who are gathered here in the cave with their friends from abroad? If all of them were to be arrested by the police and thrown into jail, wouldn't theft and robbery in Ilmorog come to an end, and the whole country be rid of man-eaters? I'll wait until I've heard what they've got to say. I'll find out what their plans are, so that when I go to fetch Inspector Gakono and his police force, I'll have plenty of evidence. I see that Mũturi is watching everything and listening to every word, as if he didn't want to miss a thing. I wonder if perhaps he'd help me in giving evidence?

She thought of asking him for help, then she paused. Her heart started beating to the rhythm of the song she had sung in Mwaũra's *matatũ* the night before:

> Come one and all,
> And behold the wonderful sight
> Of us chasing away the Devil
> And all his disciples!
> Come one and all!

The band started to play a Congolese tune:

> Babanda nanga bakimi na mobali
> Mobali oyo boto ya matema
> Nakei koluka mobali nangae . . . .

A thought suddenly seized Mũturi, he turned to Mwaũra and asked him in a whisper: 'Mwaũra, what is your connection with the killers who call themselves the *Devil's Angels*?'

Mwaũra started as if he had been pierced with a red-hot needle. 'How do you know? How do you know?' he demanded, his eyes full of fear.

But at that moment the band suddenly stopped playing. All noise ceased. There was total silence in the cave. Everybody turned their eyes to the platform.

The competition was about to begin.

93

The first competitor strode forward and sprang on to the platform. All the other thieves looked at one another in dismay.

The suit that this competitor was wearing was the kind that had been baptized Napier-Grass-Son-of-Trembling. It showed no sign of ever having been pressed. He was tall and lanky. But his eyes were big. They were like two electric bulbs hanging from a tall, thin eucalyptus tree. His arms were long, and he swung them this and that way as if he did not know what to do with them – whether to put them in his pockets, to hold them stiff, like a soldier standing to attention, or to fold them, like a man in defiant mood. He tried all these postures in turn. He scratched his head. He cracked his fingers. In the end he settled for folding his arms across his chest and gave a little laugh to drive away his stage fright as he began his story.

'My name is Ndaaya wa Kahuria. If I seem ill at ease and awkward, it's only because I'm not used to standing up before such a large audience. But these hands you are looking at . . .' and he stretched out his hands to show the audience his palms and fingers, ' . . . these hands you see are used to dipping into other people's pockets. If these long fingers were to slide into your pockets, I assure you that you wouldn't feel them. I don't think that in all of this area there is a single thief who could tell me to step aside so that he could teach me how to snatch purses from women in market-places or in buses, or how to trap people's chickens in villages.

'But by the truth of God in Heaven – yes, I swear by the Truth of Truths – I only steal because I'm hungry, because I need clothes, because I have no job and because I have nowhere to lay this small head of mine at night.

'All the same, to prove that I have a talent for stealing, let me give you a little demonstration of how I steal chickens in the villages . . . .' Ndaaya wa Kahuria's stage fright appeared to have worn off, and now he narrated how he would bore holes in grains of corn, string them together on a nylon string and throw the grains to the chickens while holding the string at one end and singing to encourage them, thus: 'Kurukurukuru . . . Kurukurukuru . . . kurukurukuru . . . .' And there and then, bending low on the platform, Ndaaya wa Kahuria began swinging his arms this way and that, as if he could see real chickens in front of him, and shouting at them: 'Kurukurukuru . . . kurukurukuru. . . .' But before he could finish his story, some of the guests started complaining and shouting, while others whistled to show their disgust at Ndaaya's demonstration on the platform. Others angrily tapped the floor with their shoes and yelled: 'How was such a wretched thief, with his dreary tales, allowed in here?'

The master of ceremonies leaped on to the platform and called for silence. He addressed the audience and told them that this was a competition for thieves and robbers, real ones – that is, those who had reached *international standards*. Stories of people breaking padlocks in village huts or snatching purses from poor market women were shameful in the eyes of real experts in theft and robbery, and more so when such stories were narrated in front of international thieves and robbers. The foreigners had not travelled all this way to meet people who stole just because they were hungry or needed clothes and jobs. Such petty thieves and robbers were *criminals*. 'Here, in this cave, we are interested only in people who steal because their bellies are full,' the master of ceremonies said, patting his stomach.

Ndaaya wa Kahuria lost all shame and fear, and he started to harangue the master of ceremonies: 'A thief is a thief. There should be no thieves with special privileges. A thief is a thief, and motive is not important. We should all be allowed to enter the competition and to compete freely. A robber is a robber . . . .'

From every corner of the cave, the congregation of thieves and robbers raised their voices in dissent, some shouting angrily, 'Tell him to get that cheap suit of his off a platform that belongs to men who know their trade! Ndaaya wa Kahuria, we don't want to look at Napier-Grass-Son-of-Trembling – let it tremble in the wind outside! Throw him out! He can take his special talent for stealing chicken to Njeruca! Master of ceremonies, do your job. If you can't, say so, and we'll soon find a replacement who can handle the situation.'

The master of ceremonies beckoned to the guards at the door. They ran forward, swinging their clubs in the air, and they hustled Ndaaya wa Kahuria towards the door, despite his loud protests about discrimination. Ndaaya wa Kahuria was expelled from the feast. The other thieves and robbers laughed and whistled with pleasure. The master of ceremonies again gestured for silence, and then he spoke.

'This is a competition for *Thieves and Robbers International, yaani*, thieves and robbers who have attained international status. So we don't want any novices or amateurs to come here and waste our time. *Time is money, and every time is robbing time.*

'So let's agree about the rules that will govern this competition from now on. Our reason for gathering here today is not as simple as some of you make out. And neither is it a laughing matter. I say this: nobody who steals only in hundreds or even thousands should bother to come up to the platform, for he will be taxing our patience for nothing.'

This was greeted with loud applause.

'That is the first rule. Your applause, which is obviously spontaneous and sincere, is a sign that we all approve of it. Here we want to see and hear only thieves and robbers who have sat down at least once to count and pocket their millions.

'The second rule is this: no one without a big belly and fat cheeks should bother to come up here to waste our time. Who could possibly argue the size of a man's belly and cheeks is not the true measure of his wealth?'

Those thieves who boasted large paunches gave him a big ovation. The slim ones shouted him down. The crowd in the cave split into two, and heated arguments developed between the clan of the fatties and the clan of the skinnies.

One man who was particularly thin jumped to his feet to disassociate himself completely from the second rule. He was so angry that his Adam's apple danced up and down at tremendous speed as he talked. He argued that although it was true that many thieves and robbers had great paunches and fat cheeks that were nourished by property, there were others whose stomachs were sunken and whose cheeks were hollow because they were always thinking about the problems raised by the extent of their wealth. 'Yes, the problems associated with its very size!' the man said, and added: 'But that doesn't mean that they aren't experts in theft and robbery. A man shouldn't be discriminated against because he is thin. He can't graft an extra stomach on to himself or borrow the swollen belly of his pregnant wife so as to be allowed to take part in the competition. To be slim is not the same as being sliced thin by misfortune ... and you don't judge a hero by the size of his calves.' The man finished and sat down. The clan of skinnies clapped him vigorously, and the clan of fatties shouted him down.

A fight almost broke out when one fatty said loudly that the man who had just spoken was as lanky as Ndaaya wa Kahuria. The man who had been insulted stood up and demanded bitterly: 'Who called me Ndaaya wa Kahuria? Who called me a wretch? Who insulted me by comparing me with a thief who deals in just a few hundreds and thousands? Let him come forward! Let him come forward, and we'll fight it out with our fists, so I can teach him that I steal *in millions*.'

Then a man stood up who was neither fat nor slim. He settled the dispute by saying: 'Let us not concern ourselves with thinness or fatness, whiteness or blackness, tallness or shortness. There is no bird of prey that is too small when it comes to hunting. Anyone who feels he has what it takes should be allowed to come forward and compete with other eaters. An eater and an eater should meet in the battlefield to settle all doubt about who calls the tune in eating other people's property. Just look at our foreign guests. Some are fat; others are slim. Some have red hair; others have hair which is not so red. One comes from Japan in Asia; others come from Europe; and their leader comes from the USA. What makes them of one age-group, one house, one clan, one umbilical cord, one kind is not slimness or fatness or language. No, what binds them together, uniting them as members of one clan, is theft, which has permitted them to spread their tentacles over the whole of the Earth, like the creeping plant that crawls into all corners of the field. Therefore we, their local watchdogs, are also of one umbilical cord, one age-group, one house, one clan, one kind. We who have gathered here today, whether Luo, or Kallenjin, or Mkamba, or Mswahili, or Mmaasai, or Mkikuyu, or Mbaluhya, are brothers in theft and robbery, related to one another through our links with these foreign experts. Master of ceremonies! We all belong to one organization. Let us always remain united. It is only among the people from whom we steal that we should create divisions of tribe and religion, so that they will never develop their own strong, united organizations to oppose us . . . . You people, a fire that blazes fiercely may destroy the meat whose fat made it jump into the flames!'

As he ended his speech, the man was greeted with applause that almost brought the walls and the ceiling of the cave tumbling down. '*Toboa! Toboa! A Daniel come to judgement!*' some of them shouted, so delighted were they with the man's words.

After a brief discussion it was agreed that a man's size, weight, religion, tribe and skin colour would have no bearing on his participation in the competition, that everybody should be allowed to fight on the basis of his cunning and skills in theft and robbery. But because of the need to exclude amateurs and novices, the following rules were agreed upon:

Rule 1   Every competitor must give his name.

Rule 2   Every competitor must give his address.

Rule 3   Every competitor must reveal the number of women he has – wives and/or mistresses.

Rule 4   Every competitor must provide information about the car he drives, the model his wife drives and the model driven by his girlfriend(s).

Rule 5   Every competitor must give a brief account of his career in theft and robbery.

Rule 6   Every competitor must show how theft and robbery can be increased in the country.

Rule 7   Every competitor must show how we can strengthen the ties between us and foreigners.

When the master of ceremonies had finished reading the rules, he sat down, amidst more thunderous applause.

'I would like to enter the competition,' Mwaŭra told Mŭturi.

'Are you a robber?' Mŭturi asked Mwaŭra. 'Where do you think my profit comes from?' Mwaŭra retorted, and then he started to laugh as if he had only been joking. But suddenly he recalled the question that Mŭturi had asked him earlier about the *Devils' Angels*. His laughter died. He turned towards Wangarĩ, and he asked himself: Does she too know what Mŭturi knows about me?

Wangarĩ sat still, torn between courage and bitter distaste. She wanted to stand up and silence the whole cave with accusations and abuse. But she remembered her resolution to endure the feast patiently, so that she could gather as much evidence as possible before going for the Ilmorog police. For about two minutes she blocked her ears to shut out the self-congratulation and mutual admiration of the thieves and robbers as they greeted the master of ceremonies with delirious applause.

And quite suddenly Wangarĩ felt as if she had been transported to Mwaŭra's *matatŭ*, where she had sat the night before, heading towards Ilmorog. She heard the voice of Mwĩreri wa Mŭkiraaĩ soothing them to sleep with the story of the man who was about to travel to a far country and who called his servants and delivered unto them five talents, two talents, one talent.... *Then he that had received the five talents went and traded with the same, and made five talents more. And likewise he that had received two, he also gained another two. But he that received one went and dug in the earth and hid his lord's money. After a long time, the lord of those servants returned, and reckoned with them, and he that had received ... talents ....*

98

The Testimony of Gĩtutu wa Gataangũrũ

The following are things that were revealed by Gĩtutu wa Gataangũrũ concerning modern theft and robbery. Gĩtutu had a belly that protruded so far that it would have touched the ground had it not been supported by the braces that held up his trousers. It seemed as if his belly had absorbed all his limbs and all the other organs of his body. Gĩtutu had no neck – at least, his neck was not visible. His arms and legs were short stumps. His head had shrunk to the size of a fist.

That day Gĩtutu wa Gataangũrũ was sporting a dark suit and a white shirt with frills. A black bow tie, which looked as if it had been stuck to his chin, stood where his neck should have been. His walking stick was decorated with pure gold. While he talked, Gĩtutu stroked the side of his belly with his left hand and swung his walking stick with his right hand. He panted as he talked, like a person carrying a heavy load.

Gĩtutu wa Gataangũrũ gave his testimony as follows.

'As for my name, I am Gĩtutu wa Gataangũrũ. That is my traditional name. But my European name – or perhaps I should say my Christian name, which is also my baptismal name – is Rottenborough Groundflesh Shitland Narrow Isthmus Joint Stock Brown. When Europeans hear my full name, they are taken aback at first, then they look at me again and again rather strangely. Some of them shake their heads, and others laugh outright. Why? Because even they have never heard of such an unusual name! You people, Europeans really fear me.

'As for matters of the flesh, I am an elder with one wife and five children – three boys and two girls. One of the boys has finished his education at all the universities in Africa, and he has now gone abroad to accomplish a similar feat there. The next boy has just secured a place at the university. My third son and my daughters are still at school, struggling with pens and books. I always say that they must get all the learning that I myself would have got if my father had had the type of cunning that I now possess. All of them go to very expensive schools, the kind that used to be for Europeans. Even today the schools they attend have only European teachers.

'But before I leave such matters, I would like to mention that besides my wife – we were joined together as man and wife at Thogoto Mission Church – I have two mistresses, for you know the saying that he who keeps something in reserve never goes hungry, and when an European gets old, he likes to eat veal.

99

'Some of you may be looking at this little belly of mine, and when you see how it droops and when you hear me panting, you may be asking yourselves: How can Gĩtutu, son of Gataangũrũ, manage one wife and two young things? Our people, I would like to ask such sceptics the following question: why have you forgotten our proverbs? As the dancer prepares himself for the arena, it's he who knows how he is going to dance. The elephant is able to carry his tusks, however huge. And again, whoever is able to resist money today is beyond human help.

'As for my address, my real home is here at the Golden Heights, Ilmorog. I call it my 'real' home because it's where my wife and children live. It's like my HQ. But I've got many other houses in Nairobi, Nakuru and Mombasa. I'm never happy staying in hotels. When I am on a smuggling mission I like to spend the night in a house that bears the name of Gĩtutu wa Gataangũrũ. *Of course*, those are the houses known to the mother of my children. But I have a few other private lairs in Nairobi. Those are for me and my *sugar girls*.

'And as for my car, I normally go about in a *chauffeur-driven Mercedes Benz 280*. But in addition I have a *Peugeot 604* and a *Range Rover*. Those are for *my personal use*. The mother of my children drives a *Toyota Carina*. That's just a little shopping basket for carrying goods from the market. There are other vehicles – lorries and tractors – that I need for my business activities. I won't waste your time counting those. Oh! I was about to forget about my young girlfriends. I gave one *sugar girl* a *Christmas gift* of a *Toyota Corolla*, and I bought the other one a birthday present, a *Datsun 1600 SS*. Modern love is inconsistent with a tight fist!

'Now, my friends! Seeing that I have been so blessed and fortune has been so generous to me, is it surprising that I should glorify and sing praises to modern theft and robbery?

'Today I saunter down smooth, wide avenues, ones without thorns, or stones, or sweat. Can't you all see that my hands have almost disappeared? They have no work to do. And my belly is becoming larger and larger because it is constantly overworked!

'When I wake up in the morning, I swallow a few eggs on top of pieces of bread and butter and a glass of milk to chase them down. At ten o'clock or thereabouts I manage to put away a couple of pounds of cooked mutton. At twelve I attack four pounds of beef (*fillet steak*) dipped in wine and then nicely roasted over charcoal, and I wash the beef down with a cool beer, one bottle. At six, I nibble at a piece of chicken, just to have something in the belly as a base for whisky, pending *supper proper* in the evening.

'I believe in the catechism of the lord in the parable that has just been narrated to us by the master of ceremonies, and particularly in all the commandments that he issued to his servants. Reap where you never planted, eat that for which you never shed a drop of sweat and drink that which has been fetched by others. Shelter from the rain in huts for which you have never carried a single pole or thatching grass, and dress in clothes made by others.

'Let me tell you this, my friends, whom I love dearly: the day I began to follow those commandments was the day all my affairs started going smoothly, without a hitch.

'My father was a court elder in the only courts black people were allowed to sit in during the colonial era, the *native tribunals*. In those days the court used to meet at Rūūwainī, in Iciciri district. It was during his tenure of office at that court that he learned how to straighten the law here, to break it there, and particularly how to bend it here and there to make it serve certain ends. He grabbed other people's lands. There was not a single black man in those days who could beat my father in court cases. Look at it this way. All the members of those tribunals, from Cura in Kiambu to Mūrang'a and Nyeri, were his bosom friends. They normally came to our house to drink beer. On such occasions, my father would slaughter the best sheep in their honour. Once or twice he even slaughtered a bull! As a result, he grabbed other people's land without fear and became a big landowner. He married several wives. He was an arrogant old man. He had only to meet a beautiful woman carrying firewood or coming in from the fields, and he would send for her: "The daughter of so-and-so must be brought to me." But my father neglected *family planning* of any kind. We, his children, were more numerous than his lands could support. I inherited only three things from my father: literacy, words of wisdom from his own mouth, and the letters he used to get from his European friends.

'I was educated at Maambere, Thogoto, in Kiambu district, and I completed *junior secondary*. I became a teacher and taught in the same school for about two years. Then I joined the High Court, Nairobi, as a *court clerk and interpreter*. Our saying is true: the young of a goat steals like its mother. I had returned to my father's origins.

'The State of Emergency found me in the law courts. My father was one of the elders who were used by the colonialists in the purges of the Mau Mau followers. But as for me, I didn't know which side I should support. I wasn't cold and I wasn't hot. I stayed like that, lukewarm, hiding in the law courts as an interpreter for those involved in murder cases.

'When Uhuru came, it found me in the same law courts, *marking*

101

time with my meagre salary. I paused to check which way the Earth was spinning, the direction of the wind. Then I started a few petty businesses, shop- and hotel-keeping. But they were never profitable. In those days I had not yet mastered the holy commandments of a man-eat-man society.

'It was then that I recalled my father's words before he died of the disease of overeating. He had summoned me to his house, and he told me: "You have been wise to start a few shops and hotels. We have a saying that a pastoralist does not stay in one spot. On a journey, nobody carries food for anyone else; each traveller carries his own. A salary is nothing for a man with a family to look up to. But at the same time we black people cannot manage petty trades that need patience. It's only Indians who have that kind of patience. My son, listen to your father's words of love. I know you have book learning. But the wise man is he who has been taught by someone who has seen it all before and has learned from the experience. A career of theft and robbery is the only one for anybody who calls himself an adult. Learn from the whites, and you'll never go wrong. The white man believes that there's no business to beat that of theft and robbery. I'll talk frankly. The white man came to this country holding the Bible in his left hand and a gun in his right. He stole the people's fertile lands. He stole the people's cattle and goats under the cover of fines and taxes. He robbed people of the labour of their hands.

'"How do you think Grogan and Delamere became rich? I would sleep with my mother before I believed that it was their own sweat that made them so wealthy. Which of us today, even though we now fly our own flag, can match the white man's wealth? I have nothing to bequeath to you. But I did send you to school. And now I have offered you words of wisdom. Here are letters from some white men with whom I have worked and who have been very pleased with my services. I am their friend. They are my friends. If you are ever in trouble, go to any one of them with a letter that bears his signature. Tell him that you are the son of Gataangūrū, and ask for his help."

'When I recalled those words, I sat down and I asked myself: Who has ever become rich by his own sweat? Who has ever become rich through his salary alone? My father never bought his property out of his salary. Cunning did it. It was not wages that provided Grogan and Delamere with their wealth. Cunning did it. Cunning, be my guardian angel. As for these miserable village shops with their *stock* of two matchboxes, two packets of cigarettes, tea bags that sell for twenty-five cents per bag, one sack of sugar and another of salt, a tin of cooking oil – whoever grew rich by owning them? Nobody.

Cunning, be my angel. Hold me by the right hand and guide me always night and day.

'I think that what made me remember my father's words was the fact that after Uhuru a few black people started buying the lands for which the Mau Mau had fought. What was very surprising – and, indeed, this delighted a lot of people who not long before had been alarmed by the news of Uhuru – was that apparently it did not matter on what side one had fought in the battle for freedom. It did not matter whether one was called Mr Hot, Mr Cold or Mr Lukewarm. The question of whether one had formerly been cold or hot or lukewarm was irrelevant when it came to the grabbing of land. What was important now was the handsome physique of money. And that money was not be had by the labour of one's hands: it was to be had through the cunning of one's mind. Cunning was more profitable than hard work.

'So I stopped working. I fell to my knees, and I prayed fervently:

Cunning, be ye my guide,
And lead me all the time,
Waking and sleeping.
And wherever I go,
I would like you to give me
The food I eat,
The water I drink,
Even the clothes that I wear.

'From then onwards I never retreated, and I have never had any regrets.

'I had hardly a cent in my pocket. But having watched the way the country was moving since the flag had been hoisted high in the sky, I was confident that for as long as I lived I would surely be able to survive by looting other people's property. I kept turning my new outlook over in my mind till the words became a song:

This is a new Kenya!
Whether you used to be hot or cold,
Don't tell us old tales.
Old perfume is no good for a new dance.
Mind, produce cunning!
Cunning, begin your work!

'I looked this way and that, and I saw that the greatest appetite

103

in the country was thirst and hunger for land. I asked myself this: Hunger multiplied by thirst – what's the answer? I took out the pen and the paper of the heart, and I calculated thus:

$$\text{Hunger} \times \text{thirst} = \text{famine.}$$

Famine among the masses = wealth for a man of cunning.

Ha! A fool's lawsuit, if unsettled, lasts for a long time. The beekeeper who postpones collecting the honey finds that the hive has collapsed. To say is to do: that is today's motto.

'So early one morning, I gathered up the letters I had inherited from my father. I went to the house of a European nicknamed Gateru, the Bearded One. He was called Gateru because during the Emergency he used to pull people by the beard until the hair and the skin of his victims came off in his hand. Gateru was one of the colonialists who used to be in the same anti-Mau Mau purging team as my father. The letter, praising my father for his faithful service, had been written during the period of the colonialist anti-Mau Mau oathing ceremonies. "Only your skin is black: you are a European at heart" was how the letter ended. I told Gateru that my biggest need was for land. When he heard that I was the son of Gataangũrũ, Gateru did not bother to ask for any other form of security. "*Yule alikuwa mzee mzuri, alipiga Mau Mau sawa sawa kabisa. Nitasaidia wewe.*"

'He told me that he had a hundred acres of land for sale near Nairobi. He would sell it to me for 100 shillings an acre. Land used to be cheap then, unlike today. The whole lot came to 10,000 shillings. We agreed on a date when I was to bring him the money in *cash* or a *banker's order* for the same amount.

'I left his house, and went to see a friend, a young man who used to work in a bank. I told him that I needed a loan of 10,000 shillings. He laughed when he saw my face, lined with worry. Only 10,000? I said, "Yes." Again he laughed. He told me not to worry. He had just been given an Uhuru fruit. Now he was *in charge of loans to promising African businessmen to help create a stable African middle class.* A loan clerk? My heart began to beat with expectation. He told me: "But remember, in this world there is nothing for free. Give to me, and I will give to you: that's the modern motto. This is the new Kenya. Give to me, and I will give to you. I'll loan you 15,000 shillings. Of that sum, 10,000 will be yours. The 5000 on top is mine. If you don't accept that arrangement, the door is over there and further on is the road."

'When I heard that, I felt anger choking me. What! He would loan me 15,000 shillings so that he could pocket 5000, and he would not even help me to repay the money? His profit was to be my debt? Then all of a sudden I burst out laughing. I saw that his outlook and mine were identical! Wealth is not the work of one's hands but the cunning of one's mind, cunning in a free market system to rob people of the fruits of freedom! "The shoe fits," I told him. "It does not need a sock."

'A week later, I had the 10,000 shillings in one pocket and, in the other, a debt of 15,000 shillings. I ran back to my European benefactor. We counted the money. He put his share in his pocket. Then the two of us went to Gateru's farm. Oh! It was an arid wasteland. Nothing had ever been planted there. No shelter had ever been erected on it. It was a desert of couch-grass, thorny weeds and stones.

'*Anyway*, a week after that I had the title deeds for a hundred acres of stones. And in all this time I hadn't forgotten my arithmetic and the answers: hunger multiplied by thirst brings about mass famine, and mass famine is the source of the wealth of a cunning grabber. The loss of the masses is the gain of the few. One portion and another portion, seized from this and that hand, become a whole meal in the belly of him who grabs from the poor.

'Now hunger for land gripped our village! I took the hundred-acre plot and divided it into fifty two-acre plots. Then I announced that only residents of the village were allowed to buy plots. The son of the homestead is always the first to be smeared with the luck-oil of initiation. I also announced that nobody was allowed to own more than one plot. Gĩtutu wa Gataangũrũ did not want to have anything to do with land grabbers.

'I sold each plot for 5000 shillings. After a week there was not a single plot unclaimed. I didn't even keep one for myself. Why should I want to own two acres of stones and thorns?

'My pocket now rang with the joyous sound of 250,000 shillings. After paying back the bank loan and meeting all my other expenses, I was left with a clear profit of 220,000 shillings. And the whole transaction had taken less than a month.

'My fame was fanned and spread like fire in the wilderness in a dry season. It was said that I was a man who acted on his words; that I was able to get land for the poor and sold it to them cheaply; and that I did not even keep a plot back for myself because of my love for the people. They started singing my praises, calling me son of Gataangũrũ, a child imbued with love of the people. Do you see what can be achieved by cunning? People had already forgotten that my father had been Gateru's home guard, that I myself had remained in hiding in the law courts that used to convict and sentence Mau Mau adherents to death.

'I learned a lesson. Before I donned the robes of cunning, I didn't have a cent to my name. But now, after wearing the robes of cunning for only one month, I had a few hundred thousand shillings in the bank, and my fame was greater than that of any man who had shed his blood for his country – and all this without a drop of my sweat falling on the land I had sold.

'The question is this. The land wasn't mine, and the money with which I'd paid for it wasn't mine, and I hadn't added anything to the land – where did I get the 220,000 shillings? From the pockets of the people. Yes, because the land really belonged to the people, and the money with which I bought it came from the people! I myself had only switched things from one hand to the other. I had done a bit of multiplication and put the answer into my pocket.

'It was then that I learned that my talents lay in juggling and multiplication and pocketing the answers. I founded *societies*, companies for buying land in the Rift Valley. This what I used to do. I would go to the Rift Valley and look for about a thousand acres of land. I and the seller would agree on the price. I would return to Central Province or, more correctly, to my village or the districts near my home. I would then announce that a piece of land of a given size and quality had been found, and that people should buy *shares* in the syndicate, the *society*, that had been formed to purchase the land.

'I remember one farm in Subukia. That was the farm that really made me! It was a thousand-acre farm, and it had on it countless cows. The owner was one of those Boers who used to swear that they would never live in a Kenya ruled by blacks. So he was selling the farm cheaply because he was in a hurry to migrate to South Africa before Congo-type chaos broke over the new Kenya. I was introduced to him by Gateru. I bought the farm for 250 shillings an acre – the whole farm cost me 250,000 shillings. As was now my practice, I divided the farm into two equal parts. One half, 500 acres, was for the *society*. The other half was divided into smaller plots of two acres each, so that each member of the *society*, on buying a *share*, would become the owner of a plot. There were 250 shares in all. A *share* cost 5000 shillings. So the contributions of all the members amounted to a total of 1,250,000 shillings. After giving the Boer his 250,000 shillings, I was left with a cool million. I put the whole sum into my bank *account*. I gave the people the farm. They were delighted. They begged me to head the *society*, but I refused.

I told them to choose their own leaders, and, of course, I advised them to choose leaders who were honest, leaders who were not greedy for money. My job was merely to acquire land for the people and to leave it to them to run it themselves.

'My fame spread throughout the ridges. And my bank *account* swelled. It was from the same gullible people that I later got a few cents to buy my many farms: coffee, tea, wheat plantations and ranches.

'Today I'm about to join hands with some foreigners from Italy, who are planning to purchase an entire county in Meru and Embu to grow rice and sugar. But I have not abandoned the lucrative business of land speculation.

'There are two ideas that I'd like to develop now. The first concerns ways and means of increasing hunger and thirst for land in the whole country; this will create famine, and the people will then raise top-grade tycoons. The masses will do that in this way: as soon as hunger and thirst for land have increased far beyond their present level, we who have the land will be selling soil in pots and tins, so that a man will at least be able to plant a seed in them and hang them from the roof of his shelter!

'My friends, when we reach the stage of selling soil to peasants in tins and pots, we'll really be making money! Imagine the whole population holding trays or plates or baskets, queuing for soil at your place! Later they will hang their few grains of soil from their roofs or verandahs and plant in them potatoes to bribe their crying children to be quiet!

'The other idea I'd like to follow up is how we, the top-grade tycoons, can trap the air in the sky, put it in tins and sell it to peasants and workers, just as water and charcoal are now sold to them. Imagine the profit we would reap if we were to sell the masses air to breathe in tins or, better, if we could meter it! We could even import some air from abroad, *imported air*, which we could then sell to the people at special prices! Or we could send our own air abroad to be packaged in tins and bottles – yes, because the technology of foreigners is very advanced! And then it would be sent back to us here labelled *Made in USA; Made in Western Europe; Made in Japan; This Air is Made Abroad:* and other similar ads!

'Our people, ponder about those ideas. When peasants and workers became restive, and they became too powerful for our armed forces, we could simply deny them air till they knelt before us! When university students made a bit of noise, we could deny them air! When the masses complained, we would deny them air! When people refused to be robbed or to have their wealth stolen, we'd simply switch off the air until they came to us with hands raised, beseeching us: "*Please*, steal from us. Rob us mercilessly...."" By the time Gĩtutu wa Gataangũrũ had finished his testimony, he was panting with fatigue. Drops of his sweat fell to the floor. His protruding belly was trembling as if it wanted to break loose and fall to the ground.

When he reached the climax of his speech, and he started shouting, 'I am the king of thieves and robbers!', Gĩtutu staggered and collapsed, completely exhausted.

The master of ceremonies and two others waddled to the platform and fanned his body with handkerchiefs till he came to. Then half the audience in the cave rose to give him a standing ovation.

'What! Are they under the illusion that we have forgotten?' Wangarĩ whispered to Mũturi.

'They appear to imagine that we are children who can be bribed into silence with sweets.' Mũturi replied.

'And furthermore, sweets that have been taken from our own pockets,' Wangarĩ added.

Watching Mũturi and Wangarĩ whisper to one another, Mwaũra became restless: Why did Mũturi ask me about the *Devil's Angels*? he wondered. What does he know about me? Who is Mũturi? Who is Wangarĩ? Gĩtutu wa Gataangũrũ returned to his table, supported by two people, but he was still shouting: 'I am the king of kings in the kingdom of cunning! My lords and masters, see what I have done with my talents...'

... And the servant who was given ... talents .....

The Testimony of Kĩhaahu wa Gatheeca

And these are the experiences of Kĩhaahu wa Gatheeca, revealed to those who had gathered at the robber's cave in Ilmorog for the competition in modern theft and robbery.

Kĩhaahu was a tall, slim fellow: he had long legs, long arms, long fingers, a long neck and a long mouth. His mouth was shaped like the beak of the kingstock: long, thin and sharp. His chin, his face, his head formed a cone. Everything about him indicated leanness and sharp cunning.

That day, Kĩhaahu was dressed in black-and-grey striped trousers, a black tail coat, a white shirt and a black tie. Standing on the platform, he looked like a 6-foot praying mantis or mosquito.

Kĩhaahu started by clearing his throat, and then he spoke the following words.

'I don't have much to tell. Too much of anything is poison. But a little is often sweet. My aim, or my *motto*, is to act on my words. My actions are the trumpet that sounds my abilities as a thief and robber. I myself am the best possible illustration of the sayings that we were reminded of earlier today: that tallness is not a misfortune, and a hero is not known by the size of his calves. For, indeed, I am the cock that crows in the morning and silences all the others. I am the lion that roars in the forest, making elephants urinate. I am the eagle that flies in the sky, forcing hawks to seek refuge in their nests. I am the wind that stills all breezes. I am the lightning that dazzles all light. I am the thunder that silences all noise. I am the sun in the heavens during the day. I am the moon, king of the stars, at night. I am the king of kings of modern theft and robbery. Crown me with the golden crown, for it is not too early for the new king to begin his reign.

'I am not praising myself for the sake of it. We came here to hold a seminar in modern theft and robbery. I'll sing a song about myself that will move our foreign guests to make me overseer of other overseers, watchdog over other watchdogs, messenger above all other messengers. Say yes, and I'll tell you a story full of wonder.

'Skills like those just mentioned to us by Gĩtutu wa Gataangũrũ *ni kama mswagi kwangu*, they are nothing at all. To head societies or companies that purchase land in such a way that one is the first to select all the healthy cows for one's own farm, or in a position to divert public money for one's own use, or to borrow from a bank on the *security* of the society's lands – these are the simple tricks through which I learned how to steal and rob. In English they would be called *amateurish tricks* or beginners' tactics.

'As for my name, I am Kĩhaahu wa Gatheeca. My foreign name is Lord Gabriel Bloodwell-Stuart-Jones. To turn to matters of the flesh, I am an elder with only two wives. I married one before I became a man of property; I married the other after acquiring property, when I started receiving invitations to *cocktail parties*. You here don't need to be lectured about the fact that old, scentless perfume is not fit for the modern dance of party talk in foreign languages. If a woman were to be out of step, she might jeopardize your whole future. So my second wife knows English, and she has no job other than decking herself out in expensive clothes and jewellery for *cocktail parties*.

'As for my children, I have quite a few. All of them speak English through the nose, exactly like people born and brought up in England. If you were to hear them speak Gĩkũyũ or Kiswahili, you would laugh until you pissed yourself. *It is so funny*. They speak the two languages as if they were Italian priests newly arrived from Rome – priests without priestly collars. But then the children are mine, and I don't mind that they speak their national languages like Italian foreigners.

'Now for my *sugar girls*. I never run after schoolgirls. Girls like those are danger itself. They may pass on diseases, and I have no *time* for penicillin injections or for swallowing preventive *capsules* before the job.

'I like other people's wives. One gets such a glorious feeling of victory. You know, don't you, that that's another kind of stealing? I am particularly good at bourgeois women. They never resist. And they have no pretensions. They want only one thing. Some are not satisfied with one or two shots – this is because their husbands are always at nightclubs with their girlfriends. And again, many of them don't have much work to keep them *busy*: today, they sing only one song – change for good seeds are not all contained in one gourd. A cunt is not salt or soap that will dissolve or disappear after use. I have baptised them Ready-to-Yield. They aren't expensive. But there is one *professional*, who has a row of degrees that stretches from here to there. She left her husband for my sake, and I felt as if I had just returned from a victorious raid. But, of course, I had to give her something in return: 1,500,000 shillings for a ten-acre plot of land that I bought for her at Tigoni, near Limuru .... That's why I've always sworn that if I catch my wife loitering on street corners, I'll make her begin to see through her arse!

'As for my car, there's not a single model that I haven't tried .... I change cars like clothes. A Mercedes Benz beats them all, but when I get tired of that, I buy a *Citroën* or a *Daimler or a Range Rover*. I have also bought toys for my two wives and older children, playthings like Toyotas, Datsuns and Peugeots.

'My *sports*: counting money in the evening, playing golf on Saturdays and Sundays and, of course, playing about with the thighs of the Ready-to-Yield when I have the *time*.

'I often contrast the way I live today with the way I used to live before I entered the field of theft and robbery, and it seems to me like contrasting sleep with death. Long ago, before Uhuru, I lived with duster and chalk in my hands, teaching children their ABC at Rūūwa-inī *Primary School*. Oh, those were terrible days! I used to eat ugali with salt as soup, or with ten cents' worth of vegetables when a bird of good omen had visited me. I used to cough all day because of the chalk dust that had accumulated in my throat, and I couldn't afford any fat to cool the pain that burned in my chest.

'I don't know, even now, how it came about that one day I opened the classroom window, and I looked outside, and I saw many people of my own generation busy picking fruit from the Uhuru tree. I heard something whisper to me: Kīhaahu, son of Gatheeca, how can you stay here like a fool, your nose clogged with chalk dust, while your contemporaries out there are munching the fruits of freedom? What are you waiting for? What will be left for you after everybody else has grabbed his share? Remember that there are no crumbs to be gathered in the wake of masters of the art of eating.

'And suddenly the scales fell from eyes. I could now see quite clearly. I, son of Gatheeca, threw the chalk through the window, put on my long coat, made the biggest *about turn* of my life and said *bye-bye* to the teaching profession. I too wanted a chance to find out what these fruits of *Uhuru wa Mwafrika* tasted like.

'Too much haste often splits the yam. Listen to this. I foolishly rushed for the very first fruit that came my way, like the girl in the story who was tricked by others into picking fruit with her eyes shut and ended up by picking only the raw ones. The fruit tasted bitter in my mouth. Had I picked crab-apples, mistaking them for real apples?

'Let me tell you about the mistake I had made, for we have come here not only to boast about our abilities but to also *share our experience*. While I was still teaching, I had already found out that the biggest thirst in the country was the thirst for education. This thirst for education oppressed the masses, but it was the basis of the wealth of a select few. Even people who could hardly read or write A or B had started their own private secondary schools, and they would get a Mercedes Benz or two out of the enterprise. The buildings were often made of mud, the teachers had been recruited from a junk yard, the desks were made from off-cuts of wood, the stationery had been collected at the road-side, and *still* the schools were able to turn a profit for their owners. I thought that I too, son of Gatheeca, should try to find out for myself the true weight of a coin picked up in that quarter. 'I thought I would start a *nursery school*, because it would not call for heavy investment. I went to a bank and got a loan. My small farm was my security. I looked for and found a building in Nairobi. Then I looked for and found an African girl who had failed her CPE, whom I employed to look after the kids: she would play with them, give them a bit of milk at ten and teach them a few songs. Then I placed a big advertisement in a newspaper, with the following wording:

111

New Black Beauty Nursery School
for Children of VIP Kenyans.
Owned, Managed and Taught
Entirely by Kenyans.
Swahili Language in Use.
Kenyan Songs, Kenyan Lullabies, etc., etc.
Cheap in Fees: Dear in Quality.
Bring One, Bring All.
Sisi Kwa Sisi, Tujenge Kenya Taifa Letu.

'Well! I never got a single child, not even a disabled one.

'I sat down and wept, remembering the amount of money that I had spent, and knowing very well that the bank might auction the piece of land I had been foolhardy enough to offer as security. I thought and thought hard. Could it be that I had not examined the Uhuru tree properly, so that instead of a sweet berry, I had picked a bitter one? But then I told myself: That which defeats a seeker after money has been turned over and over again.

'I did a bit more research to find out what was really going on. I soon found out that no prominent Kenyan, on acquiring a large farm, would employ a Kenyan as his manager: he would only employ a European foreigner. A prominent Kenyan who was a success at big business would not employ a Kenyan as his manager or accountant: he would only employ a European or an Indian foreigner. When Kenyans conversed, they never used their national languages: they only conversed in foreign languages. Whenever a Kenyan .... I noted and observed until my vision cleared. *Ugeni juu, Ukenya chini.* That was the basis of profit for the modern Kenyan bourgeois.

'I hurried back to the nursery school before the bank started harassing me. I changed its name. I baptised it: MODERN-DAY NURSERY SCHOOL. Then I looked for a white woman to be the *principal*. Luckily, I found one. She was a decrepit old woman, half-blind and hard of hearing, and she was always falling asleep. She agreed to join the staff of my school and to do her dozing there.

'Next I visited certain Nairobi shops. I bought child mannequins – those plastic human shapes – and I dressed them in expensive clothes. I fixed red wigs to their heads. I put electric machines into their plastic bellies, and then I fixed tiny wheels on the soles of their plastic feet. When I switched on the power, the mannequins would move about the floor like real human children at play. Through the big glass windows of the school building one could see them playing

112

even if one were standing by the roadside. Then I placed another big advertisement in a newspaper:

Modern-Day Nursery School.
Experienced European Principal.
Formerly for Europeans Only,
Now Open to a Few Kenyans.
Foreign Standards as Before.
National Languages, National Songs, National Names Banned.
Foreign Languages, Foreign Songs, Foreign Toys, etc., etc.
English Medium of Instruction.
Limited Places.
Telephone or Call in Your Car.
Colour is no Bar: Money is the Bar.
Fees High.

'Oh, then parents started ringing day and night to reserve places for their children. Whenever the phone rang, I would run to wake up the European principal to answer it. But the majority of parents preferred to call in their cars to make sure of a place for their children. And on finding a white woman, and on seeing the mannequins at play through the windows, the parents would pay the *fees* then and there: they didn't even bother to find out more about the school.

'I took – or, rather, I instructed the principal to take – no more than a hundred children. Each child paid 2500 shillings a month. I was overjoyed, for that meant that every month I was pocketing 250,000 shillings. After paying the rent and the salaries of the dozing principal and her assistants, I would be left with over 200,000 shillings every month. And please note, all this time I hadn't shed a single drop of sweat, and I hadn't swallowed any dust from chalk and dusters. To me the fruit from that particular tree did not taste bitter – not at all.

'I picked another fruit and yet another. I opened four other nursery schools in Nairobi, using the same trick of employing aged or even crippled white women as principals and buying white mannequins to stand in for real white children. Even here at Ilmorog and Rũũwa-inĩ I have opened a few nursery schools along the same lines.

'The fruit from that tree was certainly plentiful, and it was very ripe indeed. And sweet – but that's another story! Now, Europeans have told us that it is not good to put all your eggs in one basket. So I thought I should try to find out what the fruits of other trees tasted

113

like. Societies and companies for purchasing farms like those mentioned by Gĩtutu wa Gataangũrũ and other ways of stealing and robbing through land speculation have all yielded fruit that I have eaten gladly.

'But the tree from which I've picked fruit riper and sweeter than that on all the other Uhuru trees is — Wait, let me start the story of that special tree right from the beginning, so that all of you can see that I am not a novice when it comes to the art of theft and robbery.

'After I had picked a lot of fruit from the two trees that were watered by the people's thirst for education and their hunger for land, I began to look about me to see which fruits my contemporaries were plucking. I saw that as soon as people accumulated property, they all wanted to enter *Parliament*. With my own eyes, I've seen someone sell his farm and auction his very beautiful wife in order to meet his election expenses. I paused to think: What's in this business, which has become the object of so much in-fighting, to the extent that people are prepared to scatter millions of bank notes about and sell their wives and daughters and farms? Could it be that this tree yields more fruit than all other trees?

'I made up my mind to enter the field of politics and find out for myself: after all, it's only he who sits under the tree who knows what the black tree-ant eats. But since I was also familiar with the saying that too much haste splits the yam, I was determined not to race for a parliamentary seat – those seats, as you know, are very hot and have been the cause of bloodshed – I would go first for a seat on Iciriri *County Council*, Rũũwa-inĩ *Ward*.

'To say is to do, and it is never too early to market vegetables, before they lose their bloom. I literally poured money into the pockets of those around me. When I mean to do something, I do it in style: I don't hold back. I gathered a choir of Nyakĩnyua women about me, who sang my praises and invented stories of how I had fought for freedom and had provided people with land and education and other lies like those. I bought colourful uniforms for the Nyakĩnyua women, with my picture printed on them.

'Then I employed a youth wing, whose task was to destroy the property of my opponents and to beat those who murmured complaints about me. I had five opponents. I took two of them aside and bought them out for 50,000 shillings each. They both made public announcements that they were withdrawing in favour of Gatheeca, the hero. The third opponent refused to be bribed. One night he was kidnapped by two youth wingers and taken to Rũũwa-inĩ forest, where he was shown the barrel of a gun and told to choose between living and being elected. He wisely opted for life. The fourth one not only refused to be bribed but actually went as far as to shout his defiance even after he had been shown the barrel of a gun. I sent some youth wingers to his home. They broke both his legs.

'The fifth was a clever bastard. He quickly sent round his own thugs, who blocked the road with their car and pointed a gun at me and warned me that should I ever play with their chief, the result would be a tooth for a tooth, an eye for an eye, a leg for a leg, blood for blood. I got the message. My opponent wasn't joking. I gave in. I told them to tell their chief that eaters of other people's wealth usually meet in the field to decide which can out-eat the other. So he should agree to meet me on the election battlefield to put an end to all doubt, once and for all, about who was who. In the meantime, I warned, no eater should threaten the life another. Money is power, so he should let his money and my money fight it out in the field. In the end we arrived at an understanding: we agreed to let iron and iron clash to see whose weapon could drill a hole in the other.

'So the field was now left open to us two. Money would do the work, show which of us had stolen the most. For my part, I gave instructions that all the taps should be turned on full, so that every beer drinker could drink as much as he wanted, knowing that his vote was cast for the son of Gatheeca. I tell you, there wasn't a single trick I didn't pull, including buying *votes*. I spent a total of 2,000,000 shillings on that campaign. My opponent was no push-over. He spent 1,500,000. But eventually the seat went to the hero you now see standing before you.

'Even before I had properly taken my seat on the Council, I began to figure out how I could get back the millions I had spent on the campaign. But by now I had learned that enthusiasm for the modern dance is fuelled with money. I tried this and that. For a week or two, I hardly slept, for my time was spent seeing this and that councillor. The second campaign cost me another 50,000 shillings. The result was that I was appointed (or perhaps I should say 'elected') *chairman of the Iciciri County Council's Housing Committee*. The committee was responsible for the construction and distribution of council houses and also for the allocation of industrial and business plots to individuals or companies.

'Now I knew that I, son of Gatheeca, had really arrived. My time had come. Public property fattens the wily.

'It happened that now and then the Council would borrow money from the American-owned *World Bank*, or from European and Japanese banks, to finance the construction of cheap houses for the poor. That was a source of real fat. I can remember one time when the Council demolished some shanties at Rũũwa-inĩ. The plan was to erect a thousand houses there instead. The money was loaned to the Council by an Italian bank. The company that won the tender for building the houses was Italian. But, of course, it had first given me a small back-hander of about 2,000,000 shillings. I put the money in my account and knew that the campaign money had been repaid. Now I waited for the returns on my investment in the elections.

'It was only after the houses had been built that I found what I had been looking for. Anybody who wanted a council house first had to buy me a cup of tea worth 2000 shillings. I made another 2,000,000 shillings that way, which I stacked away in the bank.

'I hardly need to tell you that after two years, the millions that I'd invested in the election campaign had yielded quite a tidy sum. And, you will note, I hadn't shed a drop of sweat. All my money came from the very people who had voted for me. How? Because it was their tax that would go to pay back the money borrowed from foreign banks.

'What do you think of that? If you were me, would you have stopped nibbling at that fruit, which tasted more luscious than sweetness itself? I never stopped plucking it. I picked one fruit after another. The sweet juice would spill out of the corners of my mouth before I learned to eat more discreetly.

'These days I don't wait for the Council to build houses before I pocket titbits. I have teamed up with some Italian foreigners and have formed a construction company: *Rũũwa-inĩ Housing Development Company*. It is my company that usually wins tenders from the Council. But the company also borrows money from banks to construct whole *estates*, and it's able to sell the houses long before they are even completed. You people! Don't underestimate people's thirst for houses. The company builds houses to suit the different classes. Stone houses, for instance, are not all that profitable. Have you seen those barracks made of mud and wood? If you build shanties like those and then rent them out to workers and peasants, that, I assure you, is where the fat lies.

'I started receiving invitations to become a director of branches of foreign companies. I would buy a *share* here, and there I would pocket a *sitting allowance*, a kind of bakshish for attending board meetings. From all those sources I was able to take home a few cents at the end of the month – a piece here and a piece there collect in the belly of Kĩhaahu wa Gatheeca (despite his slimness) to make a whole number.

'That's why I'm very grateful to the masses of the Kenyan people.

For their blindness, their ignorance, their inability to demand their rights are what enable us, the clan of man-eaters, to feed on their sweat without their asking us too many awkward questions.

'But we shouldn't be complacent or imagine that the masses will always be as foolish. It's the possibility that things may change that has prompted some foreigners to appoint me a director of their companies – to protect them from the wrath of the masses of workers and peasants. I don't mind the assignment. It's fairly lucrative.

'That's why, these days, I never pass up an opportunity for making Haraambe donations. I might give 10,000 shillings here, 5,000 or 10,000 there and perhaps 20,000 elsewhere. It depends on my mood. But when I really mean to make an impression on people, I go first to various foreign-owned companies – you all know that they set aside money to bribe the public blind – and I ask them for a donation, 1,000 shillings, ten cents, five cents, anything, then I mount the platform to announce my generosity: "These hundreds of thousands which I have brought in sacks are from me and my friends." My Nyakīnyua women's choir immediately trills the five ululations for a male child, all in my honour. What did I say? The volume of today's applause depends on the size of the recipients' pockets. Money can flatten mountains. Today who sings in honour of the likes of Kīmathi?

'Long may the masses stay as they are, singing praises only to the size of a man's pockets. This will give us more time to live off the fat of the land – and, as you know, that which is safely in the belly never betrays its presence to inquisitive eyes and ears. I personally believe in the principle of governing by holding a carrot in the left hand and a stick in the right. Haraambe donations are our carrot. But there are a few blackguards who have had the audacity to talk about removing the scales from the eyes of the masses. Those who want to awaken the masses should be shown the whip – detention or prison – just like the fellows you all know about. But I normally send my thugs round to those who are obstinate – after plying them, of course, with drugs and alcohol and money – and then they cart their bodies along to the hyenas on Ngong Hills or to the crocodiles in the Athi River to continue their work for the masses inside the belly of a hyena or a crocodile (like the fellows you all know about). I don't believe in this democracy nonsense. In the morning the topic is democracy. In the evening the topic is democracy. Is democracy food and drink? If I could get hold of those kids at the university, together with their pygmy-sized teachers ... *Wangenijuta* ... I would load them on to an aeroplane and request them to take their communist nonsense to China or the Soviet Union.

'Sorry, gentlemen! My raging anger with that lot temporarily distracted me from the business in hand. Let me resume my story. *Oh, yes*, I was talking about theft and robbery based on housing. As for me, I'll never abandon theft and robbery that is based on housing. There's nothing on this Earth that generates as much profit as people's hunger and thirst for shelter. So I never want to see this appetite diminish, even by the slightest amount. In fact, I've often stayed awake figuring out ways and means of increasing the whole country's hunger and thirst, because the degree to which there's a property famine determines exactly the level to which the price of houses will rise and hence the level to which profits will climb like flames of fire reaching out for fatty meat. When such a famine becomes intense – of course, we don't call it famine; we give it gentler names – we, the eaters of the fat of the land, can sit down to devise ways of sharing the fat among ourselves.

'My idea is this. When the famine exceeds the limits of endurance, we need only build houses the size of a bird's nest. The nests will be constructed in such a way that they can be folded, the way tents are folded. Anyone who is desperate for a place to lay his head will be forced to buy a nest from us, which he will be able to fold and carry on his shoulders or slip into his pocket. Whenever and wherever darkness catches up with him, he will simply set up the nest at the roadside and lay down his head. And imagine, the whole night long he will be saying his prayers, asking Heaven to bless the kindhearted providers who have built him a shelter for his eyes, his ears, his lips, his nose . . . .

'Just imagine the money we could make building nests – *one man, one nest*! Ha, ha, ha! Ha, ha, ha! Every peasant inside a nest . . . ha, ha, ha! Every worker with just his nose inside a nest! Peasants and workers will be competing with the birds for air space!

'Good people, hand me the crown of victory. Hey! Wait a minute, those of you who may still be harbouring doubts about my abilities: the grass and rope for building the nests will be imported from America, Europe and Japan, foreign countries, or we could simply import ready-made nests.

'That's all I have to say. Hand me the crown!'

The Rebuttal

Kĩhaahu wa Gatheeca descended from the platform, utterly baffled about why nobody was applauding him. Before he had reached his seat, Kĩhaahu saw Gĩtutu wa Gataangũrũ heaving himself towards

118

the platform. Gĩtutu was full of bitterness. His lips were trembling, and saliva dribbled out of the corners of his mouth.

'*Mr Chairman*, we didn't come here to hurl insults at one another. We didn't come here to cast contemptuous innuendos at one another. We didn't come here to listen to filth and rubbish. We came to this cave to take part in a competition to find out which one of us is the most skilful in the art and science of modern theft and robbery. The lucky winner may find himself appointed the watchdog of foreign-owned finance houses and industries, so that while benefiting his foreign masters, he may also be able to line his own pockets. Whether one man wins or another is entirely dependent on a bird of good omen, and we should not anticipate the outcome by way of insults.

'But if this competition is designed to find out who can hurl the filthiest insults and innuendos, we should all be told now. Some of us have been circumcised, and we learned a few lessons in abuse and insulting epithets during the initiation rites.

'And if we have gathered to brag about our ability to use our youth wings to terrorize others, everybody here should know that I, Gĩtutu wa Gataangũrũ, have also employed a group of thugs more terrifying than any other youth wing I know. The group undertakes any mission I give it, including removing from the face of this Earth anybody who so much as dares to meddle in my thieving and robbing activities. My thugs, or perhaps I should say my mercenaries, have an enormous appetite for very strong bhang. My present intention is to import European mercenaries from France or Britain.

'But if there's anybody here who's anxious for a duel, I, Gĩtutu wa Gataangũrũ am ready with my gun, *wakati wo wote*.

'Why do I say that? The lanky fellow who was standing here, known by the name of Kĩhaahu wa Gatheeca, has claimed that I am a mere beginner in the art of theft and robbery. What! Son of Gatheeca! Do you really know who Gĩtutu wa Gataangũrũ is, or have you merely heard men mention his name? I swear by the Truth of Truths that you should come and kneel before me at my school – that is, you go back to *Standard One* – so I can teach you the ABC of the kind of theft and robbery that has made my belly the size it is now.

'*Mr Chairman*, what kind of theft and robbery is it that this long-legged fellow has been bragging about? Bribing opponents to drop out of the running in council elections? It might perhaps make more sense if these had been parliamentary elections! What's the other kind of theft that he bragged about? Buying plastic Europeans and deceiving people into believing that they were real European children?

'Let's go back to the question of how he intends to contribute to the development of theft and robbery in this land. Isn't it laughable that the one idea our long-legged friend can come up with is to build sparrow's nests as houses? Who'd ever agree to buy a nest just to shelter his nose and lips? Mr *Chairman*, that man who calls himself Gatheeci wa Kīhuuhia (or was it Kīhihi wa Gatheeci?) wants to rouse the workers and peasants to take up arms against us. The man wants the workers to become so angry that the scales will fall from their eyes, and they will rise up against us with swords and clubs and guns. Doesn't Gatheeci wa Kīhaahu realize that our people are sick to death of taking up arms? I know what it is: the man wants to introduce Chinese-style communism into this country.

'*Mr Chairman*, my development plans make a thousand times more sense: sell soil in tiny dishes, and trap air so we can sell it in tins or through meters! The workers and peasants would then breathe to order – our order! Grabbing all the soil in the land and all the air about us is the surest way of making workers and peasants obey us for ever, because should they make even the smallest noise, we would only need to turn off the air to bring them to their knees....

'My friends! You'd better show Waceke wa Gatheeca that you are not the kind of people who can be bribed into surrendering your votes with a glass of beer. I hope that wherever he is now seated, Gatheeca now realizes that I, Gītutu wa Gataangūrū, am not a man to run away from the battlefield and leave victory to the clan of long-shanks, even if they are experts at breaking the legs of their opponents. The crown of victory is mine!'

Before Gītutu wa Gataangūrū could stagger back to his seat, another man had already jumped up. This one did not even bother to mount the platform. Although saliva did not dribble out of the corners of his mouth, as had been the case with Gītutu wa Gataangūrū, he too was clearly bitter.

'*Mr Chairman*, I too would like to put in a word, for it has been said that wisdom locked in the heart never won a law suit.... *Sorry!* I'm known as Ithe wa Mbooi. I take it that we have all gathered in this cave to brag and to teach one another more efficient and cunning ways of stealing and robbing from the poor. But the man who was standing up there just now – I mean, the lanky, mosquito-like fellow – has slipped up very badly.

'Son of Gatheeca, don't you feel ashamed? Weren't you embarrassed, standing there in front of us bragging about deceiving people

120

of your class, shamelessly boasting about how you have stolen from people of your class? If we start robbing, thieving and cheating one another, how will our unity as a class take roots?

'For my part, I am dreadfully ashamed, and feel very sad because all my children have attended those so-called *modern* nursery schools. I have always taken it that my children were attending the same schools as European children. So they were only fake Europeans? They were plastic Europeans in wigs? And to think that I've paid hundreds of thousands of shillings for my children to be in the company of Europeans with *plastic* skin, stones for bones and electric machines for hearts? What! So when my children come home and tell me that they have been playing with their European friends, all along these friends have been plastic and electric European machines?

'I have never in all my life come across such unspeakable wickedness. Imagine an adult like Kīhaahu wa Gatheeca pocketing other people's money for nothing? So that's why my children can't speak English through the nose like real European children? And to think how often they have made me feel ashamed in front of people of my class because whenever they are spoken to in English, they normally reply in Gīkūyū?

'And, you know, their mother, Nyina wa Mbooi, has said to me from time to time: "Ithe wa Mbooi, I don't think those Europeans are real Englishmen. Why, they are always playing and doing the same thing over and over again: they spend their time running about." And I would reassure her: "Nyina wa Mbooi, the English are a hybrid race of whites of different kinds – Irish, American, German, French, Scottish – and they are a very highly principled race, not the kind to keep changing from one thing to another, day in, day out. They love games that involve running. Indeed, the English were the people who invented *football* and *rugby* and *cricket*, all based on running. Nyina wa Mbooi, let our children stay at those schools, so that they can learn true English customs. A European is a European even though he may be deformed – what matters is the whiteness of his skin!" And now it turns out it was she who was *right*? It's true indeed that a man believes a woman's word when it's too late.

'*Mr Chairman*, to thieve, to rob and to cheat the poor is *all right*. Where else would our wealth come from? Nobody worth his salt would ever question such a scheme of things, for that's how the world has always been and that's how it will ever be. But this man who thieves, robs and cheats his own class – what kind of a thief and a robber is he? Isn't it generally agreed that theft like this passes all understanding? And he dares to stand before us to make hollow

121

noises and to demand a crown of victory! A crown of victory indeed!
He should go home and put on his mother's crown!

'Kĩhaahu, from today onwards my children will never go
anywhere near your schools. I'll go straight to Nyina wa Mbooi – she
is highly educated, has even been to Cambridge – to tell her to look
for an *international* school. Kĩhaahu wa Gatheeca, do you hear that?
You have had it! You'll never again eat anything that belongs to Ithe
wa Mbooi and Nyina wa Mbooi. We shall go to *international* schools
for *international* Europeans, where *international* English is spoken,
schools without cripples for principals, schools without Europeans
made of plastic and with electric hearts and skins whitened with
Ambi acids. We want an *international* colour!'

And before Ithe wa Mbooi had sat down, another man stood up
to speak. He was so angry that as he spoke, he gnawed at his fingers
and his lips. His belly was so huge that it almost bulged over his
knees.

'*Mr Chairman*, my name is Fathog Marura wa Kĩmeengemeenge.
I don't have much to say. I move that Kĩhaahu wa Gatheeca be
expelled from this competition. How dare he come here and boast
about how he fucks other people's wives? *Mr Chairman*, my wife
has virtually run away from home. Now I know where she goes.
Now I know the adulterer who despoils and destroys other people's
homes. You, it's you, Kĩhaahu! I swear that if I had brought my gun
with me – yes, I swear by the woman who bore me – that tonight you
would have slept minus that prick that offers Haraambe to other
people's wives. I wouldn't have minded, *Mr Chairman*, if Kĩhaahu
only fucked the wives of the poor, or schoolgirls from poor homes,
but . . . but . . . !'

At that point a lump of pain blocked his throat, and Fathog Marura
wa Kimeengemeenge could only bite his lips and fingers helplessly
in rage as he sat down. The cave now became a beehive of angry
noise. Much of the anger was directed at Kĩhaahu wa Gatheeca.

And then Kĩhaahu wa Gatheeca stood up and began to defend
himself.

'*Mr Chairman*, I have been abused and insulted by those who have
just spoken, and I have listened to their insults patiently. But now
I seek and demand protection from the chair. I too am going to speak
frankly, come what may. Each man here should go home right now
and secure his wife's cunt with a padlock, and then take all the keys
to a bank *safe*, which will keep the keys safe until he is ready to
retrieve them, primed by an erection. I'm not the one who has
instructed their wives to become *sugar mummies*, or to join the club
of the Ready-to-Yield. But a woman like yours,' and here Kĩhaahu

pointed a finger directly at Marura wa Kĩmeengemeenge, 'I swear by the name of truth that I would never touch such a woman, even were I to find her thighs spread in the middle of the road, or if she and I were shut in a house together with all the lights turned out. I cannot bring myself to compete for it with schoolboys and tourists....

'I should also make the point that nobody here should brag about guns. In my house I have three *rifles* and two *machine guns*, and in the car I keep a *patchet*. And if you think that this coat pocket bulges a little, I'll have you know that it is not for nothing. Wherever I go, I am always armed from head to toe. If anybody wants to come up here and try to disarm me, he'll see stars in daylight....

'*Mr Chairman*, Gĩtutu wa Gataangũrũ has also insulted me. We came here so that each competitor could boast, in any way he chose, about his capacity for theft and robbery. I was only telling the truth, and I wasn't trying to insult anyone. What I said was that robbing the masses by means of speculation in land (the very land they fought for) was a stage through which I too passed before going on to higher things. I no longer deal with land-buying companies and societies. One does not steal and squat to eat the loot in the same place all the time, for the owner will sooner or later catch up with one.

'The only thing I deny with my heart and my life is what Gĩtutu wa Gataangũrũ said about the possibility that I might be the cause of the emergence of Chinese-style communism in this country. What, me, accept being ruled by a party of the workers and peasants? Me, accept being ruled by a party dedicated to eradicating the system of theft and robbery on Earth? Me, go back to working with my hands? Eat only what has been produced by my sweat alone, without having access to the products of other people's sweat? Find myself facing duster and chalk again? Forget that, Mr Gĩtutu....

'On the contrary, I would say that it is your plan for grabbing all the soil and all the air in the universe that's the *dangerous* one and the one that could spread the disease of Chinese-style communism more quickly. The reason is this: if you prevented people from breathing, what would prevent them from taking up clubs and swords and guns? Isn't that tantamount to showing how much you despise the masses? Better meanness that is covert: better a system of theft that is disguised by lies. Or why do you think that our imperialist friends brought us the Bible? Do you think that they were being foolish when they urged workers and peasants to close their eyes in prayer and told them that earthly things were vain? Why do you think I go to all the church fund-raising Haraambe meetings?

'Gĩtutu, leave me alone. But if you still want to challenge me to

123

a pistol duel, I would be only too happy to oblige, because your belly would make a perfect target and I'd like to find out if I can deflate it with a bullet or two. But should you prefer a war between our mercenaries, that would also give us a chance to find out which group, yours or mine, smokes the strongest bhang. I too have been circumcised. If you inquire carefully among the women, they will testify that there is no foreskin attached to my cock!

'And lastly I would like to answer the charge of Ithe wa Mbooi, who complained that I rob members of my own class. To him I say this: what kind of thief and robber are you? What is he doing in this competition if he has never learned the elementary truth that there is steel which can easily drill through steel? Let me say this to Ithe wa Mbooi: there are thieves who can out-steal other thieves; there are robbers who can out-rob other robbers; there are kings who can out-rule other kings. If Ithe wa Mbooi doesn't know this, he should pack up at once and go home to help Nyina wa Mbooi peel potatoes by the fireside and chat about ashes and embers. A piece of steel that can drill through steel itself – doesn't that indicate that the steel is of special quality and toughness? What else do you people want? The crown is mine. Let's not waste time. Give me the crown of victory!'

His last speech appeared to have created even more enemies. Several people jumped up at the same time and started shouting at one another, some in support of Kīhaahu or Gītutu or Ithe wa Mbooi, others on the side of Fathog Marura wa Kīmeengemeenge. It was as if the cave had become the site of seven markets combined.

And then suddenly silence fell in the cave. Kīhaahu, Gītutu and Ithe wa Mbooi had pulled out their guns.

People silently pushed back their chairs and stood up, each trying to keep out of the way of the bullets. For a minute or so nobody coughed or sneezed; the only noise was the scraping of tables and chairs as the occupants moved away, waiting for the whistling of bullets.

The whole feast would have broken up in disarray had the master of ceremonies not jumped on to the platform before the shoot-out could begin and yelled with all his might until people returned to their seats. Still glaring at one another, Kīhaahu wa Gatheeca, Gītutu wa Gataangūrū and Ithe wa Mbooi also resumed their seats. And again, quite suddenly, noise returned to the cave. The master of ceremonies tried to silence the people with a wave of his hand. Then he spoke to them in a soothing, conciliatory tone.

'Put those guns away in your pockets. I ask you with due respect

124

to remember what has brought us together here today. We didn't come here for a duel. We came here with the sole purpose of taking part in a competition in modern theft and robbery. I would also like to remind you that we have guests, seven emissaries from *International Thieves and Robbers*, who are here to monitor all that we say and do. Do you want to strip each other naked in front of our foreign guests? What do you imagine they think of us now, after witnessing this chaos and a threatened shoot-out in broad daylight? Our actions may make them lose faith in us and rethink their position. They must be wondering: Can these people really look after the products of our theft and robbery in their country? Are they really capable of looking after our finance houses and stores and all the industries underwritten by these? Imagine what we would lose if they were to take their leftovers to another village? What a loss for Ilmorog! Who would be to blame except ourselves? Let me be frank with you, for as the saying goes, one man can smear another out of love: too fierce a flame can cheat the fire of its meat . . . .

'I beg you, I beseech you, *tafadhali*, *please*, be patient. Every competitor will get his chance to give his testimony on this platform and to brag about his artistry in theft and robbery. Let us not look down upon one another. Testimony is testimony. We should not let testimony testify against testimony. There is no hawk too small when it comes to hunting in the modern style.

'But to restore peace to our souls and bodies, I suggest a small break to entertain our bellies, for the belly of a thief and a robber is not so foolish as to keep quiet when there is plenty of food, and it is not easily bribed into silence with a bite or two. You can all buy lunch here in the cave – we have a special *international dish* – or you can go elsewhere in Ilmorog. But I plead with you to hurry up over the eating and drinking so that we can all reassemble here at 2.30. There are plenty of testimonies to come.

'Before we break for lunch, I would like to remind the women here, whether they are wives, mistresses or girlfriends, that after the competition there will be a fashion parade, a chance for you to show off your jewellery, your gold, diamonds, silver, rubies, tanzanites, pearls. We must develop our *culture*, and you know very well that it is the way that women dress and the kind of jewellery they wear that indicates the heights a culture has reached. So when you come back, have ready your necklaces, earrings, rings and brooches, so that we can impress our foreign guests and show them that we too are on the way to modern civilization. So remember, *2.30 sharp! For now, namtakieni, bon appetit, mes amis!*'

The master of ceremonies was given a standing ovation. People were now satisfied, and they started talking lightheartedly. The *Hell's Angels* band started playing some Congolese tunes:

Babanda nanga bakimi na mobali
Mobali oyo toto ya matema
Nakei koluko mobali nangae . . . .

A few people stayed where they were, drinking and discussing the threatened shoot-out. Others moved towards the door.

Kyrie, kyrie eleison
Kyrie, kyrie eleison . . . .

Gatuĩria took Warĩĩnga by the hand and said: 'We should go outside. Let's get out, or this air will suffocate me!'

'Yes, I feel sick, 'Warĩĩnga replied, standing up. 'Let's go outside where we can breathe free air before it is turned into a commodity by Kĩhaahu and Gĩtutu,' she added, as they left the cave.

Kyrie, kyrie eleison
Kyrie, kyrie eleison . . . .

Mwaũra turned towards Mũturi and said: 'How come you know about the *Devil's Angels*? What's your connection with them?'

Mũturi took out the piece of paper which had been handed to Warĩĩnga by the thugs who had ejected her from her house in Nairobi.

'Look at this,' Mũturi said, as he gave the piece of paper to Mwaũra. 'I think it belongs to you.'

Mwaũra read it and frowned. 'Where did you get it from?' he asked.

'It was in your car last night,' Mũturi replied.

Mwaũra looked at Mũturi with eyes filled with bitter questions: What's Mũturi doing here? Who is he hunting down with his restless eyes? Could it be me? Why did he write this, only to pretend that he found it the car? Or did he want to gauge the expression on my face? Who is Mũturi? Who is Wangarĩ? Mũturi could not see the bitterness in Mwaũra's eyes, for he had, at that moment, turned towards Wangarĩ.

'We should go outside too,' Mũturi told Wangarĩ.

The *Hell's Angels* band went on playing the same Congolese tune:

Nakai Koluka banganga
Po ya Kosongisa mobali nangai . . . .

Mwaŭra suddenly decided to ask Mŭturi and Wangarĩ who had
sent them to Ilmorog. I must show them that I know about their
secret mission, he thought. I must show them that I wasn't fooled
by their tall stories last night.

'I say!' he started, and then he suppressed what was in his mind
and tried to cover it up with a different question. 'Wangarĩ, are you
going to deck yourself out with gold and diamonds and pearls and
other stones?'

Wangarĩ, Mŭturi and Mwaŭra laughed. They left the cave, still
laughing. Mwaŭra felt relieved: what had he been worrying about?

'I would rather put on earrings made of dry maize stems,' Wangarĩ
answered. 'The only problem is that I missed my chance to have my
ears pierced.'

'Why?' Mŭturi and Mwaŭra asked.

'Because ours was not a time for adorning our bodies with flowers
and necklaces. Ours was a time for decorating ourselves with bullets
in the fight for Kenya's freedom!' Wangarĩ said with pride, because
she knew that the deeds of her youth had changed Kenya's
history.

Mwaŭra suddenly stopped laughing. He was troubled. His face
darkened. His heart beat as if it were asking him: Could it be that
in your *matatŭ* you were carrying a threat to your own life, like the
louse one carries around on one's body?

But Mŭturi looked at Wangarĩ, his heart overflowing with sudden
pride and happiness. Wangarĩ, heroine of our country – all
Wangarĩs, heroines of our land! Should I reveal to her the task that
has brought me here today, so that she and I can help each other?
No, the time is not yet ripe. I'll observe her a little longer, he
muttered to himself, still gazing at Wangarĩ. But afterwards . . .
afterwards . . ., he whispered to himself. And then he recalled the
braggarts in the cave, and Mŭturi felt like weeping. 'Let's get out of
here,' he urged Wangarĩ and Mwaŭra. 'Let's leave this place!'

Chapter Five

1

When Waríínga and Gatuíria walked out of the cave, they stood for a while on a parapet. The sun shone brightly on the Ilmorog ridges and plains. The land lay quiet. No cold, no wind. 'Although I have just been in the full glare of electric lights, I feel as if I have lived in darkness all my life,' Waríínga sighed, and then she added in a sing-song voice: 'Praise the sun of God! Hail the light of God!'

'You should be singing praises to the light of our country,' Gatuíria told her.

'The light we have left behind us in the cave or another kind of light?' Waríínga asked, in a slightly ironic tone.

'No. The light that is about to be put out by those we have left behind,' Gatuíria replied.

They walked slowly and silently towards the main road. Then they began to talk. It was not really a conversation. It was more a kind of incantation, as if they were both taking part in a verse-chanting competition, citing verses remembered in dreams.

Gatuíria: Hail, our land!
Hail, Mount Kenya!
Hail, our land,
Never without water or food or green fields!

Waríínga: Hail, the splendour of this land!
Hail, the land ringed round with deep lakes,
Turkana to Naivasha,
Nam-Lolwe to Mombasa!
Hail, this necklace of blue waters!

Gatuíria: Hail, hail, the shields of the land,
From Kenya to the Mbirúirú mountains,
From Kíanjahi to the Nyandarúa ridges,
From Wairera to Mount Elgon!
Hail, nature's defence of our land!

Waríínga: And hearken to the call of the land!
The rivers flowing to the east,
Rúirú, Cania, Sagana,
Tana River, Athi River, Kerio River,
They now flow east, calling out:
Come! Come! Hurry! Hurry, and hail the land!

Gatuĩria: For this land was dearly bought,
            Redeemed with the blood and tears...
Warĩĩnga: ... of women and men,
            of parents and children.

Gatuĩria was the first to wake up from the dream-like incatations. He spoke in a voice full of bitterness: 'And this is the land that is now being auctioned to foreigners!'

Instead of answering back, Warĩĩnga began to sing the song Wangarĩ and Mũturi had sung during the ride in Mwaũra's *matatũ*:

Kenya does not belong to you, imperialists!
Pack up your bags and go!
The owner of the homestead is on his way!

'But when the owner arrives, he'll find that the entire house has been sold!' Gatuĩria said. 'So it's true that such acts of vandalism take place in broad daylight?'

'Yes, as readily as their perpetrators raise their glasses to drink!'

'Yes, as readily as they play golf.'

'And go for *sauna baths* in expensive hotels.'

'And dance in exclusive night clubs.'

'And sing boastful songs in their caves and dens,' Warĩĩnga said. 'God help Kenya, my love. What is the matter with me? My heart is so full that I feel like crying. I've never thought about these things in this way....'

'Maybe it's the effect of the whisky you've drunk,' Gatuĩria replied. 'Let's go and look for somewhere where we can get roasted goat's meat.'

'Here in Golden Heights?' Warĩĩnga asked.

'No. Aren't there other places apart from here where they want to sell air in tiny calabashes?' Gatuĩria asked.

'Buy good air, fresh from Europe!' Warĩĩnga shouted, as if she were calling out to buyers of white air.

Gatuĩria and Warĩĩnga looked at each another. Their eyes spoke to each other. They laughed together. Warĩĩnga felt her heart lighten.

'Let's go to Njeruca!' Warĩĩnga suggested.

'Is there a restaurant there?' Gatuĩria asked. 'Njeruca ... where have I heard that name before?'

Warĩĩnga laughed. She began to tell him more about Ilmorog as they walked slowly down the road.

'Ilmorog is several villages in one. Let me start with the outer edges of the town, where the peasants live and those whose strips of land have not yet been sold off by the banks or swallowed by the wealthy and the powerful. There is also the shopping area, where there are draperies, grocers, hardware stores, shops of all kinds. This part of town also houses the banks. Another area is the industrial area. That's where you'll find the big brewery, *Theng'eta Breweries*.

'The residential area is divided into two parts. The first is the *Ilmorog Golden Heights residential area*. In the past it used to be called *Cape Town*, but today it's known as *Golden Heights* or simply the *Heights*. The air there is good and clean, and that's where anyone who is anyone lives in Ilmorog. It contains the homes of the wealthy and the powerful. But do you call them homes or residences! Homes or sheer magnificence? The walls are made of stones from Njirũ. The roofs are made of red brick. The windows are of dark blue glass, like the waters of the lakes or the heavens on a cloudless day. They are decorated with iron bars shaped like different kinds of flower. The doors are made of tick wood, carved into all sorts of wonderful shapes. The floor is lined with wood, so polished, so smooth and shiny, that you can see your own reflection in it, and you can even use it as a mirror to do your hair. The residents of Golden Heights are always competing with each other. If one man builds a ten-room house with ten chimneys, the next man will build a twenty-room house with twenty chimneys. If this one imports carpets from India, the other will import his from Iran, and so on. . . .

'The other part of the residential area is called *New Jerusalem*, Njeruca. That's the residential area for the workers, the unemployed. It's where the wretched of Kenya live. But are their shacks houses, or are they the sparrow's nests that Kĩhaahu wa Gatheeca was talking about? The walls and the roofs of the shanties are made of strips of tin, old tarpaulin and polythene bags. These are the slums of Ilmorog. And this is where Maatheng'eeta, Chang'aa, Chibuku and other illegal beers are brewed – beers made more potent by the addition of quinine and aspro to knock the workers out. Sometimes I think of Njeruca as the Hell described in the Christian Bible . . . .'

'Why?' Gatuĩria asked. 'What does the place look like?'

'How can you ask that, as if you were a foreigner in Kenya? Have you never visited the slum areas of Nairobi to see for yourself the amazing sight of endless armies of fleas and bedbugs marching up and down the walls, or the sickening, undrained ditches, full of brackish water, shit and urine, the naked children swimming in those very ditches? A slum is a slum. Here in Njeruca we don't have any drainage. Human shit and urine and the carcases of dead dogs and cats – all these make the area smell as if it were nothing but pure putrefaction. Add to this decay the smoke of dangerous gases from the industrial area – all these are blown towards Njeruca by the wind – and add too the fact that all the rubbish and waste from the factories is deposited there, and you'll see why I compare Njeruca with Hell. To bury a people in a hole full of fleas, lice, bedbugs – what hell could be worse than that?' Waríínga ended her narrative with bitterness.

'Fleas, jiggers, bedbugs . . . are there more of those in Ilmorog's slums than the human parasites we have left behind in that cave?' Gatuíria asked slowly, as if he were talking to himself.

At that moment they saw a small *matatū* approaching at full speed. Waríínga waved it to a halt. It stopped, and they climbed in. After a minute or so they were at the *New Ilmorog Butchery*, owned by a one-eyed man called Tumbo. Gatuíria ordered three pounds of goat's meat. He asked Tumbo to include a few ribs but no offal. Tumbo fixed him with his one eye and told him that he, Tumbo, would never sell a piece of meat to anybody without throwing in a bit of offal. He, Gatuíria, should remember that he was now in Njeruca, the people's place, and not in Golden Heights, among the wealthy. Gatuíria asked him to include a piece of liver instead of tripe. Tumbo agreed.

Gatuíria and Waríínga went to the back of the shop that adjoined Tumbo's butchery. The room at the front was the shop, but the ones at the back were bars. Many of the customers drank their beer sitting on empty beer crates. The main bar was full of customers, but the bartender showed Gatuíria and Waríínga into an empty room. They sat down on crates. The bartender brought them two *Tusker* beers. They drank out of the bottles as they waited for their meat to cook.

'The speeches in the cave completely numbed me.' Waríínga said.

'To tell you the truth, I could hardly believe that I was actually here in Kenya,' Gatuíria said, then he shook his head and started talking as if to himself. 'Modern theft . . . modern robbery . . . . So it's really true that the edifice of progress is erected on top of the corpses of human beings?'

'Did you find the devil you were looking for?' Waríínga asked him, laughing, 'or don't you remember telling us last night that you were coming to these parts in search of plausible themes for your music? Or was your devil removed from the scene by the invitation cards that were given by Mwĩreri wa Mũkiraaĩ?'

'I think that I was probably running too fast,' Gatuĩria said. 'I think I was placing too much faith and hope in the other card. A belief is a belief, and it doesn't really need the evidence of the eyes to grow roots. What really matters is the idea from which one can develop musical themes.'

'So you didn't find a single devil, not even among the foreigners, for instance?' Warĩĩnga asked.

'What I'm saying is that it doesn't really matter if the Devil actually exists or if he's merely a certain image of the world.'

'So what about the knot that was troubling you?' Warĩĩnga pressed him. 'Or are you like the poor dancer who claims he is unable to dance because the ground is stony?'

'Not quite . . . . But . . . ,' Gatuĩria started, and then paused as if Warĩĩnga's questions had unsettled him. 'You see, music . . . or let's say musical composition . . . .' He paused again as if he were not quite sure what he wanted to say. 'The way I see it is this: an artistic composition should be inspired by love . . . love of your country . . . a love that inspires the composer to sing hymns of praise to the beauty, the unity, the courage, the maturity, the bravery, the generosity of his country. I have always dreamed of composing music to glorify the heroic deeds of our nation, in praise of our national heroes, like Beethoven composing the *Eroica Symphony* in honour of Napoleon, or Sergei Prokoviev composing an *oratorio* based on the deeds of Alexander Nevsky, one of Russia's national heroes. I would like to compose music that expresses the soul and the aspirations and the dreams of our nation . . . . But what kind of talk did we hear in that cave? Wasn't it like the morning frost that blights the shoots of patriotic love?'

'No!' Warĩĩnga replied quickly. 'Talk like that is the rain that should make buried love for one's country burgeon. There is no love that is not linked with hate. How can you tell what you love unless you know what you hate? Take a baby that cannot speak. Its cries indicate its likes and dislikes. Didn't we two emerge from that cave chanting poems to our country? Kenya has enough patriots and heroes to inspire a patriotic composition! Wasn't Kĩmathĩ born of a Kenyan woman? The biggest knot in you is the absence of love, because you've never known what hatred is. For while, it is true, a child with parents to look after him will never eat shit, if he is brought up wrapped in over-protective love, he will never learn anything. He will never learn the difference between dirt and cleanliness, hate and love . . . . It is whiteness that tells us what blackness is. Those whom we have left behind in the cave are the very people who are now identifying for us the true heroes of our land.'

'No, no, there you have confused a number of things,' Gatuĩria said quickly, as if Waríĩnga had touched a sensitive spot in his heart.

'In that case, show me what you hate and I will show you what you love. Or don't you know where you stand?'

'Ah, woman, why are you dragging me back to my home and to memories I would rather forget?' Gatuĩria asked.

'Where do you come from?'

'Nakuru. My father is a business tycoon. He owns several shops in Nakuru, and lots of farms in the *Rift Valley*, and countless other businesses to do with import and export: footwear, fabrics, flowers, seedlings. Just mention any type of trade, and my father will have a hand in it. He runs special planes for many of those exports and imports of his. I am his only son. His aim was to send me to America to learn how to manage property and profit ... *business administration* ... the kind of education that Mwĩreri wa Mũkiraaĩ was bragging about last night. But as for me, I've never wanted to follow in my father's footsteps.'

'Why not?'

'Because my heart was always with the workers on his tea plantations. They were the ones who sang beautiful songs to me, who told me exciting stories, who often played their guitars or their bamboo flutes for me .... I would look at the shanties they lived in, the food they ate, the rags they wore, and when I contrasted that poverty with the richness of their songs and the breadth of their knowledge, I would be seized with a deep hatred for my father. Weren't the workers people like ourselves? Sometimes my father would whip them, and abuse them, and call them dumb cows. And you know, on one occasion I actually found him beating my mother because she had asked him to stop whipping a man who was very old. When later I started questioning things, my father showed me the stick, and he forbade me to go near the workers' quarters. I didn't stop visiting the workers, however. I think that's why he sent me to America while I was still very young.'

'How long did you stay in America?'

'Fifteen years.'

'Fifteen years! In a foreign country!'

'Didn't I tell you that I went there soon after doing my CPE? I had no scholarship. My father paid for everything.'

'What were you studying all those years?' Waríĩnga asked.

'Lots of different things. But I ended up specializing in music,

133

playing musical instruments like the *piano*, the *organ*, the *clarinet*, the *recorder*, the *trumpet*. I studied composition, the history of Western music from the times of J. Bach and Handel in the *sixteenth century* to the more recent times of Tchaikovsky and Igor Stravinsky, who died in 1971. And I studied conducting. Things like that. What excited me most were oratorios like Bach's *B Minor Mass* and *St Matthew Passion*, Handel's *Messiah* and Mendelssohn's *Elijah*. But when my father heard that I had gone to all those universities to read for a degree in music, that I had chosen not to study business administration, he sent me a telegram the length of a railway line. He told me that he could not go on spending the thousands of shillings he had lavished on my education so that I could end up with a degree in singing and carry a guitar on my shoulders like the rogues of the Bondeni area of Nakuru. He told me to choose between music, which would condemn me to spending the rest of my life as a footloose minstrel, and business administration, which would allow me to return home as his son. *Well*, how could I explain to him that what I saw the American rich doing to the descendants of the Africans who had been taken to America as slaves about three hundred years ago was exactly what I had seen him doing to his plantation workers? How could I tell him that my long stay in America had shown me the darkness into which people of my father's class were leading Kenya? I did not answer him. But I chose music so that money should never rule my life.

'In those days, my father did not belong to the Church. But even after I had come back from America, and I found that my father was a pillar of the Church – today he has a special family pew at the front, very near the altar – he never forgave what he saw as my ingratitude and disobedience. He asked me: "Apart from money, what else is worth struggling for on this Earth? How can you bury your talent in the ground like the wicked, ungrateful servant?" And then and there he took up his Bible and he read me the very parable that Mwĩreri wa Mũkiraaĩ was telling us last night in the *matatũ*. When he had finished, I said to him: "Father, how can I eat food snatched from the mouths of the hungry? How can I drink water stolen from those who are thirsty?" He retorted: "What! Do you mean to tell me that you know better than the Reverend Billy Graham, who came here very recently and preached to us about those very talents? You are not fit even to clean the shoes of Billy Graham!"

'Next thing he knew, I was employed by the university to research into our culture, our traditions and customs, especially those connected with music, and he reached breaking-point. He summoned me once again and asked me: "How can you strip me naked before the whole church congregation? How can you strip me before God, so that even babes in arms can see my nakedness? Remember the Ham of old, who saw Noah's nakedness and refused to do anything about it – what did the Lord do to him? Do you know? He was cursed to sire the children of darkness forever. If God had not later had mercy on him and sent the children of Shem to our Africa, where would we, the children of Ham, now be? Go away. Follow in Ham's footsteps. Go and wander about the world, and return home only after you have stopped casting before swine the pearls of your talents and eating rubbish from the same plate as those swine.'

'These days I never go home. Today I am trying to save so that one day I'll be able to give him back the money he spent on my fees and will feel free of any obligation on that account.'

'That's ambitious,' Waríínga sighed. 'What's your father's name? I might know him. You know I grew up in Nakuru?'

'In that case I won't tell you who he is,' Gatuíria replied quickly. 'I wouldn't like to know that you know him because you might start to hate me as well. And even if you didn't say anything, I wouldn't be able to look you in the face, because whenever I looked at you, it would always remind me that you know my father and you also know me. No, I don't even use his name. I want to make my own way in the world and leave his trail behind me for ever.'

Before Waríínga could say anything in response to that, the meat they had been waiting for was brought to them on a wooden dish, cut into small pieces. Next came a plate piled high with a mixture of onions and hot pepper and green cloves.

They began eating the meat in silence. Gatuíria was turning over many things in his mind. He thought: I only met this woman in Mwaúra's *matatú* last night, travelling from Nyamakíma to Ilmorog, and then again this morning, and now I am telling her all the secrets that have long been lodged in my heart. Could the events in the cave have affected me?

Waríínga was having similar thoughts. The things that had happened to her in the past twenty-four hours were truly amazing. She recalled how she had been abandoned by her lover, John Kímwana; how she had been dismissed from her job by *Boss* Kíhara because she was stingy with her thighs; how she had been thrown out of her house by her landlord; how she had been given a threatening note signed by the *Devil's Angels*. She remembered . . . and at once Waríínga picked up her handbag to take out the piece of paper to show Gatuíria how the rich were employing thugs. She looked and looked, but she could not find it. It doesn't matter,

Warĩĩnga told herself, and she picked up the threads of her thoughts about Gatuĩria and the struggle between father and son. Why did he say he wouldn't like me to hate him? she wondered. Does he think we'll be seeing each another every day? Does he think he has found his own Ready-to-Yield?

Warĩĩnga was suddenly roused from her thoughts by Gatuĩria's voice, which sounded like that of man who is kicking about in the water in order not to drown.

'What! Would I ever think of giving up my involvement in our culture and participating in daydreams about selling soil to the poor in tiny calabashes?'

'Daydreams about selling God's free air to the people!' Warĩĩnga chimed in. 'People planting lilies in the air to mark boundaries and then announcing: "From here to over there, this is my air space!"'

'Daydreams about building sparrows' nests for the poor so that landlords and the banks can reap big profits!' Gatuĩria said.

'Daydreams about having dozens of girlfriends,' Warĩĩnga said in a tearful voice. 'Are they aware how many hearts they have broken into tiny pieces? Aware of the many bodies they have destroyed, the many lives they have trodden into the dust, so that every girl, examining her own body, can see only the leprosy she has caught from men? These days a woman's youth has become a rotting corpse, the warmth of her body a bonfire that consumes her life, her womanhood a grave in which her fertility is buried .... Do they know how many girls they have driven to throwing their babies into latrines or killing them while they are in the womb?

'Let me tell you. When a woman is in her youth, she has beautiful dreams about a future in which she and her husband and her children will dwell forever in domestic peace in a house of their own. There are some who dream of the educational heights they will scale, of the demanding jobs they will take on, of the heroic deeds they will do on behalf of their country, deeds that will inspire later generations to sing their praises thus: "Oh, our mother, a self-made national hero!" At the time a girl is dreaming of a bright future filled with heroic deeds, her breasts have not yet developed. But just wait for them to develop. Wait for her cheeks to bloom. Wait for the likes of *Boss* Kĩhara to start whistling at her and offering her *lifts* in their Mercedes Benzes to the bright lights and night spots of Naivasha and Mombasa. Oh, yes, just wait until she is shown all the alluring wonders of afternoons and nights in expensive hotels in Nairobi, and I can tell you that our maiden will wake up one morning to find that all her dreams lying shattered on the floor, like broken pieces of clay. There, scattered on the sandy floor, lie the fragments of her illusions. Tell me this, you who research into our people's culture: when a clay pot is broken, can it be mended? Where is the craftsman who can put back together the shards of a maiden's dream, like the dove in the story who once gave life back to a girl? No, no, no! How did the boys put it in their Mũthuũ dance-song?

An amazing sight,
The clay pot is now broken!
When I came from Nairobi,
I never knew that
I would give birth to
A child named
'Producer of wondrous courage'.

'Come, clansmen, and let us weep together! Come here and behold modern wonders. Today we can only be called the bearers of doomed children instead of the bearers of children of heroic stature. No. No. If a clay pot is broken, it can never be mended. That's how the dreams of us sugar girls are destroyed by sugar daddies . . . .'

Gatuĩria suddenly saw tears flowing down Warĩĩnga's cheeks and on to the floor.

'Warĩĩnga! Warĩĩnga, what is it?' Gatuĩria asked, surprised. What had he done to this woman?

Warĩĩnga picked up her handbag, took out a handkerchief and wiped her eyes. She tried to smile, but she could not quite manage it. She continued in the same sorrowful voice.

'It's nothing . . . but it is also something . . . . What and how can I tell you, you who are a stranger in my life? But really there's nothing secret about it – though I've never told anyone about it before – because it's happening to girls all over Kenya. It is your story that has made me look back on my life in anger, and I can see vividly where my own dreams fell to pieces like the clay pot the boys used to sing about in the Mũthuũ dance. What shall I tell you? Where shall I start?

'Truly, even today as we are sitting here, or when I'm alone, silently turning things over in my mind, or when I am typing or simply walking on the road, I can hear the heavy rumble of the train rolling along the rails towards where I stood waiting for it to take me away from all the troubles I had encountered in Nakuru. I stood in the middle of the rails, near the level crossing by Kabacia Estate, *Section 58*, Nakuru. It was about eleven on a Sunday morning. The train came towards me, belching steam, breathing hard and seemingly singing:

Going-to-Uganda
Going-to-Uganda
Going-to-Uganda
Go-ing
Go-ing
Go
Go
Go
Goooiiing ... uuuuuu-u!

I shut my eyes. I started counting, one, two, three, four, now take me....'

Waríínga covered her face with her hands. She was trembling all over as if she were actually in front of the train. Drops of sweat were forming on her forehead as if she could see the train about to crush her beneath its wheels. Gatuíria rose quickly from his seat, put his hands on her shoulders and shook her a little, asking: 'What is it, Waríínga? What is it?'

2

Jacinta Waríínga was born at Kaambúrú, Gíthúngúri Kía Wairera, in 1953. In those days Kenya was ruled by British imperialists, under very oppressive laws that went by the name of Emergency Regulations. And our patriots, led by Kímaathi wa Waciúri, had sworn an oath of unity, declaring that since death was anyway a fact of life, they would struggle against the British terrorists (codenamed Johnnies) until all torture and oppression in the land ended. The sound of guns and bombs at Nyandaarúa and Mount Kenya was like thunder. When the British terrorists, together with the homeguards, their faithful Kenyan watchdogs – you sterile bastards: you sold your country for the sake of your bellies – saw that they were about to be defeated by the Mau Mau guerrilla forces, they increased their indiscriminate torture and oppression of the peasants and workers of the whole country.

In 1954, Waríínga's father was arrested and detained at Manyani. A year later, her mother was also arrested and detained at Langata and Kamítí Prisons.

Waríínga was then only two. Her aunt, who lived in Nakuru, came for her. Her aunt's husband worked for the railways then, and afterwards for the Nakuru town council. Waríínga grew up in

Nakuru, with her cousins. In the early days they used to live in *Land Panya Estate*, but as Independence Day approached, they moved to a council house in *Section 58*.

Wariinga went to school at *Baharini Full Primary School*, near the *Shauri Yako Estate*. But her cousin went to *Bondeni* DEB, just below *Section 58*, near Majengo and Bondeni. She would go down through the grass-thatched Mithoonge huts for the destitute near the council butchery. She would then run through Bondeni, and before the last bell sounded, she would be at her place in the morning parade. Sometimes, after school or on Saturday or Sunday, Wariinga and her cousins would roam about in Bondeni to watch women hunting for men or men fighting it out with knives. At other times, they would visit all the neighbouring residential areas – Kiziwani, Kaloleni, Kivumbini, Shauri Yako, Ambongorewa (also known as the Somali Camp) – just to stare at the people and the houses and the shops. Sometimes they would go to hear concerts or to see plays in Menengai Social Hall, and at other times they would go to free cinema shows at Kamūkūnji. On some days they would walk along *Lake Nakuru* Road and down to the lakeshore to see the flamingoes and other birds, or they would go to the tracks to watch car and motorbike races.

But what Wariinga enjoyed most was not watching prostitutes fighting over men, or drunks urinating and vomiting in the open drains; no – what she loved most was going to church to pray and to listen to sermons. Every Sunday her aunt would take her to the morning mass at the *Church of the Holy Rosary*. Wariinga was baptised at the *Church of the Holy Rosary*, where she was given her new name, Jacinta. What Wariinga tried hard to avoid – though her eyes kept straying in that direction – was looking at the pictures on the walls and windows of the *Church of the Holy Rosary*. Many of the pictures showed Jesus in the arms of the Virgin Mary or on the Cross. But others depicted the Devil, with two cowlike horns and a tail like a monkey's, raising one leg in a dance of evil, while his angels, armed with burning pitchforks, turned over human beings on a bonfire. The Virgin Mary, Jesus and God's angels were white, like Europeans, but the Devil and his angels were black. At night Wariinga would have a recurrent nightmare. Instead of Jesus on the Cross, she would see the Devil, with skin as white as that of a very fat European she once saw near the *Rift Valley Sports Club*, being crucified by people in tattered clothes – like the ones she used to see in Bondeni – and after three days, when he was in the throes of death, he would be taken down from the Cross by black people in suits and ties, and, thus restored to life, he would mock Wariinga.

Wariinga's parents were released from detention in 1960 – three years before Uhuru – only to find that their small piece of land at Kaambũrũ had been sold to the homeguards by the colonial regime. They moved to Ilmorog to look for borrowed pastures and somewhere to build a shelter.

Since they found Wariinga at school at Baharini, Nakuru, they allowed her to stay there. They prayed that she would get through her schooling quickly so that one day she could free them from the chains of poverty. Wariinga was quick at learning, and she was often top of her class. In fact, it was Wariinga who often coached her cousins at maths, even those who were a class ahead. When the CPE results were announced, Wariinga was among those who had done very well. She was admitted to *Nakuru Day Secondary School*.

This was the happiest period of Wariinga's life. When she saw herself in the school uniform, a blue skirt, a white blouse, white stockings and black shoes, Wariinga felt like weeping with sheer joy.

Even her years in Form One and Form Two were happy years. Wariinga had no thoughts or worries other than the sheer love of learning and her ambition to complete school with high honour. Holding her books and ruler and pen in one hand, Wariinga would run through the grass-thatched huts to *Ladhies Road*, past the council clinic to the right. At the junction, she would leave the road to Bondeni on her left and the road to town on her right and would cross into Ronald Ngala, which would take her past the residence of the African nuns near the *Church of the Holy Rosary*. There she would cross *Oginga Odinga Road* and on to the *Nakuru Day*.

In the evening, returning home from school, she would follow *Oginga Odinga Road* past the Afraha *Stadium*, to branch off at *Menengai High School*, where she would climb up the slope past the clinic, past the butchery, to *Section 58*. But sometimes, when she was sent into town on an errand, she would go via the courts and council offices to the town centre.

But Wariinga never lingered unnecessarily. Then she knew only two stops: school and home.

Walking along those paths, in the morning on her way to school or in the evening on her way home, Wariinga often felt that she was the queen of learning in all Nakuru. She lived on sweet dreams, revelling in the little body, the warm blood and the pure heart of her blossoming youth. But her dream of dreams was to finish school successfully and win a place at the university. Her ambition was to study electrical, mechanical or civil engineering. The word 'engineer' was what made her heart beat whenever she shut her eyes

140

and tried to look into the tomorrow of her life. Wariinga could not understand why girls hardly ever opted for such challenging jobs, leaving the whole field open to men. There is no job that a girl cannot accomplish if she sets her mind to it and believes she can do it: that was what Wariinga told the other girls, who would often laugh at the daring of her thoughts. But they were convinced that Wariinga could complete an engineering course successfully; no girl or boy at *Nakuru Day Secondary* could beat her at maths. Her knowledge of maths was legendary, and her name was known in all the neighbouring schools, like *Afraha, St Joseph's, St Xavier, Crater, Lake Nakuru Secondary*, and even beyond, in schools like *Nakuru High*.

Studying night and day, going to church every Sunday, helping her aunt on the land that they were allowed to cultivate by the council at Baari and at Kilimani, near the *Menengai Crater* – that was Wariinga's routine from Monday to Sunday. Her integrity, her industry in the fields and her diligence in everything she did helped to spread her reputation to all corners of *Section 58*.

Then one Saturday at about four o'clock, as she and her cousins were returning home from the fields near the *Menengai Crater*, Wariinga saw death for the very first time in her life. They had gone past the *Annex* of the Nakuru General Hospital and had crossed the Nakuru–Nairobi road, and they were now heading towards *Section 58*. At the level crossing they found a crowd of people gathered round the body of a man who had been completely crushed on the rails by a passing train. But was it really a body, or just minced meat, blood and bones scattered on the rails? No one could possibly tell who the person had been or make out what he might have looked like when alive. Wariinga felt as if her stomach had been cut to pieces with a razor blade. She felt sick, about to vomit, and she ran home and left her cousins at the scene of the terrible accident. Wariinga had always feared the sight of blood. News of deaths and funerals gave her sleepless nights as she wrestled with the paradox of life. But to see a man's whole shape and form completely obliterated by a railway train – it was as if the man had never been, had never existed – that was something she had never imagined and the chilling sight made Wariinga unable to use that particular crossing from that day on.

That, then, was how Wariinga grew up in Nakuru – upright, always seeking the path of virtue, according to the light of her knowledge and experience. So it was, Wariinga! And so it was, Jacinta! Yes, so it was until she reached Form Three.

By that time her breasts had developed. Her hair had grown long and brilliantly black. Her cheeks had blossomed, smooth and luscious like fruits in a good season.

Her aunt's husband, whom she called 'Uncle', was the man who caused Waríínga to stray from the paths trodden by peasants into the paths of the petty bourgeoisie, the clan of tie-wearers.

Uncle was one of those who had served the whites faithfully to save their own skins. After Independence, these same people became heirs to the whites, especially when it came to land and business. But Uncle was not as lucky as the others. His salary did not allow him to climb the ladder of his ambition. It was just enough for clothes and food and fees and other domestic needs. But despite his lowly conditions, he liked to live beyond his means: he kept company with those higher up the ladder of life. His companions consisted of a few rich men from Njoro and Ngorika. His wealthy friends drank at the *Sportsman's Corner* in the *Stag's Head Hotel*, or in clubs and hotels that, like the *Rift Valley Sports Club*, had previously been reserved for Europeans only.

Uncle believed that he who walked with the rich might himself become rich, that he who searched diligently would eventually find wealth, and that the fart of the rich man never smelled foul. So he did not mind that they ordered him about, or that they gave him their fingertips for a handshake, or that they sent him on errands like those pre-colonial servants of ring-wearing feudal lords.

Perhaps because he did not mind sniffing the rich men's farts, there came a time when he was able to pick up a few leftovers. A wealthy man from Ngorika got him a house on *hire purchase*, just near the *Kíbaacia Estate, Phase Two*, and then introduced him to a bank manager, who loaned him money for the initial deposit. The same wealthy man from Ngorika got him a piece of land near the *Sambugo Scheme*.

You give, I give, so goes the saying. A good feast calls for a return feast. In the same way, Uncle did not simply pick up good fortune from the ground for free. Oh, no. He promised his wealthy friend from Ngorika some 'veal' or a 'spring chicken'. Waríínga was going to be the chicken whose feathers would be plucked one by one, leaving the flesh naked and unhampered, soft food for a toothless old man. When a white man grows old, he eats veal.

But Waríínga did not know that she had already been sold, because they did not run after her the way a late passenger runs after a bus or the way a man jumps on to a bicycle. They started at the edges, the way a man approaches a hot dish, at first cautiously but in the end swallowing it all.

Uncle started by asking Waríínga to call at the council offices

142

after school hours to collect a few items for home. But every time Wariinga called at the offices, and before she and Uncle had exchanged two words, Wariinga would see the Rich Old Man from Ngorika suddenly appear. Afterwards, the Rich Old Man would give them a *lift* to *Section 58*, or he would drive Wariinga to the council butchery.

One day Wariinga was invited by a schoolmate to a party in Bahati. She found her uncle there. The Rich Old Man from Ngorika was also present. That night Wariinga was driven home by the Rich Old Man from Ngorika in a Mercedes Benz.

Gradually Wariinga and the Rich Old Man got to know one another. He was indefatigable in his relentless pursuit of her. On leaving school in the evening, Wariinga invariably found a Mercedes Benz standing by *Oginga Odinga Avenue*, near the *Church of the Holy Rosary*. The Rich Old Man would offer her a lift, but before taking her up to the council clinic, near the butchery, he would first take her for a leisurely ride through the streets of Nakuru, or to *Menengai Crater*, or to *Lake Nakuru*, or to the race track.

Then he started giving her *pocket money*, and money for the cinema, or for the races, or for the *Nakuru Agricultural Show*. And because Wariinga had not resisted his initial smiles, she now became progressively weaker, until she was unable to refuse anything. On two occasions they met at the *Eros* cinema, on another at the *Odeon*.

Wariinga's life now changed. She felt as if a door had opened on to a Nakuru she never knew existed. Suddenly she saw the world brighten; she saw a brilliant light illuminating a road that was broad and very beautiful. Wariinga heard words of love whispered by wonderfully smooth and perfumed voices: 'Wariinga, my dear, how can you foolishly tie yourself to your books when sugary delicacies, and ripe, juicy fruits, and many other wonders calculated to stir the heart and to warm the body are to be found everywhere in Kenya?'

Wariinga grew wings. She tried out the wings and flew once with her Rich Old Man. She felt good. She flew again and again, and with every flight she felt the wonders of a Mercedes Benz multiply. Her Rich Old Man encouraged her with soothing words: he said that she should never worry, that he was perfectly willing to divorce his first wife on account of Wariinga's thighs and breasts. Wariinga was now constantly poised for flight.

She began to hate school, convinced that it was school that clipped her wings and dragged her back to earth with iron chains just when she wanted to float free, soaring through the sky towards a heaven of everlasting happiness. Her dreams of learning and of ending up at the university to read for a degree in engineering vanished into thin air like the morning dew after sunshine. In the classroom she would count the seconds, minutes, hours, days, impatient for Saturday, so that she could fly to the freedom of real *living*. She also became an expert liar. On many occasions she would deceive her aunt into thinking that she was going to Ilmorog to see her parents.

At such times Wariinga would be picked by her Rich Old Man at Nakuru bus stop, and she would be whisked along the tarmac highway towards Naivasha. At Naivasha they would take a ride around the lake in a motorboat, or they would walk along the lakeshore, watching the fishermen at work, her Rich Old Man lecturing her on how the small fishes were used by men to trap bigger ones, and how the big fishes lived on the smaller ones. 'Yes, they swallow them whole,' the Rich Old Man would add, laughing.

Sometimes they would go to the Hot Springs, ostensibly to hunt animals, though they had no hunting licence. But instead of hunting animals, they would play a game called the Hunter and the Hunted. The Hunter would take the pistol to chase the Hunted until the Hunted was worn out and exhausted, whereupon the Hunter would catch the Hunted and fire into the sky to announce his victory.

It was the Rich Old Man who normally chased Wariinga through the trees, holding a pistol in his right hand. Because Wariinga's body was agile and young, she could outrun the Rich Old Man. She would then hide in a bush until he was exhausted and started calling out for her in frustrated irritation. When Wariinga noticed this trait, she started faking exhaustion. The Rich Old Man would catch up with her, then he would fire into the sky and beam with happiness. Wariinga would then take the pistol and chase him through the trees. What always surprised Wariinga was that no matter how tired she really was, once she had the gun in her hands, she would feel infused with a new strength, and she would dash forward and catch up with him to fire the shot of victory. One day she felt fed up with the whole game. She fired the gun before she had caught him. She could never really tell what happened – as she swung her hand to fire, a branch may have jogged the gun – but at any rate the bullet missed the man by no more than an inch. It hit a pregnant antelope and killed it instantly.

The Rich Old Man was shaking and sweating. Wariinga wept. She had never killed anything in her life. She told the Rich Old Man that they should stop playing the Hunter and the Hunted. He just laughed, pretending more courage than he felt, and told her that the game would never end. But now that he had seen that she could not be trusted with guns, she was not to hunt him again. He would do the hunting all the time.

'But suppose you misfire?' Warĩĩnga asked him.

'No, I'm not like you. I wouldn't miss you,' the Rich Old Man said, as if he were joking.

They laughed. The Rich Old Man was bewitched, obsessed by the game.

The Rich Old Man would always make sure that they had a room in one of hotels along the shores of the lake. In the evening, after eating and drinking, they would retire to their room, where they would spend a night of joy. The following day he would drive Warĩĩnga to Ilmorog. He would drop her at the bus stop; she would run home; she would hurriedly greet her parents; then she would quickly run back to where her darling Rich Old Man was waiting, and they would fly back to another hotel to continue their life.

It has been said that sweetness has a mouth and a stomach of its own – and a poisonous bite. One morning, on her way to school, just before she reached the residence of the African Sisters, Warĩĩnga felt dizzy. She sat down, and she started vomiting. When the dizziness had passed, Warĩĩnga continued on her way to school, thinking that she had an upset stomach. But day after day Warĩĩnga felt increasingly sick and dizzy, and she was often sick. A month passed, and she missed her period. It sometimes happens like that, she consoled herself. Another month, and she missed it a second time.

Panic seized Warĩĩnga. Warĩĩnga had heard of many girls who had become pregnant, but she had never dreamed that it could happen to her. Now she had no doubt. What she had always thought could never happen to her had now happened.

What's done cannot be undone, Warĩĩnga told herself. In any case, the ground on which she stood was firm and solid. Her Rich Old Man had always assured her that he would marry her according to custom, that he could even divorce his wife and marry his new young wife with a proper church ceremony. So she was sure that he would not show any surprise at the news of her present condition. In any case, to be pregnant before marriage had now become the modern thing. Looking around, Warĩĩnga could see that many girls slipped on wedding rings at the altar when they were eight or even nine months pregnant. There were some who were married today only to bear a child tomorrow. Warĩĩnga had heard of one girl who had given birth in a church. Another had given birth on her way to church, keeping the bridegroom and the priest waiting at the church door in vain. Oh, Waríínga was not afraid for herself. Faith in a loved one removes all fears.

One Saturday evening, in a Naivasha hotel, Waríínga told him everything. The Rich Old Man started like one who has been bitten on the bottom by a scorpion, but he quickly composed himself, and he did not moan or voice any complaints that night. Waríínga thought that all was well. During the night she dreamed that she had been freed from the chains of schools and teachers and exams to float forever on the tides of pleasure, to paddle in the shallows of the new Kenya, enjoying a life of uninterrupted indulgence, without the repressive prospect of school tomorrow.

It was in the morning that the Rich Old Man read Waríínga a lesson she would never forget. He asked her why she had not taken care of herself, like other girls. What had prevented her from taking *pills*, having a coil fixed inside her, or being injected? And why had she not revealed her state the month she discovered that she was pregnant? It was clearly because Waríínga was not quite sure who was responsible.

'How could you possibly have conceived so soon if I were the only man who went with you? Go away and look for the young man who has got you into trouble, and tell him to marry you or to take you to the forest or somewhere else for an abortion. I thought all along that I was going with a clean schoolgirl, a girl without too many problems, a girl I would have loved to marry, so that she could be balm for my old bones. But instead I picked on Kareendi Ready-to-Yield, did I?'

Waríínga did not know whether to weep or scream or protest. She remained silent, like someone who had been struck dumb or bewitched into preserving eternal silence by powerful medicines bought from the famous Kamíri, the witch doctor. She saw the world suddenly turn hostile.

The brilliant light she had seen was no longer there. She saw the road that she had previously thought of as wide and very beautiful now suddenly become narrow, covered with thorns. The path that she had thought would lead her to Heaven now led her to a hell on Earth. So the seas of pleasure had all along been seas of fire? So the carpet of flowers on which she had trodden had actually been a carpet of thorns? So her wings had not really been wings but chains of steel?

Waríínga could not tell how they eventually got back to Nakuru. She could not remember getting out of the Mercedes Benz, the grave of her youth, her integrity and her virginity. She did not even see the

Rich Old Man rev the engine and reverse the four-wheeled tomb back towards his estates in Ngorika.

Warĩĩnga watched her future disappear with eyes that saw nothing. She was utterly alone; thorns tore at the heels, the soles and the toes of the legs of her heart, which were taking her to a hell of her own choosing.

But had she really chosen the hell, or had the hell been forced on her? Warĩĩnga asked herself, as she stood there at the bus stop, letting her eyes wander over Nakuru railway station, the road to Eldoret, the *Amigos Bar*, Kenyatta Avenue, the shops, not knowing where she should go now. She walked slowly across the bus station, went through the Nakuru municipal market, entered the Njoro Hotel, sat down alone at a small table in the far corner and ordered tea to drink while she tried to pull herself together. My God, where shall I turn now? she asked herself over and over again.

She knew that she could not turn to her aunt, or her uncle, or her cousins, or her teachers, or her schoolmates for help.

Warĩĩnga had no relatives or friends whom she could expect to appear suddenly and say, 'Warĩĩnga, I have come to help you.'

She did not drink the tea. She paid for it, left it there on the table and went out.

On arriving home in *Section 58*, she went straight to bed. She tried to say her beads, but she could not. She tried to cry, but no tears would come.

In those days of anxiety, Warĩĩnga found no one to offer her consolation, no one to say: 'Be calm, my child. Let me show you the way out of your present troubles.' On the contrary, her anguish was made more painful by the fact that at home she would strain herself in order not to show any sign of sorrow or self-pity. Only when she was alone in bed at night did Warĩĩnga have an opportunity to let her tears flow, often asking herself: Oh, what can I do to get rid of this burden of pregnancy? Warĩĩnga had no one from whom she could discover the answers to her many questions.

At school Warĩĩnga tried to seek the advice of the other girls. But she did it indirectly, approaching the subject with apparent detachment, as if it were not she who was carrying the burden. But the stories she heard – like the case of a girl who went mad after drinking a mixture of tea, quinine, aspirin and several other drugs – made her blood run cold, and her burden become heavier than ever.

Warĩĩnga had no friend or relative who could lighten the load for her.

So Warĩĩnga struggled on alone, contemplating this expedient and

147

that one, turning over this and that solution in her mind, comparing countless alternatives, trying to work out how she could vanish from the face of the Earth, never to be seen again at school, or in Nakuru, or in Kenya.

One day she thought of visiting Dr Patel, famous throughout Nakuru for the many illegal abortions he had performed.

It was a Saturday morning. She took what little money she had managed to save out of her presents from her Rich Old Man, and lied to her aunt that she was going to borrow books from one of the teachers in her school.

She took to the road, alone with her secret. She passed through the yard of the grass huts and joined *Ladhies Road*, but instead of crossing over to *Ngala Avenue* and on to *Nakuru Day Secondary*, she turned towards the centre of town. And now in the place of the dreams that used to fill her soul on the way to school, she felt only bitterness well up: the dreams of a girl in her virgin youth could blossom quickly, and then, just as quickly, droop and fall to the ground like flowers in a dry season.

She walked along *Kenyatta Avenue*, towards the Post Office and the *Stag's Head*. At the *Kenya Commercial Bank*, Warĩĩnga stopped and looked about her. Then she turned left and hurried past people and buildings without once looking behind her. But when she got to the *Mount Kenya Bookshop*, she entered, pretended to browse through the books and then went outside again. Warĩĩnga stood outside the *Bookshop* for a moment to make sure that nobody who knew her would see her enter Dr Patel's clinic. She felt as if the whole of Nakuru could guess at her intentions. Her heart was beating loudly, like the repeated hoots of an owl.

Warĩĩnga strode determinedly towards the doctor's clinic. But as she was about to set foot inside the door, she glanced down the road and saw a woman, a neighbour from *Section 58*, coming out of a tailoring school nearby. Warĩĩnga felt her whole body burn with shame, as if she had been caught in the act of stealing. She fled.

On another Saturday, at about four in the afternoon, Warĩĩnga thought of seeking help from a girl who had been her schoolmate at both Baharini primary school and *Nakuru Day*. The girl had left school after Form Two and had gone to *Nakuru General Hospital* to train as a nurse.

Warĩĩnga went to the *Annex* and luckily found the girl in her room, alone. They chatted about this and that – schools, and teachers, and students, and exams – Warĩĩnga trying to find an opportunity to pour out her problems. But just as she was about to say what was on her mind, Warĩĩnga felt a lump in her throat, and she was unable to tell

148

her secret. Instead, she asked the girl about the *Medical School*, and pretended that she was also thinking of training as a nurse at the hospital. After talking for a while Waríínga and the girl walked together towards the *State House* on the Nakuru–Nairobi road.

When Waríínga saw the girl turn back to the hospital, she suddenly felt the strength leave her legs. She wanted to shout at the girl, to beg her not leave her on the road alone.

She walked along the road towards Nairobi like someone who had taken hard liquor or bhang. She was not in full possession of her faculties. She was not aware of the cars that were heading towards Nairobi or Nakuru. She did not even notice that darkness had fallen and that the street lights were on. She simply walked, without knowing quite where she was going. At one point she just missed hitting her head against a tree.

It was the near-accident that alerted her to the fact that she had reached the turning to Bahati. She thought of taking the road to Bahati, then she skirted the hedge around *Nakuru High School*. She decided that she would go up the road towards *Menengai Crater* and throw herself into the huge hollow below, like the Indian who once drove into the cavern and died.

As a child, Waríínga had heard that the *Crater* was often visited by spirits, who would shave the whole forest and bush with razor blades early in the morning and set fire to the surrounding grass and the trees once a year. When the Indian threw himself into the *Crater*, the legend was that he had been pulled into the hollow by the spirits after he had caught them shaving the trees and playing about in the grass and on the treetops.

Waríínga longed for someone, even a spirit, to seize her and bear her away from Nakuru and from the Earth.

And then Waríínga remembered that *Nakuru High School* had a swimming pool. Waríínga decided that instead of going all the way to the *Crater* alone at night, she would end her miseries in the pool. She entered the school compound and followed the path around the buildings. Through the windows she caught sight of students reading books under electric lights, and when she recalled her present condition, she felt pain burn her heart and body. She walked faster, praying that she would not meet any students or teachers.

During the colonial days, *Nakuru High School* was reserved for European children only. But after Independence, it was turned into an expensive national school. It was a mixed boarding school. In the evening all the students had to go to class for *prep*.

Those were the students whom Waríínga saw through the windows, their heads bent over their books. Waríínga left the path

149

that led towards the boys' dormitories and took the one to the swimming pool. She did not meet anybody loitering in the compound. She thought that God had heard her prayers.

When she reached the classrooms at the far end of the compound, she took a turning to the swimming pool. It was quite dark because the light from the nearest classrooms did not reach that far. Waríínga was about to enter the swimming pool area when, from nowhere, she suddenly heard a man's voice: 'What are you doing here? Why are you not in your classroom?'

Waríínga started and looked about her, thinking that the spirits from *Menengai Crater* had come down from the mountains for her. So the spirits really existed? Then she discovered that the voice was that of the school watchman, who was half-hidden by a small hedge and had obviously taken Waríínga for one of the students. Waríínga lied.

'I am a visitor here at the school. Mr Kamau is my brother. I am staying with him this week. And I'm just taking an evening stroll to pass the time.'

'Oh, I see,' the watchman said, and walked on into the swimming pool area.

Waríínga suspected that the watchman did not believe her story. She stood there a few seconds, then she turned back to the main path, and walked down towards the road to Nairobi.

Was she fated to walk forever along thorn-covered avenues? Was she destined to carry a heavy load in her heart forever? Waríínga asked herself these and many other questions as she walked towards *Section 58*. So even committing suicide was hard? What could a human being call his own in this world if he could not end his life when he felt that it was too much of a burden? Waríínga reached the railway crossing still turning over these questions in her mind.

And then Waríínga remembered the man whom she and her cousins had found on the rails, completely crushed by a train. She recalled that the man's identity had been completely obliterated. His name was hidden forever, and it was as if he had never been born. Waríínga felt that a death like that, which would ensure that no one would ever guess who she had been, was the most suitable for her. She resolved that come what may, the next day she would offer her body to a train.

She would wait for a train on that very crossing and would throw herself in front of its iron wheels, to be wiped off the face of the Earth as if she had never been born or never visited the Earth. For the first time Waríínga was able to say her beads. With all her heart

150

she pleaded with the Virgin Mary: Virgin Mary, hear now my prayer. Mark my soul with the wounds of Jesus. Amen.

For the first time since she had caught leprosy from the Rich Old Man from Ngorika, Waríínga felt a kind of peace return to her. She even tried to whisper to herself a hymn that she used to sing when she was happy, only now she sang in sorrow.

> Peace, peace in my heart.
> I pray for peace in my heart
> At the time of Thy Resurrection,
> Peace, peace in my heart.
> I pray for peace in my heart
> In the name of Thy Resurrection.

Waríínga was not really after the resurrection of the body or soul. All she wanted was that her name should be wiped off the face of the Earth. All she wanted was to vanish as if she had never been born. All she prayed for was for the Angel of Death to come for her and to remove her name from the ledgers of Heaven and Earth:

> You who feed the hungry,
> You who relieve the tired,
> You who cool the thirsty,
> Take me across the River of Death.

The following day was a Sunday. Her aunt asked Waríínga if she wanted to go to morning mass. Waríínga declined. Her aunt and all her cousins left for the *Church of the Holy Rosary*. Waríínga remained at home to cook. But she cooked nothing. She took a bath, and she did her hair nicely, like somebody who was preparing for a long journey.

At about half-past ten, Waríínga went to the railway crossing. She glanced around her and saw that there was no one anywhere near. But a few minutes later, the watchman at *Nakuru High* passed by on his way to *Section 58*. Their eyes met. The watchman made as if to stop and talk to Waríínga. Then he seemed to change his mind and crossed the lines to the other side, Waríínga silently mocking him: You won't hold me back again . . . . There's nothing you can now do to prevent me from doing whatever I want to do . . . .

And suddenly the train appeared, heading towards Nairobi. Waríínga thought it was chanting the song that, as a child, she used to believe it sang:

Going-to-Uganda!
Going-to-Uganda!
Going-to-Uganda!

And her heart beat in time to the song of the train:

Going-to-Uganda!
Going-to-Uganda!
Going-to-Uganda!

And still the train came on, belching steam, breathing blood and death, saying farewell, on her behalf, to all the people of Nakuru.

Going....
Going....
Going....

Waríínga stepped forward on to the rails. She shut her eyes. She started counting ... one ... two ... three....

Go....
Go....
Go....

... four ... five .... *Virgin Mary, have mercy upon me....*
The train is still coming on. Its rumble is shaking the rails from their sleepers. Its roar is making Waríínga's heart and body quake. Its thunder is causing the ground to tremble as the train bears Death towards Waríínga....

Go!
Go!
Go!

... eight ... nine ... *Virgin Mary* ... Go-go-go ... ten ... take me now....
And suddenly Waríínga felt herself pulled off the rails by a man's hands and thrown on to the side of the track. She fainted.
And the train rushed past her towards Nairobi, but its whistling sounded in the sky above Nakuru, as if it were angrily demanding to know how Waríínga had escaped its crushing wheels.
Waríínga did not know who had saved her from a death she had so longed for. She could not even tell how she eventually reached

Section 58. When she opened her eyes, Waríínga found herself in bed, her aunt at her side, looking at her with eyes full of infinite pity.

Waríínga told her aunt everything . . . all about her affair with the Rich Old Man from Ngorika . . . .

Chapter Six

1

It was about three when Warĩĩnga and Gatuĩria returned to the cave for the afternoon session of the competition in the art of modern theft and robbery. They thought they were late. Robin Mwaũra was leaning against the walls of the cave, near the door. He greeted them as if he had been waiting for them.

'Ah! I thought you weren't coming back,' Mwaũra said, in a tone that suggested he was holding something back.

'Why, has the session already started?' Gatuĩria asked.

'No, not yet.'

'Where are Mũturi and Wangarĩ?' Warĩĩnga asked.

Mwaũra did not reply immediately. Standing between Warĩĩnga and Gatuĩria, he put his hands on their shoulders and turned them back the way they had come, as if he were taking them aside for a private discussion. They went a few steps without Mwaũra saying anything, until they came to a turning. Mwaũra then looked about him, as if he were taking great care not to be overheard.

'Let's run away from here – now!' Mwaũra said, in a low voice.

'Why?' Gatuĩria and Warĩĩnga asked simultaneously.

'Because . . . because fighting is bound to break in this place.'

'Fighting? *But why?*' the other two asked.

'We shall be blamed for bringing two lunatics with us last night!' Mwaũra blurted out the story. 'Even when we were still at Kineeniĩ, I had already guessed that Wangarĩ and Mũturi were not to be trusted. And this morning, if it had been left up to me, Mũturi and Wangarĩ would not have been allowed into a place where there were such important men and distinguished guests from abroad. The Mũturis of this world can bring only untold trouble to important men . . . and I bet those two are not alone!'

'But what happened after we had gone for lunch?' Gatuĩria asked. 'Were you thrown out of the cave like Ndaaya wa Kahuria?'

'Where are Wangarĩ and Mũturi?' Warĩĩnga asked, burning with impatience. 'Why are you telling us things like the chameleon that was sent to the people by God but never managed to deliver its message?'

'Let me tell you the whole story from the beginning, so we can decide what to do,' Mwaũra said, and he told them what had happened.

'When the morning speeches had ended, you two left and went your own way. We left soon afterwards, and we said to each other: "Let's take to the road to look for something to silence our gurgling stomachs. Let's go to Njeruca for some roast meat; we can't afford the food in this cave." We got into my *matatū*. Then there we were, in the heartland of Njeruca. We went into a small butchery, full of flies. But it had a self-important name, the Hilton. The sign outside read: BETTER EAT AT HIIRITONI. We ordered four pounds of meat. Mūturi paid for one half, I paid for the other. We then went into a room at the back to wait for the meat to roast and to get something to drink. Me, I had a Tusker, and Wangarī had a Tatino and Mūturi drank Whitecap.

'It was Mūturi who started the discussion. He began as if he were picking up the threads where we left off outside the cave. He said: "As Mwaūra said last night in the *matatū*, I've seen many things in this land. I have done all sorts of jobs in Kenya, I have been to many places in Kenya, and I have witnessed many happenings in our country. Once, while working as a watchman at a certain school in Nakuru, I saved a girl who wanted to take her own life. It was quite dark, and I was standing near the school's swimming pool. I saw her walking along, stealthily, close to a small hedge. When I asked her what she was doing there alone, she said that she was staying with her brother, who was a teacher at the school. Then she went away. The following day I found the same girl standing in the middle of the railway track, waiting for the train to run over her. I was on my way to Bondeni, and I passed her standing on the other side of the line. But God's case has no appeal. When I had gone a few steps towards *Section 58*, something made me stop and look over my shoulder. I tell you, I rescued her from the very jaws of death. She fainted in my arms. Luckily, in her handbag I found an envelope on which was written her address in *Section 58*. I left her there with her family, and I went on to Bondeni. Why am I recalling all this? Because what I have seen and heard in that cave beats all the miracles I've ever experienced."

Gatuīria and Warīīnga looked at one another, inwardly saying: This is a miracle indeed! Mwaūra went on: 'It was then that Wangarī joined in, and she said: "So it really is true that from the womb of the same country emerges both the thief and the witch? I too have never seen wonders to beat those in the cave."

'I kept quiet, for I know very well that a little stealing here and there is not really bad. And robbery that does not call attention to itself is not bad.

'It was Mūturi who said, "Did you know that a thief or a robber is worse than a witch?"

'There I strongly disagreed, and I told him: "A witch is worse than a thief. A thief only steals your property and leaves your heart beating. Tomorrow you can acquire more property. But a witch takes away your life, and leaves all your property for others to eat. A thief steals property, but a witch steals life."

'And at that point the meat was brought to us on a wooden dish. It was roasted very nicely! I took a knife, and I cut the meat into small pieces. While we were eating, Mūturi told us a story about a thief and a witch.

'A long, long time ago, in a certain village, there lived a very dangerous thief. He had brought misery to the whole village, but nobody could catch him in the act, for he was very cunning. Now in the same village there lived a very dangerous witch, who was also very much feared because his witchcraft was even more potent than Kamīri's. The village elders gathered at the meeting-ground. They decided to invite the witch to cast a spell on the thief that would bring about his death. The witch boasted that that was nothing to him. He collected together his potent medicines and his divining gourds and nuts. Then he lay down to sleep. In the morning, he woke up at the usual hour. He went to check his divining tools. Lo! The thief had stolen everything. The witch gathered up more paraphernalia. The thief crept in and stole it all. The witch was forced to move away from that village. That's the origin of the saying that a thief is terrible for he forces a witch to leave home. And again, a thief even steals from his own mother. A thief is like the white man, of whom it is said that he has no close friends.

'It was then that Wangarī said: "But modern thieves are worse, for they invite foreigners to rob their own mothers and in return receive a few hand-outs. But you two are wrong. A thief is no worse than a witch, and a witch is no worse than a thief. A thief is a witch, and a witch is a thief. For when a thief steals your land, your house, your clothes, isn't he really killing you? And when a witch destroys your life, isn't he stealing everything you own? That is why I say a thief is a witch, and a witch is a thief. Even Gīkūyū knew this. Long ago, the sentence imposed on a thief and a witch was the same. It carried the same punishment – death by burning or by being rolled down a hill in a beehive."

'We ate up the meat and finished it all. I told Mũturi and Wangarĩ that we should hurry up and return to the cave so that we wouldn't be late for the afternoon session.

'It was then that Wangarĩ's madness took wing. She said that she wouldn't go back to the cave, that instead she would go to the *Ilmorog police station*. To do what? I asked her. She told me: "An agreement is an agreement. A crowd of thieves and robbers like those cannot be allowed to gather and then go free!" I said: "So you were serious about the story you told us last night?" Wangarĩ said that she was a good and loyal citizen, and that she had to join hands with the police force to bring an end to theft and robbery. "If the police arrest pickpockets who snatch women's handbags in market places, and petty criminals who steal five shillings, and thieves who steal hens in villages, what do you think they will do to these men, who steal from the masses and rob the whole nation?" For my part, I tried everything I could think of to dissuade her: "Don't ruin other people's feasts. Have you got enough evidence? Wangarĩ, remember that a lawsuit can turn against a witness." Wangarĩ disagreed with me, and said: "If every time you see a thief stealing or a robber robbing, you turn the other way or shut your eyes and seal your lips, how will theft and robbery be brought to an end in this land?"

'I left her to her schemes. The case of a fool remains unsettled. And again, if a wise man argues with a fool for too long, it is difficult to tell the difference between them. A person destined for ill-fortune cannot be diverted.

'All this time Mũturi had kept quiet, like a hypocrite, listening to the argument between me and Wangarĩ. Can you imagine my surprise when Mũturi entered the fray and said that he would help Wangarĩ to catch the thieves and robbers? I asked him: How would he help? He said that he would go around Njeruca awakening the workers and the unemployed, urging them to follow him so he could show them where all the thieves and robbers of the people's wealth had gathered to compete to see who had stolen most from the people. The victims of theft were the only ones who could effectively demand the return of their stolen wealth.

'I reasoned with Mũturi. "Mũturi, you look like a sensible man. Beware of being swept off your feet by the whims of modern women. Remember how Ndaaya wa Kahuria was thrown out of the cave. Ndaaya only steals five shillings here and there to buy himself a few cakes. That shows that the rest of them are very important thieves and robbers – *Wanyang'anyi Mashuhuri; wao si wezi wa mandazi na kuku* – and they should not be disturbed."

'Mūturi shook his head and said: "I, Mūturi, do not believe in the saying that silence saves lives. Wangarī has spoken the truth. If whenever we see theft and robbery, we shut our eyes or look the other way, doesn't this mean that we support the system of theft and robbery? There is no difference between a thief and him who observes the act, Gīkūyū once said. You say Ndaaya wa Kahuria was thrown out of the cave. Yes, but what does that show us? The truth of one of Gīkūyū's sayings: that a thief in rags often becomes a sacrifice for the thief in finery. Why did Gīkūyū say that? Because in many cases we point at a thief in rags, forgetting that perhaps he steals because he is hungry and thirsty. In the old days a Mūūgīkūyū never took it out on a thief who stole only to silence a hungry belly. If in the old days you went to someone's farm and cut down sugarcane and sat down and ate it, or if you lit a fire and dug up enough sweet potatoes to satisfy your hunger and roasted them and ate them then and there, the owner of the farm would never bother you. But these modern thieves, who reap where they have never sown, to the extent of even inviting foreigners to join in the harvest, and who store all the grain in foreign granaries, leaving the owner of the farm dying of starvation, and who slaughter a herdsman's own sheep, fattening themselves on the stolen meat – have they not shat and farted beyond the limits of tolerance? Let them be arrested by the working people now that they, the thieves and robbers, have congregated in one den to parade their full bellies and to pour scorn on us. Mwaūra, you say that we should wait for more evidence? No. Procrastination destroyed the beehive. It is never too early to go to the market, before the sun scorches the vegetables.

> Come one and all,
> And behold the wonderful sight
> Of us chasing away the Devil
> And all his disciples!
> Come one and all!

Wangarī, I don't think you'll get much help from the police station. But he who has not drunk from a calabash does not know its measure. Go your way, and I'll go mine. Our aim is the same. We'll all meet at the cave, each with his own forces."

'When Mūturi had finished, he stared at me with eyes that seemed to be challenging me to a fight. But I, Mwaūra, am a man. I looked him in the face and told him very firmly that I would never support any action that was designed to increase conflict in the land. I told them this: "A person is eaten up by his own mouth. Mũturi and Wangarĩ, because you know that what is done can never be undone, leave these people alone. A thief who has not been caught is said to be eating his rightful share." Mũturi quickly replied: "*Ndio, ndio*, that's why they should all be arrested . . . ."

'That's how the two madmen and I parted company. I thought I should hurry back to the cave to tell you all about it, so that you won't be caught unawares by the drama and the chaos that are bound to follow. That's why I'm suggesting that we should race back to Nairobi now, so that at least we can share the cost of the petrol. I've also been looking for Mwĩreri wa Mũkiraaĩ, so that he can tell the master of ceremonies to end the feast before everyone is caught by the police and the workers. Those two, Mũturi and Wangarĩ, are not alone!'

Robin Mwaũra finished his story and stared about him again as if he were afraid that the police and the workers would suddenly appear. Gatuĩria and Warĩĩnga looked at one another. They did not know whether to rejoice or to pity Wangarĩ and Mũturi.

'There's nothing to worry about,' Gatuĩria said. 'Let's go inside and wait to see what happens.'

'Don't you think it would be wise of us to tell the hosts and guests at the feast what is going on?' Mwaũra asked.

'No,' Gatuĩria replied quickly. 'Let's leave them alone. Let's leave the two sides alone. We are just spectators.'

They moved off towards the cave. Warĩĩnga was thoughtful. Is it because of such coincidences that the Earth is said to be round? To come across the very man who twice saved my life – and in a place like this? Who is Mũturi? When they were close to the entrance to the cave, Mwaũra tugged at Gatuĩria's sleeve. They both stopped. Warĩĩnga went ahead and waited for them at the door.

Mwaũra whispered to Gatuĩria: 'Listen, although you say that we are just spectators, that we're not here to take sides, I'd like to enter the competition.'

'And leave Warĩĩnga and me as the only spectators?' Gatuĩria asked, checking his laughter.

'That's right,' Mwaũra said. 'But would it be a good move?'

'To give your testimony about theft and robbery, or to abandon us?' Gatuĩria asked.

'What I want is a chance to show them cunning to beat all cunning in the art of theft and robbery. Would that be a wise move?' Mwaũra asked again, forcing Gatuĩria to offer him advice.

'Well, didn't I tell you that I was a mere spectator? If you get a chance, by all means jump on to the platform and try your luck. All a competitor is required to do is to show what he has done with his talents for stealing and robbing, and what he would do now if he were given more opportunity by the foreigners . . . . But I'm not telling you to do this or not to do that. Do what you want to do. The decision is yours,' Gatuĩria said, like a judge trying to disguise his real position in the struggles of life.

But Mwaũra seemed very pleased with Gatuĩria's words. He spoke up a little. 'There, you have spoken the truth. That's why I always say that education is a good thing, a very important thing. Now, if it had been Mũturi and Wangarĩ, they would have tried to dissuade me. Why? Because they don't have much education. They have no idea what makes the world turn. I can see that you are quite impartial. In Warĩĩnga's case, take care! She seems to pay much too much attention to the words of the two madmen. But you certainly seem to know how to get to the heart of things. And you have put it well. It's not the number of one's talents that one should count. Oh, no, what's important is the quality of one's skills and the use to which one has put them. You say that I should do what I want to do . . . . Ha, ha! Do you remember what Mwĩreri wa Mũkiraaĩ told us in my *matatũ* last night? *He also that had received . . . talents came and said . . . .*'

The Testimony of Mwĩreri wa Mũkiraaĩ

'Because the white man once said *Time is money* – *yaanĩ*, hours are the same thing as money – I will only take a few minutes to offer you the kernel of my wisdom.

'As for women, I have one wife. But she is a woman with a good education, for she has a degree in *home economics* – *yaani*, a degree in how to manage money in the home and maintain a civilized way of life.

'Girlfriends? I haven't got any. Or let me put it this way: whenever I want a good time, I look for white or Indian girls. I don't believe in tribal or racial *discrimination* when it comes to women. I have always maintained that women belong to no age group, no clan, no country. *Wanawake ni watumishi kwa wote.* So if you come across a white girl, take her; if you come across an Asian girl, take her; if you come across a beautiful girl called Ready-to-Yield, take her.

'As for our children, we have only two, a boy and a girl. We won't have any more. I believe in *family planning* – *yaani*, the planning of births, the freedom of parents to say how many children they want to have or are able to support – and not in the unplanned arrival of a mass of children who will not let you eat delicacies in comfort. I am a member of an international body for regulating births (it is called the *International Planned Parenthood Association*), whose headquarters are in New York, USA. Let me tell you, children are our biggest enemy. Any increase in the population is contrary to our interests. Imagine if the whole world belonged to you and your wife alone? *You see what I mean?* The greatest threat to us is the increase in the number of people who will be demanding food, clothing and shelter. For if those people fail to land jobs, fail to find food, fail to buy clothes, what is to prevent them from taking up clubs and swords and guns to split open our own well-fed bellies? We of the *Planned Parenthood Association* have only one desire: to find ways and means of decreasing conflict between nations, and especially conflict between those of us who have grabbed wealth and those from whom we have grabbed. That's why we who belong to the *Association* maintain: let the wives of the poor bear only the number of children that they can support with the food we have left them in their granaries, or according to the size of their salaries. If a man is without a job, then let him not burden himself with women and children.

'As for my education – and here, good people, I crave your indulgence: if I brag a little, don't take it that I am being arrogant – as for my education, I am a man with three degrees in his pocket or, rather, in the head you see before you. A hero is not gauged by the size of his calves, and fame is often greater than its owner, and wisdom is innate and not attached like a patch of cloth.... If anyone's in doubt, I still have a small stack of my *business cards*. In the cards you'll see all my degrees in a row: *B.Sc. (Econ.) (Mak.); B. Comm. (NRB); MA (Bus. Admin.) (Harvard, USA); MRSocIBM*. The last one is not really a degree; it is an honour, and it stands for: *Member of the Royal Society for International Business Management*. The card shows clearly that my knowledge is concentrated in the fields of business management and economic development. All that skill and knowledge is contained in this small body you see before you. That's why I say that fame is often greater than its owner.

'I don't believe in *foreign ideology*. But I believe in the *ideology* of modern theft and robbery. But in order that you should know —'

Before he could continue, Mwīreri wa Mūkiraaī was interrupted by a man who wanted to ask a question. The man had seen Mwīreri wa Mūkiraaī merge from a *matatū* that morning, and he had serious doubts about whether Mwĩreri had reached the necessary standard in theft and robbery to qualify him to enter the competition.

'Mr Chairman, the speaker on the platform has waxed eloquent on the subject of his degrees. That's very good. Even the system of theft and robbery needs educated people. But Mr Chairman – and remember, one can hit out at a loved one – could the speaker please let us know first what make of car he drives? That's the kind of fame we understand. Tales about education are all fiction to us.'

The man sat down. He was given a big ovation. And now, because Mwĩreri wa Mũkiraaĩ did not know that the man had spotted him getting out of Mwaũra's matatũ, he was a bit confused and did not know where to start. And then many of the guests shouted at him, demanding details: 'His cars, let him tell us all about his cars! Hatukujui bila kitambulisho chako ... your identity card ...!'

'Mr Chairman,' Mwĩreri wa Mũkiraaĩ, 'Mr Chairman, my car .... I am sorry that I forgot to mention that. As for my car, I've only got one, a Peugeot 504 (with petrol injection). I tell you, though, that car is very fast, faster than the swiftest arrow. The same car acts as my memsahib's shopping basket. But now I am thinking of getting her a small plough, a Toyota Hilux pick-up, only two tons, just a plough that she can also use as a shopping basket.'

Mwĩreri was interrupted again by the same person. 'Mr Chairman, could Mr Mwĩreri please let us know if he drove to this feast in the Peugeot 504 (with petrol injection), or can I take it that it died in flight, the way an arrow does?'

The man was given another ovation. He was filled with fresh strength, and he continued to ask questions edged with sarcasm. 'Yes, how did he get to the cave this morning? Which was the car that brought him to Ilmorog yesterday? Or did he come in a borrowed car? Mr Chairman, a man who owns only one car, even granted that it is swifter than an arrow, is he fit to stand up before mature people to talk about the art of modern theft and robbery? I move that Mwĩreri be thrown out, together with his collection of degrees. He should be thrown out like Ndaaya wa Kahuria!'

The man sat down. Mwĩreri wa Mũkiraaĩ took a handkerchief out of his pocket and wiped beads of sweat from his face. He cleared his throat and stared challengingly at the people, then he raised his voice and spoke with all the courage of wounded pride.

'Mr Chairman, I did not come in my car. You, Mr Chairman, you know me, and you certainly know my car. Was I not the main distributor of these invitation cards in Nairobi?'

'Mwĩreri wa Mũkiraaĩ!' The master of ceremonies cut him short. 'Let me remind you of what you have just been told, that it is not easy to recognize a man without his car. A car is a man's *identity*. I once met my wife on foot because she had left her car at home. I didn't recognize her. She told me about the encounter later. Now, if I can't recognize my own wife without her car, do you think that you're an exception? Show these elders your identity card so we can get on with the feast.'

'*Mr Chairman*,' Mwĩreri cried out in desperation, '*Mr Chairman*, my car stalled at Kikuyu. I left it outside the *Ondiri Hotel*. If we rang the hotel, we could ask someone to check whether or not a *Peugeot 504* is standing in the yard. I came in a *matatũ*, Matatũ Matata Matamu. You can ask the owner whether or not I told him about the problem with my car, for I wouldn't want you to think that I'm entirely dependent on *matatũs* for transport! Robin Mwaũra, *please* stand up!'

Robin Mwaũra stood up, grinning broadly. Mwĩreri wa Mũkiraaĩ started asking him questions as if Mwaũra were giving evidence in a court of law.

Mwĩreri: What is your name?
Mwaũra: Robin Mwaũraandũ. Mwaũra for short.
Mwĩreri: Do you own a *matatũ*?
Mwaũra: Yes, I'm owner and driver. Matatũ Matata Matamu, Model T Ford, registration number MMM 333. Motto: If you want to hear rumours, enter Matatũ Matata Matamu. If you want gossip . . . .
Mwĩreri: Can you recall last night?
Mwaũra: Yes.
Mwĩreri: Tell this gathering of modern thieves and robbers what happened.
Mwaũra: It was about six o'clock. I found you outside *Sigona Golf Club*, near Kikuyu, just before Njoguinĩ, standing at the bus stop. I had four other passengers from Nairobi.
Mwĩreri: Did I tell you anything about a car?
Mwaũra: Yes. You told me that your *Peugeot 504 (with petrol injection)* had stalled at Kikuyu, that you had left it outside the *Ondiri Hotel*, and that therefore you were looking for a *lift* because you did not want to be late for this competition.

Another man jumped up and told the chairman that they had not come to settle a lawsuit.

'Let Mwĩreri continue with the tale of his theft and robbery. Come to think of it, his face is beginning to assume the shape of a *Peugeot*

163

504 (with petrol injection), and I doubt that it could acquire that shape if he did not own such a car.' He sat down.

Mwĩreri wa Mũkiraaĩ was very pleased with the man's words. 'That's all, Mwaũra. The elders are now satisfied,' he told Mwaũra. 'You can now resume your seat. Mwaũra, you can now sit down.'

But Robin Mwaũra remained standing. Everybody turned towards him.

'*Mr Chairman*, our foreign guests and elders,' Mwaũra began, 'I beg to be allowed to say a word. I too would like to enter the competition, for, as was once said, men meet in battle to test one another's mettle in order to resolve all doubts about who is who. But before I begin my story – I started stealing and robbing long before the Emergency – I would like to reveal a small matter that could be the ruin of this feast. At about two o'clock, I looked for Mwĩreri wa Mũkiraaĩ to tell him that two of the people to whom he gave invitation cards, a worker and a peasant, are planning to spoil this competition. The two are utterly without gratitude, seeing that they were given those invitation cards by Mwĩreri wa Mũkiraaĩ. The brain behind the whole thing — '

Several people stood up to speak, but the man who managed to shout down the others took the floor. He said that they had not come to the cave to listen to stories about workers and peasants. Mwaũra should be told to keep his rumours and gossip to himself and to let the feast proceed. The sun never waited for anybody, not even a king.

Mwaũra sat down, his face dark, his heart heavy. Mũturi is after me, and now I have missed the chance to harm him, Mwaũra said to himself. He had thought that once he had given away Wangarĩ's and Mũturi's secret, he would be accorded an opportunity to testify and perhaps to earn the crown. Despite his humiliation, Mwaũra did not lose heart. He bolstered his spirits with three proverbs: to a beggar, a rich man's fart has no smell; he who loves beauty does not complain while he is pursuing it; he whose stomach is upset is the one who goes to the forest.

The other guests were waiting patiently to hear Mwĩreri's testimony. His face was now less anxious and the beads of sweat on his forehead had dried.

The following is the testimony given by Mwĩreri wa Mũkĩraaĩ B.Sc., B. Comm., MA, MRSocIBM.

'I'll pick up the tale where I left off. We shouldn't mind too much how many cars a man owns. What's important is the make of a car. We know a bee does not begin with the honeycomb. A bedbug grows fat even when it is living in a crack in a piece of wood. We should

164

only worry about a man's beliefs and about where he stands – *yaani*, his stand – in relation to the development and exploitation of the wealth of a nation.

'I don't have much to say. I believe in the god of modern theft and in the lord of modern robbery. I say this because my education has shown me that all the nations and countries that have made progress and have contributed to modern *civilization* have passed through the stage of exploitation. Among such nations, power has been taken away from the workers and peasants and given to the heroes of theft and robbery – in English, we might say, to those who have *capitalist business know-how*.

'Our modern heroes are those who know about *creative invest-ment, yaani*, those who know how to market their talents so that they'll bear fruit. This simply means those who are experts at sniffing out that rare delicacy called profit, *yaani, the rate of profit*. That in turn means this: if you steal five shillings today, tomorrow you must steal more than five – say, ten shillings; and the day after tomorrow you must steal more than ten – say, fifteen shillings. You must steal more, rob more all the time: five shillings today, ten tomorrow, fifteen the day after, twenty-five two days after that, and so on, until you find that the rate of profit is growing at a tremendous speed day by day, like a progressive graph to paradise. The profit curve should go up and up all the time. In English we say that *you look for conditions that will ensure an ever-increasing rate of profit*. So you have to be knowledgeable about fertile fields, fields that will ensure that the rate of profit does not fall below the level of yesterday and will not remain static. And where but in the sweat of workers and peasants can you find such fertile fields?

'But, friends, modern theft is of two kinds. There is the kind of theft that is a domestic or, let's say, a national affair. In this case, expert thieves and robbers of a given country steal from the workers and peasants of their own country. But there is another kind of theft that involves foreigners. In this case, the thieves and robbers of one country go to another country and steal from the masses there and take the loot back to their own country. This means that such thieves and robbers steal both from their own workers and peasants and from the workers and peasants of other countries. Such foreigners are able to feed on two worlds: theirs and other people's. Today, for instance, American, European and Japanese thieves and robbers steal from their own masses, and then go on to Africa, Asia and Latin America to rob the peoples there, and take their plunder back to their own granaries. These foreigners are, of course, aided in their enterprise by bands of local thieves and robbers.

165

'Sometimes these foreign thieves and robbers build stores and granaries in the countries they loot, and they employ a few of the thieves there to look after them. What all that means is this: when foreigners such as the ones we have here come to our land and build stores and granaries, their plan is simply to rob our country and take the spoils back to Japan, Europe and America.

'I, Mwĩreri wa Mũkiraaĩ, believe only in the first kind of theft and robbery: that is, the theft and robbery of nationals of a given country, who steal from their own people and consume the plunder right there, in the country itself. But to the second kind – the theft of foreign thieves and robbers who come to our country and build lairs here, helped by some of us – I say no, *hapana, a thousand times, no*!

'We, the national experts in theft and robbery, should not join hands with foreigners to help them to seize our national wealth and carry it back to their own countries, leaving us only a few crumbs, the price of the heritage they have taken from us.

'Let's not be their spies, their watchdogs, their disciples, their soldiers, the overseers of their lairs and stores in our own land. Let them leave us alone to exploit our own national fields.

'Why do I say that?

'I'll speak very frankly, come what may. These people are hypocrites, though you might not believe that as you watch them now, peacefully smoking their cigarettes and pipes.

'I, Mwĩreri wa Mũkiraaĩ, have studied thoroughly the system based on the theft of the sweat and blood of workers and peasants – what in English we call *capitalism*. The system is this: the masses cultivate; a select few (those with talents) harvest. Five rich men grow roots in the flesh of fifty workers and peasants. I've got the learning, and I don't need anybody to teach me more about it. I believe that we who are here today are capable of building our own lairs and stores in which to stack the products of the sweat of our masses. I am very sure that we, the Kenyan thieves and robbers, can stand on our own feet and end forever this habit of sharing our loot with foreigners. Let me repeat myself, for a word hidden in the heart can never win a lawsuit: we should not rob our workers and peasants – I should really call them our slaves – and then hand over the spoils to foreigners to do the sharing out, returning a little to us and exporting the rest to their own countries! Why don't they allow us to steal from their America, their Europe and their Japan so that we can import their loot into our own country? Why don't they allow us to build lairs and stores in their countries so that ours becomes the decisive voice in the distribution of the products of the sweat of their people?

'Let us steal from among ourselves, so that the wealth of the country remains in the country, and so that in the flesh of ten million poor we can plant the roots of ten national millionaires. We shall then be able to blind the masses with the following words: "*Wananchi*, don't complain! When the foreigners were eating, did you ever moan? Did you ever scratch yourselves? Our people, the plague that is stalking the country is not as alien as the one in Europe. You should be rejoicing at the fact that your sweat and blood has produced ten native millionaires."

'I'm a man of few words. You can tell the food that will cook well from the first lot of boiling water. My story is short. It concerns my struggles against companies owned by foreign thieves and robbers.

'After finishing school, I started working for various imperialist companies. There are very few foreign-owned companies in which I haven't set a foot as an employee – oil companies, pharmaceutical companies, coffee- and tea-processing companies, finance houses, tourist hotels, motor companies and several agricultural firms. In some I was a *sales manager*. In others I was a personnel *manager*. Generally, however, I was employed as a *public relations manager*.

'But in none of these firms was I ever allowed into the secrets of the inner circle – you know, where the real decisions are made, where the decisions about money and the distribution of profits are made, for instance. Membership of the inner circle was reserved for Europeans.

'But whenever there was a crisis in the country – when the workers became restive and impossible, or Parliament was debating income tax measures that might curb the constant rise in the rate of profit, or the Cabinet was about to agree on certain measures concerning foreigners – I was the one who was dispatched to act as the eyes and ears of the foreigners. In some places I would appeal to national chauvinism to put out the dangerous fire; in others I would smooth away wrinkles in the skin with modern oils; and in yet others I would change the minds of those in power with a bit of hard liquor. And so on and so forth. But on many occasions I would buy a good public image for the foreigners through Haraambe contributions.

'One day I stopped to ask myself: Are these foreigners employing me as an individual, or are they employing the colour of my skin? Are they buying my abilities or my blackness? And all at once I realized that I was being used as window-dressing. If our people looked out for foreigners, they would see me at the window of the enterprise; and on seeing me, they would think they saw a bit of themselves reflected in me, and they would think they had a share in the enterprise, and so they would continue to acquiesce in the foreigners' theft, in the belief that they were becoming wealthy bit by bit.

'I took counsel with myself. The wealth of a nation is produced by the workers of that country. For it is true that without the hand and the head and the heart of a worker there is no wealth. What do foreigners bring into the country? A bit of machinery and a bit of money to pay the workers' first month's salary. That is the kind of lure that is thrown to a monkey to fool it into allowing itself to be robbed of the young it is holding. The machinery is a kind of a trap, and the salary is the piece of meat that is used to trap a mouse. Or the machinery is the fishing line, and the salary is the worm used as bait to attract fish. The machinery is a machine for milking the sweat, blood, energy and skills of a worker, and the banks are the vessels – the calabashes, tins, drums – in which the milk is stored.

'So I asked myself: Mwĩreri wa Mũkiraaĩ, how can you allow the imperialists to milk their country and yours? Don't we have people of our own who can milk the masses, soothing the workers with a little fodder as they are being milked? Are foreigners the only ones with skill at milking? Are they the only people who know how to eat what has been produced by others? Can't you, Mwĩreri wa Mũkiraaĩ, step forward to exploit your own people's sweat, use it to produce things and then sell the things back to the owners of the sweat, so that they produce them first and then have to buy them, grow crops and then buy the same crops? We don't want eaters of what has been produced by others to come from foreign countries: we can encourage the growth of a class of eaters of other people's products – yes, a class of man-eaters – in our own land.

'With all my heart I shouted at the foreigners: Now we shall see who is who, you fucking bastards! I'll show you that even here we have men who have been initiated into the modern art of stealing and robbing the workers! You foreigners will have to go back home and rape your own mothers, and leave me to toy with my mother's thighs!

'I refused to take any more jobs. But because of the weakness of my position, I had to go to the foreign-owned banks to negotiate a loan – oh, yes – so that I could buy fodder for the workers and still be left with enough to buy the machine for milking their sweat.

'I set up a factory for manufacturing cooking oil from wild spinach. Ah, listen to me in silence. That was the beginning of all my woes: but it was also the beginning of my knowledge of the way the world works. Now, when I went out to sell the oil, I found the market completely flooded with cooking oil imported by foreign-owned companies. And to add insult to injury, they cut the price of their oil. I saw quite clearly that I, Mwĩreri wa Mũkiraaĩ, was on the verge of bankruptcy. I sold the factory and all the machinery. It was bought by foreigners.

'Then I started a factory for manufacturing skin-lightening creams. My reasoning was this: if foreigners are growing fat by wrecking the skins of black people, why can't I do likewise? The story was the same as before. I found that creams to destroy black people's skins had been poured on to the market at throw-away prices. I saw ruin stare me in the face. Again I sold out to foreigners.

'And yet I set up another factory, this time for manufacturing rubber condoms – you know what I mean, sheaths for men to wear when they don't want a girl to become pregnant. In this case, our own customs got in the way. Our men don't like covering their things with those rubber contraptions. They like feeling flesh against flesh. As for the Europeans and Asians, they preferred imported ones, ones manufactured abroad by companies in their own countries.

'This enterprise too was devoured by foreigners.

'So, as I stand here, I can promise you that I tried to make a success of many different types of manufacturing. But no matter what I attempted, I would find that the foreign manufacturing firms and their local allies had ganged up against me. If I sold my product at five shillings, they would sell theirs at three shillings, and of course all the buyers would flock to buy their goods. Sometimes the foreigners would ensure that certain types of machinery were not sold to me. At other times they would sell me outdated machinery, and even then the machines would take years to arrive in this country. Sometimes I couldn't get spare parts, or they would be delayed, or they would suddenly vanish in transit and my factory would grind to a halt.

'It was this that made me realize that foreigners are not ready to relinquish their hold on our manufacturing industries – fed, of course, by the sweat of our workers. For a worker's sweat is the source of all profit. I thought that I ought to give up manufacturing for a while. But that was only a temporary setback. To slip is not to fall.

'I went back into the service of foreigners. I started up a wholesale business – well, a business to sell things manufactured by foreigners. It is not a bad business. For when a man transfers something from here to there and adds nothing in the process, not a single drop of his own sweat, he's able to enjoy a few goodies. Today I am a wholesaler and *importer* of fabrics, hard liquor, shoes, secondhand clothes and pills to prevent the poor from producing babies like rats and rabbits.

'Today I, son of Mũkiraaĩ, am still in the service of the foreign owners of industries. The foreigners still monopolize the whole field of the theft of the sweat of our workers. But I have never abandoned my ambition to drive them out of the arena.

'Therefore, *Mr Chairman*, when I got an invitation to this gathering and a letter asking me to spread the news of this great competition to judge thieves and their plans for increasing theft and robbery in this land, I was delirious with joy.

'Now, listen carefully. I am going to tell you a secret. All these years I, Mwĩreri wa Mũkiraaĩ, have kept this very important secret to myself. It's a secret that could allow us to soar above Japanese, American, British, French, German, Italian and Danish thieves, *the whole of the capitalist Western world*, in the art of theft and robbery. It is a secret the mastery of which could break the chains that have bound us to foreigners. Now I'm going to share the secret with you because if my plan is to work effectively, it will require complete unity among those of us who seek to build *true native capitalism*, free from *foreign ideologies*.

'The secret is this. Our country has iron ore. Our country has workers in metal. The skills needed to smelt iron ore and turn it into pig iron has been with us for generations. Before imperialism these were the very skills that were marshalled to make spears, swords, hoes and different types of ring. But this knowledge did not spread for two reasons. The guild of metal workers tended to keep their knowledge to themselves, for in those days the small class of people who know the delicious taste of the sweat and blood of workers gathered into factories had not yet emerged. When the foreigners came here, they deliberately suppressed this native knowledge of metal working to make us buy things made abroad and thus help the growth of their industries.

'So today I say this. Let us unite, big and small, to develop our own machine tools, because the sweat and the blood of our own people is in cheap and endless supply.

'Don't be deceived by anybody into thinking that we have no iron ore. There is no natural resource that is not available in this country, oil included. But even if we had no large supply of iron ore, we could still develop what in English has been called *maintenance technology*, *yaani*, the knowledge of turning used iron into usable smelted iron. What do you think has permitted Japan to survive as an industrial power?

'The sweat of our workers would enable us to manufacture machine tools to make pins, razor blades, scissors, matchets, hoes, axes, basins, water containers, tins and corrugated iron sheets, motor vehicles, tractors, steam and diesel engines, ships, aeroplanes, spears, swords, guns, bombs, missiles, missile-launching rockets or rockets for launching people into space – in short, to make for ourselves all the goods that are now made by foreigners. Then we would see if we too could not benefit from modern science and technology.

'Think about it, good people: *Kenya's own millionaires, billionaires, multi-millionaires, multi-billionares, Kenya's own industrial capitalists, like Japan's . . .* and all through iron ore or maintenance technology washed clean by the sweat and blood of the workers; What more could you want?

'National robbers, national thieves, I have shown you the way. Now let every thief among us take home his talents and use them on his own mother.

'Who gets the crown of glory then? Mwĩreri wa Mũkiraaĩ! For he has offered us words of wisdom, both natural and learned. I didn't go to school for nothing. I want to end with the following battle cry: every robber should go home and rob his own mother! That's true democracy *and equality of nations! Per omnia saecula saeculorum. Amen.*'

Chapter Seven

1

A dream. It was surely a dream in broad daylight. Gatuĩria pinched his thigh to see if he could feel pain to prove that it was not all a dream. The pinch hurt. No, it was not a dream. But even so, Gatuĩria could not quite believe that what he was seeing with his own eyes was really there. A man may well dream he is pinching himself and that he is feeling pain. Or he may dream that he is dying, and he may even see himself being buried and actually going to Heaven or to Hell.

Gatuĩria looked over at Warĩĩnga. He stretched out his hand, and took Warĩĩnga's fingers, and pressed them gently, and he felt that Warĩĩnga was really there, in the flesh. Then Gatuĩria believed that he was awake and that the cave was not the illusion of a malaria-ridden patient.

Even today, Gatuĩria still remembers with a shudder the chaos that erupted in the cave following the testimony of Mwĩreri wa Mũkiraaĩ. It's true that some of the guests did clap him, but the majority gnashed their teeth and shouted and roared with rage. Women too. A small group ululated for him, but the vast majority cried out in protest.

2

The leader of the foreign delegation, the one who carried the sign of the USA on his crown, was the first to speak out. The noise and the chaos subsided as the people strained to catch every word.

'*Mr Chairman*, speaking on my own behalf and on behalf of the other foreign experts, I wish to express my horror at the abuse and insults that have been hurled at us by Mwĩreri wa Mũkiraaĩ. We did not come here for insults and abuse. No, we came here to find ways of strengthening the partnership between American, European, and Japanese thieves and robbers and the thieves and robbers from the developing world, that is from those countries that have been given their own flags very recently. We who come from the developed world have had many years' experience of modern theft and robbery. I might also remind you that we are the owners of the houses and stores and granaries that contain all the money that has ever been snatched from the peoples of the world. You can see for yourselves that even our suits are made of bank notes. Today money is the ruler of all industry and commerce. Money is the *field marshal* of all the forces of theft and robbery on Earth. *Money is supreme. Money rules the world.* We came here to see if we could acquaint a few of you with our secrets so that you could become the eyes and ears of the international community of thieves and robbers here in your country. But we did not know that we were coming to listen to the speeches of the politically naive, the speeches of thieves and robbers who dream of walking before they have even learned to crawl, the speeches of thieves and robbers who are envious of plunder that has already been stolen and stored by those who have been at the game for a long time. In coming here we thought that we were visiting people who understood that all the thieves and robbers of the world belong to the same age-group, the same family, the same nationality, and that they share the same ideology. We believe in *freedom*, the freedom that allows one to rob and to steal according to one's abilities. That's what we call *personal initiative and individual enterprise*. And that's why we have always stated that we belong to the *Free World*, a world where there are absolutely no barriers to stealing from others. Why, then, does Mwĩreri wa Mũkiraaĩ want to cause divisions among us? What makes him say that there are two kinds of theft? Theft is theft. And why does he say that you should build your own missiles and bombs and rockets? Don't you believe that we are capable of guarding and protecting your theft and ours, as we have always done in South Korea, Brazil, Israel and South Africa? We are eating and drinking from the same table and yet you have no faith in us. Now, because of the abusive language and the insults we have had to endure at the hands of Mwĩreri wa Mũkiraaĩ. we have decided that we shall not wait until the end of the feast. We are leaving now, and we are going to take with us all the gifts we brought with us and leave you Kenyans to scramble for the iron ore Mwĩreri was so enthusiastic about.'

The leader of the foreign delegation sat down.

3

The atmosphere in the cave grew cold. Many of the robbers felt their impending loss in their bones. They all turned bitter eyes towards Mwĩreri wa Mũkiraaĩ.

The master of ceremonies was the one who saved the day again.

173

He mounted the platform and spoke with a heart full of repentance, begging the foreigners not to take any notice of what had just been said because there was not a single thief or robber in the whole cave who was not searching for ways and means of improving his relationship with such *important* guests, to the greater glory of the system of theft and robbery on Earth. Mwīreri wa Mūkiraaī's call to the thieves and robbers of every country to be self-reliant and to stand aloof in a corner, patting their stomachs alone, was just adolescent talk.

The master of ceremonies then swore by all the gods that there was not a single local thief or robber present who supported the ideas of Mwīreri wa Mūkiraaī. He reminded the foreign guests about the parable with which he himself had opened the proceedings that very morning.... *The flag of Independence can be likened unto a man travelling unto a far country, who called his own servants, and delivered unto them his goods* ....

The master of ceremonies paused in the middle of the parable, and he turned towards the foreign thieves, and, smiling ingratiatingly with his golden teeth, he declared: 'Distinguished guests, we are your slaves. You have come back to see what we have done with the talents you bequeathed to us in grateful recognition of the services we rendered you in suppressing those of our people who used to call themselves freedom fighters. That is good. I would like to remind you that even today we have continued to hoodwink our people into believing that you did actually leave the country. That's why we don't call you foreigners, or imperialists, or white robbers. We call you our friends. Therefore I beseech you, please resume your seats and be patient, so that you can hear the stories of all the other man-eaters. Don't worry about Mwīreri wa Mūkiraaī. We shall take care of him. His fate will be decided here today. I hope that this apology is adequate. What remains is the apology of actions.'

He sat down. The leader of the foreign delegation of thieves and robbers accepted his apology and said that they were content to wait for the apology of actions. He said: *Justice must not only be done, but must also be seen to be done. Asante.*

The thunderous applause that broke out in the cave almost brought down the ceiling and the four walls.

Gatuīria held Warīīnga's hand. He still felt as if he were in a dream. Warīīnga squeezed his hand. They sat in silence, both engrossed in their own thoughts, but each feeling that were he or she to let go of the other's hand, they would both drown in the darkness of the cave.

Gatuīria was not able to pursue his ideas to their logical conclusion. An idea would come into his head and dance about there for a while, then it would be driven out by a new thought. And the new thought would leap about for a time before it too was driven out by another. His relentless desire for a suitable theme for his music seemed to have evaporated. What worried him most now were thoughts about Warīīnga's past troubles. But as he turned over Warīīnga's story in his mind, the knowledge that Wangarī had gone to fetch the police and Mūturi the workers intruded and bothered him. What would happen when all the forces met in the cave? The noise and the chaos generated by the testimony of Mwīreri wa Mūkiraaī also troubled him. *And he didn't even condemn the system of theft and robbery. All he said was that each thief should steal from those in his own country. Suppose, then, a man like Mūturi should come here and reject the whole system of theft and robbery?*

And suddenly Gatuīria felt like telling Warīīnga that they should flee, for his mind's eye was seeing images that made him tremble. And at the centre of these images was Mwaūra.

Gatuīria thought he saw Mwaūra look at him with eyes full of ravenous greed. Then he saw that it was not Mwaūra alone who looked at him in that manner. All the people around him wore the same expression. Whenever one of the thieves yawned, Gatuīria thought he saw his teeth transformed into blood-soaked fangs that were turned towards where he and Warīīnga sat. He heard a voice whisper to him: These are the eaters of human flesh; these are the drinkers of human blood; these are the modern Nding'ūri's; take this girl and flee this place.

But another part of him urged him not to flee, to wait until the very end so that in future they would not have to listen to yarns about how the feast had ended. For if Gatuīria had been told that there were still professional murderers and eaters of human flesh in the world, he would not have believed it. So the old man from Bahati, Nakuru, had really been telling him stories of modern-day ogres?

Gatuĩria shook his head to stop himself from pursuing this line of thought. He stared hard at the platform to prevent himself from looking at the terrifying pictures he saw on the faces of the people around him.

He started thinking about Mwĩreri wa Mũkiraaĩ, comparing his testimony with the story he had told them the evening before about the man who was going to a far country and left five talents, two talents and one talent to his servants, and who, after he had stayed away for some time, returned and called his servants to him....

And the one who had received ... talents came and testified....

The Testimony of Nditika wa Ngũũnji

Nditika wa Ngũũnji was very fat. His head was huge, like a mountain. His belly hung over his belt, big and arrogant. His eyes were the size of two large red electric bulbs, and it looked as if they had been placed on his face by a Creator impatient to get on with another job. His hair was parted in the middle, so that the hair on either side of the parting looked like two ridges facing each other on either side of a tarmac road. He had on a black suit. The jacket had tails cut in the shape of the wings of the big green and blue flies that are normally found in pit latrines or among rotting rubbish. His shirt had frills all down the front. He was wearing a black bow tie. His eyes rolled in time to his words. His hands rested on his stomach and he patted it gently, as if beseeching it not to stick out towards the people with such arrogance.

'I don't have much to say. I am not going to get excited counting degrees that can find no better transport than a *matatũ*. We shall leave insulting foreigners to the wretched who have nothing to boast about in front of well fed eaters except their hatred of foreigners.

'I am called Ngũũnji wa Nditika – sorry, Nditika wa Ngũũnji. As for my wife, I have only one. My girlfriends? I belong to them, ears, horns and all. I suffer from two diseases: I can never get enough of that or of food. Good food makes for a fine, healthy body, and the smooth thighs of young girls make for a fine, healthy soul.

'As for cars, I have several, from *Mercedes Benzes* to *Range Rovers*, from *Volvos* to *Peugeots 604*. When I go out hunting young girls, I take my *BMW* (which stands for *Be My Woman*), and it's quite true that if a young woman gets into your *BMW*, she can never say no! My wife's shopping basket is a *Fiat 1600*. But the other day she complained bitterly that a woman with a wicker basket also needs a small sisal basket, so I bought her a *Mazda*.

'My children ride horses. They learned to ride at *The Nairobi*

High-Class Riding School, previously owned by Grogan and Delamere. Before Independence, no black man was allowed anywhere near the school compound. You people, to think that some blockheads have the audacity to roam from hotel to hotel saying, "Not yet Uhuru"! What other Uhuru do people want? As for me, I am delighted whenever I meet my children on the road or near my home, and I'm driving this car or that, and they're riding their horses, and they wave at me, and stick out their tongues, and call out, "Daddy! Daddy!", just like European children! Uhuruuu!

'All these joys have grown out of modern theft and robbery. Today, for instance, I own several farms in Njoro, Elburgon and Kitale. I pay my workers seventy-five shillings a month, plus a daily ration of flour and a weekly bottle of separated milk. Ha! ha! ha! Do you know what? One day they went on strike, demanding higher wages! I tell you, they all ended up seeing through their mouths instead of their eyes. I dismissed them all on the spot, *without notice*, and I went into the villages and engaged new hands then and there. Ha! ha! ha! You know, those villages are our granaries for *reserve labour*! Ha! ha! ha! Why am I laughing so much? Excuse me, let me wipe away these tears of laughter. You'll laugh too when I tell you that most of the labourers who dig up the grass on my farms are the very people who once took up blunt swords and home-made guns, claiming they were fighting for freedom! And you know, even in those days I never hid anything from them, and I used to tell them my mind: "We are lording it over you during the Emergency, and when freedom comes, we shall continue to lord it over you!" And they used to retort, scornfully: "You stop that nonsense! You deserve a bullet through the heart." Today I look at some of them when they come to my office for their wages, with their hats off and their hands behind them in deference, and when I recall their taunts, I could die laughing. Ha! ha! ha!

'But all that's history now. We all fought for freedom in different ways, for different sides. What's wrong with the way things are? Let's all forget the past. All that business of fighting for freedom was just a bad dream, a meaningless nightmare. Let's join hands to do three things: to grab, to extort money and to confiscate. The Holy Trinity of theft: Grabbing, Extortion, and Confiscation. If you find anything belonging to the masses, don't leave it behind, for if you don't look after yourself, who'll look after you?

'My success at stealing and robbing has been restricted to the field of smuggling and the black market. Let me explain briefly. I have many sources of expensive stones – pearl, gold, tanzanite – rare animal skins like those of leopards and lions, elephant tusks and rhino teeth, snake poison and many other things, all from the public mines and the game reserves. I export them. I get particularly big orders from Japan, Germany and Hong Kong, orders that reward my effort very nicely. I've certainly got no complaints. These deals are only possible because of my partnership with foreigners, who own big hotels and other tourist enterprises. They are experts at handling the *Customs*, the shipping lines and the airfreight companies; they also have good contacts with receivers overseas. You know, our people don't imagine that the whites engage in smuggling or play the black market, but I know better, and I have established a lucrative relationship with them. That is why when I see somebody standing here arrogantly demanding that white foreigners should leave our country, I feel like .... Oh, I'm going to leave *matatū* university degrees out of this!

'The other commodities that I smuggle overseas and to neighbouring countries are salt, sugar, maize, wheat, rice, coffee and tea. Personally speaking, Amin's departure was a loss. During his rule Uganda coffee brought me in more than 50 million shillings. I also export beef to Arabia and to Europe. I have a special ship at Mombasa, which is always on stand-by.

'But I've got many other *shughulis* that bring me in money. Sometimes I buy food at harvest time. Ah, but do I buy or do I pick it up off the ground? When famine spreads throughout the land, I sell the food back to the very people who grew it. But is that really selling, or is the word extortion? Gĩtutu wa Gataangũrũ spoke the truth: mass famine is jewellery for the wealthy!

'Sometimes, when I know Budget Day is near, I try as hard as I can to buy information about the goods that will go up in price from those close to the secret, be they clerks or whoever. I then buy and hoard large quantities of these goods. When the new prices are announced, I flood the market with my goods. Sometimes I buy them in a store and sell them in the same store the following day – for a profit.

'What's wrong with this method of accumulating wealth is that you can never be absolutely *sure*. I remember one year a clerk told me that the prices for both ground and unground pepper would go up. I bought enough of both types of pepper to supply the whole country for over a year. People, I saw through eyes that watered. Instead of the price going up, it went down. I had to burn all the pepper. Today I never want to see or smell any kind of pepper again.

'Now, all these activities really opened my eyes, and I learned certain truths. Book learning is not as important as Mwĩreri wa

178

Mũkiraaĩ was trying to make out. Education is not property. Take me, for instance. I did not complete primary school, and here I am, employing arts graduates as my clerks. And their degrees are the old-style, reliable BAs, not like the ones awarded at Nairobi these days by fellows who think they are highly educated just because they have dropped their precious foreign names and call themselves wa, Ole, Arap, or Wuodh *this or that*. My girlfriends are all of university or Cambridge standard! So Mwĩreri wa Mũkiraaĩ should forget all this hullabaloo about degrees and education. I challenge him to take his degrees to the market for girls (including the market for those European and Asian girls he was bragging about), and I'll take my *BMW (Be My Woman)*, and we'll see which of us ends up screwing most girls.

'I would even say that too much education can be a form of foolishness. For instance, what was Mwĩreri wa Mũkiraaĩ telling us just now? That we should spend all our time on rubbish heaps and in scrap yards, collecting old tins to build *matatũs*? That we should be self-reliant in modern theft and robbery? And where are we going to acquire *international* experience in the art of stealing? From the rubbish heaps and scrap yards of *maintenance technology*? Mwĩreri, *you must be joking!*

'I can only repeat what has already been said by others: that what's profitable to us is our partnership with foreigners. Let's strengthen it. Now, despite the fact that I don't have any *matatũ* degrees, I recently had a brilliant idea that could improve the quality of all our propertied lives. But the idea cannot be realized unless foreigners are involved, for it is they who have the *knowledge* of *modern technology*. That's why I wholly agree with those who are always telling the whites to hurry up with the *transfer* of their *technology* or to sell us *appropriate technology* of our own.

'I would now like to share my brilliant idea with you, so that you'll see I'm the only man fit to wear the crown of slavery!

'The idea suddenly came to me one night, as I lay asleep. My heart leaped with joy, and I felt that the secret of a new life for us propertied people had been revealed to me.

'It was during the visit of *Professor* Barnard – you know, our Boer friend from South Africa – when he spoke about transplants in the *human body*. I was present when he talked to the doctors at *Kenyatta Hospital*. It was then that I was seized again by a worry that has always plagued me.

'Whenever I, Nditika wa Ngũũnji, contemplate my extraordinary wealth, I ask myself sadly several searching questions. With all my property, what do I have, as a human being, that a worker, or a

179

peasant, or a poor man does not have? I have one mouth, just like the poor; I have one belly, just like the poor; I have one heart, just like the very poor; and I have one ... er, you know what I mean, just one like the poorest of men.

'I have enough money and property to supply food for a thousand people, but I am satisfied with one plateful, just like other people. I have enough money to wear a hundred suits at a time, but I can only put on one pair of trousers, one shirt, one jacket, just like other people. I have enough money to buy fifty lives if lives were sold in the market, but I have only one heart and one life, just like other people. I have enough property and money to enable me to make love to ten girls every night, but one girl exhausts me after only one go, and I end up falling asleep without being completely satisfied.

'So, seeing that I have only one mouth, one belly, one heart, one life and one cock, what's the difference between the rich and the poor? What's the point of robbing others?

'It was revealed to me that night that in this country we should have a factory for manufacturing human parts like mouths, bellies, hearts and so on, spare parts for the human body. This would mean that a rich man who could afford them could have two or three mouths, two bellies, two cocks and two hearts. If the first mouth became tired of chewing, and his belly could hold no more, then the spare mouth and belly could take over. When an old man like me had a sugargirl, instead of falling asleep soon after the first engine had stalled, he would simply start up the other engine and continue with the job in hand, the two engines supporting each another all night long, so that on waking up in the morning he would feel that his heart and body were completely relaxed. We could coin some new sayings: a rich man's youth never ends. When a man possesses two hearts, he virtually possesses two lives. This would mean that a really rich man would never die. There's another possible proverb: a rich man never dies. We could purchase immortality with our money and leave death as the prerogative of the poor.

'I was delighted with that idea. But I made a mistake in telling my wife about it. Too much haste can split the yam. Women have no secrets.

'At first my wife was very pleased with the idea, and she hugged me, and praised me in English ("*my clever little darling*"), and showered me with kisses. She said that if the idea ever bore fruit, it would be wonderful, for it would be possible to distinguish the wife of a man of property from the wives of the poor. These days all women, be they rich or poor, look alike, thanks to the *mass production* of clothes. But after the factory was built, the wives of

180

the rich would be distinguished from those of the poor by their two mouths, two bellies, two or more hearts and . . . two or more female things.

'When I heard her mention two female organs and say that she would be able to have two instead of one, I was horrified. I told her quite frankly that I would not mind her having two mouths, or two bellies, or multiples of any other organ of the body. But to have two . . . no, no! *I told her to forget all that nonsense.* Then she started arguing, and said that if that was to be the case, then I wasn't going to be allowed two cocks. I asked her bitterly: "Why do you want to have two? Tell me: what would you use two for?" She retorted: "Why do you want two? What would you use two for? If you have two, then I must have two. *We must have equality of the sexes.*"

'By this time, I was really very angry! I told her to take her *equalities* to Europe or America. *Here we are Africans*, and we must *practise African culture.* I struck her a blow on the face. She started crying. I struck her again. But just as I was about to strike her a third time, she surrendered. She said I could have three, or ten. She would be satisfied with just one.

'People, think about that vision! Every rich man could have two mouths, two bellies, two cocks, two hearts – and hence two lives! Our money would buy us immortality! We would leave death to the poor! Ha! ha! ha!

'Bring me the crown. At long last, it has found its rightful owner!'

Chapter Eight

1

Waríínga could not bear the scene in the cave any longer. The talk sat heavy on her mind, like a log of wood. The breath of the speakers smelled worse than the fart of a badger or of someone who has gorged himself on rotten beans or over-ripe bananas. Nausea swept over her. She excused herself to Gatuíria and lied that she was going out to answer the call of nature. But what she wanted most was a breath of clean, fresh air.

Waríínga went around to the back of the cave. She walked across a grass court and slipped through a hedge of roses. Then, on the other side of the hedge, she strolled towards a small bush that marked the beginning of the golf course. Waríínga sat on the grass and leaned against a black wattle tree, breathing a long sigh, as if the load were being lifted from her heart. But the pain remained.

She regretted having gone back to the cave for the afternoon session. The speeches, the thieves' attire, their hymns of self-praise, all these things reminded her of the problems she had faced since she became pregnant by the Rich Old Man from Ngorika and gave birth to a baby girl.

Ah, Wambũi . . . .

By that time, Waríínga's parents had emigrated from Kaambũrũ, established a home in Ilmorog and had more children. The burden of looking after Wambũi still fell on Waríínga's parents. But they had never beaten Waríínga or even criticized her for getting pregnant before marriage or for trying to throw herself in front of a train. On the contrary, they were very hurt by her attempted suicide, and they looked at Waríínga with inifite pity in their eyes. Waríínga was always to remember her mother's words to her: 'Our forefathers said that only a fool sucks at the breasts of his dead mother. Waríínga, do you know how many women yearn for a child of their own without ever having one? A baby is a special gift to a man and woman – even an unmarried woman. To have a child is not a curse, and you must never again think of taking your life because of it.'

After giving birth to Wambũi, Waríínga continued to burden her parents with requests for money to pay for a correspondence course at the university. She studied at home for a year. She sat her School Certificate exams, but when the results came out, she had only managed to scrape into the fourth division. It was then that she took the secretarial course in Nairobi, after which, having roamed the city streets in search of work, she got the job with the *Champion Construction Company* from which she was dismissed after rejecting the advances of *Boss* Kīhara.

Leaning against the black wattle tree on the Golf course, Warīīnga went over the details of all that had happened to her since her dismissal: John Kīmwana . . . her landlord . . . the *Devil's Angels* . . . her aimless wanderings through Nairobi . . . the loss of her handbag . . . the Kaka Hotel bus stop . . . her crazy longing to throw herself under a city bus . . . her rescue by the stranger.

Where was the stranger now? Why hadn't he come to the feast?

Warīīnga felt as if all those things had happened to somebody else many years ago. But as she realized that not even two days had passed since then, she suddenly felt ill at ease. In her mind's eye, she saw her meeting with Gatuīria, Mūturi, Wangarī and Mwīreri wa Mūkiraaī the night before. She saw them all riding in Mwaūra's *matatū*, telling one another stories, and their meeting at the cave, like people who had known each other all their lives. As she remembered her talk with Gatuīria over lunch, she felt her heart lighten a little: where had she found the courage to tell him all about her affair with the Rich Old Man from Ngorika, an affair which she had never mentioned to anybody outside her family?

The lens in her head showed her the watchman who had rescued her from the wheels of the train. What a coincidence that Mūturi and the watchman were one and the same person! Who was Mūturi? An angel in rags? Could he be the angel who had rescued her from the bus in Nairobi? The one who had given her a fake invitation card?

No! The lens showed her a close-up of the man who had given her the card. She saw the clothes he was wearing, and she recalled his voice and words. Warīīnga said to herself: Even if the man refused to come to the feast, he still did me a good turn by giving me a card so that I could see this wonder for myself and never try to take my own life again on account of this vile class of men who are determined to oppress the whole land!

The lens showed her Njeruca – the shelters with cardboard and polythene walls . . . the drains. Then it showed her contrasting images of the Golden Heights – the nice, spacious houses . . . the clean, fresh air . . . . Then it drew her back inside the cave to show her the faces of the seven foreigners, the greedy expressions of the competitors, and again she asked herself: What will happen when Mūturi and his workers and Wangarī and the police gather at the cave?

Waríínga yawned, stretched her arms and leaned back against the tree, feeling drowsy, as if sleep were stealing upon her. But her mind was executing strange drills, as though it had been given licence to roam wherever it chose and to do whatever it wanted.

Waríínga spoke to herself out loud: '*Local* and *international* thieves gathered in the same lair, debating ways and means of depriving the whole nation of its rights – that's a wonder that has never been seen before! That's like a child planning rob its mother and inviting others to join in the crime! It has certainly been said that there are two worlds . . . .'

Before she could complete the thought, Waríínga heard a voice say: '. . . and there is a third, a revolutionary world.'

2

Waríínga was startled. She looked about her but could see no one. With sleepy eyes she could make out only the green grass of the golf course as it spread out before her, rolling up and down, losing itself in tiny bushes on the horizon. Waríínga was afraid. She tried to stand up, but she felt tied to the ground and to the tree by invisible wires of fatigue. She gave up the attempt. And suddenly she felt herself completely free of fear, and she said to herself: Come what may, I'm going to stop running away from life's struggles. With great courage, she asked the invisible voice: 'Who are you?'

Voice: I am a roaming spirit. I walk about the Earth, planting the tree that grows the fruit of the knowledge that enables him who eats it to tell good from evil.

Waríínga: The Tempter?

Voice: Oh, of course, you used to be a woman of the Church. *The Church of the Holy Rosary* in Nakuru, wasn't it?

Waríínga: So?

Voice: That's how you guessed who I am so quickly,

Waríínga: I don't know you.

Voice: Are you going to deny me, you who have always tried to crucify me on the Cross?

Waríínga: I said I didn't know you. Who are you?

Voice: I told you. I am the roaming spirit who distributes the knowledge that enables men to tell the difference between good and evil. I am also a Tempter and a Judge.

Waríínga: A Tempter and a Judge?

Voice: Yes, of souls.

Waríínga: And what are you doing here? Or are you planning to try the souls of those who are competing in the art of stealing and robbing?

Voice: And you, what are you doing here? He who keeps the company of the corrupt becomes corrupted.

Waríínga: I came here to see a truly amazing sight —

Voice: Is there a difference between a thief and a man who looks on?

Waríínga: Ilmorog is home.

Voice: Why is it home to you?

Waríínga: My father and mother .... Our home .... It's home because my home and family are here.

Voice: Big deeds make for a big mouth, but a big mouth does not make for big deeds ....

Waríínga: What are you trying to say? That Ilmorog is not my home?

Voice: Those who looked on Ilmorog as their home showed their loyalty through their actions. When they saw their home burning, they cried out for help. They went to seek help.

Waríínga: Who are these people?

Voice: Wangari and Mũturi – didn't you know?

Waríínga: I had nowhere to turn.

Voice: Because you are neither hot nor cold. You said just now that there are two worlds.

Waríínga: I was only repeating a saying.

Voice: You don't know which the two worlds are?

Waríínga: The two worlds? No!

Voice: But you claim to be educated.

Waríínga: Just Cambridge, EACE When I was young I used to dream of learning all there was to know in the world. I wanted to climb the mountain of knowledge, the highest mountain on Earth, to climb and climb until I stood on the highest peak, the whole Earth below me. But today my education can't even fill one small stomach for a day.

Voice: Education up to EACE level is still education. What's wrong is the teaching. For today children are taught to shut their eyes and block their ears so they'll never see the needs of the people or hear their cry. He who used to hear has become deaf. The products of such schools are the ones of whom it has been said: Woe unto this generation, for they have eyes and they cannot see, and they have ears and they cannot hear! For they have been taught to see and to hear only one world. What were

185

you saying about two worlds? You mean the world of the robber and the world of the robbed; the worlds of the lords of theft and the victims of theft, of the oppressor and the oppressed, of those who eat what has been produced by others and the producers themselves.

Warĩĩnga: Who are you? You are repeating the things we said last night in Mwaũra's *matatũ*. Aren't those words the very ones that were voiced by Mũturi last night?

Voice: Those two know all about it, for they have been robbed all their lives.

Warĩĩnga: Mũturi, robbed? Of what? He is not one of the rich people of this country.

Voice: What did I tell you just now? That you have ears and you can't hear; you have eyes and you can't see.

Your kind of learning has turned you upside-down. You have come to believe that the *clouds* are the *Earth* and the *Earth* is the *clouds*; that black is white and white is black; that *good* is *evil* and *evil* is *good*.

You ask what has been stolen from Mũturi. Aren't his sweat and blood worth anything? Where did they teach you the wealth of nations comes from? From the clouds? From the hands of the rich?

Those gathered in the cave know the source of the wealth of nations well enough. For they know where they can drink water that they have not gone to fetch. They know where they can dam the water so it does not reach those who are downstream. They know where they can dig canals to divert the river so that it waters only their own fertile fields.

That's why whenever they gather together, they talk openly and frankly. They share the wisdom of 'I eat this, and you eat that.'

You don't believe me? But haven't you been inside the cave? As you and I are talking here, what do you think they are saying in there? Listen, and I'll tell you, for it is said that even the wise can be taught wisdom. Just now, as we are talking, Kĩmeendeeri wa Kanyuanjii is standing on the platform. You should be there to see Kĩmeendeeri wa Kanyuanjii. His mouth is shaped like the beak of the red-billed ox-pecker, the tick bird. His cheeks are as smooth as a new-born baby's. His legs are huge and shapeless, like giant banana stems or the legs of someone who is suffering from elephantiasis. But his disease is simply the grossness that comes from over-eating. His neck is formed from rolls of fat, like the skin of the hairy maggot. But this astonishing body, these legs and neck, have been completely covered by a white suit and a bow tie.

He was given the name of Kīmeendeeri during the Emergency because of the way he used to grind workers and peasants to death. Kīmeendeeri was then a District Officer. He used to make men and women lie flat on the ground in a row, and then he would drive his Land Rover over the bodies. When Independence came, Kīmeendeeri quickly climbed the administrative ladder to become a Permanent Secretary. Then he worked with foreign companies, especially those connected with finance. He now owns countless farms. His import–export businesses are equally numerous. He has dozens of tricks up his sleeve. His skill at theft and robbery is visible from a great distance.

Today it is possible that Kīmeendeeri will be crowned king of modern theft, robbery and service to foreigners.

The ideas that will win him his victory over the other thieves and robbers show quite clearly that Kīmeendeeri understands that the sweat and the blood of the workers are the wellsprings of wealth. Kīmeendeeri is not even attempting to disguise the fact. He is telling the other delegates: 'Our drinking of the blood of the workers, our milking of their sweat, our devouring of their brains – these three activities should be put on a scientific basis.' The scientific plan he will outline is this: Kīmeendeeri wants to set up a research farm – the first stage in a long process – to experiment with his idea. The idea itself is both simple and complex.

Kīmeendeeri intends to fence off the farm with barbed wire, just like the wire that was used to fence off detention camps during the state of Emergency in colonial Kenya. He plans to pen the workers in there like animals. He will then fix electrically operated machines to their bodies for milking their sweat or the energy that produces the sweat, their blood and their brains. The three commodities will then be exported to foreign countries to feed industries there. For every gallon of sweat, or blood, or brains, Kīmeendeeri will get commission at a fixed rate.

Warīīnga: And how will he export the three commodities?
Voice: He'll construct pipelines. The blood will be poured into them and a machine will pump it to the importing foreign countries, just like petroleum oil! The company handling the trade will be called *Kenyo-Saxon Exporters: Human Blood and Flesh*.

Wariinga: But won't the workers refuse to let their bodies be exploited like that? Won't they refuse to be robbed of their lives?

Voice: Why have you never prevented your own body from being exploited? ... *Anyway*, the workers will never know what's being done to them. They'll never see or feel those machines and pipes in their bodies. And if they should ever chance to see them, they won't mind the burden ....

Wariinga: Why?

Voice: Because the Kīmeendeeris of this world are not as foolish as you think they are. Kīmeendeeri will show them only two worlds, that of the eater and that of the eaten. So the workers will never learn of the existence of a third world, the world of the revolutionary overthrow of the system of eating and being eaten. They will always assume that the two worlds of the eater and the eaten are eternal.

Wariinga: How will he manage to fool them like this?

Voice: On the farm he'll build churches or mosques, depending on the religious inclination of the workers. He will employ priests. Every Sunday the workers will be read sermons that will instruct them that the system of milking human sweat, human blood and human brains – the system of the robbery of human labour power and human skills – is ordained by God, and that it has something to do with the eventual salvation of their souls. It is written in the Holy Scriptures: Blessed are they that mourn, for they shall be comforted. Blessed are they that hunger and thirst after righteousness, for they will be filled. Blessed are they that think ill of no man, for they shall see God. Blessed are they that daily observe the four commandments 'Thou shall not kill', 'Thou shall not lie', 'Thou shall not steal', 'Thou shall not covet other people's property', for they shall inherit wealth in Heaven. The main farm song, *the Shamba's anthem*, will run like this:

> Even if you cry and moan
> Because of your sins,
> Unless you carry the Cross,
> You'll never find rest.

Kīmeendeeri will also build schools in which the workers' children will be taught that the system of drinking human blood and eating human flesh has always held sway since the world was created and will always hold sway until the end of the world, and that there is nothing people can do to put an end to the system. The children will be allowed to read only those books that glorify the system of drinking human blood and eating human flesh. They will not be allowed to ask questions about the conditions of their lives or those of their parents, or that might raise doubts about the sanctity and necessity of drinking human blood and eating human flesh. They will sing only those songs and hymns and read only that literature that glorify the system of drinking human blood and eating human flesh.

Kĩmeendeeri will also build a hall, where the people will be shown films and will be entertained by concerts and plays, but all these diversions will glorify the deeds, traditions and culture of the drinkers of human blood and the eaters of human flesh. The victims of cannibalism will always be presented as happy and contented people.

Kĩmeendeeri will also publish newspapers, whose role will be to denigrate those opposed to the system of drinking human blood and eating human flesh, and to celebrate the charitable hand-outs of Kĩmeendeeri and his friends. He has not yet chosen a name for the newspapers, but titles like the *Shamba Times* or the *Shamba Daily Flag* or the *Shamba Weekly News and Views* will probably be considered suitable. Kĩmeendeeri will also build breweries, and clubs for hard liquor and other alcoholic drinks, like chang'aa and lager, so that alcohol will make idiots out of those who have not already been crazed by Christian and Muslim ritual.

This means that the churches, the schools, the poetry, the songs, the cinema, the beer halls, the clubs, the newspapers will all act as brain-washing poisons whose purpose will be to convince the workers that in this world there is nothing as glorious as slavery to the Kĩmeendeeri class, so that each worker will look forward to the day he dies, when his body will become fertilizer to make the farm ever more productive. The intellectual and spiritual and cultural brain-washing poisons will make the workers believe, literally, that to obey the Kĩmeendeeri class is to obey God, and that to anger or oppose their overlords is to anger and oppose God.

But to be on the safe side, Kĩmeendeeri will build prisons and law courts and will hire armed forces, so that anyone who opposes the *Shamba's* system of laws or wishes to leave the confines of the farm will be punished by being jailed or detained

189

in pits of total darkness or shot and thrown to hyenas on Ngong Hills.

Waríínga: Eaters of men! Is that possible?

Voice: Jacinta, have you already forgotten that this is the teaching of your own Church?

Waríínga: Which is?

Voice: That the eating of human flesh and the drinking of human blood is blessed on Earth and in Heaven? You beat your breast three times, and what do you say?

> *Agnus Dei, qui tollis peccata mundi,*
> *Miserere nobis.*
> *Agnus Dei, qui tollis peccata mundi,*
> *Dona nobis pacem.*

Waríínga: No! No! That's not the way it is!

Voice: Remember the Sacrament that you, Waríínga, used to eat at the *Church of the Holy Rosary* in Nakuru? The priest, after giving you a piece of bread, would say:

> *Ecce Agnus Dei,*
> *Ecce qui tollis peccata mundi ....*

Then he would tell you to do this as Jesus instructed:

> Take, eat, this is my body.
> Do this until I return.
> *Corpus Christi. Amen.*

And the same priest would then give you red wine, and he would tell you to drink it as Jesus once commanded:

> Drink ye all of it, for this is my blood. Do this until I return.
> *Dominus vobiscum,*
> *Per omnia saecula saeculorum.*
> *Amen.*

Waríínga: That's only religious ritual. It's not a question of eating one another. The Sacrament symbolizes the Feast of the Passover.

Voice: What's the Passover?

Waríínga: I don't know. It's just one of the festivals of the Jews and of the Christian Church.

Voice: Never mind. The Kīmeendeeri class is only acting out the central symbolism of the Christian religion. The Kīmeendeeris are the true Christian disciples.

Warīīnga: It's not the same thing . . . .

Voice: Why isn't it the same thing? Isn't it that same religion that argues that the slave can never be equal to his master? Isn't it that same religion that tells the oppressed not to observe the law of an eye for an eye and a tooth for a tooth?

Warīīnga: An eye for an eye and a tooth for a tooth? What would the world come to if there were so much violence?

Voice: Oh, it becomes violence only when a poor man demands the return of his eye or his tooth. What about when the Kīmeendeeris poke out the poor man's eyes with sticks, or lacerate him with whips? What about when they knock a worker's tooth out with a rifle butt? Isn't that violence? That's why the Kīmeendeeris, the Gītutus and the Ngūnjis will go on living it up all their lives on the backs of millions of workers. And you people will continue going to church or to the mosque every week to listen to the catechism of slavery.

> I say unto you
> That ye resist not evil.
> But whosoever shall smite thee on thy right cheek,
> Turn to him the other also.
> And if any man will sue thee at the law,
> And take away thy coat,
> Let him have thy cloak also.

Take, yourself, for instance. When the Rich Old Man from Ngorika snatched your body, what did you do? You decided that you wouldn't put up a fight. You said to yourself that since he had taken away your body, he might as well take your life too.

Warīīnga: What else could I have done?

Voice: You could have demanded the return of your eye and your tooth.

Warīīnga: I'm a woman. I'm weak. There was nothing that I could do, nowhere that I could go and no one that I could turn to for help.

Voice: What were you hoping for? That men who had preyed on you would rescue you from slavery imposed by themselves? The trouble with you, Warīīnga, is that you have no faith in yourself. You have never known who you are! You have always

191

wanted to remain a delicate flower to decorate the lives of the class of *Boss* Kīhara. Warīīnga, Jacinta Warīīnga, look at yourself. Take a good look at yourself. You have a young body. The joys of life are all before you. If you hadn't taken to singeing your hair with hot combs and your skin with lightening creams like *Ambi*, the sheer splendour of your body would have been pulling a thousand and one hearts behind it. The blackness of your skin is smoother and more tender than the most expensive perfume oils. Your dark eyes are brighter than the stars at night. Your cheeks are like two fruits riper than the blackberry. And your hair is so black and soft and smooth that all men must feel like sheltering from the sun in its shade.

Now add to the power of youth and beauty the power of property, and you'll rid your heart of all the troubles that poverty is heir to. Men will kneel before your body, some of them content merely to touch the soil on which your feet have trodden, others driven to standing by the wayside, hoping to be touched by your shadow as you pass by.

Warīīnga: So what must I do?

Voice: Come. Come. Follow me, and I'll take you up into the big Ilmorog mountains, and I'll show all the glories of the world. Let me show you palaces hedged round with flowers of all the different colours of the rainbow, take you on a tour of golf courses carpeted with green, guide you to night clubs where there is music that lures birds from the sky, sweep you up for a ride in a car that moves smoothly over tarmac highways with the grace of a young man sliding across the perfumed body of a woman. All those wonders will belong to you . . . .

Warīīnga: To me?

Voice: I'll give them all to you.

Warīīnga: You'll give them to me?

Voice: Yes, if you'll kneel down before me and sing my praises.

Warīīnga: What is your name?

Voice: Oppressor. Exploiter. Liar. Grabber. I am worshipped by those who love to dispose of goods that have been produced by others. Give me your soul, and I'll guard it for you.

Warīīnga: Those voices that I hear raised in self-praise in the cave – are they singing hymns to you?

Voice: Ah, those. Those are all my followers. Their cunning is a gift from me, and in exchange they have given me their souls to keep. So I know everything they have done in the past, everything they are doing today and everything they'll do tomorrow, and the day after tomorrow, and in years to come. Why are you holding back?

Waríinga: Go away! Leave me alone, Satan! Take your wiles and offer them to your own people. If I were to give you my soul, what would I be left with?

Voice: You don't believe me, do you? Even after all that you've heard with your ears and seen with your eyes. Weren't you there in the cave?

Waríinga: Yes, I was.

Voice: And you heard Mwíreri testify?

Waríinga: Yes.

Voice: And you rode in the same car as he did last night?

Waríinga: Yes. And I must say his testimony surprised me, because in the *matatū*, it was he who was telling us the parable of the man who was going to a far country and he called his servants, and gave them his goods. Unto one, he gave five talents, unto the second two talents, and unto the third . . .

Voice: . . . he gave one talent. I know the parable. I am an avid reader of the Bible. And there is nothing hidden from me under the sun. I was there at the very beginning of the conflict in Heaven. God and I are twins. He is the Lord of Heaven. I am the Lord of Hell. This world is our battlefield; it is where God and I fight over the mastery of human souls.

Waríinga: Proof. I need proof.

Voice: Today I am waiting to receive Mwíreri wa Mūkiraaí, who is about to be hurled down into my kingdom by those who want to buy my blessings.

Waríinga: What?

Voice: You will never see Mwíreri wa Mūkiraaí on this Earth again.

Waríinga: He's going to be murdered? For what? By whom?

Voice: His mouth will cost him his life. Wasn't he the one who called for national self-reliance in theft and robbery? Didn't he argue that the national thieves and robbers should refuse to share their loot with foreigners, and that every thief should steal from his own mother? The foreign thieves from America, Europe and Japan became very angry, and they said to one another: 'Weren't we the people who introduced modern theft and robbery into this country? Didn't we show these people all the arts of modern theft and robbery? And weren't we the people who gave them the necessary talents to start with? And now Mwíreri wants to turn against us, and demands that we should leave his mother to him? Weren't we the ones who kept his mother as our mistress – although, admittedly, we had to rape her in the first place? And today aren't we still keeping her? And now Mwīreri is telling us to pack up and leave him his mother's thighs' It was decided that Mwīreri wa Mūkiraaī should be sacrificed to soothe the foreigners and to persuade them not to take away their talents and the crumbs from their table. Mwīreri will be murdered today by . . . .

Warīīnga: By?

Voice: Robin Mwaūra.

Warīīnga Mwaūra? The owner of Matatū Matata Matamu or some other Mwaūra?

Voice: Mwaūra is a member of the *Devil's Angels*.

Warīīnga: The *Devil's Angels*? Mwaūra? How can that be? This is a marvel to beat all marvels! The thugs who kicked me out of my house in Jericho yesterday?

Voice: Why are you so amazed? Did you imagine that Mwaūra couldn't do a thing like that? Don't be surprised. Don't be astonished. That's a job Mwaūra has often undertaken. He started during the Emergency. In those days he was a very cruel home guard. He used to work with a killer squad led by the European nicknamed Nyangwīcū, who used to terrorize people in the *Rift Valley*. But before he joined Nyangwīcū, he worked with another killer squad led by Kīmeendeeri, the very man who is singing his own praises right now. Mwaūra used to get five shillings for the head of every Mau Mau follower he killed. Mwaūra would scout the villages at night. Old women, children, young men, young girls, old men – Mwaūra did not mind. After all, the Mau Mau didn't wear identity badges. In the morning, Mwaūra would take the heads to Nyangwīcū, who would give him the bounty for murder. In fact, it was Nyangwīcū who gave Mwaūra the car he uses as a *matatū*. Now consider this: if he could kill for five shillings then, why not now, when he has just been promised a new vehicle by Kīmeendeeri?

Warīīnga: I don't believe it. I don't believe anything. Why are you distressing me with stories that will keep me awake when I need a good sleep above all? I've hardly slept at all the last four nights.

Voice: Because . . . because I would like to give you a job.

Warīīnga: A job? Where?

Voice: In Nakuru. Ngorika.

Warīīnga: No! No! Get thee behind me, Satan . . . .

194

Waríínga woke up, her body tense with fear.

'Here you are, sleeping peacefully, and I've been rushing about all over the place looking for you,' Gatuíria said.

Waríínga had never been as happy as she was the minute she opened her eyes and saw Gatuíria standing beside her.

'I leaned against this tree, and I must have dozed off,' Waríínga told him, yawning. She stood up, stretched and yawned again. She glanced about her. 'I didn't get enough sleep last night. When I got home, I had a long talk with my mother.'

'Last night's journey was rather long,' Gatuíria observed, 'and Mwaúra's *matatú* crawled along the road like a dung beetle.'

Waríínga thought of telling Gatuíria about her strange dream and then decided against it, telling herself that a dream was a dream, and that there was no one who didn't have nightmares now and then.

'Is the feast over?' Waríínga asked Gatuíria, laughing to drive away her fears.

'No, but let's get away,' Gatuíria said. '*Let's go*,' he added in English. 'The firebrand is burned at the handle.'

'What did you say?' Waríínga asked.

'The cave is in chaos,' Gatuíria said gloomily. 'The police came.'

'And did they arrest the Gítutus and the Gatheecas?' Waríínga asked excitedly. 'Oh, that would really be wonderful!'

'No,' Gatuíria replied in a low voice. 'They arrested Wangarí.

'Wangarí? They arrested Wangarí? Didn't she go to fetch them herself?'

'Yes, Wangarí made the mistake of going to look for her lost sheep with the henchmen of the thief who had stolen it,' Gatuíria said angrily. 'I have just seen them chain her hands and throw her into the back of a *Black Maria*.'

'But why?' Waríínga asked.

'Because, they claimed, she was spreading rumours and hatred and planting seeds of conflict in a country that is committed to peace and stability.'

Waríínga recalled her recent dream.

'What peace?' Waríínga asked. 'Whose peace? Will the nation's peace always be said to have been shattered only when the poor demand back their eyes or their teeth?'

Warĩĩnga's questions pierced Gatuĩria's heart, and his words poured out like a river in full spate that finds a weak spot at which to burst its banks.

'Oh, you should have been there to see the sight of the Ilmorog police – shepherds of peace, indeed! – attacking a defenceless woman. They came with batons raised, shields ready, guns cocked, as if they were at war, led by *Senior Superintendent* Gakono. Warĩĩnga, it's a tale I would never have believed had I not been present and seen the whole drama with my own eyes. Listen. Kĩmeendeeri wa Kanyuanjii had just left the platform —'

'Wait a minute!' Warĩĩnga interrupted Gatuĩria. 'Who did you say? Kĩmeendeeri wa Kanyuanjii? Was there really someone called that, or were you dreaming?'

'I wish it were a dream,' Gatuĩria replied. 'Kĩmeendeeri wa Kanyuanjii was certainly there, but it was difficult to tell whether he was a human being or a fat, hairy worm with a beak. *Anyway*, Kĩmeendeeri had just finished his monologue (monologue or verbal diarrhoea? you might ask). He started by giving us details of his wealth, then he bragged about how he wanted to set up an experimental *farm* to investigate the feasibility of exporting the labour of our workers to foreign countries through pipelines, and to discover whether their bodies could eventually be made into fertilizer to ensure the continued productivity of rich people's farms here and abroad. And suddenly I saw all the people in the cave open their mouths, and they looked at me with eyes that seemed hungry and thirsty for human blood and human flesh, and fear seized me, and I desperately started looking for an escape route....'

'*Please*, let's sit down,' Warĩĩnga cried out. 'My legs are shaking.'

Gatuĩria and Warĩĩnga sat down on the grass. Gatuĩria went on with his story.

'It was then that the police came. Wangarĩ was the first to enter the cave, followed closely by *Senior Superintendent* Gakono. Oh, I've never come across a woman with so much courage! Wangarĩ calmly walked up to the platform, and she silenced the whole cave with the power of her eyes – it was as if they were flames of fire – and then she denounced the thieves in a voice that did not betray the slightest trace of fear: "These are the men who have always oppressed us peasants, denying us clothes and food and sleep. These are the men who stole the heritage bequeathed to us by Waiyaki wa Hiinga and Kĩmaathi wa Waciũri, and by all the brave patriots who have shed their blood to liberate Kenya. These are the imperialist watchdogs, the children of the Devil. Chain their hands, chain their legs and throw them into the Eternal Jail, where there is an endless gnashing of teeth! For that's the fate of all those who sell foreigners the heritage of our founding patriarchs and patriots!"

'Waríínga, how can I describe the scene adequately? It looked as if everyone in the cave had been transfixed by the electric power of Wangarí's words. Oh, Wangarí was beautiful, I can tell you. *Oh, yes,* Wangarí's face shone as she stood before us all, and it looked as if her courage had stripped years from her body and given her new life. It was as if the light in her face were illuminating the hearts of all those present, and her voice carried the power and the authority of a people's judge.

'Then I saw the master of ceremonies stand up and look over at the *Superintendent,* who was standing there silent and immobile. "What's all this about, *Superintendent* Gakono? *Is this a coup or what?*" he demanded angrily. Gakono, springing to attention, saluted and started offering apologies and begging for forgiveness in a trembling voice. He spoke as if fear had penetrated his flesh and bones, and he did not understand the use of the comma or full stop: "*I am sorry sir truly sorry* to tell you the truth I did not know that you were the people who had gathered here I thought it was the ordinary small-time thieves and robbers from Njeruca *you know* those who play about with your property and sometimes break into banks that belong to foreigners like the guests we have here that woman brought us reports that the thieves and robbers who have troubled and bankrupted the whole country were hiding in this lair bragging about their exploits and again *please* I would like you to know that it was not really my fault for on Saturday I got a call from Nairobi telling me that there was a woman who was expected to bring vital information about thieves and robbers and so when I saw the woman over there —"

'"*Never mind,*" the master of ceremonies interrupted him, "we'll talk about that later and pin down the enemy who has planned all this to sow seeds of discord between us and our foreign masters. *Kitulacho Kimo Nguoni Zetu.* We ought to be more *self-reliant,* eh? We'll face them squarely and root out those who think they're smarter than the rest of us. We are very embarrassed about this shameful drama which is being enacted before our international guests. *Superintendent* Gakono, do your job. *Wembe ni ule ule.* Act as you do when you are angry, then come back and greet our foreign guests over a glass of whisky."

'Gakono blew his whistle. The police swarmed into the cave, armed with clubs and guns. Gakono pointed at Wangarí, and they rushed up to the platform, and they attacked her, and they chained

197

her hands. But even when fate had turned against her, Wangari did not display any fear. She merely asked, in a voice that was quite steady: "So you, the police force, are the servants of one class only? And to think that I stupidly went ahead and entrusted my love of my country to treacherous rats that love to devour patriotism!" Then Wangari raised her voice in song as they prodded at her and shoved her with clubs and batons and spat at her:

If ever you hear drip, drip, drip,
Don't think it's thundery rain.
No, it'll be the blood of us peasants
As we fight for our soil!

And she was led out, still singing her defiance, her chained hands raised high above her head, the links gleaming like a necklace of courage. Wangari, heroine of our land!'

Gatuiria paused, as if Wangari's courageous voice were ringing in his ears.

'Wangari, heroine of our nation!' Gatuiria said again, slowly. 'It was then, as I was sitting there, dumbfounded by the crime that had been committed before my eyes, that I saw Gakono return to the cave. Muttering, "*Crazy woman, crazy!*", he went over to the table occupied by the master of ceremonies and the foreign guests, and sat down, and started talking and laughing over a glass of whisky. Mwireri wa Mukiraai stood up and asked for permission to defend himself against certain words that had been uttered by the master of ceremonies. He was not allowed to speak. He turned away, fuming, and stopped at Mwaura's table. He told Mwaura to follow him to the *Green Rainbow* Hotel, as he wanted to be taken home this evening in the Matatu Matata Matamu. He promised that they would not fall out over the hire fee.

'As Mwireri wa Mukiraai was about to go out, he looked at me, halted, then said with bitterness: "Now you see the danger of putting too much faith in women like that! Never cast your pearls before swine!"

'He didn't wait for an answer, but left immediately. And suddenly I felt a burning anger inside me, and I ran after him so that I could tell him a thing or two even if it meant that we came to blows. But I couldn't find him.

'While I stood there, wondering where Mwireri wa Mukiraai had gone, I saw Robin Mwaura and the master of ceremonies and Kimeendeeri wa Kanyuanjii come out of the cave, talking animatedly like old friends. Kimeendeeri was saying to Mwaura: 'Yes, yes,

198

I knew you the moment I saw you. I remembered the sort of job you used to do before you joined Nyangwicu....' They went a little further and then stopped, deep in private conversation. I couldn't hear all they said, but a few words were blown by the wind towards where I was standing. "*Devil's Angels* ... *private businessmen* ... one of them ... today ... tonight ... phone them ... Yes, they'll meet you on the way ... Kīneeniī...." I didn't wait to hear more. I just started looking for you, to take you away from here. What I have seen so far is more than enough for me!'

Gatuīria fell silent. As for Warīīnga, her heart was thumping, for what had occurred in the cave corresponded almost word for word, action for action, with what had gone on in her dream. Or could it be that it was not a dream but a revelation?

'What about Mūturi and his people?' Warīīnga asked Gatuīria.

'Mūturi hadn't arrived by the time I left the place,' Gatuīria replied.

'If he comes to the cave now, won't he be arrested as well?' Warīīnga asked.

'I don't know. I don't seem to be sure of anything any more,' Gatuīria said. 'Things are bubbling away in my head like porridge cooking in a pot.'

And not in Gatuīria's head alone. Warīīnga was also turning over several things in her mind. She was considering a number of questions. Should she tell Gatuīria about her dream? How could they help Mūturi to escape from chains and police custody? And what could she do to prevent Mwīreri wa Mūkiraaī from being murdered by Robin Mwaūra and his group of *Devil's Angels*? How could she be certain of anything in what, after all, had been a dream?

Warīīnga decided that she would not tell Gatuīria about the dream, but she would do her best to prevent Mwīreri from travelling in Mwaūra's *matatū* that night. What they had to do straight away was to prevent *Mūturi* from coming to the cave.

'Let's go and meet Mūturi to warn him about the danger ahead!' Warīīnga suggested. 'Let's save him from Wangarī's fate before it's too late.'

Gatuĩria and Warĩĩnga began to walk towards Njeruca, each carrying a private load of thoughts and doubts.

Gatuĩria was preoccupied by the image of Wangarĩ in a police cell, her hands and feet in chains.

Warĩĩnga's thoughts were dominated by the voice of Mwĩreri wa Mũkiraaĩ as he told them the story of the man who was travelling to a far country and how, on his return, he called all his servants to account for the talents he had left them . . . .

Then he that had received one talent came and said, Lord, I know thee, that thou art à hard man, reaping where thou hast not sown and gathering where thou hast not reaped . . . .

Warĩĩnga suddenly halted and tugged Gatuĩria by the sleeve. Gatuĩria stopped too and asked Warĩĩnga: 'What is it?'

'Listen to the voices of the people singing a new song!'

Chapter Nine

1

The rays of the setting sun fell on Ilmorog's Golden Heights like flames reflected in the shiny steel of swords and spears. Waríínga and Gatuíria stood on the grassy carpet of *Ilmorog Golf Course*, ears and eyes straining towards the road to Njeruca, from which came the sound of singing voices:

> Come one and all,
> And behold the wonderful sight
> Of us chasing away the Devil
> And all his disciples!
> Come one and all!

'That must be Mũturi and his crowd,' Gatuíria remarked.

'Let's hurry then,' Waríínga replied, and she started running towards the voices. And the voices came nearer and nearer, still singing:

> Come one and all,
> And behold the wonderful sight
> Of us chasing away the Devil
> And all his disciples!
> Come one and all!

After a few minutes, Waríínga and Gatuíria were standing by the side of the road that ran through Ilmorog, astonished at the strange sight before them.

A long procession of women, men and children met their eyes. The procession was winding along the road towards the cave. Many of the children were running along beside the column, some prancing about and others joining in the singing.

'What a long procession!' Gatuíria said.

'It looks as if Mũturi has collected the whole of Njeruca together!' Waríínga replied.

'I don't know if we'll be able to find Mũturi,' Gatuíria said.

'Let's just stand here and hope that if he sees us, Mũturi will come over to us,' said Waríínga.

'Even if we tell him about the police, it won't make any difference,' Gatuīria said.

'Why?' Warīīnga asked.

'Because I can't see this crowd retreating!' Gatuīria replied.

They stood there by the roadside, watching the long procession, waiting for Mūturi. And the people still came on, some singing, some whistling, some blowing penny whistles and horns, but all in time to the song. Their footsteps and their gestures matched the rhythm of the song. Many had rags for clothes. Many more had no shoes. But there was a small group in the procession that was better dressed, with clean shirts, coats and trousers.

Suddenly Warīīnga felt her heart miss a beat. She did not know whether to believe the evidence of her eyes. It was as if she had gone back to a dream that had no beginning and no end.

'Look! Look!' she shouted at Gatuīria. 'Look at him!'

'Who? What is it?' Gatuīria asked quickly. 'Mūturi?'

'Look at the man I told you about last night! Look at the man I saw yesterday!' Warīīnga said, as if she were chanting a song.

'But who?'

'The man who gave me the fake invitation card at the Kaka Hotel bus stop! Can you see him?'

'Where?'

'Over there, among the group that seems to be slightly better dressed. The one with a goatee beard.'

'*Wait a minute!*' Gatuīria said. 'I know him!'

'Who is he?' Warīīnga asked.

'He is a student at the university!'

'A student?'

'Yes. He's the leader of the *Ilmorog University Students' Association*, ILUSA.'

'And what's he doing in the procession?' Warīīnga asked.

'He's probably one of them,' Gatuīria replied.

'So Mwīreri wa Mūkiraaī's claim that the fake cards that called this a Devil's feast came from the students was true after all?' Warīīnga asked.

And then and there, she opened her handbag and took out the card given her by the student and the card given her by Mwīreri wa Mūkiraaī. She compared them quickly, as if she were seeing them for the first time, and then returned them to the bag.

'I know now, without a doubt, who the people were who put the fake card into my pigeon hole at the university!' Gatuīria said, nodding as if everything had just dawned on him.

They watched the procession, their minds preoccupied with questions.

Some people carried placards bearing different slogans: WE REJECT THE SYSTEM OF THEFT AND ROBBERY; OUR POVERTY IS THEIR WEALTH; THE THIEF AND THE WITCH ARE TWINS – THEIR MOTHER IS EXPLOITATION; THE BEEHIVE IN WHICH WE WILL ROLL THIEVES AND ROBBERS DOWN THE SLOPES OF THE HILL OF DEATH HAS ALREADY BEEN BUILT BY THE WORKERS; WHAT'S THE BIGGEST THEFT? THE THEFT OF THE SWEAT AND THE BLOOD OF THE WORKERS! WHAT IS THE BIGGEST ROBBERY? THE ROBBERY OF THE BLOOD OF THE MASSES! and many others not easily discernible to a person on the roadside. Those who did not have placards carried sticks on their shoulders as if they were guns.

'This is really an army!' said Gatuĩria.

'An army of workers?' Warĩĩnga asked.

'Yes, and peasants, and petty traders, and students. . . .'

'. . . led by the workers. . . .'

'And taking the battle to the cave!' Gatuĩria added.

Warĩĩnga laughed as she contemplated the battle that would be fought out in the cave between the forces of the workers and the forces of the thieves and the robbers.

By now many of those at the front of the procession had passed Warĩĩnga and Gatuĩria. Warĩĩnga said to Gatuĩria: 'Maybe Mũturi isn't among them?'

2

As if in answer to Warĩĩnga's question, Mũturi caught sight of them at that moment, left the procession, and came over to where they were standing. Mũturi spoke quickly, without a pause, as if the river of his words had flooded and burst its banks.

'Are you leaving so soon, when the struggle has only just started? Do you want to miss the extraordinary spectacle of us chasing away the class of exploiters from their den in the cave? Look at our people stamping firmly and proudly on the ground as if they were hearkening to the call of the masses! I found that most of the preparatory work had been done by the Ilmorog workers themselves. I just helped a bit. You see that small group that seems well dressed? Those are Ilmorog students from the schools around here and the university. This is really wonderful! Future generations will sing about this day from the rooftops and treetops and mountaintops, from Kenya to Elgon, from Elgon to Kilimanjaaro, from

Ngong Hills to Nyandaarwa. I, Mŭturi wa Kahonia Maithori, found the students and the workers already forming a procession, urging all those who live in Njeruca to join them to attack the local thieves and robbers and their foreign friends. I passed on the information I had already collected, and I was asked to put in a word. We toured every corner of Njeruca. Whenever anybody learned that I had actually heard the thieves and robbers bragging, he would immediately go for a stick and come back to join the procession and the singing. What more can I tell you? Bring your horns so that we can trumpet the glory of this great day. Come, and let's rejoice together. Come, and let's stride about in pride, for some of our educated youth have opened their ears, and they have started listening to the cry of the people! They have opened their eyes, and they have started seeing the light that shines from the great organization of the workers and peasants! Has Wangarĩ come back?'

'We've come to meet you!' Gatuĩria said as soon as he found a chance to slip in a word.

'Why? Where is Wangarĩ?'

'Wangarĩ was arrested by the police,' Warĩĩnga told him.

'Arrested?'

'Yes, for spreading rumours that might start violence and endanger peace and stability in the land!' Gatuĩria said.

'Where was she arrested? In the cave?'

'Yes,' Warĩĩnga replied.

And now Mŭturi spoke with pain and bitterness: 'As a worker, I know very well that the forces of law and order are on the side of those who rob the workers of the products of their sweat, of those who steal food and land from the peasants. The peace and the order and the stability they defend with armoured cars is the peace and the order and the stability of the rich, who feast on bread and wine snatched from the mouths of the poor – yes, they protect the eaters from the wrath of the thirsty and the hungry. Have you ever seen employers being attacked by the armed forces for refusing to increase the salaries of their workers? What about when the workers go on strike? And they have the audacity to talk about violence! Who plants the seeds of violence in this country? That's why I wanted Wangarĩ to fetch them and see for herself, so that all her lingering doubts would vanish, and she would ask herself: Have I ever seen the police being sent to silence the rich?'

'Listen,' Gatuĩria said hurriedly, 'we came to warn you that you might be arrested as well. The Ilmorog police chief is at the cave.'

'I'm glad you came to warn us,' Mŭturi replied slowly, obviously moved by the gesture. 'Your action is a source of great joy to me.

You and I met in a *matatū* only last night and yet you've come to save me from danger. But I will not run away. We shall not run away. For us workers, there's no turning back – where could we run? Let me tell you, I'm sure that the system of theft and robbery will never end in this country as long as people are scared of guns and clubs. We must struggle and fight against the culture of fear. And there is only one cure: a strong organization of the workers and peasants of the land, together with those whose eyes and ears are now open and alert. These brave students have shown which side education should serve. My friends, you should come and join us too. Bring your education to us, and don't turn your backs on the people. That's the only way.'

3

As soon as he had said this, Mūturi left Gatuīria and Warīīnga and ran to rejoin the workers' procession.

Warīīnga and Gatuīria looked at one another. Both were shaken by Mūturi's call to arms.

A while before, as they were eating meat and drinking beer in Njeruca, they would never have thought that they could possibly join a procession of ragged, barefooted workers on their way to attack the cave with sticks and placards. But now the voice of a worker was calling upon them to choose the side on which they would use their education.

A while before, though both were nauseated by the talk in the cave, they were inclined to view those things as happening in a world quite unrelated to their own lives. But now the voice of a worker was calling to them, telling them that nobody could walk along two roads at the same time.

A while ago, they regarded themselves as spectators of a dance danced by others. But now the voice of a worker was urging them to enter the arena, not to stand on the edge and watch now that the dance of the people was being danced.

Gatuīria asked himself: We, the intellectuals among the workers, which side are we on? Are we on the side of the producers or the side of those who live on the products of others? Are we on the side of the workers and peasants or the side of exploiters? Or are we like the hyena which tried to walk along two different roads at the same time?

Warīīnga was experiencing similar emotions and was pursuing

similar thoughts: We who work as clerks, copy typists and secretaries, which side are we on? We who type and take dictation from *Boss* Kĩhara and his kind, whose side are we on in this dance? Are we on the side of the workers, or on the side of the rich? Who are we? Who are we? Many a time I've heard women say: '*Our* firm does this and that', 'In *our* firm we employ so many workers, who earn this much', '*Our* company made this much profit', and as they speak, they may not have a cent for their bus fare in the evening. Yes, I've often heard girls bragging about their *bosses*, and when you check carefully to see what they're bragging about, you can't find a thing. A few hundred shillings a month for a woman with children to feed, and we proudly call that a salary? And in exchange for so little we have sacrificed four things.

First, our arms. Yes, for it is we who type all their documents and all their letters. Our hands become their hands; our power becomes their power.

Second, our brains. Yes, because there is no *boss* who wants a girl with independent thoughts and an independent stand; no *boss* is happy with a secretary who questions things, or who opens her eyes wide to see what is being done to her by *Boss* Kĩhara! *The Boss is always right*: hang your brain from your fingers or your thighs!

Third, our humanity. Yes, because *Boss* Kĩhara and his kind work out their frustrations on us. When they quarrel with their wives at home, they bring their anger to the office; when something goes wrong with their business, they bring all their fury to the office. We are insulted, but we keep quiet because we are supposed to have hearts that are not easily moved to tears.

Fourth, our thighs. Yes, because except for the lucky few, most of us can get jobs or keep them only by allowing the likes of *Boss* Kĩhara to paw our thighs. We're their real wives . . . but, of course, not their legal wives! Yes, we are wives installed in a *BMW* for a weekend drive to an abattoir! After all, there's a difference between a goat for slaughter and one for grazing.

Who are *we*? Who are *we*? Who are *we*? Warĩĩnga's heart beat in time to her question, raising problems to which nobody could provide her with solutions because they concerned the decision she would have to make herself about the side she would choose in life's struggle.

Wariinga and Gatuiria found the whole cave reeking of burnt debris and smoke. The whole place had been completely surrounded by the Njeruca crowd, which was still singing:

Come one and all,
And behold the wonderful sight
Of us chasing away the Devil
And all his disciples!
Come one and all!

The drama at the door to the cave, as several thieves and robbers attempted to squeeze their fat bellies through it at the same time, was both comic and sad. Any thief who managed to squeeze through would lumber across to his car like a hippo and, after a second, would raise dust as he speeded away, saying his prayers with all his soul. Those who did not have fat bellies – the clan of the skinnies – would jump through the windows and, touching the ground, would dart away like arrows. And the workers would run after them shouting: 'There he is! There he is! Hunt him down! Hunt him down! Catch thief! Catch thief!'

From where she was standing, Wariinga did not have a clear view of what was happening on every side. The yard was a chaos of running feet as the owners of the palaces and mansions in Ilmorog's Golden Heights were chased by the Njeruca shanty dwellers. But Wariinga was able to witness the wonderful spectacle of Gitutu wa Gataanguru and Nditika wa Nguunji, trying to run away, like two spiders with eggs, while their buttocks were lashed by their pursuers with sticks. By the time they reached their cars, they were panting, and the sweat of pain and fatigue and fear fell to the ground in drops like rain during a heavy downpour.

Wariinga was not alone as she smiled. The air was full of the noise of the good-humoured laughter of the Njeruca people as they mocked the Heights dwellers in flight, trying to remove jackets, ties, shoes, belts, anything that would make them lighter.

But when the crowd saw the foreign thieves about to leave the cave, their laughter turned into menacing roar. The people roared like a thousand angry lions whose cubs had been taken away from them, and they seized their sticks and clubs and iron rods and pressed forward towards the foreign thieves, who were surrounded by their local home guards. One local thief took out his gun to shoot, but the angry hiss of the crowd made his hand shake, and the bullet flew up harmlessly into the air. The crowd halted. Then it surged forward again, the footsteps of the people running together making the ground shake.

The seven foreign robbers from Western Europe, the USA and Japan were saved from being torn to pieces only by the fact that their cars were nearby, and their drivers had the engines revving, ready for a quick get-away.

There were two thieves who forgot that they had cars and fled on foot. The cars were set alight. After a while, not a single thief or robber was left in the area of the cave. All of them had managed to flee, as if they had suddenly grown wings of fear.

5

The people now gathered outside the cave, expecting speeches and guidance from their leaders. Mūturi wa Kahonia Maithori was the first to speak.

'Friends – or perhaps I should call you clansmen, for we who are gathered here now belong to one clan: the clan of workers – I think all of us saw the incredible spectacle of those who have bellies that never bear children come to scorn us. Those bellies are not swollen by disease. They have been fattened by the fruit of our sweat and blood. Those bellies are barren, and their owners are barren. What about us, the workers? We build houses; others occupy them; and we, the builders, are left out in the rain. We make clothes; others take them, and dress well; and we the tailors go naked. We grow food; others eat it; and we, the farmers, sleep with our stomachs growling through the night. Look here. We build good schools; other people's children find places in them, and ours go looking for food in rubbish heaps and in dustbins. Today we are taking a stand. Today, here, we refuse to go on being the pot that cooks but never tastes the food.'

Mūturi stepped aside. The crowd gave him a big ovation. The women ululated.

The Ilmorog students' leader was the next to speak.

Seeing him, Warīīnga felt a strange sensation. How could this be? How could it be that Mūturi, who had once rescued her from death under a train in Nakuru, was being followed on the platform by the

208

man who rescued her from death under a bus in Nairobi yesterday? Waríínga watched his goatee beard move in time to his words.

'We, the mass of students in Ilmorog, whether in primary or secondary schools or at the university, support the workers fully in their just struggle against the system of modern theft and robbery. The workers are at the forefront of the fight against neo-colonialism, the last stage of imperialism. When the organization of Ilmorog workers got wind of the gathering of local and international thieves, they informed us, as a student organization. And we, the students, sat down and asked ourselves: What can we do to show our solidarity with the workers? It was then that we printed cards to indicate to people the nature of the feast, to show them that it was going to be like a Devil's feast organized by Satan, the king of devils. Let us all now join hands with the working people in their just war against the drinking of human blood, the eating of human flesh, and the many other crimes perpetrated by imperialism in its neo-colonial stage. Let us join hands with the workers as they struggle to build a house that will benefit all the builders. What greater thing can our education do for our nation? That's why we, the students, said that we would not be left behind, that we must join hands in this wonderful drama in which we, the people, were to throw out the Devil and all his followers!'

He too got a big ovation, and the women's ululations were like the trumpets of war.

The third to speak was the Ilmorog workers' leader. He had on a large overcoat and a cone-shaped hat. Before he spoke, he took off his hat. He had a few grey hairs.

'First, I would like to pay tribute to the courage of the students from the university and the schools around here. If our youth were to hang up its arms, what would happen to the defence of the land? Where would the nation be? A word of gratitude is also due to all those, from Nairobi to Ilmorog, who hearkened to our cry. Now, I'm going to say only one word and to ask only one question. We have two types of unity: the unity of workers and the unity of the rich. Which side are you on? Which principles do you uphold, for each side has its own doctrine?

'The Beatitudes of the rich and the imperialists go like this:

Blessed is he who bites and soothes,
Because he will never be found out.
Blessed is the man who burns down another man's house
And in the morning joins him in grief,
For he shall be called merciful.

209

Blessed is the man who robs another of five shillings
And then gives him back half a shilling for salt,
For he shall be called generous.
As for the man who bites and doesn't know how to soothe,
And the one who steals from the masses
And does not attempt to deceive them with honeyed words,
Woe unto him!
For should the masses ever awaken,
Such people will see through their arses,
And may even pass on their disease to us,
Who have been able to disguise our wicked deeds
With the religious robes of hypocrisy.

The workers' catechism goes like this:

I believe that we, the workers, are of one clan,
And hence we should not allow ourselves
To be divided by religion, colour or tribe.
I believe that in the organization of the workers
Lies our strength,
For those who are organized never lose their way,
And those who are not organized are scattered by the sound of
   one bullet.
I therefore believe in the unity of the workers,
Because unity is our strength.
I believe that imperialism and its local representatives are the
   enemies of the progress of the workers and peasants and of
   the whole nation.
I therefore vow always to struggle against neo-colonialism,
For neo-colonialism is the last vicious kick of a dying
   imperialism.

Let us now all sing together the worker's anthem!'
   He then started singing, and all the others joined in, their voices
raised in unison making the ground tremble where Wariinga stood.
While the song was going on, Wariinga felt somebody tug at her
dress from behind. She turned quickly and found that Mūturi was
trying to attract her attention. She followed him, and they retreated
to a hidden place behind the cave.
   'Listen,' Mūturi started immediately, his eyes fixed on Wariinga's
face and eyes, as if he could read all the hidden corners in her heart,
'can I trust you with a small burden until tomorrow?'
   'What kind of burden?' Wariinga asked.

'A piece of metal pipe that emits fatal fire and smoke,' Mūturi said, still watching Warīīnga.

Why not? Warīīnga asked herself.

'Yes, if you promise you'll collect it tomorrow,' Warīīnga said.

'There's no time to lose,' Mūturi urged. 'I observed you last night in the *matatū*, and I've watched you throughout the day in the cave, and I've decided that you can be trusted with a worker's secret. As soon as I left Gatuīria and you standing by the roadside, I went and joined the people in their battle with the thieves. Did you see the power of a people united? Those thieves were armed, but none was able to use his gun because they were terrified by the eyes and the massive roar of the crowd. Kīhaahu wa Gatheeca was the only one who tried to shoot at me. I had chased him round to this side, where we are now. But I was too quick for him, and I hit his arm before he could fire. Kīhaahu cried out in pain, dropped the pistol, took to his heels and flew like an arrow. I picked up this iron pipe with which he intended to kill me. Here it is. It's so tiny that it will fit in the palm of your hand or in a shirt pocket. See how beautifully it gleams! This is the product of a worker's hands! But, you know, it doesn't go to defend the worker. We, the workers, have always made things that end up oppressing us! But now look at the product of a worker's hands back in his own hands. It was iron pipes like this one, in the hands of the workers, that saved Kenya from the old colonialism. Even today guns like this should really be in the hands of the workers so that they can defend the unity and wealth and freedom of their country. But let me stop . . . preaching. Tonight there's bound to be more trouble. Take this pistol. Put it in your handbag. Let's meet tomorrow morning at ten o'clock at the Nairobi bus stop. And don't show this to anyone or tell anybody about it, not even Gatuīria. Those educated people are often not sure whose side they are on. They sway from this side to that like water on a leaf. Go now. Take care. This gun is an invitation to the workers' feast to be held some time in the future.'

Mūturi gave Warīīnga the gun and turned away. Warīīnga felt a strange sensation come over her. Her heart trembled. Then she felt courage course through her whole body. She thought that there was not a single danger in the world that she could not now look in the face. All her doubts and fears had been expelled by the secret with which Mūturi had entrusted her. She thought of asking him about the occasion when he rescued her from death under the train long ago, in Nakuru. But another thought seized her, and she called out to Mūturi. Mūturi stopped.

'Tell me something that I'd like to know before you leave,' Waríínga began. 'Who are you?'

'Me?' Mũturi replied. 'I'm a delegate from a secret workers' organization in Nairobi. But don't ask any more questions. Wherever I am, I am working for that organization. Look after yourself – and remember, you're not alone.'

They parted company.

Waríínga returned to Gatuíria, carrying with her Mũturi's secret. And then she decided that it would be better for her to take the secret home immediately.

The workers were still singing.

Waríínga told Gatuíria that she wanted to go home before darkness fell, as she was very tired.

Gatuíria's heart sank. His face darkened. He was disappointed because he had thought he would be able to take Waríínga home, but he could not think of a way of suggesting himself as her escort. He said: 'I'd like to stay here to see the end of this drama. *But how can I see you tomorrow?*'

They agreed to meet at the *Sunshine Hotel* at twelve o'clock the following day. Waríínga wanted to sing Gatuíria a song that she used to hear on the eve of initiation into a new life:

Now you see me!
Now you see me!
Dawn is breaking!
Death and life are the same to me
Dawn is breaking!

As she walked along the road, Waríínga's heart acquired new wings, ready to fly. She thought of waiting for a *matatũ*. Then she suddenly remembered Mwaũra and his Matatũ Matata Matamu and the fate awaiting Mwíreri wa Mũkiraaí. She decided to go first to the *Green Rainbow Hotel* to see if she could prevent Mwíreri wa Mũkiraaí from going to Nairobi tonight.

Waríínga could not tell what was urging her on to do this. But she felt that she owed a debt of some kind because she herself had been rescued from death by strangers on two occasions. She recalled her recent dream. Had it really been a dream or a revelation? Waríínga put the same question again: Had the voice been real or had it been an illusion?

No. It had been the voice of Satan, the voice of temptation. For although the voice had painted a true picture of what was going on in the country, and it had made pertinent observations about neo-colonial Kenya, the way that the voice had shown her as the escape route from the prison of neo-colonial life was misleading and would have cost Warĩĩnga her life. It had tempted her to walk along a broad highway carpeted with the flowers of self-seeking individualism. It had tempted her to sell her body for money again! Was she going to consider selling the Devil her soul and being left a shell, like Nding'uri wa Kahahami? For mere money? *God, no*! One fall was enough for her, Warĩĩnga resolved firmly, as if the secret she was carrying for Mũturi had given her indomitable courage to fight and defeat the Devil with all his tempting propositions designed to persuade patriots to sell their country down the river.

Just before she reached the *Green Rainbow Hotel* Warĩĩnga saw two army lorries, filled with soldiers armed to the teeth, driving towards the cave. Behind the two lorries were three armoured cars. Oh, God, there'll be death at the cave now, Warĩĩnga said to herself. She thought about the workers gathered outside the cave. She thought about Gatuĩria, about Mũturi, about the lives of the people.

Warĩĩnga remembered the secret she was carrying. She hurried on. The sun had set, but it was not yet dark . . . .

Because of the conflicting thoughts that were seething in Warĩĩnga's mind, she did not realize that she had already reached the *Green Rainbow Hotel*, where Mwĩreri wa Mũkiraaĩ was staying, until she suddenly saw its neon-lit sign.

'Mwĩreri wa Mũkiraaĩ?' the receptionist asked Warĩĩnga, as if he had not heard her question clearly.

'Yes.'

'He has just left. He checked out of the hotel not five minutes ago.'

'How did he go?' Warĩĩnga asked.

'By Matatũ Matata Matamu Model T Ford, registration number MMM 333. I have never seen a *matatũ* covered with so many grotesque slogans. 'If you want true rumours, ride in Matatũ Matata Matamu', 'If you want true gossip. . . .'

Warĩĩnga left the receptionist, who was beside himself with laughter.

What's all this about? What's all this about? Warĩĩnga was asking herself.

Suddenly Warĩĩnga's blood froze in her veins. Throughout Ilmorog, the whole of Ilmorog, nothing could be heard but gun shots and the blood-curdling cries of the people.

The following day Warĩĩnga went to the bus stop to meet Mũturi.
Mũturi was not there.

Then Warĩĩnga went to see Gatuĩria at the *Sunshine Hotel*. Her
heart was heavy because in Njeruca and in Ilmorog as a whole, the
only topic was the feast at the cave and how it had all ended in many
deaths. Some said twenty people had died; others claimed fifty; yet
others set the figure at a hundred. But what was common to all their
claims was the fact that some people had been killed by the military
and the police, and others had been arrested by *Superintendent*
Gakono.

It was Gatuĩria who told Warĩĩnga the exact position.

'Five workers were killed by the forces of bourgeois law and
order. And the workers killed two soldiers. But there were lots of
injured on both sides.'

'And Mũturi?' Warĩĩnga asked anxiously.

'Mũturi? Mũturi was arrested, together with the students' leader.
They couldn't arrest the workers' leader because he was hidden by
the others. He has gone underground, but they are still looking for
him.'

Gatuĩria and Warĩĩnga fell silent, like bereaved parents. They sat
outside, at a table in one of the hotel gardens filled with green grass
and flowers. The tea that they had ordered grew cold in their
cups.

Before Warĩĩnga could say anything, Gatuĩria added, slowly: 'But
what made me very bitter was this. This morning the Ilmorog radio
station didn't even mention the death of the five workers and the
many fatal injuries. But the same radio station found time to tell
listeners about the death of the two soldiers and the death of Mwĩreri
wa Mũkiraaĩ.'

'Mwĩreri wa Mũkiraaĩ?'

'Yes. It said that he was involved in a car accident at Kĩneeniĩ on
his way to Nairobi last night.'

'And Mwaũra? Robin Mwaũra?' Warĩĩnga asked, stunned.

'He's alive. He had a narrow escape.'

Chapter Ten

1

Another Saturday. It is two years since Warĩĩnga rejected the temptations of Satan at the Ilmorog golf course: two whole years since the Devil's feast at the thieves' and robbers' den gave birth to the sorrow of jail and death: two years of great change in the lives of Warĩĩnga and Gatuĩria.

Two years....

Where shall I begin? Or should I stop involving myself in other people's lives?

He who judges knows not how he himself will be judged.

The antelope hates the man who sees it less than him who betrays its presence.

But I too was present at Nakuru. I saw with my eyes and heard with my ears.

How can I deny the evidence of my eyes and ears? How can I run away from the truth?

It was revealed to me.
It was revealed to me.

Where shall I pick up the broken thread of my narrative?

Listen. Two years had passed....

No, I shall not proceed at the same pace as before. The seeds in the gourd are not all of one kind, so I will change the pace and manner of my narrative.

So, come, my friend. Come, my friend, come with me so I can take you along the paths that Warĩĩnga walked. Come, let us retrace her footsteps, seeing with the eyes of our hearts what she saw, and hearing with the ears of our hearts what she heard, so that we shall not be hasty in passing judgement on the basis of rumour and malice.

Truth can break a bow poised to shoot!
That is good, my friend.
Let it be.
Oh, let it be. Come, peace of God!

Hurry up, my friend. And you too, lover of justice, hurry up. Run faster, for one should get to the market early, before the vegetables begin to wilt in the sun. . . .

2

Here is Waríínga!

She now lives in the Ngara area of Nairobi, in a single room on the fourth floor of a seven-storey building. The whole building is called *Maraaro House*.

The first storey has been partitioned off into several residential rooms for anybody who can afford the rent. Each single room is kitchen, sitting room and bedroom combined. Even so, every room is taken. A bird exhausted by flight lands on the nearest tree.

Outside the building there are quite a number of service stations owned by foreign oil companies: *Esso, Shell, BP, Caltex, Mobil Oil, Agip, Total*. A few yards away, near the Múrang'a Road, are several kiosks selling raw and cooked food.

Maraaro House is situated at a road junction. So the noise of cars makes it very difficult to get enough sleep, especially if you happen to be a visitor.

But Waríínga doesn't mind the noise.

She is used to it now, for the noise of cars is her livelihood.

Oh, Waríínga, work harder to develop our land!

This Waríínga is not the one we met two years ago. This Waríínga is not the one who used to think that there was nothing she could do except type for others; the one who used to burn her body with *Ambi* and *Snowfire* to change the colour of her skin to please the eyes of others, to satisfy their lust for white skins; the one who used to think that there was only one way of avoiding the pitfalls of life: suicide.

No, this Waríínga is not that other Waríínga.

Today's Waríínga has decided that she'll never again allow herself to be a mere flower, whose purpose is to decorate the doors and windows and tables of other people's lives, waiting to be thrown on to a rubbish heap the moment the splendour of her body withers. The Waríínga of today has decided to be self-reliant all the time, to plunge into the middle of the arena of life's struggles in order to discover her real strength and to realize her true humanity.

Cleanliness is bathing. A hero is known only on the battlefield. A good dancer is known only in the dance arena.

Waríínga, heroine of toil, the heroism of life can be discovered only in the battle of life....

This Saturday, for instance, Waríínga wakes up very early, pumps pressure into the primus stove, lights it and puts on a pot of water to make tea. And before the water has boiled, Waríínga has washed her face and gone to do her hair in front of a mirror, gathering it into four plaited knots. Her hair is long and black and soft. What did I tell you? The present Waríínga stopped singeing her hair with hot iron combs long ago. There, now she is tying a scarf over her hair. She puts on her blue weather-beaten *jeans* and a khaki shirt. Look at her! Her clothes fit her so perfectly, it's as if she was created in them.

Waríínga goes to a cupboard. She chooses the dress she will wear later, after work, and another that she will wear tomorrow, Sunday. She puts them in a small safari suitcase. For today, after work, Waríínga intends to go to Ilmorog to see her parents. And tomorrow she is going on another journey, to Nakuru, to see Gatuíria's parents.

But the two journeys do not prevent Waríínga from concentrating on her job. Today she is changing the engine of a car, and she must finish that task before one o'clock.

Waríínga, our engineering hero!

She has drunk her tea. Now she is rummaging through her handbag to make sure that everything she needs is there, a comb, some cream, a hand mirror, a handkerchief ... and a small spanner. How did she come to put the spanner in her bag? She must have done that by mistake. *Yes*, the gun she was given by Mũturi to keep is also there. Waríínga never leaves the gun behind. It is so small that someone who knew nothing about guns might take it for a child's toy. She is ready to go. At the door she suddenly remembers that she has left a *phase tester* on the windowsill. She goes back for it. She normally hangs it from one of her shirt pockets, like a pen. She never leaves it behind, not even at her workplace with the rest of the tools. It is as if the *phase tester* and the pistol were her two most important shields.

There goes Waríínga! She walks along Ngara Road. She turns into the path that goes past the Shan Cinema, crosses the Nairobi River and walks up through the Grogan Valley. Now she is in River Road, walking towards the garage between Tom Mboya Street and River Road, near Mũnyua Road.

As Waríínga walks along, people stop to watch her. Her faded blue *jeans* and khaki shirt and blue waistcoat, also faded, fit her beautifully. And not only these clothes. These days all her clothes fit her perfectly. For today Waríínga has dresses made for her or she buys them ready-made, but they always suit the shape, colour and movement of her beautiful body. It's her own body that now dictates how she'll dress, and not other people's figures and taste.

But it's not simply her clothes that have made her what she is now.

Today Waríínga strides along with energy and purpose, her dark eyes radiating the light of an inner courage, the courage and light of someone with firm aims in life – yes, the firmness and the courage and the faith of someone who has achieved something through self-reliance. What's the use of shuffling along timidly in one's own country? Waríínga, the black beauty! Waríínga of the mind and hands and body and heart, walking in rhythmic harmony on life's journey! Waríínga, the worker!

Those who are not acquainted with her might not guess straight away that this girl is a mechanical engineer who specializes in motor vehicles and other internal combustion engines. Those who like to belittle the minds, intelligence and abilities of our women might not believe that Waríínga is also an expert at fitting and turning, at forging and welding, at shaping metal to suit a variety of purposes.

People love to denigrate the intelligence and intellectual capacity of our women by saying that the only jobs a woman can do are to cook, to make beds and to spread their legs in the market of love. The Waríínga of today has rejected all that, reasoning that because her thighs are hers, her brain is hers, her hands are hers, and her body is hers, she must accord all her faculties their proper role and proper time and place and not let any one part be the sole ruler of her life, as if it had devoured all the others. That's why the Waríínga of today has said *goodbye* to being a secretary and has sworn that she will never type again for the likes of *Boss* Kíhara, *bosses* whose condition for employing a girl is a meeting for five minutes of love after a hard drink.

So Waríínga went to the *Polytechnic* to study the very engineering course she had always dreamed of while she was a student at *Nakuru Day Secondary*, long before the Rich Old Man from Ngorika came into her life and initiated her into the dance of the hunter and the hunted. Whenever she entered the engineering *workshop* and felt her whole body being shaken by the drills, as they sent out sparks of fire in every direction, or she hammered the iron that had already been smelted in the huge blast furnaces, Waríínga was always filled with the joy of someone who watches the power of her mind and body struggling against nature, turning molten iron, for instance, into products designed to enhance human lives.

218

But the skill that thrilled her most was her ability to take apart and re-assemble internal combustion engines. The smell of burning diesel or petrol was the most intoxicating perfume. The noise of machines in a workshop, of iron drilling into iron, of iron filing iron, of iron hammering on iron, of workers raising their voices above the noise of metal on metal – to Waríínga these noises were like a beautiful song sung by the best of choirs.

The music of a modern factory! That is good!

Waríínga has now done two years at the *Polytechnic*. She has one more year to go to the complete the course.

The first year was the hardest for Waríínga. The male students in her class used to laugh at her. But when they saw her struggling with heavy metal tools, just as they did, or sweating by the blast furnaces, just as they did, and facing up to every challenge, they began to laugh less and less and to swallow their sarcastic remarks. But all the laughter and the remarks came to a sudden end when the results of the first term's test were announced, and Waríínga came fourth out of a class of twenty-five. Instead of laughing, their respect for her increased, and they started treating her as one of their comrades in their journey's struggle.

She also had financial problems. Most students at the *Polytechnic* were sponsored by employers, who paid all their fees and other costs. But Waríínga had no sponsor. She was paying her own way. The money she had saved while working as a secretary at the *Champion Construction Company* was not enough to meet her fees, rent and food.

Gatuíria had offered to help with her fees and rent, but Waríínga refused. She did not want to bind herself to Gatuíria or to anyone else with strings of gratitude for charity. Self-reliance was self-reliance. So Waríínga managed only by undertaking all sorts of odd jobs, like hairdressing in a *Beauty Saloon*, or typing research papers and dissertations, which Gatuíria brought to her from the university.

During that first year Waríínga did not get enough rest. When she was not at school, she was at her books, and when she was not bent over her books, she was busy trying to earn money from odd jobs here and there, and when she was not doing any of these, she was attending judo and karate classes at the *Kenya Martial Arts Club* in the Ngara area. Waríínga had resolved that she should be able to defend herself and stand on her own in every way.

The problem of money eased in her second year. That was when Waríínga got a chance to offer her services as a self-employed mechanic at *Mwíhotori Kiwanja Garage*, near Múnyua Road.

Wariinga was always to remember the very first day she passed the open-air garage. It was a Friday afternoon, about two. She was very hungry. But when she saw men working on motor vehicles, she suddenly decided to ask them if she could join them to earn a few cents. When they heard her request, the mechanics were beside themselves with laughter. One of them, who was stooping under the open bonnet of a lorry, straightened up and looked at Wariinga with hatred, his mind searching for words to wound her. 'Woman, why don't you go and sell beer in a bar? Here there's no juke box to stand beside so that you can swing your skirt to attract men.' Wariinga suppressed her anger, for a beggar cannot afford to be too sensitive to insults. But she was determined to go on, for it's the man who wants a shit who goes to the toilet and not the toilet to him. 'I'm not standing here because of any desire to swing skirts or attract men,' she retorted.

A mechanic who was lying underneath another lorry stood up and announced in a deliberately loud, sarcastic voice, so that all those around could hear: 'Why don't you come over here and remove and dismantle this engine which has given us a headache all day, and tell us what the problem is?'

Wariinga steeled herself, and she suddenly felt courage flood through her body. Without moving from where she stood, Wariinga told the man that there was no need to dismantle the engine. 'Just start the engine,' Wariinga ordered him, with authority. After the engine had been started, Wariinga walked over to it, and for a full minute she just looked at it. By now all the other mechanics and even several passers-by had stopped whatever they were doing and had crowded around the lorry to watch a woman daring to storm a man's citadel. Wariinga took her eyes off the engine, and she started looking about her on the ground where the lorry was parked, as if she were searching for something. She found a piece of wood shaped like a spoon with a long handle. She picked it up and banged it on a stone to remove the dust. She placed one end of the spoon against the side of the engine, and she put the other end to her ear, just as a doctor places a *stethoscope* on the chest of a patient and listens to his heartbeat. Wariinga placed the end of the spoon at different points on the engine. The onlookers around her could not understand what she was doing. Suddenly Wariinga paused, and for a time she concentrated on the odd movement of the third cylinder. Then she called over the man who had been working on the engine, gave him the piece of wood and asked him to listen. He did as he was told. Some of the spectators laughed at him, while others made sarcastic comments about men who obeyed the childish orders of crazy women. Who had ever seen such madness as trying to find out what was wrong with an engine with a stick?

Waríínga asked him to describe what he could hear. The man promptly replied: 'I can only hear a kind of grinding noise, like the sound of dented pieces of metal eating into each other.'

Waríínga asked him: 'So what's the problem?' Now everybody held their breath, quite silent.

The man who only a moment ago had acted like the expert now looked about him wildly, as if seeking help from those around. Failing to find help in his test, he lowered his eyes. He felt a lump block his throat, and he stammered out: 'I don't know.'

Waríínga told him that the unpleasant noise was being caused by a loose bolt that joined the conrod to the crankshaft. The people round started clapping their hands. Others went away, shaking their heads, saying: 'Really, I've yet to see anything to beat that! So our women have acquired that much learning!' The other workers welcomed her as one of them, and they allowed her to use their tools until she could buy her own set.

From that day on, a deep friendship developed between Waríínga and the other workers. The more they saw Waríínga at work and observed that she did not avoid any type of work, the more they respected her.

One day a man brought in his car for a check. When he saw that it was Waríínga who opened the bonnet, he was clearly doubtful. But noticing Waríínga's beauty, he started teasing her light-heartedly, and then he touched her breasts. Waríínga raised her head, looked at him with eyes that held no laughter, and in a voice that indicated neither mirth nor anger, she calmly but firmly warned him against teasing her: 'I am a worker. You should respect or despise my work according to my performance. But my breasts are not part of this task. My beauty or ugliness has nothing to do with the job in hand.' The man took this to be the usual woman's come-hither pretence at offence, intended to lure him on. So when Waríínga bent over her work again, he fondled her buttocks.

Let me tell you, the lesson Waríínga taught that man, wherever he might be, he has probably never forgotten. For Waríínga turned like lightning, and in a twinkling of an eye, she had assaulted him with so many judo kicks and karate chops that for a time he saw stars. When he was finally felled by her judo kicks, he beseeched her to stop: 'I'm *sorry*.' The man got to his feet, took his car keys, started the engine and literally raised dust on the tarmac as he drove away.

Waríínga's fame spread to every corner of the city. The respect

221

of the other workers for her increased, and they sang of her diligence, perseverance and courage.

Wariinga, daughter of the Iregi rebels!

The fruits of each worker's labour went into his own pocket. But at the end of every month each worker would contribute a fixed sum to a common pool, from which they paid the ground rent for the garage to the Nairobi City Council and their other common expenses. And if one of the workers had an unexpected problem, he or she was allowed to borrow from the common pool to meet his or her needs. No one in that community of workers lived on the sweat of another. Everyone received according to his ability, his reputation and the quickness of his hands. When one of them had a lot of customers, he would pass on some of the work and the benefits to others with less work. The enterprise would never have made them rich, but self-employment did provide them with clothes and food and shelter. Their ambition was to build a modern, communally owned garage on that very site one day. Their leader had contacted the City Council and had been promised the site.

And so, during her second year, Wariinga was to be found at the Polytechnic, attending classes, or in her room at Ngara doing drawings as part of her homework, or at the *Mwihotori Kiwanjani Garage*.

It is to the garage that Wariinga is going this Saturday to finish her job before setting off on the journey to Ilmorog.

Wariinga enters a hotel near the garage, for that's where she keeps her overalls and her tool kit. Most of the workers who come to the hotel for a morning cup of tea know her. They exchange good-humoured remarks and jokes, including some that touch on the subject of men and women. But the playful remarks and the ribald jokes are based on mutual respect. They take her to be one of them. They feel she belongs to them all.

Wariinga changes into her greasy overalls. She hands her safari suitcase and her handbag over for safe-keeping at the hotel.

Wariinga goes out. She crosses the road.

Across the road stands the garage.

Her heart begins to beat faster. Why have all the other workers gathered together in a silent group, with faces set like those of people bereaved? Why are they all looking so anxious at such an early hour?

Hurry up, Wariinga! Faster, Wariinga! Move, Wariinga!

'Why are all you people looking so sad?'

'Don't ask any questions, friend.'

'No, tell me!'

222

'Our site has just been sold off.'

'Sold by whom?'

'By the City Council, of course.'

'To whom? To whom has our inheritance been sold?'

'To *Boss* Kĩhara and a group of foreigners from the USA, Germany and Japan.'

' To *Boss* Kĩhara?'

'He owns almost the whole of Nairobi. They intend to build a big tourist hotel on this site.'

'So that our women can have facilities for selling their flesh to foreigners!'

'Why can't they admit that they're building a factory for modern prostitution!'

'That's quite true. These tourist hotels are meant to nurture a nation of prostitutes, servants, cooks, shoeshine boys, bed makers, porters. . . .'

'Sum it up in a phrase, and say: to nurture servants to meet the whims of foreigners.'

Boss Kĩhara, the Devil's feast, foreigners, finance houses – and now tourism? Thoughts of these dance in Warĩĩnga's mind. And suddenly Warĩĩnga remembers Mũturi and Wangarĩ and the student leader. When will they be released from detention, if ever? Warĩĩnga feels as if she is suffocating with anger.

'When the bracken has been cleared from the land, fig trees often replace it, and they are both bad for the land. I ran away from cold only to run into frost!' one of the workers says, as if he were talking to himself.

'It would be terrible if we were to let them cut off our hands without offering any resistance!' Warĩĩnga says in a voice heavy with tears, as if replying to the other worker.

But her heart rages with the courage of a rebel.

3

It's the afternoon of that same Saturday. Warĩĩnga and Gatuĩria are on their way to Ilmorog. Gatuĩria is at the wheel of a red *Toyota Corolla*. They want to spend the night at Ilmorog and drive to Nakuru tomorrow morning.

They want to tell her parents about their decision to get married.

Gatuĩria is wearing grey trousers, a white shirt and a brown leather

223

jacket. Wariinga has changed out of the *jeans* she put on at Ngara earlier in the day. Now she is wearing a long kitenge dress of red and white flowers. Her hair is tied in plaits running from the front of her head to the back. Who could tell that this is the Wariinga who was dressed in *jeans* earlier today? Who could tell that this is the Wariinga who put on greasy overalls earlier today? And who would guess that this beautiful girl is an expert at judo and karate? Who would guess that those hands move more swiftly than lightning when they are holding a gun?

Gatuiria steals glances at Wariinga. His eyes have never tired of her beauty. And his inner eye is telling him: Not many months from now, this lovely woman will be known as Wariinga wa Gatuiria. When such thoughts strike him, Gatuiria feels a sharp pang in his stomach and back; his heart rises as if it had wings to fly; and his body feels all warm with the blood of love. His heart begins to sing: Happy is the woman whose heart beats to the sound of the loved one calling out at the gate as he returns from the victorious defence of his country against enemy attack. Happy is the man whose heart beats in time to the voice of his love drawing water or gathering greens in the valley. Happy are the men and women whose hearts beat in unison as they sit on a platform at night to scare away birds from the millet fingers. Happy are men and women when youthful blood courses through their veins, their hearts crying out to each other: What can I do, my love, now that my love for you has weakened me so?

At such moments, the talker feels as if he or she were speaking beautiful verse like the poetry of a gicaandi singer, and the listener feels the words of the loved one plucking at the golden strings of the harp lodged in the heart. That's how Gatuiria and Wariinga feel now, as they travel to Ilmorog asking each other riddles of love.

Gatuiria is talking about music. It was soon after the Devil's feast that Gatuiria decided that the period of searching was over and that the clan those who cry of 'I'll do it tomorrow' would wait forever for a morrow that will never come. Gatuiria decided then that he would never again talk about the composition of a national oratorio until he had accomplished the task, a score to be sung by hundreds of human voices, with an orchestra of hundreds of instruments. He also decided that he would never discuss the issue of marriage or even introduce Wariinga to his parents until he had successfully crossed the river of his intended composition.

For two years Gatuiria concentrated exclusively on his work, and he would literally lock himself into his study whenever the Muse visited him. At such times Gatuĩria never allowed anybody to enter his study. A task is a burden only when it has not been tackled.

Gatuĩria has now accomplished the musical feat. And he has also won Warĩĩnga's heart. When Warĩĩnga accepted his proposal, he sent a letter to his father immediately, telling him that after years of wandering he, Gatuĩria, would now like to return, bringing home the darling of his heart and the fruits of his research in music.

And his father promptly replied: 'My only son, your decision to come back home and ask your father's blessing is a fine one. My extensive property still cries out for a manager with modern know-how. Come back home quickly, so that I can have you fitted out with the best robes and a ring to put on your hand, and so that a fatted calf can be slaughtered for you. We will eat and be merry together, for you were dead and are alive again; you were lost and are now found. Bring home your intended, so that our bodies and souls can rejoice together. God has hearkened unto the cry of our hearts!'

'And so tomorrow the fatted calf is to be killed for you,' Warĩĩnga tells Gatuĩria.

'More than one,' Gatuĩria replies, laughing. 'His letter suggests that he is taking me for the prodigal son who went into a far country and there wasted his substance on riotous living, music and prostitutes. I am sure he has been deep in prayer, beseeching God that I may return home and stop throwing the pearls of my life before swine!'

'What if they should find out that you haven't stopped casting your precious pearls before swine?'

'I'm not afraid. When he sees what I've brought him, his heart will break with sheer joy.'

'Over me or the score?' Warĩĩnga asks, with laughter in her eyes.

'How can you compare your own beauty with mere sheets of music!' Gatuĩria demands, pretending to be a little angry. 'You don't seem to have any idea. Since the Devil's feast, it's as if you have been transfigured, body and soul. Your skin has a depth of blackness that is softer and more tender than the most expensive perfume oil. Your dark eyes shine more brightly than the stars at night. Your cheeks are like two fruits riper than the blackberry. Your hair is so black and soft and smooth that all men feel like sheltering from the sun in its shade. Your voice is sweeter than the sound of a thousand and one musical instruments. Warĩĩnga, my love, you are the music of my soul.'

His words suddenly startle Warĩĩnga. A shadow crosses her face

225

and laughter disappears from her eyes. How can words she heard two years ago now spring from Gatuīria's own lips? Words spoken in a dream two years ago. . . . Warīīnga does not want to tell Gatuīria about the fear that has suddenly seized her, and she does not want Gatuīria to go on about her beauty. She tries to divert the conversation into different channels.

'Tell me about the oratorio,' Warīīnga says. 'To tell the truth, I'd never thought that any music could take a whole two years to compose.'

'Music that tells the story of one's country? Music to be played by an orchestra of hundreds of instruments and sung by hundreds of human voices? And remember, you have to indicate where each instrument and each voice comes in. My friend, there is music and *the* music; there is song and *the* song! In fact, if I hadn't met you and gazed into your eyes, and if love hadn't given my heart wings, I don't know if I could ever have completed this score. But when I locked myself away in my study, I could see your lovely face beckoning me, urging me, telling me: Finish it, my love, so that we can go away together. The gift that will be waiting for you when you have completed the task is very special. . . .'

And because of that, Gatuīria had decided that his score would be Warīīnga's engagement ring. He had decided that on completing the score, he would offer it to Warīīnga in front of his own parents at Nakuru. He had also decided that the first performance would take place on their wedding night. Tomorrow would be the first stage towards the union of their hearts: during tomorrow's ceremony Gatuīria intended to offer her the two hundred sheets of music, the fruits of two years of the labour of his heart. . . .

'I asked you about the music and not about my face,' Warīīnga tells Gatuīria, still trying to change the subject.

Gatuīria is turning over in his mind all the problems he faced as he composed the music. He wonders how to explain a work that runs to two hundred pages in a handful of words. How can a work that took two years to complete be summed up into two minutes?

In his mind, of course, Gatuīria can reconstruct the whole process of mixing the various voices and the various sounds in harmony: how and where all the voices meet; how and where they part, each voice taking its own separate path; and finally how and where they come together again, the various voices floating in harmony like the Thīrīrīka River flowing through flat plains towards the sea, all the voices blending into each other like the colours of the rainbow. The same is true of the instruments. In his mind, Gatuīria can hear where the instruments meet to create a single sound; where the instruments part; and where each instrument carries the theme on its own. But most clearly Gatuĩria can hear the voices and the instruments joining together in a single chorus of harmony, sometimes lifting the hearts of the audience to peaks of joy, at other times hurling their hearts into depths of sorrow. Gatuĩria can even visualize the audience surging out of the concert hall, angry at those who sold the soul of the nation to foreigners and babbling with joy at the deeds of those who rescued the soul of the nation from foreign slavery. Gatuĩria hopes above all that his music will inspire people with patriotic love for Kenya.

All these things are seething in Gatuĩria's mind, each sound image chased by other sound images, as if they were all fighting for dominance in the arena of Gatuĩria's thoughts and imagination. As he steers the red *Toyota* towards Ilmorog, Gatuĩria can hear the voices and the sounds of men and instruments calling him. . . .

First Movement

Voices from the past, before the coming of British imperialism
> The gĩcaandĩ calabash
> The one-stringed violin
> Drum, flutes
> Rattles, horns
> Stringed instruments
> Wind instruments
> Percussion instruments

Dancing	**Our women**	Clearing forests
Asking riddles	**Our men**	Clearing the bush
Telling stories	**Our children**	Digging
Praying	**Young men**	Breaking up clods
Settling disputes	**Young women**	of clay
Taking part in ritual	**Boys**	Planting
ceremonies	**Girls**	Cultivating
Birth	**The crowd**	Protecting millet
Second birth	**The masses**	from the birds
Initiation		Harvesting
Marriages		Grazing
Burials		Building houses
		Working with iron
		Making pottery

And the sound of the feet of young men
At the cattle kraal,
Defending the wealth of the land
From foreign foes,
To prevent them from eating
That which has been produced by others.
The sounds of spears and shields.
The voices of patriots.

Second Movement

Foreign voices
Voices of imperialism
Drums
Trumpets

After our land **Foreigners** Their aims:
After our labour **and** Our wealth
After slaves **their armies** Our herds
After all the Our harvest
   shadows of the Our industries
   land Our creations

The struggle against the foreign forces.
The voices of patriots.
   Horn trumpets
   Drums
   Flutes
The sound of the foreign forces retreating.
Patriotic songs of victory.
Songs of Waiyaki, Koitalel, Me Kitilili,
Gakuunju . . .

Third Movement

Foreign voices, oily, smooth with hypocrisy
Drums
Flutes
Piano, organ
   Christian choirs

They secure loyalty from:	Foreigners	Their aims:
Chiefs	Priests	Wealth
Bishops	Educators	The means:
Feudalists	Administrators	Divide and rule
Sellers of the soul of the nation	Armed soldiers	Capture their souls

The imperialist flag

The struggle of cultures.
People taken captives.
The nation divided.
Revolutionary activities banned.
Some young men have hung up their arms;
Now they have no weapons.
Voices of the soldiers of imperialism.
The sounds of chains on our people,
Chains on hands,
Chains on legs.

Fourth Movement

The voices of slavery
Piano
Guitar
Saxophones
Drums and trumpets
The voices of the people picking tea.
The voices of the people picking coffee.
The voices of the people picking cotton.
The voices of the people harvesting wheat.
The voices of workers in a factory.

Fifth Movement

Sounds and voices of a new struggle,
To rescue the soul of the nation.
Horns
Drums
Flutes

Voices of rebirth.
Voices of our heroes.
Voices of Mau Mau.
Voices of revolution.
Voices of revolutionary unity of workers
    and peasants . . .

Gatuĩria is trying to explain to Warĩĩnga the movement of the different voice and sounds. He is trying to explain to Warĩĩnga the kinds of instrument that might be made to represent the workers and peasants as they rescue the soul of the nation from imperialist slavery. He is trying to explain the difficulties of writing down African music, for the notation of African music has not yet been sufficiently developed and differentiated from that of European music.

And suddenly Gatuĩria notices that Warĩĩnga is not listening. 'What's the matter?' he asks.

'You mentioned workers and peasants, and it reminded me of Wangarĩ and Muturi and . . . and. . . .'

'The student leader?'

'Oh, yes, and the student leader.'

'Do you ever forget the Trinity?' Gatuĩria asks.

'The Holy Trinity of the worker, the peasant, the patriot,' Warĩĩnga replies, pauses and then continues: 'No, no, I have never forgotten them. I have never forgotten their court appearance. God, I shall never forget the trial of the Holy Trinity. . . .'

4

Virtually the whole of Ilmorog had attended the trial. The Ilmorog courtroom was filled to capacity with two types of listener. On the one side were people like Kĩhaahu wa Gatheeca, Gĩtutu wa Gataangũrũ, Nditika wa Ngũũnji, Kĩmeendeeri wa Kanyuanjii and many others who had attended the Devil's feast. On the other side was the crowd of workers, peasants, students, petty traders and so on. The judge was a white man, and he wore a blood-red gown. The court clerk scribbled things down as he interpreted.

In the dock sat Mũturi, Wangarĩ and the student leader, guarded by prison warders and policemen. The three were charged with the offence of disturbing the public peace at Ilmorog Golf Course during a meeting of some *private businessmen* and, in the process, causing the death of seven persons.

Gatuīria and Warīīnga had been summoned to Ilmorog police station, and after being questioned, they had been asked if they would act as witnesses for the prosecution. They refused. The prosecution's witnesses now consisted of the likes of Gītutu and Kīhaahu and the police. But the principal witness for the prosecution was Robin Mwaūra, *owner*-driver of Matatū Matata Model T Ford, registration number MMM 333.

Mwaūra told the court that on a certain Saturday he picked up two passengers, Wangarī and Mūturi, in Nairobi in his car. But right from the start, Mwaūra could see that Wangarī and Mūturi were not trustworthy. Wangarī had even refused to pay the fare, beating her breast and claiming that everything in Kenya should be provided free. Mūturi was clearly in league with Wangarī, for it was he who had paid her fare. Mūturi and Wangarī had talked all they way from Nairobi to Ilmorog, and they had talked of nothing but the unity of workers and peasants and the need for the kind of communism advocated by university students. He himself, with his own ears, had heard Wangarī bragging about how she was going to ruin the feast at the cave by deceiving the Nairobi and Ilmorog police into believing that it was a gathering of thieves and robbers. Mwaūra also heard Mūturi boasting that he would rally the workers and peasants and destroy the feast in revenge for being dismissed from his job by the directors of the *Champion Construction Company*.

Mwaūra then told the court that these two were clearly in league with a certain Mwīreri wa Mūkiraaī. Mwīreri had been silent for most of the journey. But the silence was pure hypocrisy because towards the journey's end, it was he who had given Wangarī and Mūturi invitations to the feast. When Mwīreri wa Mūkiraaī saw that the disturbance he had planned with the two accused was about to erupt, he had very cleverly left the cave and rented Mwaūra's *matatū* for a night journey back to his home, but unfortunately the vehicle had overturned at Kīneeniī. Mwīreri had died on the spot. The vehicle was a write-off. He, Mwaūra, had had a very narrow escape. . . .

Mwaūra was in the middle of his story when a note was handed to the prosecutor. The prosecutor read the note, then he walked up to the bench and whispered something in the judge's ear. The judge immediately announced that the charges against the accused had been withdrawn, and that therefore Mūturi, Wangarī and the student leader were now free. People did not even wait to hear under what

231

Section of the Penal Code the accused had been released. Workers, peasants and students shouted with joy.

Warĩĩnga ran outside the courtroom to embrace Wangarĩ, Mũturi and the student leader.

She almost fell to the ground with shock. The whole courtroom was completely surrounded by soldiers armed with guns and shields and batons. When Wangarĩ and Mũturi and the student stepped outside the courtroom, they were met with guns and chains.

It was only two weeks later that people learned that Mũturi and Wangarĩ and the student leader had been detained – and a month after that, Mwaũra bought three brand-new vehicles, which he converted into *matatũs*. The company he formed was called the *Matatũ Matata Matamu Modern Transport Company*. The master of ceremonies was one of the directors of the company; the other was Kĩmeendeeri wa Kanyuanjii. . . .

5

'Are they still alive?' Warĩĩnga asks Gatuĩria. 'Sometimes I feel that they were probably taken to Ngong Hills.'

'Who knows?' Gatuĩria says, still steering the red *Toyota*. 'Let's wait for 12 December. They might be released along with the ordinary convicts.'

'Amen!' Warĩĩnga says, with all her heart. 'That will be the day when real music will sound in my soul!'

Chapter Eleven

1

Our Ilmorog, it appears, does not change much. Two whole years after the Devil's feast, Ilmorog manifested the same divisions as before. The Golden Heights had gone on expanding. Mansions with walls decorated with candles in gold candelabra and Persian carpets on the floors were still being built with the wealth that local tycoons had in excess. The same was true of beds made out of silver and gold: this had become so common and normal that nobody would have thought that the other residents of the area would even be surprised at it. Foreign companies, especially those from the USA, Canada, West Germany, France, Britain, Italy and Japan, had increased. The car was a good measure of the increased dominance of foreign property over our lives. (The truth of the matter is that today there is not a single make of car – *Toyota, Datsun, Mazda, Honda, Subaru, Ford, Cadillac, Vauhxhall, Volvo, Fiat, Peugeot, Rolls Royce, Bentley, Jaguar, Alfa Romeo, Mercedes Benz, BMW* and many others – you will not find spinning along Ilmorog's roads.) Foreign finance houses and stores – the ones that call themselves insurance companies and banks – that gathered in people's money had virtually overrun Ilmorog. Two American banks, from Chicago and New York, were the latest to build stores, money-trading bases, in this heartland of wealth.

Njeruca too had expanded. Cardboard shelters, trenches filled with foul water, detritus from the foreign-owned factories, shit and urine had expanded Njeruca slightly. Even the villages that used to be on the outskirts of Njeruca – like Ngaindeithia Village, where Waríínga's parents lived – had been swallowed up by Njeruca. Workers, the unemployed, the very poor, sellers of illegal brews and sellers of oranges and Mandazi, traders in their own bodies were all crammed into the vast Njeruca slumyard. Njeruca also had several tiny shops that sold meat, eggs, *sukuma wiki* vegetables, salt, beer, pepper, onions and flour.

The owners of these shops and slum shelters were the Golden Heights residents. Some visited Njeruca to collect their *rent* and profit, but most of them employed thugs to collect *rent* for them. Even the *Devil's Angels* had established a branch in Ilmorog.

Waríínga's parents lived in Njeruca. But they still referred to their section as Ngaindeithia Village. Their house was slightly larger than most, for when Warĩĩnga worked as a secretary, she had helped them to extend it. With the little money she had been earning at the garage, she had also helped them to pay school fees and to buy food.

It was in Ngaindeithia Village, in Njeruca, Ilmorog, that Gatuĩria and Warĩĩnga made their first stop.

2

It is Saturday, about five in the evening. Warĩĩnga's father is out. Wambũi, Wariinga's daughter, and the other children have gone for a walk in Njeruca. But all is well. Warĩĩnga's mother is in.

Warĩĩnga and Gatuĩria tell Warĩĩnga's mother of their intention to marry, so they can start a home of their own like other people. Warĩĩnga's mother clears her throat. She is elderly, but she is one of those people who never seem to age. Her white-and-black flowered frock, though it is a little faded, fits her well. She showers her breast with saliva, by way of blessing, but she has a question to ask, just one question.

'I'm going to put my question to you, Warĩĩnga. And I am going to ask you the question in front of this young man so that he can hear the answer too, because you modern girls are difficult to fathom. Have you told this young man that you have a daughter old enough to be initiated into womanhood – that is, if girls were still circumcised, as they used to be?'

'Is my little Wambũi the girl you're calling a woman?' Warĩĩnga asks, laughing. 'She's not something I've covered up. I've told Gatuĩria everything. Besides, he met her when he was last here, during the feast two years ago. But nobody will ever be able to tell that Wambũi and Gatuĩria are not related by blood. Don't you think they look alike? They could be twins – only Gatuĩria's an old man!'

'You're quite right,' Warĩĩnga's mother agrees, without hesitation. 'They really do look alike.'

'What is a blood relation?' Gatuĩria asks, slightly irritated. 'What does it matter if people are alike or not? A child is a child. We all come from the same womb, the common womb of one Kenya. The blood shed for our freedom has washed away the differences between that clan and this one, this nationality and that one. Today there is no Luo, Gĩkũyũ, Kamba, Giriama, Luhya, Maasai, Meru,

234

Kallenjin or Turkana. We are all children of one mother. Our mother is Kenya, the mother of all Kenyan people.'

'You've spoken up well, young man!' Waríínga's mother replies. 'May God help you always to cultivate fertile fields. Today our girls think only of throwing their babies into latrines or leaving them in rubbish bins so that they won't be rejected by their young men.'

'I almost killed myself,' Waríínga says, 'and all because of being rejected by a Rich Old Man. Really! Fancy throwing myself in front of a train on account of the clan that consigned Múturi and the others to detention!'

'Only a fool sucks at the tits of his mother's corpse,' Waríínga's mother says. 'Youth is nothing but foolishness at times.'

'*Forget it!*' Gatuíria tries to restrain Waríínga from reviving the issue. 'What's past is past.'

'I don't any longer lose sleep over what I lost,' Waríínga says, laughing. 'If I'd married my hairy-chested Waigoko, where would I ever have found a young man like you? But I was told by someone that modern Waigokos have their chests shaved smooth by money. Money is the modern youth.'

'Money isn't life,' Waríínga's mother says. 'Whether it's an old man or a young man, what's important is the happiness that springs from a person's deeds on Earth. Waríínga, why don't you take Gatuíria for a walk around Ilmorog, while I cook something? Go away and by the time you come back, you'll find your father in, and then you can tell him all about your plans.'

'That's a good idea, mother,' Gatuíria says, standing up. 'I haven't walked around Ilmorog since that feast. . . .'

3

Once again Waríínga and Gatuíria are heading towards the Golden Heights for a breath of cool, fresh air. It is evening. The grass in *Ilmorog Park* is soft and green. The trees there spread their branches and leaves like umbrellas.

Gatuíria stops the *Toyota* at the side of the road, as they both want to walk on the green grass and through the trees. They climb to the top of the ridge to look at the plains lying below, with their wheat and barley plantations, the property of Theng'eta Breweries.

This is joy: when the blood of youth flows in harmony down the valley of love. Waríínga and Gatuíria are standing together, their shoulders touching, looking at the plains below and at the distant hills.

'I'm always glad when I hear you say what you said when we were at home,' Wariinga begins.

'What did I say?' Gatuiria asks. 'I said lots of things.'

'That there's nothing shameful about a girl becoming pregnant. That a baby born out of wedlock is not a disease,' Wariinga replies promptly.

'Didn't I tell you to forget the past?' Gatuiria asks her. 'Let's be happy today and tomorrow. We have jumped one hurdle on our journey: your mother has blessed us. My heart is bubbling over with joy. Who could claim to be luckier than me? I have composed the music that it has always been my ambition to compose. And now I have a special gift – a beauty to beat all beauties.'

'You are giving the same kind of testimony as those thieves and robbers offered us in Ilmorog!' Wariinga tells him, laughing. 'You should wait for someone else to sing your praises!'

'But I'm telling the truth. I'm singing the praises of joy. What do you think is the one thing that I need to make my joy burst its banks?'

'I can't read a letter that's sealed in the envelope of your heart,' Wariinga says, holding back her laughter as she remembers *Boss* Kihara's words in the office. 'Tell me what you're waiting for, so that when I see your joy in flood, I can jump to one side so that I'm not carried away.'

'I'm waiting for the blessing of my parents at Nakuru tomorrow,' Gatuiria answers.

'What do your parents look like?' Wariinga asks suddenly. 'Do you look like your father or your mother?'

Gatuiria has never heard Wariinga ask that kind of question before. He does not know how to answer her. In his heart of hearts, Gatuiria has always felt ashamed of his parents because of the way they cover themselves in the robes of foreign customs at all times, equating European culture with the culture of God. Even now Gatuiria is not quite sure how his parents will receive Wariinga tomorrow, especially when they learn that she has had a child by another man. But he has made up his mind about one thing: no matter how they receive her, Wariinga is his chosen bride. More to the point, he does not know whether Wariinga herself will accept his parents. Will she despise them when she sees their behaviour tomorrow? Will she change her mind about him after discovering that the foreign customs that she and Gatuiria have often discussed and condemned are entrenched in his parent's home?

236

These are the doubts that have prevented Gatuīria from showing Warīīnga the invitation card that his parents have sent out to friends, asking them to attend a tea party to welcome Gatuīria and his fiancée. To begin with, Gatuīria would not like Warīīnga to see the names that his father has assumed. The card is printed in letters of gold and decorated at the edges with golden flowers. But what makes Gatuīria even more ashamed than the fact that the card advises the guests how to dress for the occasion is that on the card are listed the names of the shops from which the guests may buy gifts.

A Feast! A Feast!

NGORIKA HEAVENLY ORCHARDS

Mr and Mrs Hispaniora Greenway Ghitahy have the pleasure of inviting Mr and Mrs/Miss/Dr/Prof./The Hon. MP/ ....
to a tea party to welcome home their son,
Master Gatuīria Ghitahy, and his fiancée,
on Sunday .... at exactly two o'clock.

Dress:
Men – Dark suits
Ladies – Long dresses, hats, gloves.
If you care to bring a gift, you can get one from the following VIP shops:
Men's and Ladies' London Shop, Ilmorog;
The Shop with the Parisian Look, Nairobi;
The Woman of Rome VIP Shop, Nakuru.

RSVP: Mr and Mrs H.G. Ghitahy,
Ngorika Heavenly Orchards,
Private Bag,
Nakuru, Kenya, EA
Tel. HCOV 10000 000

I look up unto the hills from whence cometh my help.
Psalm of David.

As he thinks about the card, Gatuīria feels like weeping. There is nothing as terrible as a people who have swallowed foreign customs whole, without even chewing them, for such people become mere parrots. The doubts that have prevented Gatuīria from showing Warīīnga the card are those that are now making him hesitate over replying to Warīīnga's question.

'Have you forgotten what your parents look like? Why are you so quiet in response to my question?' Warīīnga prompts him.

'Shut your eyes until two tomorrow afternoon,' Gatuīria replies, trying to adopt a light-hearted tone. 'And when you open them, guess who you'll see! Gatuīria's parents. And lo, it will come to pass that all Warīīnga's doubts shall be washed away.'

As Gatuīria talks, his arm is around Warīīnga's waist, and Warīīnga leans her head on Gatuīria's shoulder.

'Ah . . . tomorrow. Let it dawn soon so that we can share the fresh water with the early bird,' Warīīnga sighs. Her voice seems to come from far away.

Two tears run down her cheeks, like dew drops forming on the smooth skin of ripened fruit when the sun is rising. Only now the sun is setting over the Golden Heights.

'What is it? What's the matter, my love?' Gatuīria asks, worried. 'What has burdened your heart so suddenly? Are you angry? Because I was only joking.'

4

'It's not that,' Warīīnga replies. 'Don't take any notice of my tears. I sometimes find myself crying for no particular reason. Did I tell you that today we were informed that we have to quit our Mwīhotori garage premises?'

'Leave your site? Move? And abandon the site to whom?'

'To *Boss* Kīhara and his new company, the *Tourists' Paradise Development Company*.'

'The man who sacked you for refusing to sleep with him?'

'Yes, he and his foreign friends have stripped us in broad daylight,' Warīīnga says, and then, remembering the parable told them by Mwīreri wa Mūkiraaī, she adds in the tone of a priest, 'so that the words of the Prophet will be fulfilled, when he told us: Unto every one that hath shall be given, and he shall have abundance . . . .'

' . . . but from him that hath not shall be taken away even that

238

which he hath,' Gatuīria finishes the sentence, adopting the same priestly tone.

Warīīnga and Gatuīria laugh together. Then, at the same moment, they stop laughing. For a minute each is alone with his separate thoughts. Warīīnga sighs.

'Do you remember that I told you once, in Njeruca, about a dream I used to have when I was a student at the *Nakuru Day Secondary*?'

'About the Devil being crucified on the Cross by people in tattered clothes?'

'Yes. And on the third day he would be lifted down from the Cross by people in dark suits and ties.'

'And they would then kneel down before him, and cry "*Hosanna! Hosanna!*" Yes, I can remember you telling me something of the sort. But remember what I told you. Many churches have paintings and engravings on their walls and windows. Pictures like those can give a person nightmares. But why do you ask?' Gatuīria says, looking Warīīnga in the face.

'Because I had the same dream last night. And you know, these days I hardly ever go into a church. But last night's dream was a little different from the usual one. In last night's dream, the tie-wearing tribe didn't even wait for three days to elapse. And they didn't approach the Cross stealthily. Last night the men in ties came as soon as the Devil was on the Cross. They were led by armoured cars with big guns. They lifted him down and started singing his praises, guarded on every side by the armoured cars.'

'And the people in rags?' Gatuīria asks. 'What did they do when they were caught in the act?'

'I couldn't see clearly. But I think they scattered and went to the forests and to the mountains, singing songs that I had not heard before. I woke before the nightmare was over.'

'Don't let the nightmares worry you.' Gatuīria tries to Warīīnga's spirits. 'Don't forget that two years ago you saw armoured cars chasing away workers and peasants and students who had come to the court during the hearing of the case of Mūturi and company. You had the dream about armoured cars because your brain knew that today you were coming to Ilmorog. Q.E.D.'

'That seems to be the case,' Warīīnga says, with a lighter heart.' You'd make a good Yahya Hussein! Why don't you set up in business and interpret people's dreams? You could earn a bit from the trade.'

'I could call myself *Prof.* Gatuīria, interpreter of dreams and nightmares. "If you need a herb to cure all ailments, come to *Prof.*

Gatuīria! If you need love potions, come to me! *Past achievements* ... I was the first to predict that a day would come when the sun would rise in the morning and set in the evening!"'

Warīīnga and Gatuīria laugh together.

5

It is true that love has no fear. It is true that love knows no pain or trouble or bad dreams. Love knows not yesterday or the day before; it knows only tomorrow and the day after tomorrow, the beginning of eternal happiness. Gatuīria's and Warīīnga's future will begin tomorrow. . . .

'But it's not those two things – being thrown off our site and having nightmares – that are making me cry,' Warīīnga explains to Gatuīria.

'Then wipe away your tears,' Gatuīria replies.

'These tears can't be wiped away today,' Warīīnga says, 'for they are born of a mixture of sorrow and joy.'

'What do you mean?'

'I have never been back to Nakuru since I tried to take my own life. I have been telling myself: Nakuru was the beginning of my sorrow. Tomorrow the same Nakuru will mark the beginning of my joy.'

'What's wrong with that?' Gatuīria asks. 'The Nakuru of tomorrow will avenge the Nakuru of yesterday.' Gatuīria tries to smooth away the weight in Warīīnga's heart.

'Yes, that's it. Nakuru is to become the source of both tears and laughter.'

'Amen,' Gatuīria says. 'So wipe away your tears, for Nakuru is a source of miracles. It produces joy out of sorrow. Why don't you wipe away your tears? Let me wipe them away with love.'

'You, professor of lies!' Warīīnga cries, pushing Gatuīria away with a hand that does not quite mean it. 'Where did you learn this foreign habit of kissing? Confess that you've never given up foreign habits!'

'Confess that you want black people's kisses!' Gatuīria retorts, smiling and moving closer to Warīīnga. Warīīnga leans away from him, but they are talking all the time. 'Kisses and whispers in a bed of love,' Gatuīria says, and he starts to sing a Mūthūūngūūci verse:

Gatuĩria:	Where I now hold you,
	Where I now hold you,
	Do you feel I am pressing too hard?
Warĩĩnga:	Where you now hold me,
	Where you now hold me,
	It is good so.
	Man, hold, and don't let go.
Gatuĩria:	Dance, and we'll go home together.
	Dance, and we'll go home together,
	My love.
	For I won't let you leave me out in the cold.

As he sings the last line, he grabs and embraces Warĩĩnga.

'And who taught you Mũthũũngũũci songs and dances?' Warĩĩnga asks.

'The old man I told you about, the one from Bahati, Nakuru, who told me the tale about Nging'uri, who sold his soul to an evil spirit and was left an empty shell,' Gatuĩria replies.

'But he didn't tell you to use the song for wicked ends, on a hill over which darkness is falling.'

'Haven't you heard that darkness makes even a poor dancer to dance with confidence?

I'll dance here on the surface,
I'll dance here on the surface,
Oh, Warĩĩnga,
For the valley below belongs to the owner....'

'Go away, you wicked man!' Warĩĩnga says, laughing. 'Can't you see there's dew on the grass and darkness has fallen?'

'Come to me, my love!' Gatuĩria whispers in her ear, pulling her to the ground. 'The grass is a free bed given us by God, and the darkness is his blanket!'

Chapter Twelve

1

When Gatuĩria came to collect Warĩĩnga on Sunday morning he found her ready, beautifully dressed from head to foot. Gatuĩria was struck dumb, unable at first to recognize Warĩĩnga.

Warĩĩnga was dressed the Gĩkũyũ way. A brown cloth, folded over a little at the top, had been passed under her left armpit, the two ends gathered together and held at the right shoulder by two flower-shaped safety pins, so that her left shoulder was bare. The cloth was long and fell to her ankles; its edges were held together on her right side with safety pins. Around her waist Warĩĩnga had tied a knitted belt of white wool, the two long, loose ends of which fell the length of the cloth to her ankles. On her feet she wore leopard-skin sandals. Around her neck were necklaces of white, red and blue beads, which sat beautifully on her breasts. She had Nyori-like earrings. Her hair was smooth, soft and black.

As she walked, Warĩĩnga appeared to be the child of Beauty, mother of all beauties, just created by the creator of the twins, elegance and beauty.

'Can a simple length of cloth really turn out to be so beautiful?' These were Gatuĩria's first words on recovering his speech.

'You mean the cloth is more beautiful than I am? In that case I should take it off at once!' Warĩĩnga said lightheartedly.

'A smooth body is made of perfume oil,' Gatuĩria replied in the same bantering tone, 'but perfume oil is not made out of a beautiful body. *Mke ni nguo . . . . Lakini nguo si mke.*'

'Sometimes I feel guilty about decorating my body,' Warĩĩnga said, in a slightly sad voice.

'Why?' Gatuĩria asked.

'These are not times for decorating our bodies with necklaces and perfume,' Warĩĩnga replied. 'These are times for keeping our bodies and minds in a state of readiness.'

'For . . .?'

'The struggles ahead.'

'Those will come soon enough,' Gatuĩria replied promptly. 'Today is today. Don't take off the cloth. The struggle for national cultures is still a relevant struggle.' He broke off to sing, and Warĩĩnga joined in.

Gatuīria: If God's Heaven were close by,
             I would file a lawsuit against women.
             Beautiful bodies given you free by God –
             Why do you ruin them with skin-lightening creams?
Warīīnga: Young man, hurry! Hurry! We are leaving!
             Run! Run faster! We are leaving for the Court in
                Heaven!
             Eyes given you free by God –
             Oh, our people, why are they only pleased at the
                sight of foreign things?

In a gay mood, they climbed into their *Toyota* to drive to Nakuru
to put an end to all doubts.

Gatuīria kept stealing glances at Warīīnga and praising the way
she had dressed in her cloth and beads, till Warīīnga was forced to
warn him: 'Concentrate on the steering-wheel, young man. Or do
you want us to overturn like Matatū Matata Matamu?'

'Earthly life is a passing cloud,' Gatuīria replied. 'If we
overturned now, I'd be very happy, for if you stood at the gates of
Heaven dressed as you are, the angel who keeps the keys would rush
to open the gates wide. And as you entered, I, the sinner, would get
a chance to enter Heaven too and live forever with you and the
Lord.'

'This Earth is my home. I am not passing through. So drive
carefully because I'm no longer in such a hurry to get to Heaven.'

'You're quite right. But as your Earth is my Heaven, I have to look
at you over and over again, for nobody is satisfied with just one
glance at a beauty.'

They stopped off in places like Naivasha and Gilgil for tea or soft
drinks just to pass the time until two. Gatuīria was not unhappy
about that. His heart overflowed with joy at the sight of Warīīnga
walking along, dressed in that cloth and her necklaces and earrings,
with a handbag hanging over one shoulder, the backs of her heels
just showing. And Gatuīria was not alone. Several passers-by
stopped to watch Warīīnga.

'Oh, that's a fine-looking woman,' some said.

Others commented: 'You see, there's no tradition that can't be
developed. Wherever she goes, people will defer to the beauty of
that young woman.'

Back in the car, Gatuīria elaborated on their comments. 'Those
people are simply telling the truth. There's no national tradition that
we, the people of Kenya, can't develop and build on – our
architecture, our songs and our way of singing them, our theatre, our

literature, our technology, our economy. Although Mwīreri wa Mūkiraaī didn't reject the system of eating what has been produced by others, some of what he said was true. The essence of his speech was right: that we shouldn't always run after foreign things, following in the footsteps of other people, singing only songs that have been composed by others, joining in the chorus of songs sung by soloists from other lands. We can compose our own songs, produce our own soloists, sing the songs to ourselves.'

'Your own composition could start a revolution in Kenyan music,' Warīīnga told Gatuīria, and then added with a laugh, 'Gatuīria Juu!'

'I am not a politician, so don't pay lip-service to my talent,' Gatuīria said. 'Revolution? Your words remind me of what a Russian composer, Igor Stravinsky, once said in his book *Poetics of Music*. He argued that there was no real revolution in music: each composer only adds something to what others have done before. But I say amen to your thoughts. We, the Kenyan youth, must be the light to light up new paths of progress for our country.

"You, for instance, are a very good example of what I am trying to say. Your training in mechanical engineering, fitting and turning and moulding, is a very important step. It is a kind of signal to indicate to other girls their abilities and potential.'

For a minute Warīīnga heard not Gatuīria's voice, but the voice of her lecturer at the *Polytechnic*, talking to them about the workings of an internal combustion engine, especially a motor vehicle engine . . . .

'A motor vehicle has several parts that make it work. The power that makes it move comes from the internal combustion of fuel. An engine is to the motor vehicle what a heart is to the human body. It is the engine that converts a mixture of air and fuel into the power that makes the vehicle move. There are two types of internal combustion engine, the diesel and the petrol, but today we shall only discuss the one that consumes petrol. An engine has a block with four or six cylinders. Each cylinder has a piston that is connected to the crankshaft by a conrod. A piston is like a pestle for crushing a mixture of air and petrol. There are two valves in each cylinder: the inlet for the mixture of air and petrol, and the outlet for the exhaust. Each cylinder has a spark plug. Petrol and air are mixed in the carburettor.

Combustion has four main stages: induction, compression, ignition or firing and exhaust. Let us take one cylinder, to see how it works. Now, the vehicle has been started by switching on the starter motor. The crankshaft begins to revolve. The piston is pulled to the bottom of the cylinder. The inlet valve opens. A mixture of air and petrol is injected into the cylinder and fills up the empty space. Now the piston which is at the bottom of the cylinder begins to move upwards, in the process compressing the mixture of air and petrol, and the inlet valve closes. The spark plug sparks. The compressed mixture of air and petrol explodes. Now, since all the inlets and outlets are closed, the power from the explosion pushes the piston down. The crankshaft revolves. Before the piston begins to move up again, the outlet valve opens; the exhaust gases are released and so on. The power from the engine is taken up by the clutch, gearbox and drive shaft, which distribute it to the axles, which in turn distribute it to the wheels. But we shall go over all this again in detail. Today's lesson is only the beginning of greater things to come....'

Warĩĩnga was jolted out of her memories of the past by Gatuĩria, who was speaking with sudden bitterness: ' ... What about today? The abilities and potential of our women are enslaved to the typewriter, the bar or the beds in those hotels we have put up in every corner of the country for the pleasure of tourists. How insulting to our national dignity that our women should have become mere flowers to decorate the beds of foreign tourists, so that when they go back home to their own countries, they can praise the generosity of our women in bed! Is that real praise or contempt?'

'The foreigners are not entirely to blame,' Warĩĩnga replied. 'Even you, the Kenyan men, think that there is no job a woman can do other than cooking your food and massaging your bodies. The other day I told some young men that my ambition was to design and build a simple machine to ease the burden of rural women, a simple machine that would exploit the greatest source of energy on the Earth – solar energy. And you know, the men laughed! Why have people forgotten how Kenyan women used to make guns during the Mau Mau war against the British? Can't people recall the different tasks carried out by women in the villages once the men had been sent to detention camps? A song of praise begins at home. If you Kenyan men were not so scornful and oppressive, the foreigners you talk about so much would not be so contemptuous of us.'

'*Haidhuru! Haidhuru*!' Gatuĩria said quickly, mollifying Warĩĩnga. 'Let's agree this is a new beginning for better things to come,' he added, his optimism springing from conviction that things were bound to change.

Then Gatuĩria remembered the invitations to the day's celebration and the way the guests had been instructed to dress, and he fell silent as he contemplated the shock his parents would have when they saw the way Waringa was dressed – a cloth, bead necklaces and Nyori-type earrings.

Gatuiria laughed inwardly. He thought of showing Waringa the card, then dismissed the idea.

'The dawn of new and more productive things to come,' he repeated, speaking more to himself, to bolster his spirits, than to Waringa.

'Let's hope so!' Waringa said, but after a pause, she took back what she had said: 'No, let's not be content with hoping. We aren't going to wait for things to happen by themselves any longer. Why can't we make things happen the way we want them to happen?'

'Let's make them happen then,' said Gatuiria.

'Let's make them happen,' Waringa repeated.

'The revolution of the Iregi rebels!'

'A new beginning for a new Earth!' Waringa said.

'So be it!' Gatuiria shouted, pressing his right foot hard on the accelerator . . . .

2

It is true that their journey to Nakuru was pleasant.

And their journey was still pleasant as they went past Lanet, and as they branched off towards Ngorika in their red Toyota.

And their journey was pleasant even when they drove into the home of Mr and Mrs Hispaniora Greenway Ghitahy, *Ngorika Heavenly Orchards* . . . .

You who were there, what more can I say?

3

Gatuiria and Waringa's journey was pleasant even as they walked through the gates of the homestead; was still pleasant when they entered the yard and their eyes met the faces of Kihaahu wa Gatheeca, Gitutu wa Gataanguru, Nditika wa Nguunji, Kimeendeeri wa Kanyuanjii and many others whom they had last seen at the Devil's feast in Ilmorog two years before. Robin Mwaura, of the *Matatu Matata Matamu Modern Transport Company*, was also present, as he had brought some foreign guests in his brand-new taxis.

Waringa almost refused to accept the evidence of her eyes. But

246

her eyes were not deceiving her: her uncle and aunt were there....

4

What are you saying? That such things cannot be? Give me strength, you who asked me to tell this story. Give me the tongue. Give me the words....

5

What happened then is a story that has been told over and over again, but it is one that those who were not there find difficult to believe. Give me the tongue ... give strength, you who commanded me to tell this tale. Give me the words....

6

When Gatuīria and Warīīnga walked into the courtyard, they were met by servants in uniform: striped trousers, dark tail coats, top hats and white gloves. Gatuīria and Warīīnga were escorted towards a special room, where Gatuīria's father, together with a select inner circle of elders, was waiting to receive them. Things had been organized so that Gatuīria's father would be the first to receive his son's bride, would be the first to touch her. The owner of the homestead had to be the first to receive the bride of his only son, according to modern tradition.

The guests had lined up on either side, and they clapped as Gatuīria and Warīīnga passed by.

The men had on dark suits, white frilled shirts and bow ties. The women wore very expensive clothes of different colours. But they all wore hats and white gloves.

On the outer edges stood foreign guests and tourists, dressed very lightly for a sunny day and bemusedly watching the drama unfolding before them as if they were studying the ridiculous products of their own civilizing missions.

Warīīnga glanced at her aunt and uncle to dispel the doubts she now felt. She saw them hide their faces; she assumed that they were ashamed of the way she was dressed....

A red carpet had been laid at the entrance to the special room. On the floor of the special room was green carpet four inches thick. From the ceiling hang chandeliers like bunches of glass fruit.

Gatuīria's father sat on a high seat covered with cushions of different colours. On either side of him his elderly friends were sitting on seats similar to his, only theirs were smaller.

The news of an only son returning home had reached every corner of the area, and this was borne out by the crowds of people who had come to the feast. Yes, the news of him who had been lost returning home for the blessing of his father and of all the other elders around had spread far and wide.

Warīīnga felt as if she were an actor in a film.

That was how she felt as she stepped on to the red carpet.

That was how she felt as she entered the special room and stood on the green carpet.

That was how she felt as she let her eyes wander around the room . . . .

And suddenly Warīīnga's eyes met those of Gatuīria's father.

Gatuīria's father? Oh, no!

Warīīnga's eyes had met the eyes of the Rich Old Man from Ngorika, who was sitting on the high seat, ready to receive her.

Gatuīria's father? Wambūi's father!

7

'Father, this is —,' Gatuīria started to make the introductions. His father stopped him with a wave of his hand. He was a sturdily built old man. His bald patch, which now divided his grey hairs into two sections, gleamed in the light.

His face betrayed nothing.

Even his voice gave nothing away as he asked everyone to leave the room, including Gatuīria, so that he could become acquainted with his son's fiancée, so that father-in-law and daughter-in-law could get to know each other.

'Gatuīria, go and greet your mother, and take these guests to join all our other guests. Shut the door behind you, please, and tell your mother that I would be grateful for *strictly no disturbance*.'

The guests left the room, glancing lasciviously at Warīīnga, some of them muttering to themselves: 'The young of today really are beautiful! What a terrible calamity old age is!'

They imagined that everything was going according to plan. None realized that there had been an unexpected development – none, that is, except Wariinga and Gatuiria's father.

Gatuiria's father? Wambui's father!

8

The hands of the Rich Old Man from Ngorika were trembling. He stretched out his arms and laid his hands on a Bible that was lying on a table in front of him. And all this time his eyes were fixed on Wariinga's face. His lips trembled too. He did not know where to start.

The firebrand of words was burned at the handle.

Wariinga stood on the same spot, her fearless eyes meeting the gaze of the Rich Old Man. She shifted her handbag from her right shoulder to her left.

'Won't you sit down?' The Rich Old Man asked her, standing up and pushing a chair towards her.

But Wariinga remained where she was. She did not utter a word.

The Rich Old Man from Ngorika sank back into his seat, his eyes still on Wariinga's face. 'Did you . . . did you know that Gatuiria was my son, my only son?'

Wariinga shook her head.

The Rich Old Man stood up again and said to Wariinga: 'Let's kneel down and pray together.'

Wariinga shrugged her shoulders. She remained on her feet.

'*Please*, I beg you, let's pray together so that the Lord can show us the way.'

Wariinga did not move. The Rich Old Man from Ngorika knelt on the carpet in front of Wariinga.

Wariinga looked at him like a judge at an unrepentant prisoner who is pleading for mercy.

The Rich Old Man tried to pray. No words of prayer came to him.

Wariinga's lips parted slightly, as if she were about to laugh, but she did not.

The Rich Old Man from Ngorika opened his eyes and looked up at Wariinga, but he was greeted by eyes that danced with laughter and irony.

The lips of the Rich Old Man trembled. He abandoned his prayers, stood up and began to pace about on the carpet, his hands clasped together behind him, but every few steps he would stop to touch the table or the chair on which he had been sitting.

Waríĩnga did not take her eyes off him for a moment.

And then suddenly he stopped pacing and stood in front of Waríĩnga.

'This is a trial,' he said, with the voice of a drowning man. He lowered his gaze, as if he did not want to look directly into Waríĩnga's face, and went on in the same tone: 'You know that all that you and Gatuĩria have planned is not possible now?'

Waríĩnga said nothing. She just looked at him.

Drops of sweat glinted on his smooth bald patch.

And suddenly Waríĩnga felt sorry for the man. She started to speak and then stopped. But a sharp arrow tip of pity pierced her heart.

The Rich Old Man sensed a slight change in the atmosphere. He thought he saw a crack in the walls of a hard heart, and he hastened to widen the crack with words.

'Jacinta! Waríĩnga! There is not a thing I would not do today ... truly, there is not a thing I would not do for you today if you remove this burden from me. *Please*, Jacinta, I beg you in the name of the woman who gave birth to you! My happiness, my status, my faith, my property, my life, all these are now in your hands. *Only* take this burden from me!'

Waríĩnga felt laughter rise in her heart. The sharp sting of pity no longer pierced her. But she did open her mouth and say one word: 'How?'

The Rich Old Man from Ngorika had not heard Waríĩnga's voice for a long time. He raised his eyes at once, as though he had been struck in the heart by the spear of Waríĩnga's one word. He gazed at Waríĩnga's dark eyes, and he began to talk faster and faster, imagining that he would succeed in widening the crack of pity within her.

'Leave Gatuĩria. He is my only son, and I love him dearly, although he is wayward and tries to map his own independent path instead of following in my footsteps. Besides, Gatuĩria is almost your child. So your plans are impossible as long as I'm alive, for it would be like a child marrying his own mother. It would be like my son marrying my wife while I am still breathing. I would not be able to breathe a day longer for shame before my people and before God.

'My home would fall apart. My property would be left without a manager. My life would break into seven pieces. Jacinta, save me!'

'How?'

And once again the Rich Old Man was struck by the sound of Waríínga's voice. He started pacing about on the carpet again. He took two or three steps. Then he stopped and struggled for control.

'I would like you to leave Gatuíria.'

'How?'

'Go back to Nairobi together. When you get to Nairobi, tell him that your love affair is over. He's only a child. He won't feel a thing.'

'And me?'

Suddenly he felt as he had in the old times, when he used to overpower Waríínga with words. He felt the blood surge through his veins; he felt his old virility return. He stretched out his arms as if to place his hands on Waríínga's shoulders, but meeting Waríínga's blazing eyes, he quickly let his hands fall to his side. However, he did not suppress the words on his lips.

'Be mine. Remember, you once belonged to me. I believe I am the man who changed you from a girl to a woman. And you are the mother of my child, although I've never set eyes on it.'

'And what about your wife, Gatuíria's mother?'

The Rich Old Man was overwhelmed by Waríínga. Lust dominated him. Sweet words began to flow with effortless ease. He moved nearer her. He spoke exactly like *Boss* Kíhara. It was as if both had attended the same school of seduction or read the same book containing a hundred love letters from a father to his daughter.

'Jacinta, she doesn't count. No one applies old perfume that has lost its scent. *Please*, my little lady, my fruit, listen to my words. Release me from this shame today. Be my woman, and I will rent a house for you in Nairobi, Mombasa or wherever you choose. I will furnish the house with the kind of furniture and carpets you see in this house, and with mattresses and curtains and other things imported from abroad – from Hong Kong, Tokyo, Paris, London, Rome, New York. *Name it, and it's yours.* I'd like you to take off this cloth and these necklaces and these earrings made of dry maize stalks and to put on clothes and jewellery made in Europe. I will also buy you a *shopping basket*, a basket to take to market, like a *Toyota Corona*, a *Datsun 16B*, an *Alfasud* or any other car of your choice. Jacinta, my baby, my fruit, my orange, come back to me and solve the problems of your life, of my home and of my child!'

'Which child?'

'Gatuíria, of course!'

'And Wambũi? Is she not your child?'

'I am not as stupid as you think. Gĩkũyũ said that to hate a cow is to hate its hide. And now I say to you: to love a cow is to love its calf.'

'And what if I refuse to become your flower, a flower to sweeten your old age?'

The Rich Old Man from Ngorika paused a little, as if deep in thought. His face darkened; he was angry at Warĩĩnga's words. He cleared his throat and spoke in the harsh, bitter voice of a man who is not used to having his words and wishes challenged.

'Let me talk to you in parables. A long time ago Satan (or the Devil) was an angel dearly loved by God. He was then called Lucifer. But one day Satan was seized by an evil spirit, and he yearned for the seat on the right hand of God. As you know, that seat had been reserved for God's only Son. What did God do to Lucifer? Even we, the followers of God on Earth, have ways of fulfilling his wishes. You are not a baby, so I don't need to explain to you what that means. I was not present at the feast in Ilmorog. But I do know that there was someone there by the name of Mwĩreri wa Mũkiraaĩ. He was one of the most respected guests at the feast; I hear that he had been given the largest number of invitations to distribute. But after eating and drinking his fill, he started abusing God and showing his scorn for the people of his class. He refused to abide by God's laws on Earth. Highly respected he may have been once – but where is Mwĩreri today?'

'He was murdered by Robin Mwaũra, in Matatũ Matata Matamu, registration number MMM 333, at Kĩneenĩĩ, near Limuru.'

The Rich Old Man from Ngorika was startled.

'So you know? Then I don't have to hide anything from you. Mwaũra used to be the leader of a group called the *Devil's Angels*. Perhaps you've heard of them. Their task is to liquidate those who prevent the work of God from being done on Earth. Right now, I would only have to open my mouth, and you would not reach Gilgil . . . . But what are we talking about, Jacinta? We have strayed from our path. I know you are not a fool. I know you won't reject riches. If what you want is a farm in the Rift Valley that you can manage by telephone from Nairobi or Mombasa, all right. Just say what you want, and it shall be done.'

'And the people outside? What shall we tell them?'

'Leave that to me.'

'*Mr* Gĩtahi, I wonder if you have ever once stopped to think about other people's lives. May I ask you a question?'

'Certainly. One is never prosecuted for asking questions.'

'You want the love between me and Gatuīria to end, don't you?'

'Yes, I do.

'All right. Do you want to marry me? That is, do you want to go through a wedding ceremony so that I become your second wife?'

'*Please*, Jacinta, stop pretending that you don't understand. I am a man of the Church. I just want you to be mine. I'll find my own ways of coming to visit you. Just like the old times, *don't you remember? Please*, save me! Save the honour of my name! Save the honour of my son! Jacinta, save the honour of my home, and you'll see before you a man who knows what gratitude is.'

And then the miracle happened. The Rich Old Man gazed at Warīīnga, and he was suddenly struck by the full splendour of her beauty. His heart and body were scalded by Warīīnga's youth. He lost all control, and he fell on his knees in front of Warīīnga, and he began to plead with her. 'I have never seen beauty that shone with such brilliance. Save me!'

He clutched Warīīnga by the knees, while words poured from his lips like a river in flood.

Warīīnga was standing exactly where she had stood since she had entered the room. She began to speak like a people's judge about to deliver his judgment.

'You snatcher of other people's lives! Do you remember the game you and I used to play, the game of the hunter and the hunted? Did you imagine that a day might come when the hunted would become the hunter? What's done cannot be undone. I'm not going to save you. But I shall save many other people, whose lives will not be ruined by words of honey and perfume.'

The Rich Old Man interrupted Warīīnga: 'I knew you would agree! My darling, whom I love dearly! My little fruit, my little orange, my flower to brighten my old age!'

He went on, carried away by his words. He did not see Warīīnga open her handbag. He did not see Warīīnga take out the pistol. 'Look at me!' Warīīnga commanded, with the voice of a judge.

When Gatuīria's father saw the gun, his words suddenly ceased.

9

The people outside heard the shots. When they entered the room, they found Gatuīria's father kneeling, still clinging to Warīīnga by the knees. But three bullets were lodged in his body.

'What is it? What is it, Warĩĩnga?' Gatuĩria asked.

'There kneels a jigger, a louse, a weevil, a flea, a bedbug! He is mistletoe, a parasite that lives on the trees of other people's lives!'

10

Warĩĩnga left the room. People gave way before her. Outside the door she met Kĩhaahu wa Gatheeca and Gĩtutu wa Gataangũrũ. And suddenly, remembering Wangarĩ and Mũturi and the student leader – the people who had roused her from mental slavery – she felt an anger she had not felt as she killed Gĩtahi.

'You too, and you!' And she shot at both Kĩhaahu and Gĩtutu, splintering their kneecaps.

People scattered in every direction, some shouting, 'Arrest her! Catch her! She is mad!' as they ran for their lives.

Two people who tried to capture her were greeted by judo kicks and karate chops, and they were felled. Warĩĩnga calmly walked away, as the people watched her from a safe distance.

Nguunji wa Nditika was the only person who was seen running, holding his belly in both hands to prevent himself from falling and shouting for Robin Mwaũra: 'Where are you? Where are you and your men?' But Mwaũra had already started up his taxi and he sped away.

Gatuĩria did not know what to do: to deal with his father's body, to comfort his mother or to follow Warĩĩnga. So he just stood in the courtyard, hearing in his mind music that lead him nowhere.

He stood there in the yard, as if he had lost the use of his tongue, his arms, his legs.

Warĩĩnga walked on, without once looking back.

But she knew with all her heart that the hardest struggles of her life's journey lay ahead . . . .